SEA MISTRESS

IRIS GOWER

SEA MISTRESS

BCA

LONDON NEW YORK SYDNEY TORONTO

This edition published 1995 by
BCA
by arrangement with
Bantam Press
a division of Transworld Publishers

CN 9054

Printed and bound in Great Britain by
Mackays of Chatham PLC, Chatham, Kent

To Christopher, Emily
and JoJo with love.

CHAPTER ONE

Her husband had taken a mistress, she knew it as surely as if the word 'betrayal' was written in blood upon his forehead. Bridie Marchant lay beside Paul in their large bed, her emotions in turmoil, jealousy searing her, and stared at his naked back.

When he had come home from sea (was it only yesterday?) he had been as warm and as happy as he'd always been to see his two young sons. His presents had been lavish, his gifts of silks from the East and perfume from the Americas were, as always, generous but when he took Bridie in his arms, something about him was different.

They had made love, if you could call their quick coupling that. It had seemed more of a duty to him rather than the passionate response of a man returned to his wife after a long absence at sea. Once he would have been eager for her, he would have taken his time, made her sing with happiness but this time it was different. When it was over, Paul had promptly turned away from her and fallen asleep leaving Bridie feeling disappointed, bewildered and used.

Bridie had been unable to sleep; usually, after one of his trips, they sat up in bed, he talking of his adventures in foreign lands. She had enjoyed the moments of closeness when he would listen with rapt attention while she brought him up to date on the progress of his sons.

Was this the normal pattern of marriage after several years, a case of familiarity breeding contempt? Had Paul tired of her already?

Bridie felt tears on her lashes and brushed them away,

she was the one who was always in control of her emotions. Bridie Marchant, sensible mother to her children, partner in a large shipping fleet, the senior partner to all intents and purposes, she reminded herself sternly. The thought gave her a small feeling of security. To keep control of the shares left to her by her father was something she had made a decision on before her marriage even though Paul had protested vigorously. He felt that women knew little or nothing about business, especially a business that involved the sea. And yet hadn't there been some instinct warning her even then, that she would need to keep an ace in her hand where her husband was concerned?

As though aware of her scrutiny, Paul stirred, muttering words that Bridie strove to hear. He was between sleep and wakefulness as he reached out for her. He drew her close and she lay against him, listening to the strong beat of his heart, miserably contemplating the identity of the woman he had last held this way. Had he fallen in love or had the long weeks at sea made him eager for release? Questions worried at her mind, she imagined him making love to some faceless hussy, kissing unknown lips and anger raged through her.

She disentangled herself from his arms and slid from between the sheets. She stood looking down at him for a moment, his curling hair hung over his brow, his broad shoulders were golden from the sun, she loved him so much she ached.

Softly, she padded across the room. Soon her sons would be awake and, in spite of an undoubted fondness for Annie their nurse, it was their mother the boys turned to first thing on rising in the morning. Her features softened; her sons, Andrew and Christopher were so dear to her, they were her life. She clenched her hands into fists; for them, she would do anything to retain her interest in the shipping line, she would protect their future. For somehow she felt it might prove necessary one day.

8

'Where are you going?' Paul was sitting up in bed, watching her as she stood, hand on the doorknob.

'To the children, of course.' She knew her voice lacked warmth and Paul knew it too. For a moment, his violet eyes were guarded and then, he held out his hand and smiled. 'Come back to bed, it's early yet.'

'The boys . . .' Her words died away as Paul held back the blankets invitingly.

'The children have a nurse, that's what she's for, to take care of our sons while we . . . while we.'

'Make love?' She supplied the word he seemed reluctant to say aloud. 'It's all right, Paul, it's quite legal, we are married.'

'Come here.' He was assessing her, he sensed something was wrong but he had no intention of recognizing her mood. Slowly, Bridie returned to the bed and climbed into the warmth beside her husband.

'Paul . . .' There was a question in her voice but Paul, clearly, didn't want to enter into any sort of discussion. His mouth was on hers, silencing her.

This time there was more warmth in his approach, more tenderness and she tried to tell herself that she had been foolish, imagining a problem which didn't exist.

His hands were caressing and in spite of herself she responded to his touch with her usual rush of desire. She loved Paul, she wanted him desperately. He took his time, he kissed her eyelids, her cheeks, her lips, and then his mouth tantalizingly moved to her breasts. Her breathing became ragged.

'Do you love me, Paul?'

'Of course, Bridie, you are my wife.' His voice was thick with emotion and mingled with Bridie's passion was a great thankfulness. His reassurances were like water to her parched senses, she wanted to believe him so much. She must believe him.

She flung back her head, her back arching to enjoy all the more his possession of her. Her hands clasped his

9

back, sliding silkily over his skin, feeling with delight the firmness of his buttocks. She wanted the moments of happiness never to end, for Paul, her husband was hers once more.

CHAPTER TWO

The mill was filled with wood dust. In the slant of the early sun the motes appeared as snow drifting and falling in the cold spring air. The sound of the machinery macerating plates of oak bark reverberated around the mill, seeming to shake the frail wooden structure with the force of its power.

Ellie Hopkins stopped the mill and made her way down the rickety wooden stairs to the room below, to where the chute was discharging the slivers of bark, and with an effort shifted the overflowing basket away from the foot of the machine. She sighed and rubbed at her spine before bending to place an empty basket beneath the chute. She paused for a moment, day-dreaming in the relief of the freedom from noise. It was a fine day, a good day for being out of doors, she thought wistfully.

The splash of sunlight from the doorway was suddenly blocked by the huge bulk of Jubilee Hopkins. '*Duw*, Ellie, you're like a little ghost there, standing silent in the dust. Pull your finger out girl or the work will never be done.'

Ellie looked up and smiled, she knew the rebuke, though harsh-sounding was good naturedly given. 'So? Why not do a bit of graft yourself then, Jubie?' She looked at him with fondness, his craggy brows formed a grey forest over his lined eyes, his hair hung around his shoulders in a white cloud. He appeared, Ellie thought, like a prophet from the Old Testament.

Jubilee Hopkins came further into the mill and sat down on an upturned box. 'Now I've stopped work for a minute, I'll have a smoke, I deserve it, those skins I'm cleaning are giving me callouses on top of my callouses.'

'Do you have to smoke that foul thing in here?' Ellie demanded, her hands on her slim hips. She pushed back her fair hair, which was damp with perspiration, and stared at this man, this old man who was her husband.

'Don't grumble, girl, the tobacco covers the stink of the yard, you should be grateful.'

Ellie had long since been unaware of the animal smell of the tannery where she had worked ever since her marriage. Even the sight of the stray dogs eating the debris of flesh from the skins newly in from the abattoir had ceased to offend her.

On an impulse, she crouched on the ground beside her husband and took his roughened hand. 'Jubilee, you will tell me if the work gets too much for you, won't you?'

'Aye, girl, don't fret, I'll be put in my box when I can't work in my own tannery.' He looked at her wryly, 'Not much good for anything else am I, not at my advanced age?'

Ellie felt her colour rise, theirs was a marriage that was not consummated, she had never expected it to be; Jubilee Hopkins had been in his seventies when he'd slipped the gold band on her finger.

'Don't talk like that.' She said the words almost without thinking, they were her usual response to any suggestion that her husband was mortal.

'Oh, love, I know what the men say about me, that I'm an old man without bullets in my gun.' Jubilee ruffled her hair. 'There's not one of them out there as wouldn't like to service old Jubilee's wife given half a chance.'

'Aye, well that's what none of them will get, there's no chance for any of them. I'd never risk going through all that anguish again.'

'Don't dwell on the past, Ellie,' Jubilee rose, 'what's done is done and can't be righted, see? Now, I'm going in to Swansea, got to buy some more skins, business is brisk this time of the year what with saddles and horse-collars and such. See you later, my little sweetheart.'

When Jubilee had left, Ellie thought about him with a warm affection; he was a fine man and she was lucky to have him. Old he might be but he was twice the worker that any of his men were. Oh, she had seen them, the casual labourers in the yard giving her the eye, knew that they watched her, expecting her to fall into the arms of one of them but they were wrong. Ellie Hopkins wanted none of them, once bitten twice shy. She sighed, pushing back memories of her past. In any case, it was high time she got on with her work, the oak bark would not grind itself.

Later, in the large house Jubilee had built for himself many years ago, Ellie put the big black kettle onto the fire and prepared to make tea for the four workers and the two casuals. They would take it out in the yard or if it was raining they would gather in the currying house where it was warm and dry.

The two older men were no problem, both Luke and Harry were much older than Ellie, in their forties and happily married with buxom wives who sometimes helped out at the mill. And Boyo was a young boy from the workhouse, he was so shy he could scarcely bring himself to speak to Ellie and when he did, he touched his forelock as though she were some fine lady. Her face softened; Boyo, young though he might be, was fiercely protective of her, trying his best to ward off the attentions of the one man who gave her trouble.

Matthew Hewson was handsome, young and with a fine tongue for the poetry but he had one conceit, he fancied his chances with any woman who came his way.

Ellie would have liked to have been indifferent to him, that sort of reaction would offend him more than anything. But she felt a deep mistrust of him and a scorn for the way he lived his life, the way he used women and tossed them aside. She could hardly help knowing that he was a womanizer, he spoke often enough about his prowess and in a voice loud enough for everyone to hear.

She went outside in the sparkling spring air and banged on the gong that hung outside the door. The tea was brewed, the bread and cheese set out on the plain wooden table in the kitchen. The men would pick up their grub packs and place a few coins on the table in payment. It was an arrangement that Jubilee's long dead sister had instituted and which Jubilee had wished Ellie to continue.

Ellie clattered the enamel mugs on the table, side by side and lifted the brown shiny teapot.

'Let me do that, Mrs Hopkins, it's too heavy a job for the likes of you.' The voice spoke directly behind her shoulder and Ellie sighed in resignation.

'I'm perfectly capable of pouring a cup of tea, haven't I done it these past years well enough?'

'Why so prickly?' Matthew Hewson was close, too close and Ellie moved away from him but not before he saw the pulse beat in her neck. He smiled. 'Why won't you let me be friends with you?' he said softly, 'I mean you no harm.'

Ellie looked at him steadily. 'Friendship is not what I'm offering, nor anything else. You work for my husband, that's the only reason I'm civil to you.'

'You don't like me, even a little?' Matthew picked up his bread and bit into the thick brown crust with white, even teeth.

'I neither like you nor dislike you.' Ellie poured the tea with a steady hand, 'You have enough to do with the village girls chasing after you from what I hear.'

'Ah, jealous is it? Well you needn't be, the girls are silly giggling creatures, you, Ellie Hopkins, are what I'd call an enigma, a beautiful, delicious woman.'

Ellie suddenly felt old, she was past twenty, her youth had vanished some years ago when she had put her trust in a man she had loved. Just look where it had got her.

'Stop your silly nonsense.' She put down the teapot

and refilled it with hot water from the kettle. With a sense of relief, she heard the sound of Boyo's light footsteps as he came towards the house. She supposed he had a proper name but she had never known it and neither had he.

Boyo stepped into the kitchen and looked from Ellie's impassive face to take in Matthew's twitching smile. He frowned and placed himself directly between them.

'The master's on his way back, missus, I heard the sound of the cart from down the lane.'

Ellie concealed a smile, she knew that Boyo wished he was strong enough to punch Matthew on the nose but he was a youth, his muscles scarcely showing beneath the sleeves of his flannel shirt.

'Good.' She poured the boy's tea and watched as he took up his grub pack. The bread and cheese was wrapped in muslin to keep it fresh and Boyo undid the cloth and bit, with a delicacy rarely seen in a young boy, into the yellow cheese.

Ellie wished sometimes that the men ate in the kitchen. It would be good to listen to the interchanges of banter between them. Harry had a fine, dry sense of humour; he often poked gentle fun at Matthew, teasing him for his pride at being a bard. Matthew took it mostly in good part but sometimes, his colour would ebb, his fists would clench themselves into white-knuckled weapons and then Harry would smile.

'Come on now Mat, only teasing, I am, mun. Wish I had your way with words not to mention with the women.'

Ellie had come to realize that Matthew was unable to resist flattery, he was a vain man but there was about him a warning that he could also be a dangerous one.

Jubilee came into the kitchen, his bowler awry, his pipe jutting from under his moustache.

'There's such talk in Swansea.' He sat, scraping back a chair, mindless of the polished slates of the floor and sinking down into it gratefully. 'Seems this new

Bible-puncher is come to town, setting the place on its ears he is, with his talk of the wonders of the baptism of the Holy Spirit.'

Ellie smiled indulgently, it was a rare occurrence when her husband didn't come back home from town with a new piece of gossip.

'What's he like?' she asked, pushing the kettle onto the flames of the fire. 'A Methuselah like you, is he?'

'Don't be rude, girl.' Jubilee was not offended by her reference to his old age, rather he revelled in her affectionate insolence; it was a sign that she was a woman of spirit. 'Young as a sapling, he is, handsome and with a way with the ladies that would take your breath away.' Jubilee glanced at Matthew who had paused in the doorway, half inclined to beat the other men to the currying house and get the best place to sit and yet fascinated in spite of himself.

'Is it that Evan Roberts you're talking about?' he asked, his tone derogatory. 'Preaching like a maniac, telling us all to get saved, trying to run the lives of Christian people he is, mind. Why doesn't he go and convert the heathens, not tell respectable folk how to live?'

Jubilee barely glanced at him. 'Come from a place near Loughor, so it seems, got the *hwyl* all right, folks are going to the chapels in droves just to hear the word from him.' He looked directly at Ellie, 'Do you want to go and see him, *merchi*?'

Ellie considered her husband's words. Jubilee must be interested in hearing this new preacher for usually he favoured the Church of England's pomp and dignity. 'Where's he preaching next, then?' She sat down at the table and pushed a mug towards Jubilee. Her back ached and she wanted to kick off her boots but there were still some hours of work to do yet. The prospect of a day off was appealing.

'I hear he's going up to Tabernacle in Morriston, I could drive us there in the cart, be a good break for you, Ellie, looking a bit peaked you've been lately.'

'Perhaps she's with child.' Matthew's voice was overtly innocent and Jubilee looked at him sharply.

'*Darro* haven't you got work to do? Perhaps there's not enough jobs here to warrant the employment of three men and a boy, perhaps I'd best get rid of a full-time worker and employ another casual labourer.'

Ellie wanted to reach out and cover Jubilee's hand with her own; he was stung, his manhood imputed by Matthew's jibe. She glared at the man in the doorway and he had the grace to look abashed.

Boyo stood beside Ellie, he was puzzled by the charged atmosphere and a little dismayed, not understanding it. How could he know that Jubilee Hopkins was a man who could not father a child? An illness, the swelling of the glands in his neck when he was a young man had done the damage, at least that's what the doctor had told Jubilee.

'Get out of here, leave me and my wife to eat in peace.' Jubilee rarely lost his good humour but now, his mouth was drawn down, his eyebrows met across his brow and he suddenly looked like the old man he was.

When they were alone, Ellie smiled reassuringly. 'Don't notice the men, especially Matthew, he's all talk that one.'

She stared into Jubilee's eyes and saw a tear there. 'Love, don't be unhappy, we've got a good marriage, haven't we?'

'But I wanted sons,' he said flatly. Of course, it was the reason he had married her, taken her off the hands of her shamed family, made her respectable. He'd wanted the twins she was carrying.

'I'm sorry.' Her voice was scarcely audible and he shook off his bad mood as though it was an unwanted garment. 'No, it's me that's sorry, behaving like a big kid, I am. You suffered more than me when you lost the babbas and I should be the first one to recognize that. Wasn't I there holding your hand, poor little girl?'

17

A pain filled Ellie's body and filtered into her mind. Her children, her sons. Born too soon as was the way of twins, they died without having lived. Jubilee saw her stricken look and rose, taking her into his arms, holding her against his barrel chest. 'Damn Matthew Hewson,' he said.

She was comforted by his nearness, Jubilee was a good man and she loved him. It might not be the love of a wife for a husband but it was a strong love nevertheless. And Ellie was grateful to him, Jubilee had given her a life of respectability that she had no right to expect, only now and then when someone like Matthew stirred the muddy waters did she remember her past.

On an impulse, she made up her mind. 'We'll go and hear this wonderful new preacher man,' she said. 'I think we both need a day off from work, Jubilee my love.'

'Right then,' he moved to the door, 'it's settled. But for now I suppose I'd better make sure the skins are getting worked properly, can't trust young ones to be as fussy as us old ones are. Good leather needs proper treatment from the grinding of the oak bark down to the last soaking in the pits. Three long years it takes to make fine leather that will last the course and I don't want any of my workmen ruining my reputation.'

Alone in the kitchen, Ellie washed out the teapot at the huge white slab of a sink and stared through the window to the fields beyond. The Hopkins tannery was separated from the house by a few acres of scrub land; it needed to be because the stink of it was worse than anything produced by the plethora of works along the banks of the Swansea river.

Ellie remembered her shock when she had first come here as a bride, a bride with a large belly, she thought ruefully. She had never been used to hardship. She had been the pampered daughter of a respectable, if not too thrifty, merchant.

She had fallen in love, had become even more pampered as the mistress of Lord Calvin Temple. He'd given her everything she wanted, money, clothes, an apartment of her own. But what he wouldn't give her was marriage.

Ah, well, it had taken Jubilee to give her that and she owed him everything. Her face softened for a moment, dear Jubilee, he'd been kinder to her than her own father in the end.

She left the cottage and hitched up her skirts as she walked, tucking the hem into her belt. She had enough trouble washing the stink of skins from the clothes on a Monday without dragging her skirts in the dust.

In the mill, Boyo was thrusting a slice of wood into the grinder, he glanced at her shyly, his dark eyes sliding away from her exposed ankles. 'Master sent me in by here to help you, missus,' he explained, 'thought you was looking a bit tired, like.'

'Thanks, Boyo. Perhaps you'll take that basket of oak bark out to the pits for me then.'

She sighed as she watched him drag the basket towards the door, struggle to lift it and then stagger out into the sunlight with it. Everything was the same, every day was like another, hard days and long nights spent lying beside Jubilee like father and daughter not husband and wife. Was this what she really wanted from life? Was there nothing more to look forward to?

Shame filled her, she should not be moaning about her lot, she should be going down on her knees and thanking Jubilee Hopkins for all he'd done for her. The knowledge was there inside her head, why then did her soul and spirit cry for something more?

The church was packed to the door, there were men standing in the aisle of Tabernacle, the fine building built on the main road in Morriston.

'Man must be good.' Jubilee looked unfamiliar in his best suit and his white shirt with its pristine starched collar. His white hair had been brushed back as a token of respect for the occasion and his moustache was neatly trimmed. He was a fine man, must have been a very handsome man in his prime. It was a great pity that he was not sitting there with a brood of children and grandchildren around him, Ellie thought soberly.

Ellie remembered her wedding, perhaps it was the heady aura of expectation in the church that brought it to mind. The ceremony had been quickly performed, the preacher had no time for a bride who revealed her sin for all to see. The breakfast had been a simple one, with no guests present, just Jubilee and his new wife eating ham and cold chicken at their own fireside.

The night had been a strange one, Jubilee had held Ellie in his big arms, had rocked gently, calming her trembling. 'I won't touch thee, girl,' his voice was reassuring, 'got no seed to give you, no passion either.'

She was relieved and immediately felt ashamed. 'What are you getting out of all this, Jubilee?'

Her question had remained unanswered for a long time. At last, he'd spoken. 'I heard all the talk about you, *merchi*, carrying twins they say. I want them babbas you got in there.' He rested his hand on her stomach, 'I need sons, see, can't get 'em myself so I'm content to take another man's offspring as my own. Give me boys and you'll have repaid me a thousand times.'

The organ burst quite suddenly into life and Ellie blinked, trying to reorganize her thoughts. She had come to love Jubilee. She never had, and never could, repay Jubilee for all his generosity.

Evan Roberts was in the pulpit, he was a man of the people, decently but not richly dressed. When he spoke, his words were plain; he was not a gifted orator yet Ellie, watching him was fascinated, and in spite of herself, moved by the message he was proclaiming so forcefully. She glanced up at her husband as he took out a large handkerchief.

'*Duw*, he's bringing tears to my old eyes.' Jubilee's whisper carried around the church. 'A man of God I'm not but I can't help but be impressed by all this "come to Christ" business.'

Ellie smiled up at him. 'I know,' she mouthed the words, Jubilee's hearing was not what it used to be. 'So am I.'

Behind them, a man rose to his feet and waved his arms above his head. 'Forgive me, God, I have sinned.'

He moved towards the pulpit and sank to his knees. He had begun a reaction that seemed to spread through the congregation. 'Praise the Lord!' The words passed from mouth to mouth and Ellie saw one young girl fall into a swoon on the floor. Willing hands rushed to help her and she was lifted and carried towards the preacher.

'Let's go, I can't abide theatricals.' Jubilee took Ellie's arm and led her outside. She understood exactly how he felt, the emotion within the church had been over-powering, even a little frightening.

'He's a good man, though, Jubilee, a sincere man, you've got to admit that.'

'I'm not saying that I didn't listen to what the man was preaching. I suppose he can't help it if people start babbling and throwing themselves on their knees before him or that a silly woman chooses to swoon in the middle of the sermon but I like a bit of decorum myself, give me the Church of England any time.'

Ellie smiled. 'Old stick in the mud,' she said and kissed him on the cheek.

The words of the preacher stayed with Ellie over the next days. She had a great deal of time for thinking, working as she did in the mill. Mostly she was alone though sometimes Boyo helped her, bringing in the oak bark from the yard and thrusting the pieces into the blades of the mill. Boyo had a fancy for her, she knew it but it was perfectly harmless, the fancy of an unformed lad. He respected her, held her in high esteem and his manner was entirely devoid of the insulting familiarity with which Matthew treated her.

As if drawn by her thoughts, Matthew came into the mill and stood near the door, his hands thrust into his pockets beneath his leather apron, his waistcoat jauntily unbuttoned.

'You went to hear this new preacher man, then, what's he like?' He made even the most innocent words seem implicit with hidden meaning.

'He's very good.' Ellie wished Matthew would go away, she was uneasy in his presence, fearing him, though she didn't know why. What harm could he do when there was a yard full of men outside?

'Hear he likes the women.' Matthew's smile beneath his moustache was thin. Ellie lifted her head and looked directly at him.

'And if he does, is that a sin, then?' She realized she was rising to the bait by the gleam that came into Matthew's dark eyes. 'It's natural enough for a man to like women, doesn't mean there's any harm in it.'

He came closer to her. 'Well said. No harm at all. I like women very much indeed. Usually, they like me, too.'

She felt threatened by his masculine aggressiveness, he towered over her, his shoulders broad, his eyes running over her as though his gaze could penetrate her clothing.

'Married women, too?' Her tone was sharp and immediately she had spoken, she regretted the words. As she'd expected, he misinterpreted them.

'*Especially* married women.' He was so close she could almost taste the smell of leather about him. He rested his hand on her shoulder. 'In particular women married to senile, useless old men.'

Her hand lashed out and caught his face with a resounding slap. The sound echoed around the wooden walls of the mill and Ellie felt alarmed at her action. She had lost her dignity, admitted to this man that his words had stung.

'Go away.' She moved around the mill putting the machinery between them. 'Haven't you any work to get on with?'

22

He rocked back on his heels but there was no anger in his eyes, only amusement. 'Right you are, missus.' He touched his cap and looking at his clear-cut features and square chin Ellie wondered why she never found him attractive. Perhaps it was his coarseness, she wasn't used to men of his sort.

He swaggered from the mill and paused for a moment, held in the motes of sunlight beyond the door. All Ellie could see was his outline, the square bigness of his frame, the booted feet firmly planted on the ground as though he was master of all he surveyed. After a moment, he turned and left her.

She returned to work, thinking of the turn her life had taken. She was to all intents and purposes leading the life of a nun. She was as cloistered as if she was hidden away in some crumbling abbey. She was wife in name only to an old man, in that Matthew was right, but she loved her husband in a way that even she found difficult to understand. And it must be enough for her.

Passion she had shared with her lover, the young, hot-blooded passion of a girl believing herself in love with a sophisticated man. Calvin Temple had been a vigorous lover and perhaps he had loved her just a little too. But not enough.

Ellie became aware that the sun was fading from outside the door. Her arms ached as she moved the basket of oak bark, full to overflowing now, away from the sloping chute of the grinding mill. The wood had an earthy smell that reminded her of winter fires when the logs blazed in the hearth of the home she shared with Jubilee, the home he had so generously given her.

In return he'd received nothing, nothing except her undying gratitude and the determination to work her fingers to the bone if necessary.

'Come on, missus, it's time to knock off.' Boyo was standing in the doorway, a pathetically slight figure looking much younger than his fifteen years. As he came further into the mill, she saw that his face was blotched

23

with weariness, his eyes half-closed as though he could scarcely keep awake.

'Aye, so it is.' She dusted her hands on her skirts and put her arm around his thin shoulders. 'My back is in half, I suppose it's about time I called it a day.'

She watched as Boyo made his way towards the loft above the stable, where he slept at night, his small frame stretched across the old bed Jubilee had given him. Boyo had no family, no kin to care for him. Glyn Hir Tannery was where he worked, ate and slept; not much of a life for a boy scarcely grown from childhood.

This was yet another example of Jubilee's kindness; he had taken Boyo in, given him a home, a job and a fair wage. More he had given Boyo the benefit of his wisdom, urging him to put away his money for the future.

In the kitchen of the rambling house, Jubilee was seated in his big rocking-chair near the fire. The logs lay dead and unlit, no warm flames reached out to warm the cool of the spring evening. This was unusual, Jubilee saw to it the fire was built up in good time for Ellie to make the evening meal.

His eyes were closed, his skin appeared grey in the dark of the evening. He didn't seem aware of her watching him and as she looked, she saw not Jubilee, her strong-willed husband, but an old man sitting there. Suddenly she was afraid.

CHAPTER THREE

'I want to put an advertisement in *The Swansea Times*, please.' Ellie smiled at the clerk behind the desk. He was handsome and very young and he was gazing at her in open admiration.

'What ad is that, miss?' He leaned over the counter and his eyes were sparkling. He must be a new addition to the staff of Arian Smale's daily for quite obviously he didn't recognize Ellie, didn't know she was a married woman and in a way she found that strangely moving.

She usually accompanied Jubilee when he came to *The Times*, today she was alone and so, to give her courage, she was wearing her best clothes. The much worn, outdated hat with its ostrich feathers and the heavy, winter coat and skirt had seen better days but the muted colours of peach and fawn suited her fair complexion.

She pushed the piece of paper across to him; on it Jubilee had scrawled the usual bald phrases that offered to the wholesalers leather suitable for the making of harnesses, boots and shoes.

'Your dad a tanner, is he?' The young man was openly flirting with her and Ellie smiled at him, warmed by his admiration. She had no intention of being unfaithful to her vows of marriage but a little attention from a handsome young man was very flattering.

'I'm Mrs Hopkins,' she said quietly. 'My husband is Jubilee Hopkins, we put an advertisement in the paper every month.'

He sat up straighter and Ellie became aware that his gaze was now focused on a point beyond her shoulder.

'Mrs Hopkins, it's good to see you again, how is Mr

25

Hopkins?' Arian Smale, proprietor of the most successful newspaper in Swansea, stood at Ellie's elbow. She didn't wait for Ellie's murmured pleasantries, she plucked the paper from the hands of the young man and scanned it quickly. 'That's fine,' she said briskly, 'give it to Mac, he'll see that it's passed on to the right department.'

The business dealt with, she turned to give Ellie her full attention. 'Would you come up to my rooms for a moment, there's something I need to talk to you about.' Though her smile was polite there was a wariness in Arian Smale's beautiful eyes. Ellie knew why. Ellie had once been Calvin Temple's mistress and Arian was in love with Calvin Temple. Their affair was the worst kept secret in Swansea.

On an impulse, Ellie put out her hand to touch Arian's arm. She liked Arian, respected her. In a way she was sorry for her. 'It was never very much, you know, the affair between me and Calvin. I think, on reflection, he only ever saw me as a pale substitute for you.' She was babbling, regretting her outburst as well as her over-familiar gesture, there was an air of reserve about Miss Smale that was slightly unnerving.

Arian made no comment but led the way upstairs with a straight back, every line of her body forbidding any further mention of Ellie's alliance with Calvin. No doubt the thought of the affair still had the power to hurt her.

Arian's private quarters were situated above the offices of the newspaper. Once Arian had occupied the building next door. Now, it was simply an annexe to the main newspaper office. Ellie looked around, the rooms were almost opulent, the décor tasteful, more sparse than was usual in an Edwardian home.

'I like your place,' Ellie said. 'It's so . . .' she struggled to find the right words, 'so dignified.'

Arian gave a short laugh. 'Not quite the way the citizens of our fair town see me, more the hussy than a lady of dignity is how I'm perceived.'

'You deserve some happiness whichever way you find

it.' Ellie could have bitten off her tongue as soon as the words were spoken, once again she felt she was on dangerous ground.

Arian's eyes were difficult to read, 'Nothing comes easily in this life.' The hard line of her jaw softened. 'Still, I have my newspaper, seeing it flourish is most satisfying.'

Ellie bit her lip and looked down at her work-roughened hands. Suddenly, it was as if she had no business to be sitting in a fine room surrounded by beautiful things. She was the wife of a tanner, her home was spartan, her husband worked back-breaking hours to make a living.

And yet, she was lucky, she could have ended up in the workhouse or even on the streets. It was as though Arian had picked up something of her thoughts because she leaned forward, her voice when she spoke was softer, kinder.

'You have something I'll never have, you have respectability.' She shrugged, 'I have a husband in the asylum and a lover who visits me under the cover of darkness. Not an entirely happy arrangement.'

Ellie felt the urge to open her heart to Arian, it seemed a very long time since she had a woman to talk to. She began to speak before she could lose her nerve.

'I may be respectable now but you know as well as I do it wasn't always like that.' She hesitated to put into words her feeling of rejection when Calvin had refused to marry her, no need to upset Arian again with reminders of her lover's chequered past.

'I'm married now, I have a ring on my finger but it was put there by an old man.' Immediately she had spoken, Ellie felt disloyal. 'Mind, Jubilee is kindness itself.' She frowned. 'It's true he can't love me in the way I'd like to be loved,' she shrugged, finding she was floundering into deeper water. 'He's sick, that's why I'm here alone today and I'm frightened for my future, is that very selfish of me?'

27

'It's natural enough, you've been alone once. When your family turned you out, it must have seemed as though everyone had deserted you. No wonder you are frightened and insecure.' She paused and it was as though the words were forced from her lips. 'Do you hate Calvin very much?'

'I don't lay blame at anyone's door, it's just the way my life has turned out and now, I have a great deal I must be thankful for. Calvin never lied to me, he never said he would marry me. It was my decision to leave him when I fell pregnant. He honoured his obligation to me financially until the day I married Jubilee. No, I don't hate him for what happened.'

'It's strange,' Arian said. 'If only we could fall in love at will and with suitable people, life would be much easier.'

'Anyway,' she spoke briskly now, 'to business.' She rested against the plump cushions of her chair, a woman more at ease now, a woman in charge once again. 'It's just that my advertising rates have to be increased at the end of the month by quite a large amount. If this inconveniences you, especially in the circumstances, with your husband indisposed, then I'm more than willing to accommodate you – for a while but I'm afraid I must move with the times.'

'Of course.' Ellie moved to the edge of her chair feeling the point of the interview had been reached, 'I shall tell Jubilee when I get home and then he can decide what to do about it.'

'You can take a copy of our future prices with you,' Arian said as she rose to her feet and moved towards the door. 'I hope you'll feel you can still patronize us, you are one of our most regular customers.'

Ellie could not help feeling dismissed even as Arian accompanied her down the stairs and right to the door of the office. She studied Ellie for a long moment in silence as though weighing her up. 'I hope to see you again, Mrs Hopkins,' she said at last.

'Yes, of course. Thank you for your time.' As Ellie turned she came face to face with Bridie Marchant. Her head high, her neck stiff, she looked every inch the lady; her eyes swept past Ellie's unfashionable figure without interest.

Bridie Marchant was the wife of one of the richest shipping merchants in Swansea, part owner of the fleet and she appeared determined to let everyone know it. Her carriage stood near the kerb, the paintwork gleaming, even the wheels looked as though they had been polished. The horses, immaculately groomed, stood as if to attention and Ellie wondered if Bridie's formal, almost regal air had affected the animals as much as it affected her.

'Morning, Mrs Marchant.' Arian had stepped back to allow Bridie inside the door and for a moment, the three women stood as though posed for a tableau.

'It's about the tide tables,' Bridie Marchant began without preamble, it seemed she had no time for pleasantries. 'They have been wrong on two occasions over the past week. We shipping folk rely on you people at *The Times* to get it right. I'm sure you will appreciate that if our loads miss the tides the delay costs us good money.' She sounded cross and Ellie, feeling she was eavesdropping on a private conversation, stepped outside into the street.

'Good day to you, Mrs Hopkins.' Arian sounded pleasant, unruffled by the attack on her paper and Ellie watched for a moment as the two women disappeared into the offices of *The Swansea Times* and the door swung shut as if to exclude her.

Ellie smiled, coming to Swansea certainly made her realize how the other half lived. Once she had been part of the other half herself. But that was some years ago now, when she was single, when she was the pampered mistress of Calvin Temple. Then her family had turned a blind eye, after all, the inclusion of lord into their circle was a welcome event. It was only when Ellie was alone,

29

alone and with child, that her father showed his disapproval in no uncertain terms.

In marrying Jubilee Hopkins Ellie had married beneath her but, even as her father had digested that information, he had been relieved that he no longer need feel any responsibility for his daughter or the twins that the local midwife had assured them Ellie was carrying.

Would she ever learn to forgive her parents? Ellie turned towards the seashore, it would be good to breathe in the clean air and watch the waves if only for a few minutes. Perhaps one day she would forget her father's rejection of her but she imagined it would be a long time before she could forgive.

Her mother was weak, subservient to her husband's will. She could no more help her attitude than she could abandon her comfortable lifestyle. Her mother Ellie could understand, she was a victim of her own strict upbringing and failed totally to understand her modern-minded daughter.

The waves were washing the golden sand of Swansea bay. The curving stretch of coastline was breathtakingly beautiful on this crisp spring morning. Suddenly Ellie felt an excruciating sadness for all the things she would never have; a young, vigorous husband, a brood of children round her skirts.

She turned in sudden determination towards home, she would just have to be content with what the good Lord had chosen to give her.

'It really isn't good enough, you know.' Bridie knew she sounded sharp, shrew-like even but she couldn't seem to help herself. She sat in Arian Smale's private rooms in the same chair Ellie had occupied a little earlier, but unlike Ellie she didn't admire the décor, didn't even see the good furniture and rich carpets. Her own home was palatial, the shipping industry was booming and that was a result of Bridie's acumen rather than that of her husband.

'I apologize. I shall see to it, Mrs Marchant,' Arian's voice was soothing, controlled and for some reason it served only to incense Bridie so that she clenched her hands tightly together.

'If the mistakes continue I shall feel obliged to take my custom elsewhere.'

'That would be a great pity, we are the largest paper in these parts and *any* advertisement you should choose to place with us would find the widest of audiences.'

Bridie flushed as Arian's meaning became clear. Bridie placed little or no advertising in *The Swansea Times*. Come to think of it she couldn't remember the last time she had put any business of that sort Arian Smale's way. Arian clearly knew that and was making a point.

Bridie rose to her feet, 'I must be going.' She drew on her gloves. 'I apologize if I sounded a little harsh but . . .' she shrugged.

'That's your privilege as a reader of our paper,' Arian spoke softly, 'you are quite right to point out any errors we make, I'm grateful to you.'

Was there an edge of sarcasm to Arian's words? Bridie could not quite decide. When Bridie left the offices of *The Times* she stood for a moment looking back at the large, elegant building and she felt, uncomfortably, that she had come out of the encounter with Arian with considerable loss of face.

'Take me home.' She snapped at the driver as she climbed into her carriage and closed the door impatiently behind her, the man was so slow, perhaps he was getting too old for the job. She sank back into the seat and pondered on the unsatisfactory direction that her marriage, indeed her whole life, seemed to be taking.

Paul was in the drawing room; he was sitting, legs spread out before him, reading the paper. It was *The Swansea Times*.

'Not looking up the tide tables are you?' She pulled off her gloves and threw them down on the well-polished occasional table beside her.

31

Paul took his time looking up at her. 'I am as a matter of fact. I'm sailing the day after tomorrow as well you know.' He sounded irritated, he seemed quite often irritated by her these days.

'Where are the boys?' she asked tossing aside her hat. Paul watched her, his eyes narrowed.

'With the new tutor, of course. I want them to go to a good school later on, in the meantime they need preparation, you must realize that, surely?'

She didn't reply and he spoke again, his tone revealing his irritation. 'Can't you let the maid take your things in the hall? Or else go up to your room to change, it's not very seemly of you to be flinging your clothes about the drawing room.'

'*You* talk to me about being seemly?' Bridie was, for a moment, lost for words. Paul was an upstart, a self-made man while she was from a good family background.

'Why the question, do you think me so much of a peasant that I'm not able to discern what is seemly and what is not?' He sat forward in his chair, any moment now they would be heading for a full-scale row. There had been too many rows lately.

'Of course not,' her tone was conciliatory. 'It's just that I'm annoyed by the wrong information contained in that rag you're reading, Arian Smale should be sure to get her facts right and I told her so to her face.'

'You seem to be handing out home truths left, right and centre lately.' Paul subsided in his chair, it seemed he'd had enough of the matter as he put the newspaper deliberately close to his face, effectively shutting Bridie out.

She suddenly felt lost and alone. 'What's happening to us, Paul?' She was close to tears. He didn't reply but the way he shook out the folds of the newspaper indicated he wanted nothing to do with any such discussion.

Disheartened, Bridie left the room and went upstairs

to the master bedroom. Paul's bag was packed, it was as if he couldn't wait to get away from her. On an impulse, she knelt down and tugged at the clasp, the bag gaped open and there were Paul's clean, crisp shirts and fresh underwear and socks. Not much to take when he was going to sea for a month or more. But then he had another wardrobe aboard his ship. He always sailed with a full complement of kit on the *Marie Clare*.

Bridie could understand the wanderlust that drove her husband, she sometimes heard the call of the sea herself, and yet she was growing tired of the gap that was between them. What had happened to all that love they'd shared? Or was she mistaken, was it only her ships Paul had wanted and she had been a necessary part of the package?

Something was jutting out of the inside pocket of the bag, a leather-bound book, a diary she thought with a sudden sense of discovery. She drew it out and saw that it was much used. Paul's fine handwriting was small, difficult to decipher but at once Bridie could see that it was no record of any amorous adventures. She sank onto the bed and began to read.

It seemed to make little sense, there were notes concerning odd cargos which brought little profit, things like boxes of candles and leather horse-collars. There were dates, apparently of meetings and the name Monkton appeared several times and Ireland was mentioned on almost every page.

Baffled, she returned it to the bag and snapped the catch shut. Perhaps she was growing obsessed, her reasoning distorted by jealousy. Well, she would go downstairs and discuss with Paul which school he would like their sons to attend when they were older, that approach was sure to put him in a better frame of mind. She left the room and closed the door quietly behind her.

★　　★　　★

Ellie carried the laden tray up the stairs to Jubilee's room. She had insisted he rest after what he called his 'funny turn' and though he'd protested, she could see he was grateful to spend a few days in bed. This in itself was worrying, it was seldom Jubilee was indisposed.

' 'Bout time you brought my grub.' Jubilee was resting against the pillows, he was still pale and the flesh hung around his jowls. 'A man could starve to death by here in this bed while his wife gallivants round Swansea.'

Ellie knew he didn't mean a word of it. 'Stop your complaining, man.' She placed the tray on the washstand and brought a bowl of soup to the bed. 'Shall I help you?'

'Good Lord, no. When the day comes I can't feed myself I'll be ready for my box.'

Ellie remembered when he'd said the same thing about working the tannery and she bit her lip trying not to show her anxiety. She waited while Jubilee bent his head to say grace and then placed the soup in front of him. But his hands were shaking and after a moment, Ellie took the spoon.

'Come on you stubborn old goat, if you don't eat you won't get well again and then what will I do?'

'I'm not ready to go, not for a while yet, so don't go looking for my nest egg.'

Ellie smiled. 'I'd be lucky to have a nest egg after your days, Jubilee Hopkins, spent it all in drinking and riotous living, you.'

A sparkle came to his eyes. 'Aye, once maybe, the drinking anyway but those days are long gone, my girl.'

Ellie saw that he ate most of the soup before she took away the bowl. 'I've made some nice bread pudding would you like some?'

'Not now, couldn't manage anything more, perhaps I'll have some for tea, what about that?'

'All right then for tea, but you must eat some of it, mind, there's four good eggs in that pudding, it will stick to your ribs, bring back your strength.'

34

'Kill me off, more like. Oh, damn! I've spilt some soup on the bedclothes,' he said frowning. Ellie said nothing, she just wiped the bedcover with the tea cloth as surreptitiously as she could. She was getting used to his clumsiness now, prepared for his moments of weakness, at least that's what she told herself.

Jubilee put out his hand to cover hers. 'I won't be a burden to you, my girl.' His voice was unusually gentle, 'I'd die rather than put any weight on those lovely shoulders of yours.'

'Don't talk like that.' Ellie pulled the covers over him. 'I won't have it, you've got a small chill, nothing to worry about, you'll be out and about in the yard again soon, don't you fret.'

'Talking about the yard,' Jubilee sank back onto the pillows grateful that the effort of eating was over. 'Hadn't you better get down there, see what those men are up to?'

'Aye, all right, nag.' Ellie took up the tray and moved to the door. 'Try to have a little nap, I'll get down to your precious yard straight away.'

'Oh, Ellie, make sure there's enough oak bark, don't want to be running out. It's spring time, should be fetching in a fresh stock by now. Organize some of the men to take out the wagons to collect a load of oak bark, take a time to dry the plates do.'

She moved to the door and was stopped by his voice. 'And remember, Caradoc is coming to do the books for us.' He paused for breath and Ellie took her opportunity.

'Don't fuss and worry, I've been here longer than five minutes, mind.'

Downstairs in the kitchen, Ellie placed the dishes in the sink, they could wait. Tonight, she would tidy up the place while Caradoc Jones worked in Jubilee's study adding up figures, making sense of the columns of profits and losses. Fortunately, there were few losses because Jubilee was a shrewd businessman. It was all an uncharted land to Ellie; the buying, the selling and the

35

finances of the tannery, all this she preferred to leave in the hands of the experts.

It was chilly in the yard and Ellie was glad to make her way to the comparative warmth of the grinding house. Matthew was thrusting plates of bark into the mill, while down in the room below Boyo was carrying half-hundredweights of oak bark to the tan yards for the dusting.

'Enjoy it, then, your jaunt into town, I mean.' Matthew was eyeing her coolly, his tone was a little censorious for Ellie's liking.

'I beg your pardon?' She held her head high and her eyes challenged him. With Jubilee sick, it was vital she keep the reins of the place firmly in her own hands. It was not a situation she relished and one she wasn't competent to handle but it was a case of take charge or allow the men to do as they liked. Only one was likely to take advantage and he was standing before her now. As Jubilee was fond of saying, one rotten apple could ruin a good barrel.

His eyes flickered away from hers. 'I should have come into town with you, it's not seemly or safe for you to be walking the streets of Swansea alone.'

'That is not your concern,' Ellie's voice was cold. 'This is the new century, women are having to get out in the streets alone every day, how else do you think they get to work?'

'I only meant . . .' His voice trailed away into silence and Ellie took a deep breath.

'Matthew, if you wish to continue working here then please accept that I'm your boss, at least while Jubilee is sick. If you remember that and give me the respect I deserve we'll get on much better. Now, I'll take over here, you go out and help the others dust the oak bark on the leather.'

Matthew gave her a long look, he seemed about to protest but after a moment, he moved from the grinding house and she was alone. Ellie found she was trembling,

36

it was an effort to assert herself, she who had always been content to take a back seat in life. But no, not always. Once she had refused to accept Calvin Temple's terms for staying in his life, she had wanted the commitment of marriage, he had not. She had left him. It had taken courage but in the eyes of her family, her decision had been ill-judged.

Perhaps her family were right, had she stayed with Calvin as his mistress might she not be living in luxury right now? Or, alternatively, perhaps she would have been cast aside anyway once Arian Smale had found a place in Calvin's life. Anyway, it was all past history. Here she was, wife of a tannery boss and, for the moment at least, she was in charge of the yards.

'Missus Hopkins, there's no bits of bark coming down the chute, the grinder must be empty.' Boyo's voice echoed up from the room below the grinding house. 'Want me to fetch more plates in from the drying house?'

Ellie gathered her thoughts and looked around her. 'That would be a good idea, Boyo,' she called. She moved to the window and stared outside into the yard, watching as the slight figure of the boy crossed the open ground. He was a good worker, small but strong for his age. At least he would be loyal to her if she was forced to take over the running of the mill completely. But no, that wouldn't happen, Jubilee would be well soon, he would take up the reins again and life would go on in the same way as it had these past years.

The future seemed to stretch in drab monotony before her. She would have no children, she would have no young man to sing her love songs and make her feel beautiful. No strong body next to hers in the bed. Her flesh would never again sing with desire the way it had when Calvin Temple had held her and made love to her. She felt with a deep sense of conviction that she would never love again. Suddenly there were tears on her lashes and even though Ellie recognized them as tears of self-pity, she couldn't stop them slipping down her cheeks and into her mouth.

By the evening, Ellie's mood of despondency had been alleviated by young Boyo's stories. He told her how the men working in the yard talked of their lives at home. Luke's mother-in-law was living with him, so he complained and he was being nagged by two sets of jaws simultaneously. Ellie could well imagine Luke's dry humour that would be much in evidence even while he grumbled.

Harry had other problems, his wife had found she was expecting again and had banished Harry to the slope where he shivered alone at night. The way Boyo repeated the tale was so funny that Ellie found herself laughing aloud. She appreciated the men; through all the trials and tribulations of life they were good natured and did an honest day's work for their pay. The older man kept in line the casual labourers who worked only intermittently when there was extra work on at the yard. The casuals caused little problem, glad of a few hours labour for a more than generous pay.

Ellie knew the men could be relied upon in a crisis, both Luke and Harry were loyal to Jubilee. It was Matthew who made her afraid she would fail to keep the tannery running smoothly.

Jubilee was asleep when she went into his room and she stood for a moment looking down at him, her heart filled with an almost painful love. He was more of a father to her than her own had ever been. Jubilee, if he'd had a daughter would never have cast her aside for fear she would disgrace him. He would stick by his own against all odds not caring what anyone else thought.

As though aware of her presence, he opened his eyes. 'Hello, love,' he smiled. 'I feel a little better now, mind, the sleep did me good.' He gestured for her to sit beside the bed. 'When I go, you'll be well cared for, it's all done, the will, legal like. In any case, there's no other kith or kin of mine to come and try to take a penny from you. What I've earned is yours, it's all in the hands of Bernard Telforth, he's a good man, he'll advise you.'

'Hush, please Jubie, don't talk like that.' She took his hand and traced one of the blue, jutting veins with her finger. 'I don't know how I'd manage without you, I love you, you must know that.'

'Aye, I do, that's why I want to leave you well provided for. You'll be free some day soon and then you can do just as you please.'

'Being with you pleases me.' Ellie felt close to tears. 'I need you Jubie, don't give up on life.'

'Look, girl, I'm an old man, I've had my life. These years we've been together have been some of the happiest any man could wish for.'

She put her free hand across his lips. 'No more. I'm not having you talk like that. Now, let's change the subject, what about a bit of that lovely pudding then, all I've got to do is warm it up?'

Jubilee smiled. 'Aye, that sounds good, go on with you then, less talk and more action, right?'

He ate very little of the pudding and Ellie's concern grew. Perhaps it would be as well to call in the doctor in the morning if Jubilee was no better.

Later, Caradoc Jones came to the house and stood in the kitchen before the fire; a young, rotund man, his fresh face wreathed in smiles beneath a hat that appeared too small for him. 'Cuppa before I start on the books wouldn't go amiss, mind.' He thrust his hands into his pockets and leaned back towards the fire, his belly hanging ripely over the waistband of his trousers. There was a dusting of fuzz above his mouth and more around his chin, it seemed Caradoc was unable to grow either a moustache or a beard.

Ellie's feet ached, she longed to kick off her boots and sink into a chair before the fire but the sooner she gave Caradoc his ritual cup of tea, the sooner he would start work.

'How's Mr Hopkins?' he asked looking round

questioningly, 'Gone out to the public is he?'

'He's not feeling too well.' The kettle began to pour steam from the blackened spout and Ellie deftly hauled it onto the hob and made the tea.

'I think I'll have one with you.' She put out the cups and watched as Caradoc spooned sugar in a generous measure into his cup.

'I don't know how you can drink it like that.' She took her tea without sugar. 'It must be sweet as honey.'

He nodded affably, 'Aye, just about.' He drank it standing up before the fire, his face alight with almost feline contentment. 'Can't beat a good fire, my mother, rest her soul, used to make sure that the maid kept our grates well stocked with coal. Can't abear being cold, me.'

Ellie would have imagined, looking at him, that his bulk was enough to keep him warm, but she was too polite to say so.

'Jubilee in bed, is he?' His rapid change of subject was bewildering, Caradoc's mind was like a butterfly hopping from one subject to another with amazing swiftness.

'Yes, he's in bed.' Ellie wished he'd get on with his work, she wasn't in the mood for making polite conversation, she was far too tired.

'Had the quack in to him?' Caradoc put down his cup and lifted the tails of his coat to give the flames of the fire more access to his large backside.

'I will in the morning.' Ellie put her cup down beside Caradoc's, she could hardly keep her eyes open she was so weary.

'Best thing.' He talked in the briefest of sentences and Ellie found herself doing the same. It must be an idiosyncrasy that was catching.

'By far.' She waited patiently in silence and at last he moved away from the fire.

'Best get on. Shall I go through?' Without waiting for a reply, he left the kitchen and, with a sigh of relief, Ellie sank into a chair.

She must have dozed because when she opened her eyes once more, the fire had fallen in the grate, the flames almost extinguished. She looked at the clock, it was past ten, time she was in bed. The door to the kitchen opened and Caradoc's stomach preceded him into the room.

'All done for this month,' he rubbed his chubby hands together in satisfaction. 'Good books Jubilee Hopkins keeps, no need to worry about discrepancies where he's concerned.' He moved towards the door.

'See you again then and take care of that husband of yours, give him my regards, mind.'

Ellie damped down the embers of the fire and poured what was left of the hot water from the kettle into a bowl, she would have a quick wash and then she would go to bed.

Later, lying beside Jubilee in the double bed, Ellie lay wide-eyed staring at the patch of light cast on the wall from the window. In spite of her weariness, sleep wouldn't come. She was worrying about Jubilee. She wished she had called the doctor at once, when Jubie had taken to his bed. With a man the age her husband was, it didn't do to take chances.

At last, when she finally slept, it was to dream of graveyards and coffins and black-garbed mourners and interminable rain streaming down into her eyes.

When she woke in the morning, she turned at once towards her husband and caught her breath in relief, Jubilee was breathing easily, he had a good colour and as though aware of her scrutiny, he opened his eyes. They were bright and clear. Well, hadn't her mother told her when she had nightmares as a child that nasty dreams always meant the opposite and that something good was going to happen the morning after a bad dream?

'Hungry?' She slid out of bed and stood bare-footed on the wooden floor, feeling the chill of the spring morning wrap itself around her.

'I'm starving.' Jubilee smiled, 'Fetch me my trews, I'm getting up, I've got work to do.'

As she knelt before the hearth, building the fire, listening to Jubilee's heavy footsteps on the boards upstairs, Ellie closed her eyes for a moment in relief.

'Thank you God,' she whispered fervently and as though in reply, a shaft of morning sunlight slanted, like a benediction, across her face.

CHAPTER FOUR

Arian Smale locked the door of the newspaper offices with a sigh of relief; the last few days had been trying, to say the least. Customers had complained *en masse* of the rise in the advertising rates, giving voice to their protests in no uncertain terms; anyone would think she was proposing to take the last penny out of their pockets.

In her own rooms, she kicked off her boots and sank into a chair. The maid, conscientious as always, brought in her tray holding a carafe of sherry. She had only been with Arian for a few months but already she was proving invaluable.

'Thanks, Mary, you're a wonder.' Arian stretched her toes towards the fire gratefully; although spring was bringing swaths of daffodils through the parklands of Swansea, the evening air was still misty and chill.

Arian picked up her mail, slicing the envelopes open with a paper-knife. It really was time she engaged the services of a secretary, she had enough to do without answering customers' letters personally.

The first one was from Bridie Marchant, reiterating her complaint concerning the tide tables. Arian bit her lip, it really was too bad of her reporters to get it wrong, it wasn't difficult to consult the experts down at the Swansea shipping offices. Blast Bridie Marchant!

Strange, Bridie used to be a very nice person. When she had come to live in Wales and had stayed with her cousin Jono in his modest home at Clydach, Bridie had been kindness itself. But then Arian had been a nobody, a shoemaker and not a very good one at that so perhaps

43

Bridie had found her no threat. Did that mean that now she did?

Arian looked around at her lush apartment with a critical eye. As her newspaper had flourished she had been able to expand her business, taking on the building next door and adding to her living-quarters so that they were large, almost sumptuous. True she had no grand house, no flower-filled garden in which to walk, but she had the town of Swansea right on her doorstep.

It was just possible that Bridie resented her success. But it went deeper than that, Bridie Marchant was a woman who was very unhappy. The lines etched deeply around her mouth, the small frown that was always present between her brows revealed her state of mind much more than any words could do.

Arian drank a little sherry, allowing the mellow flavour to roll over her tongue, then she rose to her feet stretching her hands above her head. She would have a bath, she would revel in the luxury of her newly built bathroom. She would prepare herself for Calvin's visit.

She was just like a courtesan, she thought soberly, washing, perfuming her body in readiness for her lover. But unlike a courtesan, she had a husband who had tried to kill her. She also had the need to earn her own living.

Lying in the scented water, Arian felt the tensions wash from her. It was good to forget the petty irritations of her day, even better to anticipate the moment when Calvin would hold her in his arms.

A long time ago, she had come to a decision about what was important in life. Facing death at knife-point, confronted by Gerald Simples, her husband, a madman, she had decided that if she was allowed to live she would make the most of her days. So, here she was, waiting for her lover as eagerly as any untried maiden.

Calvin was late. Arian stood at the window watching, waiting for him to come to her, as she had done so many times before. He was all she desired in a man; he was kind, generous, a lover and a friend. What a pity he could never be her husband.

When he turned the corner into her street, anticipation flared through her. She resisted the temptation to rush down the stairs, waiting for his key in the lock and the sound of his footsteps on the stairs with barely contained excitement.

When he entered the room, he carried with him the freshness of the spring air. He took her into his arms and held her close. She didn't admonish him for his lateness, she closed her eyes and breathed in the scent of him and knew she loved this man more than she had ever loved anyone.

'Take me to bed,' she whispered. He held her hand in his and led her through the upper hallway and towards the narrow stairs to her room.

'Arian, I have waited for this moment all day.' His voice was tender and she kissed his mouth. She loved the way his lips curved upwards at the corners, she touched them lovingly with her fingertips.

'Damn it! I can't wait, will I never get enough of you, Arian?'

His flesh was warm against hers and as they lay beneath the blankets, Arian held him close to her, closing her eyes, happiness flowing through her.

'I love you,' she said the words against his mouth as he kissed her. 'I love you, Calvin Temple.'

He took her with vigour and yet without aggression. She held him close, enjoying the silk feel of his skin against hers. He was so dear to her, had such power to thrill her. She revelled in their passion, losing herself in the dizzy happiness of the moment.

Afterwards they remained side by side, propped up against the pillows and talked. 'I've had a written complaint from Bridie Marchant about the error in the tide table.'

'Is it important?' Calvin held her hand, his fingers warm around hers.

45

'It is to me, I hate making mistakes.'

'Well, you know what Bridie's trouble is, don't you?' He was being mischievous, Arian could tell by the smile in his voice.

'No, tell me.'

'Her husband is a sailor, he has a girl in every port. Well, at least in one port.'

'How do you know this?' Arian turned to look at him, her interest aroused.

'Men gossip too, especially sailors in drink. Call yourself a newspaper hound and you don't know the latest bit of scandal? I bet old Mac knows all about it.'

'Ah, Mac.' He was Arian's partner as well as being a very good reporter. 'I sometimes think he knows everything.'

Calvin was silent and Arian punched him lightly on the shoulder. 'Come on, then, tell me.'

'Paul Marchant is being unfaithful to his wife as is the wont of footloose sailors.' He turned to look at her. 'It's common talk among the society ladies of the town, brought to them by their servants, I've no doubt.'

'I wouldn't know from first hand experience.' Arian's tone was dry. 'As the wife of a madman, I don't warrant invitations to any fancy events. In any case, I suppose I'm the subject of a great deal of gossip myself.'

Calvin raised her hand to his lips and kissed the palm. 'Do you mind?'

Arian shook back her long hair. 'No, I suppose not. Sometimes it rankles though, I'm not accepted for myself, Arian Smale, businesswoman, and I should be. All right, I haven't a husband who's made his mark in the town, instead I have a husband who is capable of violence, who killed a young girl.' Her face softened. 'Who would have killed me if you hadn't been there, my darling.'

'Hush, don't rake up bad memories.' Calvin slipped out of bed. 'I'm going to take a bath, come with me?'

'Not now,' Arian smiled. 'I don't want to throw

46

caution entirely to the wind. I wouldn't like Mary to hear my gurgles of delight as she sits in her room.'

'She's discreet enough, isn't she?' Calvin stood naked, a tall well-muscled man, looking down at Arian.

'I suppose so, I think I can trust her. I don't really care either way. I live my life as I see fit, even if I wanted respectability I'd hardly be able to achieve it, would I?'

'Am I enough for you, then? The little bit of time we have together, is it making you happy?'

'I have you and I have my newspaper, that's all I'll ever want.' When she was alone, Arian pondered on her own words. Was it enough for her, this hole in the corner affair? In any case, had she any choice but to accept such a compromise?

Calvin was free of encumbrances, he had divorced his first wife in spite of the furore it had caused. Since then, he'd taken mistresses, no-one blamed him for that, and now she was one of them.

Arian sighed. She was still married to Gerald Simples; whatever he was, whatever he had become, he was her husband and nothing could change that. It was something she had told herself many times before but it didn't get any easier.

She rose from the bed. She would wash in the water from the basin, it would be cold but later she would luxuriate in her bath once more, remembering every little detail of how Calvin had looked and what he had said, going over and over it in her mind. Precious memories, was that all she would ever have?

Bridie stood in the window watching as the cab carrying Paul away from her disappeared along the drive. Once she would have gone with him to the docks, stood waving to him as his ship prepared to put to sea. Now it was different.

She turned away and moved towards her desk. She took the key from her belt and unlocked the roll-top desk. Seating herself comfortably, she pulled her notebooks towards her and began to study them. Here she kept her private records of the business transactions carried out by the main body of the fleet of ships she owned. Steel, tin-plate, coal, she wasn't fussy what the cargo was so long as it made her money.

The accountant was very efficient, he worked diligently over the regular books but Bridie did not wish to trust anyone entirely. So she kept her own accounts.

Paul might not be aware of it, but lately, Bridie had taken to relegating the cargos on board his ships with the less profitable loads. Instead of letting him take the long haul trips to China and India, she had manipulated matters so that he took the short runs to Bristol and Ireland. These brought in little return but strangely he made no protest, indeed, he seemed happy to accommodate her wishes. What he failed to realize was that her fortune was growing and his was diminishing; it was one way of keeping her husband in line.

If there was any bitterness in the way she thought about him, she chose to ignore it. Paul was being unfaithful, she was sure of it. Oh, it would be difficult to prove, he was too careful to allow any evidence of his infidelity to become apparent. But he was not the shrewd business man he believed himself to be, or else he trusted his wife implicitly, because while he was betraying her, she was finding ways to arm herself against his possible desertion.

She doubted he would go so far as to cause an open split in their marriage, he wanted the regard of his sons, his fine home, the acquiescent wife he supposed Bridie to be. Well, she was not so gullible, he would find that out one day to his cost.

She pored over the books for a time, adding figures, making calculations and then, carefully, she closed her desk and locked it. Let Paul Marchant try to get one up on her and he would learn that she was not such easy prey as he imagined.

She wandered into his room; this last trip he had made

an excuse to take one of the other bedrooms for his own so as not to disturb her. Disturb her indeed! Did he think she was a fool?

Systematically she searched through the drawers; there were his clothes, his underwear, his socks and in the wardrobe his pristine shirts hung stiffly in a row. She smelled them, wondering if she could detect perfume on the fine linen but no, they were freshly washed, there was nothing but the scent of soap and the hot iron.

At the bottom of his wardrobe she found an old cloth bag that he'd left behind this trip. She had bought him a new one, ashamed of the shabbiness of the one he usually carried, finding it distasteful for a man in his position to be so careless of his possessions.

On an impulse, she picked up the bag and carried it to the bed. Perhaps she would find his notebook again and this time make more sense of it. In the depths of the battered bag, she found a jacket which Paul must have overlooked. She pulled it free of the bag and as she did so she heard a crackling in the pocket. Her mouth was suddenly dry as she took out the piece of paper and unfolded it.

If she had hoped to catch him out, to prove his infidelity, she was disappointed, there was nothing written on the slip of paper but the time of the outgoing tide from Swansea docks.

But wait, it wasn't in Paul's hand, his writing was strong and bold, with large loops and curls. This was small, cramped, the handwriting of a woman. On an impulse, Bridie thrust the paper in her pocket and glanced at the ornate clock on the mantelpiece. There was over an hour yet before the ship sailed, why had her husband left too early? He had a master to see to the preparations for hauling anchor and preparing the ship for sailing. Well, she would take a look down at the docks, try to find out just what Paul was up to.

★   ★   ★

49

Ellie walked towards the docks feeling the softness of spring cool her hot cheeks. Shortly, she reached the entrance to the harbour where the pier jutted out to sea like a long arm reaching for the distant shore across the water.

The scents of tar and rope mingled with the over-powering smell of the fish market as she walked rapidly past the open shed where the fishermen had displayed their wares. A few housewives and serving maids were bartering loudly beside the boxes of cod and whiting and no-one noticed Ellie as she made her way to one of the shipping offices situated in the streets surrounding the docks.

Her spirits were light because Jubilee was up and about again, his illness vanished as quickly as it had come. The doctor was amazed at Jubilee's powers of recovery, declaring him a tough old bird. The sickness and fever, which remained undiagnosed, had vanished as if it had never been and though Jubilee was still a little unsteady, his powers of leadership were as strong as ever.

The reason she was here now, making for the offices of Marchant and James shipping line, was because of Jubilee's fussiness that his payments for goods delivered be made on time.

He had lately sold stocks of leather to Paul Marchant, undertaking to deliver the skins to the saddler and thereafter to pick up the finished goods and have his waggons deliver the horse-collars directly to the docks.

Jubilee's orders were that Matthew should accompany Ellie on the journey to the shipping office but Matthew had been out with one of the wagons collecting more timber. In any case, Ellie didn't want to give the man any encouragement at all, though she could hardly tell Jubilee that. So she had come alone and now she was feeling a little foolish and at a loss.

She looked up at the elegant buildings, at the ornately decorated porticos and felt intimidated. She wasn't used to doing business, she usually left all that to Jubilee. Still, it was about time she took some responsibilities from the shoulders of her husband.

The tannery at Glyn Hir, though not a large one, was flourishing and had a reputation surpassed by none in Swansea or its environs. He was probably speaking the truth when Jubilee claimed that the leather from Glyn Hir was among the finest in the entire Principality.

The offices of Marchant and James were smaller than she had imagined, less imposing. But the woodwork was newly painted and the sign above the door was bold, striking a chord of confidence in Ellie that gave her some measure of relief. At least she would not be dealing with charlatans.

She knocked on the door and a masculine voice called for her to step inside. If she had expected to see Bridie or her husband Paul Marchant she was disappointed. An elderly man with huge side whiskers sat behind a desk, looking at her in obvious surprise. She saw him rise to his feet in an excess of politeness and gesture to the rather capacious wooden chair that stood facing him.

'I'm sorry, young lady,' his eyes, set deep in plump creases, sparkled. 'We don't see very many of the fairer sex in this office. I'm Mr Elias, by the way.'

Ellie felt foolish. 'My husband hasn't been well,' she said, feeling the need to make excuses for her presence there. 'It was necessary for me to come to see you. It's rather embarrassing, it's about an outstanding bill, as a matter of fact.'

'I see, sorry to hear it indeed. Well can you give me some details Mrs . . . ?'

'Mrs Hopkins,' Ellie supplied, 'I'm sorry to have to come to the offices but the bill has been outstanding for some time and now, it seems, Mr Marchant needs more stocks of leather. I'm sure it's all just a mistake, an oversight on Mr Marchant's part.'

'How much leather?' Mr Elias turned some papers over on his desk. 'I need to know a little more about this before I can look in to it. When was the load delivered and what was its destination? Do you have a bill with you stating the amount owed?'

Ellie felt foolish, she could see now that she had come to town ill prepared, she should have been business-like, had all the necessary information at her fingertips.

'I haven't brought anything with me, I haven't gone into it very thoroughly, I'm afraid, I can see that now.'

'Well, Mr Marchant would not want the leather for delivery to France, that's for sure.' Mr Elias leaned back in his chair, 'They send us the most lovely calfskin, want to export more, not import any leather, that's the French for you.'

Ellie was feeling more foolish by the minute. 'I think I should go, it was silly of me to have come here so unprepared.'

The outer door opened and the rush of salt breeze carried with it the tang of the sea. Paul Marchant was suddenly in the office filling it with his presence. 'Elias, we'll be sailing soon and . . .' his eyebrows lifted when he saw Ellie sitting there, looking up at him in some agitation.

He was a handsome man, broad of shoulder and with the healthy complexion earned by years of weathering in the sun and sea air. 'Good morning.' He stood beside Ellie's chair, looking down at her, his eyes full of interest. 'I wasn't expecting to see anything so lovely when I walked into my office this morning.'

Ellie felt her colour rising, she was used to Matthew's rather blunt approaches, but coming from a gentleman of Paul Marchant's standing, such charm disconcerted her.

'I'm afraid I may have wasted Mr Elias's time,' she said. She moved her bag on her lap, uncertain whether to leave and after a moment's hesitation, she rose to her feet.

'The young lady, Mrs Hopkins,' Mr Elias paused, was there an emphasis on her married name, Ellie wondered? 'Mrs Hopkins was enquiring about an unpaid bill. Her husband owns a tannery, you see, sir.'

'Yes, I do see,' Paul thrust his hands into his pockets and studied her, he had a subtle air about him which managed to convey the impression that Ellie was the one woman in the world he wanted to talk to. At this moment, she certainly seemed to be the sole object of his interest. His charm was palpable and what's more he was aware of it. He was the same type as Matthew Hewson except he was garbed in gentleman's clothes.

'How much leather are we talking about and in what quantity?' Paul smiled disarmingly. 'When was the delivery date?'

'I'm afraid I came here quite unprepared.' Ellie's embarrassment increased, 'I'm sorry, I don't know answers to any of your questions.'

'Don't look so worried, I'm sure we can sort this out.' Paul leaned slightly closer and Ellie resisted the temptation to step away from him.

'Our tannery is called Glyn Hir, we . . .'

'Ah, yes, of course, very good stuff comes out of your place. Old Jubilee Hopkins is well known around Swansea, his name is synonymous with quality. Think no more about it, the matter will be dealt with as soon as I return from my trip to Ireland.'

'I'd better go,' Ellie moved towards the door, 'I'll speak to Jubilee, he hasn't been well or he'd have called to see you himself. He knows much more about the business side of things than I do,' she added apologetically.

'I insist I accompany you past the entrance of the docks,' Paul's voice indicated it was a casual gesture. Somehow, Ellie knew that the move was quite calculated.

'Can't have you being carried off by any of the foreign sailors who come ashore here, can we?' Paul was exerting his charm, smiling down at her, his strangely violet eyes full of meaning.

53

'It's all right, really.' Ellie drew her gloves more tightly over her fingers, she was ill at ease with this man, she was aware that he posed a threat without really knowing why.

Mr Elias rose from his chair, 'Good day to you, Mrs Hopkins.' His practical attitude broke the tension, 'I trust you'll soon sort matters out to your satisfaction.'

There was nothing for it but to allow Paul Marchant to accompany her on her departure from his office. But as Ellie walked along the cobbled roadway with Paul Marchant at her side she was feeling far from comfortable with the situation. She could think of nothing to say but that didn't seem to matter, Paul Marchant was in complete control of the moment.

'I shall make it my business to come to Glyn Hir and see Jubilee Hopkins for myself. I shall also make it my business to ensure the bills are paid on time in future.' His smile inferred that the oversight was not his own. Ellie found him far too confident of his own charm and she was beginning to be irritated by him.

'I need your leather,' Paul said more seriously, 'it's a very important part of my trade. As is the extra service done by Mr Hopkins. It saves me so much time to have the skins delivered to the saddler's and made up into the required loads of tack.'

'But surely there are larger tanneries than ours?' Ellie said, trying to keep the surprise out of her voice. Why was Paul Marchant bothering to flatter her? Glyn Hir's contribution to his business enterprise must be very small indeed.

He seemed to read her mind. 'Your price is competitive and your goods are of an excellent quality, that's why I need to buy your leather.'

Perhaps he was right but Ellie doubted it. She wished she had never come, it was embarrassing walking along with this man who was a stranger to her and who was so sure of his own ability to charm her. There must be something in the transaction for him, he was the type who never did anything without good reason. Still, he was a customer and she must not be downright rude to him.

As they passed the entrance to the docks, where, thankfully, Ellie could take her leave of Paul Marchant, a carriage drew to a sudden halt and a woman alighted. Her face was flushed, her eyes narrowed.

'Paul!' Her voice was harsh, her features so contorted with anger that for a moment Ellie didn't realize she was face to face with Bridie Marchant. 'And what may I ask are you doing walking openly along the docks with some cheap whore? You thought you'd fooled me didn't you?' She was gasping with anger. 'I knew you were up to something, I felt in my bones that there was another woman in the offing somewhere.'

Ellie felt herself blanch, how dare Bridie Marchant assume she was a loose woman?

'Excuse me, you're quite mistaken,' she forced herself to speak. 'I came here on business, I . . .'

'You are alone, aren't you, here on the dockside with a sailor? And what sort of business are you conducting, I wonder?'

'I came to see about a bill for leather, an unpaid bill for money owed by your firm.' Ellie was growing angry, she had asked for none of this.

'A likely story, you're acting more like a prostitute than a lady out and about on business. Oh you may talk in a fancy voice but that doesn't make you a lady.'

'I'm a respectable married woman.' Ellie was outraged by Bridie Marchant's attitude, 'I don't deserve this . . . abuse.'

Bridie rounded on her. 'I know who you are, you're the wife of the tannery owner aren't you? Shows what sort you are, married to improve yourself did you? Well you just keep your hands off my husband if you know what's good for you. Go back to your disgusting old man.'

55

Incensed beyond reason, Ellie found herself lashing out, the flat of her open hand catching Bridie full across the face. Immediately, Ellie was appalled by her own reaction, by responding in such a way to the woman's goading she had lowered herself to Bridie Marchant's level.

'How dare you touch me,' Bridie put her hand to her cheek, 'you bitch!'

'Bridie,' Paul stepped forward, his face set, 'you are making an exhibition of yourself. Be calm, let's all get a grip on our tempers. I assure you Mrs Hopkins came to see me on a business matter.'

'On what business matter? The business of how much she was going to charge you for her services, I suppose. You disappoint me Paul, I didn't think you were the sort to pay for your pleasures.'

'Be reasonable, Bridie,' Paul urged again. 'Let me just explain things to you.'

Suddenly Bridie shot a question at Ellie, her voice full of venom. 'Very well, explain, then, what sort of load did you have in mind, how many tons of leather are involved and where is this leather being taken?'

'I don't really know . . .' Ellie realized how feeble her story must seem.

'So you want me to believe that your husband sent you alone to see my husband about a so-called load that you know very little about, is that it?' Bridie's voice was bordering on the hysterical.

'I know it sounds strange but it's the truth,' Ellie said, feeling her hands begin to tremble.

Bridie came close to her face, there was sheer hate in her eyes. 'Leave my husband alone, you might think it great fun to be his doxy, profitable too, but you are going to find out it doesn't do to cross Bridie Marchant, you'll pay dearly for what you've done this day.'

With a shake of her head, Ellie moved a step backwards. 'There's nothing to say, you're obviously not prepared to listen to reason so I might as well go.'

56

'Aye, go, run home but you won't be safe from me, not anywhere, be warned.'

Paul Marchant caught his wife's arm trying his best to restrain her. He looked apologetically towards Ellie and shook his head.

She hurried across the roadway and headed into the centre of town, finding that she was trembling from head to toe. How appalling to be involved in such a scene. Bridie Marchant had provoked her but losing her temper and lashing out was unforgivable. Ellie's hand stung from the strength of the blow, she must have really hurt Bridie Marchant and she was ashamed.

Bridie was to be pitied, she must really be frightened of losing her husband and she must have good reason. Well Ellie was well out of it, she wouldn't ever go near the docks alone again, it had been a foolish move on her part. Had she taken Matthew as her husband suggested, all this wouldn't have happened. Now she had roused Bridie Marchant's bitterest anger, and in that instant, Ellie felt a deep sense of unease.

'I must go Bridie, be reasonable, I want to catch the tide.' Paul's voice was soft, he was attempting to conciliate her but Bridie was beside herself with anger, she was past being reasonable.

'If you don't come home with me now and sort this all out then it's over between us.' Her voice was raised and people were turning to look at them.

'But, Bridie, I—'

'No buts, you come home right now.'

'All right, if it means that much to you, I'll come home. It was just a short trip anyway, I seem to be doing quite a few of those lately. You go home and I'll follow as soon as I can.'

Bridie hesitated and Paul seeing his advantage spoke again. 'What has given you this foolish idea that I am interested in another woman, Bridie?'

She held out the handwritten note she had found

and he took it and studied it with a puzzled frown.

'This is old Mr Elias's handwriting, you are a silly girl to make out anything suspicious from this.' He attempted to hold her close for a moment but she remained rigid in his arms.

'Look,' his tone held a note of resignation. 'I'll have to let the master know I'm not sailing, otherwise the man will miss the tide.' Paul turned away with an air of determination and entered the docklands, his hands thrust into his pockets, his head high.

Bridie returned to the coach and climbed aboard, she would go home and wait for Paul and woe betide him if he didn't follow, she would throw him out on the street without compunction. They were living in the house she had bought with her own money, he would do well to remember that fact. Whatever excuses he made, she intended to nip this little affair in the bud, teach Paul that he couldn't trifle with other women and still enjoy all the luxuries *her* money had brought him.

She pursed her lips angrily. As for Ellie Hopkins, she could look out, she would have to learn it wasn't wise to make an enemy of Bridie Marchant.

CHAPTER FIVE

Arian sat in the small room that lacked any sort of luxury and looked towards the preacher who was standing near the window, his hands thrust into his pockets. Beside her Mac, his notebook in his hand, was scribbling swiftly.

Arian had expected Evan Roberts, the great revivalist, to be verbose, had expected flowery phrases to pour from his lips, but there was a simplicity about the man that was more impressive than the greatest of oratory.

'You feel God has called you to this work then, Mr Roberts?' Arian asked gently. 'When did you know that you were cut out for the ministry?'

Evan Roberts looked at her with strangely compelling eyes. He was slow to speak, almost as though the thoughts were turning over in his head and being sifted before he replied to her question. 'The principal of the grammar school which I attended urged his pupils, myself included, to listen to the preachings of Seth Joshua. I was greatly impressed by the man and subsequently took the Lord into my heart.'

He paused, the words did not come easily to him. 'Thereafter, I wept and prayed without ceasing and when I came out of my own Gethsemane, I knew that a great revival was about to begin.' He paused, his conviction that he was right was impressive. 'I was charged by God with going out and spreading the gospel. I gave up my preparation for the ministry to lead the nation to Calvary.'

'Strong words,' Mac said. 'Coming from someone else, sir, they would seem like boasting but I've heard of your great following in your own village and of your influence on Loughor. Indeed I've seen the effects of your work on the good citizens of Swansea and though I might not agree with your views, I certainly feel the need to respect them.'

Arian's eyebrows lifted a little, it wasn't like Mac to admit to being impressed. And yet, didn't she too feel the presence of this man Evan Roberts who spoke of his faith so simply?

'You are quite willing to be quoted in my newspaper?' Arian felt obliged to ask.

Evan Roberts inclined his head gravely. 'If my words can reach out to people, bring them to their maker in humility and love, then I will be grateful to you and your newspaper.'

He moved towards the door. 'Now, if you will excuse me, I have people waiting who need my council and my prayers. This work is important, you see?'

Arian rose at once. She felt that Mac wanted to extend the interview but she looked down at him, where he remained stubbornly seated and shook her head.

'We've kept Mr Roberts long enough.' She smiled to soften her words. 'Let's go back to the office, you can knock the piece into shape ready for tomorrow's edition.'

In the hallway, Evan Roberts paused, a strangely youthful man for such a calling and yet one who appeared to have the wisdom of the ages engraved into his face.

'God be with you, friends.' The door closed and Adrian felt as if she had been granted a rare gift.

'He's a holy man, there's no doubting his sincerity or his conviction.' She looked up at Mac who was adding a few words to his hastily scrawled notes.

'I can only agree,' his tone was dry, 'much as I hate to admit it even an old reprobate like me felt the power of the man. I think he's going to take the whole of Wales by the throat and make them follow him and his God.'

Arian pulled on her gloves. 'Well, it's our place to

report the news not to make any predictions,' she smiled. 'Not that you'll worry about that, you'll write your piece as you see fit as you always do and I will doubtless agree that it's a work of genius.'

That evening she talked about the interview with Calvin; he was seated in the large chair near the window that looked down onto the teeming life in the Strand below. Arian stood beside him and rested her hand on his shoulder and leaning forward saw a line of Chinese men, undoubtedly off one of the ships, walking one behind the other, large plaits hanging down their backs.

'It's a strange world all right,' she said. 'The Chinese have their own sort of God, the Egyptians theirs, who can say who is in the right?'

Calvin turned her to face him and took her in his arms, drawing her into a chair to rest on his knee. 'I love you, Arian Smale, especially when you're so serious and grave, I love your little nose, your beautiful eyes and most of all I love your silver hair.'

He pulled at the pins and Arian's hair fell in shining waves over her shoulders. Calvin moved the strands aside and kissed her neck.

'You must agree, though, Calvin, it's a strange thing, this religion. Do you know, I almost envied Evan Roberts, so sure of his faith, so filled with peace.'

'Stop talking and pay a little attention to me,' Calvin whispered in her ear and Arian felt herself responding to him with a warmth and languor that never seemed to diminish.

She kissed his mouth, her tongue probing his, she ran her hands over the broadness of his shoulders and desire began its slow course through her blood. But even as he touched her breast, she knew that the desire was heightened because she loved Calvin deeply, loved him for his unconditional acceptance of the little she had to give him.

'Come to bed,' she said softly. Arm in arm, they left the sitting room, leaving the fire to spit and the coals to

61

shift in the grate until the embers burned with only a faint glow.

'Sorry I didn't seem to get very far with Paul Marchant.' Ellie took Jubilee's gnarled hand in her own. 'I was ill prepared, I should have known more about the quantity of goods he owed us for, I felt a real fool, believe me.'

'You should never have gone alone,' Jubilee grumbled. He was seated at his desk in the study of the old house, his account books before him. It was a shabby room but warm with books lining the walls and the scent of pipe tobacco that was Jubilee's hallmark.

'I worry when I think of you down at the docks with all those foreigners flocking around you.' Jubilee's aversion to anyone from outside British shores was well known and Ellie hid a smile.

'It might seem amusing to you, my girl,' Jubilee was not fooled by her attempt to conceal her laughter. 'But you could have been abducted, harmed in some way. Don't you ever do such a thing again, mind.'

'I won't, I promise, but then you're well enough to do the errands yourself now, especially if you take one of the men with you.' She forbore to tell him of her heated encounter with Marchant's wife. It would be more ammunition for him to use against her for being so pigheaded as to go to the offices without Matthew for company.

'Aye, that's as maybe.' Jubilee sounded noncommittal and Ellie looked at him thoughtfully.

'You *are* all right, aren't you, love?' She pressed his hand with hers.

'I'm well enough but I'm not getting any younger, you've got to face facts, girl, I can't live for ever. I worry about you, you've got no head for business, you don't know how to make two and two add up to four.'

'Well teach me then,' Ellie said reasonably, 'perhaps I can learn.'

Jubilee shook his head. 'No, some women are not cut out for it and you are one of them. A brood of babbas you should have round your skirts, a natural mother that's the sort you are.'

'Well, it wasn't to be, was it?' Ellie tried to smile even as she acknowledged her weakness. She might as well face it, she was one of life's failures.

'You're a good wife to me,' Jubilee said softly. Sometimes, Ellie thought, it was almost as if he could read her mind.

'It's easy to be a good wife to you, Jubie,' she kissed his brow, leaning a little on his shoulder. 'You're a fine handsome man, a good man.'

'I don't know about good.' Jubilee said dryly. 'I would like to be good but I'm too fond of the ale and the smoke of my pipe and the lewd talk of the men in the yard when you're not there to be good.'

'Perhaps we should go to listen to the preacher again.' Ellie was only half serious. 'It seems he's having a great effect on those who go to his meetings.'

'Perhaps you're right,' Jubilee said, 'the nearer I get to the grave, the more I think I should look for an afterlife while there's still time.'

Ellie hugged her husband impulsively. 'I wish you wouldn't talk like that, I need you, Jubie, I can't manage without you.'

'Of course you'd manage.' Jubilee spoke firmly, 'Matthew could run the tannery perfectly well, he's got the way of a leader, the men would listen to him. To show my confidence in him I've sent him down to the docks to see the accountant in Marchant's office about that dratted bill.'

'See, I failed even in that simple task.' Ellie pressed her cheek against Jubilee's and felt the dryness of his skin with a sense of alarm. 'You're sure you are feeling well, love?'

'As well as a man my age has the right to feel. Now go on, do some sewing, anything, but leave me in peace.

63

I must get these figures in order for Caradoc Jones, you know how I take a pride in my books.'

Obediently, Ellie left the study and made her way into the small sitting room. Everywhere, even here in the house, the tang of the tannery yard permeated the air. It was in her clothes, on her skin, however much she bathed, she couldn't rid herself of the smell of leather.

She sat down before the ancient organ and began to pump with her feet. She knew only a few tunes, hymns most of them, melodies she had learned from her mother. Those were the days when her mother cared about her, before Ellie had disgraced the family by becoming a cast-off mistress who was bearing the fruits of her sin for all to see.

She should not be bitter, it did no good and yet Ellie found it difficult to be anything else. Her hands fell idle as she tried to envisage her future without Jubilee. Matthew in charge, Matthew free to make advances to her, it didn't bear thinking about.

Of course Jubilee would know nothing of Matthew's overtures to her in private, he trusted the man, probably believing him happy with the girl he was walking out with. What Jubilee didn't realize, Matthew had a different girl for every month of the year, or so it seemed to Ellie who had to listen to his boasting.

She shook the thoughts from her mind, Jubilee was all right, he would live to a ripe old age. And yet, her eyes were misted with tears that fell onto the worn ivory keys beneath her hands that suddenly trembled.

When Matthew came to the door of Jubilee's house, he was smiling with such an air of confidence about him that Ellie knew instinctively he'd succeeded in his task. 'Good news, boss,' he stood in the hallway, his cap twisted in his hands, his bold eyes taking in his surroundings as though he could picture himself occupying them. 'I think I've persuaded the people down at Marchant's shipping office to buy a regular load of leather from us.

What's more,' his smile was triumphant, 'the bill is paid in full, I have the money here.'

'Come into the study, Mat,' Jubilee said clapping the younger man on the shoulder, 'tell me all about it.'

The door closed on the two men and Ellie was excluded from the talk of business which did not concern her. Well, she couldn't blame Jubilee for shutting her out, she had had her chance and failed dismally.

She thought with a sense of discomfort of the scene between herself and Bridie Marchant, how unjust the accusations Bridie had flung at Ellie had been and how undignified her own response to them. Well, it was not an incident that was likely to be repeated, she should put it out of her mind once and for all.

She moved into the garden, in spite of the buds fresh on the trees, the air was chill with a hint of rain. It would have been good to breathe in the scent of the spring flowers but the all pervading smell of the tannery encroached even so far as the house and garden.

Jubilee would have done well to build his home well away from the yard, it would be worth the inconvenience of travelling every day to be free from the stink of rotting flesh and soaking leather. Ellie supposed that Jubilee no longer noticed it. He had grown up with the tannery, the very skin of his face and hands were as one with the leather, his fingers stained with much dipping in the residue of oak bark and water in which he worked.

Now, with his health failing, he was working much less and yet it irked him to be idle, he wanted nothing more than to be out at the pits or in the currying house with the men. Ellie was sad for him, understanding his frustration only too well, she had frustrations of her own to contend with.

Later, when her husband emerged from the study, he was smiling. Behind him, Matthew was looking at her with something like triumph in his eyes.

'I've given Mat promotion, Ellie.' Jubilee rested his

arm around her shoulder. 'He's done well, hasn't he, love?'

'Very well.' Ellie lowered her glance, she did not wish to meet the triumph in Matthew's face. 'I expect you're very pleased Matthew aren't you?'

'Aye, missus,' he was so respectful when Jubilee was around. 'Especially now that the boss has promised to make me a shareholder in the business.'

Ellie forced herself to be calm, was Jubilee out of his mind? He would be giving the man some of his own profits as well as power and for what?

'Are you putting money into the firm then, Matthew?' she asked coolly.

'Course not love,' Jubilee answered for him, 'Mat is putting in something far more precious, his strong back, his good brain and his loyalty.'

Ellie remained silent, Jubilee had made up his mind, there was nothing more to be said on the subject.

Later, he took her to task, something he never did. 'You don't like Matthew, do you, Ellie?'

'I don't really care about him one way or another.' Her reply was carefully framed but Jubilee pursued the point.

'But come on, admit it, you don't like the fact that I've planned to make him a shareholder, have you a reason for that?'

'I just don't think you should give any of your business away, Jubie,' Ellie said.

'I've no boy of my own, Mat's been with me a good many years now, I took him on when he was little more than a child, who else should I take into the business?'

'I'm sorry.'

'No Ellie, love, I wasn't getting at you, not in any way.' Jubilee took her hands in his. 'You know I've no room to criticize, I'm a man who had no pips, as they say. Even if I was up to making love to you, I couldn't give you a baby.'

'Oh Jubilee, don't let's say any more on the subject,'

66

Ellie pleaded. 'I don't want to quarrel about it, if you want Matthew brought into the business then it's your privilege to do so.'

'I want to know you'll be protected, love,' Jubilee spoke softly now. 'When I'm gone, Matthew will be here to take care of you.' His voice changed, became more robust, 'By then, Mat will be married, have a brood of kids, he'll be that much more responsible, I've acquainted him with my wishes in that respect. Everything will be above board, you'll see it's for the best then.'

Ellie knew there was nothing she could say, Jubilee felt he was doing his best for her, how could she disillusion him?

'I'm going up to bed. I'd like some hot milk, please love.' Jubilee appeared tired, quite suddenly, and he had dark circles beneath his eyes. 'Good night, God bless, Ellie.'

On an impulse, Ellie went to him and hugged him. 'I love you, Jubie, you're a darling man.'

'There's a flatterer if ever I saw one, go on with you, get about your business, woman.'

She listened to his footsteps on the stairs, they were slow, heavy, those of an old man. Ellie sighed, she really should not upset Jubilee, if it eased his mind to take Matthew into the business then she would have to put up with it.

She measured out some milk and edged the pan onto the fire hob in the kitchen. The milk hissed against the bottom of the vessel and Ellie watched as it began to boil. She sighed, she was tired too and she would have to dampen the fire down before she went to bed, cover the flames with small coal just enough to keep the embers alight until morning.

As she climbed the stairs with the mug of steaming milk in her hands, she felt uncertainty settle over her. Jubilee had worried her with his talk of dying, did he know something she didn't? It would be just like him to make every effort to protect her from what he might see as an unpalatable truth.

'Here we are then, my darling.' As she entered the room, she saw that Jubilee was almost asleep. She put down the mug and sat beside him, wondering if she should disturb him. He opened his eyes slowly and smiled sweetly at her.

'Come to bed, love,' his voice was dry, 'give your old man a bit of fussing, I feel the need of it tonight.'

'I'll just see to the fire, Jubie,' Ellie handed him the mug, 'and then, I'll be with you, don't you worry.'

She did her chores as quickly as she could and returned to her bedroom. She washed in the water from the jug on the stand and, shivering a little in her cotton nightgown, she slid into bed beside her husband.

'My precious little girl.' He kissed the top of her head. 'Have I ever told you how happy you've made me these past years?'

'Aye, you have. We'll have many more happy times, too, Jubie, don't you worry.'

'Put out the lamp, love, let's get down under the blankets and keep warm together. It's not much to offer a red-blooded girl is it?'

Ellie was silent, there was nothing she could say. Even if she protested to Jubilee that she wanted nothing of men ever, that she would never fall in love again, he wouldn't believe her.

'Will you marry, after a decent interval, of course?' He spoke in a matter-of-fact way and yet Ellie felt fear crawl along her spine. 'Don't talk like that, Jubilee, I won't have it.' Her effort to sound stern failed dismally. 'I can't imagine a life without you in it,' she added almost pleadingly.

'There, there, I didn't mean to upset you. I've had a good innings, I'm grateful to God for what he saw fit to give me. I'm not even bitter about what he saw fit to withhold,' he sighed heavily.

'No more talking now, I'm tired.' He held her close

68

and, as she listened to the beat of his heart, Ellie had difficulty holding back the tears.

'The piece on the preacher went down very well with the public.' Mac was standing before the windows of *The Swansea Times* staring out into the street. 'I wrote it rather well considering I've no time for religious claptrap.'

Arian was drawing off her gloves, she had been out shopping, a rare event indeed; these days she seemed too busy to even keep her wardrobe up to date.

The coat and skirt she wore now were good worsted but too heavy for the fine weather that was promised by the cloudless skies. Her hats were old-fashioned without the flair of the modern milliner. And her shoes! Looking down at her feet, she felt her mouth quirk with amusement, what would her old friends, Eline and William Davies, both of them excellent cordwainers, make of the shabby, down at heel boots she was wearing?

'No comment?' Mac's dry tones intruded into Arian's thoughts, 'I expected a little praise for my efforts or is that asking too much?'

'You did a fine piece of writing, Evan Roberts should be grateful to you.'

Arian moved through the busy offices hearing distantly the noise of the printing presses. She breathed deeply, this was the stuff of life to her; the pressure, the constant crisis, even the harassment from townspeople who thought *The Swansea Times* had maligned them, she looked upon it all as a challenge.

The inner office was strident with the noise of clacking typewriters; here her army of editors, sub-editors and juniors worked at producing decent copy, free, it was to be hoped, from errors of the kind Bridie Marchant had complained of.

Arian paused, scenting the atmosphere of industry, brought about, no doubt, by her appearance. Sometimes her reporters took time off to smoke, or to drink the

69

coffee, which was now becoming more fashionable than tea, from the pot constantly bubbling on the stove. But these practices, considered indulgent by some, seemed to Arian conducive to producing good copy. Well written pieces that had flair and verve.

One of her best writers was Daniel Bennett, a young man scarcely able to grow a moustache let alone a beard, who gazed up at her now in open adoration. He was about twenty years old, she guessed, fresh out of college, an intelligent young man from a fine Swansea family. The fact that she was at least five years his senior didn't seem to worry him.

Arian concealed a smile, that the boy had a fancy for her was apparent to anyone who worked alongside him. But, Arian mused, he would get over it. Once Daniel met a suitable young lady he would forget his infatuation for the proprietor of *The Times*.

'Afternoon, Daniel,' she stopped at his desk and saw with a dart of pity that his face had become bright red above his immaculately starched collar. She took up the sheet of paper from his desk and read it with interest. 'I think you are going to make a very good reporter. Have you mastered that infernal machine, then?' she pointed at the gleaming typewriter. 'You seem very quick at it.'

'I found it quite easy to pick up, Miss Smale. It helps me get my thoughts down more quickly than my hand-writing would allow.'

'Perhaps you should learn Sir Isaac Pitman's method of writing at speed, Daniel, I'm sure it would be of great value when you're out interviewing.'

'I do know some shorthand, Miss Smale.' Daniel volunteered the information slowly as though reluctant to appear too eager. No doubt the epithet 'teacher's pet' had been thrown in his direction more than once by some of the more seasoned reporters.

She supposed there would be more than a little scepticism shown by her employees to the young college boy. Many of her reporters had come up the hard way by sheer initiative, not to mention guts. It wouldn't help the young man at all if she were to pay undue attention to him.

'Keep up the good work, then.' She walked on and through to the passage that led to the stairs. It would be good to get into her own apartment and kick off her boots.

Later, she would bathe, she would prepare herself to receive Calvin into her home and into her bed. The thought brought her a fleeting happiness and then the moment was gone. That was the pattern of her days, brief interludes of happiness with Calvin. Wouldn't it be wonderful if she could show her love openly? For that to happen she would have to be married to Calvin, something that was outside the scope of her wildest dreams.

Guilt seared her; it was high time she visited Gerald, her flesh and blood husband, not mooned about someone she could never have. Tomorrow, she decided, tomorrow she would go to the asylum. What a stark name but then it was a stark place. A place of doors with locks, a place of misery and lost souls. Arian shuddered, it was just as well that her husband was not in his right mind, otherwise, finding himself in a mad house, he would surely kill himself.

And yet wasn't she, deep down, glad that he was locked away from her? Arian became aware that she was standing poised at the foot of the stairs leading to her rooms. She took a deep breath and made her way upstairs, anxious to leave the dimness of the passageway.

Her memories brought her only unhappiness, the despairing memories of a marriage that she had never wanted, that had been forced upon her. How many times had she lain with her husband dreading his touch upon her breast, her thigh?

In her rooms, she turned up the gas lamps and shifted the coals in the fire. The maid had heard her and brought a pot of hot tea and a tray bearing a fine china

71

cup. Arian nodded her thanks absently, she was still in the thrall of the past, still feeling the repugnance of body and soul that belonging to Gerald Simples had brought her.

'Tomorrow,' she murmured, she would go to see him tomorrow, it was no more than her duty to make sure that he was being adequately cared for.

Sedated, that's how he spent his life; his senses, his angers, his illusions, his dreams drowned under the effects of his medication.

'Run me a bath would you, please, Mary?' Arian said not looking at the maid who was, she knew, bobbing her acquiescence. 'Don't make the water too hot, mind.'

It was as though she could bathe away her memories. But even when she was lying in the scented water, staring up at the whitened ceiling, she felt again his hands upon her, his cold insistence that she do her wifely duty, that she please him in the marriage bed. She would never be free of him, she thought dully, the touch of his hand, the look in his eyes as he took his pleasure of her, his insistence on her subjugation, these were memories that would always be with her.

That night, she told Calvin something of her feelings, he drew her close in his arms. 'I could kill him, I wish I had killed him when I had the chance.'

Arian shook back her hair. 'No, you know you couldn't have done such a thing, even though he had threatened both of us with a knife. How ever much of a danger he was to me, to anyone who stood in his path, you could no more kill him than I could.'

'I wish I was as sure of that.' Calvin was leaning up on one elbow now, looking down at her. She caught sight of the dark shadow of hair beneath his arm and she was unaccountably touched by the sight.

'I love you, Calvin, I don't tell you often enough.' She turned her face into his chest and closed her eyes, breathing in the scent of him. Her being melted with love, it seemed to surround her with happiness.

'The past is over and done with,' she said forcefully, 'let's be grateful for the present.'

Even as Calvin bent to kiss her, to possess her once more, she knew that for her the past would never be dead, not while Gerald Simples lived.

Ellie woke slowly, early rays of sun spread prying fingers into the room, catching the side of a flower vase, touching the lace cloth of the table with slivers of gold. It was going to be another fine, spring day. She would have liked the window to be open, to watch the soft breeze ruffle the curtain but that was not possible, not if the stink of the tannery was to be shut out from the bed chamber.

Slowly, she stretched out her limbs, careful not to disturb her husband, she would slip out of bed, mend the fire that hopefully would still be alight, so that when Jubilee rose he would find the rooms downstairs warm and welcoming.

She washed quickly, the morning air was chill in spite of the sunshine, and dressed in her Sunday clothes. Today, there would be no work in the tannery, it would be a quiet day spent reading the Bible and if Jubilee was up to it attending morning and evening service at St Mary's church situated at the centre of the town.

Ellie tied a fresh linen apron over her good skirt and stood for a moment staring down at Jubilee. He was breathing heavily in his sleep. His eyelids fluttered as though he was beset by dreams. Ellie smiled indulgently, he was so precious to her, her buffer against the world.

It was cold in the kitchen, the rag mat before the blackleaded fire grate offered little protection from the bare flagstones beneath. It was surprising that in such a finely built house, so gracious in its proportions, there was little comfort.

When the fire in the kitchen was glowing with life, Ellie moved to the parlour and lit the fire there. It was lit only on Sundays, to save coal, most of the weekdays and nights were spent in the kitchen.

She cursed the cold fire grate and tried again to kindle the sticks. She was as inept at this sort of work as she was at any other but then she had never been used to manual labour, not of the rough kind.

In her parents' house, there had been servants to do the menial tasks and Ellie had accepted the everyday luxuries her comfortable way of life had afforded her without a second thought.

It took some time to set fire to the sticks and the paper and lumps of strategically placed coal but at last there was a cheerful glow in the parlour.

Back in the kitchen, the kettle danced and spat, issuing forth steam. She poured some of the boiling water into an enamel bowl, she would cool it with water from the jug in the bedroom, then she poured hot water into a mug ready for Jubilee to shave.

She wished for a moment that she could afford the services of a cook and a maid but Jubilee would have laughed at such an idea.

Jubilee liked his day of rest to be special, Ellie liked it too, the ceremony of Sundays made a happy break in the working week. She would rouse Jubilee from his sleep and then, when they'd talked awhile, she would cook him a huge breakfast of bacon, eggs and fried bread. Or maybe today he'd like some salt fish for a change, she had a few pieces soaking in a bowl overnight just in case.

She climbed the stairs, balancing the bowl on her arm and pushed the door open with her foot. The sun was filling the room with bars of light now. She rested the bowl on the table near the sunwashed window and turned to the bed. Jubilee's eyes were open but he didn't appear to see her.

Ellie sat down on the patchwork quilt beside him and stroked his face. His eyes seemed to focus then, lucidity returned.

74

'This is it, my love, time to say goodbye.' His voice was thin, his chin under the stubble of his beard quivered but with weakness rather than fear. 'Time to say goodbye,' he repeated.

Ellie felt a moment of sheer panic. 'No, Jubie, you were fine yesterday, you were talking about the future, about Matthew being married with a brood of children. Oh, I must do something, I must call the doctor.'

'Don't bother with the doctor,' Jubilee was struggling to speak, 'too late for that, my lovely girl.' His eyes closed for a moment with the effort. He opened his eyes very slowly again, staring into her face, as though memorizing it.

'I've loved you the best way I knew how, Ellie. I'm sorry I'm going to leave you before I've sorted everything out.' He sighed softly, 'Matthew will be married soon, he told me, it will be all right . . .' His voice faltered a little, 'You must think only of what's best for you now, my girl.' His chest heaved once and then the light slowly faded from his eyes. He looked, Ellie thought abstractedly, like a small boy fallen asleep.

'Jubilee!' she said his name urgently but there was no response. In truth, she had expected none. She put her head on his chest where only hours ago she had felt the beat of his heart, now there was only stillness.

Ellie wished she could cry, tears would bring some relief but her pain went too deep, she had lost the man who had become dearer to her than her own father. She tucked the covers under her husband's chin as if, even now, she could warm him to life.

She didn't know how long she sat there with the spring sunshine patterning the bed, the walls, the ceiling, in a mockery of lightness and hope, she only knew there was a great emptiness inside her, love had gone completely from her life. But then love was a painful thing, it was best done without.

At last, she rose to her feet; there were matters to attend to, she must occupy her thoughts and her hands with necessary arrangements, arrangements that would remove the last vestiges of her husband for ever from her life. Perhaps, she thought, though with faint hope, once the funeral was over, once Jubilee was laid properly to rest, the pain within her would ease but she did not believe it.

At the door she turned and stood for a long moment, looking back at her husband. Already he had changed, he was a mere shell, he was no longer her Jubie.

'God bless, my love,' she whispered the words before she closed the bedroom door firmly behind her.

CHAPTER SIX

'You want me to go to see Mrs Hopkins, just me?' Daniel felt excitement flow through him. He squared his shoulders, this was his first real assignment for *The Times* and though he would only be writing an obituary, at least Miss Smale was evincing a measure of trust in his abilities that was gratifying.

'You will handle it sensitively, of course.' It wasn't a question, Arian was speaking matter of factly and Daniel was flattered.

'I will choose my words with care, you may be sure of that, Miss Smale.' He picked up his pen from the desk and tucked his notebook into his pocket. 'How many words would you suggest?'

'I'll leave that to your judgement, Daniel.' Arian looked beautiful this morning, Daniel could hardly keep his eyes from her. She wore a crisp white blouse with a frilled neckline and the black, rather plain skirt emphasized her slimness.

He was well aware that she looked on his regard as nothing more than puppy love and perhaps she was right but he had never met a woman he admired more than he did Miss Smale.

Daniel came from a good background, his parents were not rich by any means, certainly not in Arian Smale's league but the Bennetts were a well respected Swansea family with a modest property on the edge of the Uplands. He'd been to the college on Mount Pleasant hill and had enjoyed his studies tremendously. But all the while he'd been learning Geography and Mathematics, he'd wanted more from life. He had always harboured a love of words and so it seemed the sensible course to pursue was to learn the art of journalism.

'Well, off you go then,' Arian Smale looked away from him as Mac entered the office in a rush of fresh air. Daniel recognized that Mac was a brilliant writer, he had a gift for words that Daniel envied. He was sometimes dour and unapproachable but then, out of the blue, he would offer a gem of good advice which Daniel would seize upon eagerly.

'Right. I'll do my best, you can be sure of it.' Daniel picked up his hat from the stand near the door and Mac looked at him with large brown eyes filled with something very much like amusement.

'You're going to do the obit on Jubilee Hopkins, then?' He allowed the smile to creep across his mouth. 'Beware of the stink up at the tannery, it's to be hoped that you've got a strong stomach, lad.'

Daniel hated being called 'lad' especially with Arian standing there looking on. Still, he was determined to allow nothing to spoil his moment of triumph. 'Strong enough,' he said smoothly. 'I know enough about tanneries to understand it's no bed of lavender.'

There was silence and Daniel had the feeling, suddenly, that he'd been a trifle too confident, this was after all his first lone assignment.

'I'd better go then,' he still hesitated wondering if there was something he could say to retrieve the situation, he didn't want anyone, especially Arian, thinking he was conceited.

'It's a long walk.' Mac's laconic remark goaded Daniel into movement and he left the office determined that he would come back with some unusual angle on this old man and then he would write the best obit he was capable of.

It was indeed a long walk out to the tannery but even before he reached the folds of Kilvey Hill and passed beyond, he thought he could detect the faintly nauseating smell of drying animal skins.

He would be spared actually going into the tannery itself, the yard was no place for a lady. He guessed he would find Mrs Hopkins weeping within the confines of her house. And so it turned out to be when he enquired after her at the tannery entrance.

From the outside, the house appeared quite grand, sprawling across a large piece of ground higher up than the tannery boundary. The curtains were drawn against the morning sun, a sign of mourning and suddenly Daniel felt ill equipped to deal with the pain of a bereaved old lady.

The door was opened to his knock quite quickly and a petite young woman dressed in black looked out at him shading her eyes with her hand, apparently dazzled by the sudden fall of sunlight across her face.

She was very pretty in a fair, rather delicate way, her hair was caught back in a bun and her breasts swelled becomingly beneath the dark pleating of her bodice. Daniel breathed a sigh of relief, at least he would not be seeing the widow alone. This young lady, he presumed, was a daughter of the deceased.

'I'm from *The Swansea Times*, miss, Daniel Bennett, I'm sorry to intrude on such a sad time but I would like to write an obituary that will do justice to Mr Jubilee Hopkins. Are you his daughter?'

She stood back to allow him to enter and he could see that the proportions of the hallway were impressive. At some time, years ago, this would have been a very much sought after property but now with the adjacent tannery it would be less than desirable.

'Come into the parlour won't you?' The girl spoke in cultured tones and looked up at him with large beautiful eyes and he felt a wave of protective warmth sweep over him. She seemed so vulnerable and yet so dignified in her grief.

The room was empty. The grate was swept clean, innocent of coal, there was no fire and the air was chill

79

in spite of the sunshine outside. Also, he noticed, it was surprisingly shabby.

'Please sit down,' she gestured to a chair and though her hands were small, Daniel could not help noticing that they were work roughened and stained. It must be that the girl was obliged to carry out manual work in the tannery but this was not unusual where a business was a family concern. And yet, she was so soft, so delicate, she should be spared the toil of the yards.

How Jubilee Hopkins conducted his affairs was none of his business, he reminded himself. He was here to do a job, nothing more. The first rule of journalism was not to get involved and he was in danger of breaking it already.

'Would you like some cordial, perhaps?' She moved to the door as though anticipating his acceptance and he smiled.

'That would be lovely, thank you.' It might be easier to talk if his mouth wasn't so dry. He recognized that he was nervous. This was a part of writing he'd not anticipated. This was dealing with real flesh and blood people, people who were grieving and he wasn't sure he was experienced enough to cope with such a situation.

She returned after a few minutes with a tray, apparently there was no maid and, handing him a glass, she sat down opposite him. 'Sorry there's no fire in here, we're waiting for a delivery of coal. Jubilee usually brings in a stock but he's had other things on his mind lately.' She looked at him with those large, lovely eyes and he swallowed hard. He desperately tried to think of something to say.

'I'm Mrs Hopkins, Ellie,' she broke the silence. 'I'd be pleased to give you any information about my husband that you need. I want you to do him justice, he was a fine man.'

Shock waves ran through him, this pale girl was wife to the old man, that was a surprise. He made an effort to marshall his thoughts. To give himself time, he consulted his sparse notes. 'Mr Hopkins was past eighty, is that correct?'

'Yes,' her voice was low. 'My husband was hale and hearty until a few weeks ago.' Her voice trembled, 'It was only lately that he . . . well I'd never seen him sick before, it was dreadful.'

She put her hand up to her face for a moment as if overcome and then she seemed to draw a deep breath and regain her self-control. 'Sorry, I didn't mean to sound self-pitying.'

'It's quite understandable in the circumstances,' he coughed. 'I'll personally take care to give your husband his due, I do assure you, Mrs Hopkins.'

It seemed scarcely credible, this girl looked little more than his own age, how could she bear to be married to an old man like Jubilee Hopkins, however fine he was? Was her grief genuine? It certainly seemed it.

'Perhaps you can tell me when he was born and where, that sort of thing.' Daniel searched his mind for the information usually contained in obituaries. 'And what works he did for the community, you know the sort of thing.'

'I don't really.' The girl, he couldn't think of her as Mrs Hopkins, seemed at a loss and Daniel knew it was his fault. He should be asking pertinent questions not expecting her to know the form.

'Just tell me all about him, I'll write it down and sort it out when I get to the office,' he tried to sound reassuring but he didn't quite succeed.

Ellie smiled at him then and he saw the charm and beauty of her, the fragile loveliness illuminating her pale skin. Her hair was fair, almost silver. She was like a madonna. He was embarrassed by the extravagance of his feelings and coughed again to hide the rush of colour to his face.

'Have you any children, Mrs Hopkins?' He tried to sound business-like but it was difficult with her looking down at him so appealingly.

She shook her head, 'I've no children.' She regarded him steadily for a moment, assessing him, and he met her gaze knowing that he wanted to learn more about her.

'This is my first assignment,' he blurted the words, his intentions of appearing confident, in charge of the situation, disappearing, 'I want to get it right, I want to do you and the deceased gentleman justice by what I write.'

'I understand,' Ellie spoke softly. 'Perhaps it would be best if we look at the family Bible, I think you'll find all you need in its records.'

They stood together leaning over the large open Bible resting on the table, he could smell her fragrance and was moved by it. Ellie seemed unaware of his feelings as she ran her finger along the dates written in careful hand.

'There, see, Jubilee was born in September 1824 to Mary and Jasper Hopkins.' She turned and looked over her shoulder, her eyes were large in her pale face. 'It seems such a long time ago.'

'Indeed,' Daniel wrote the date in his notebook, 'but then Mr Hopkins was a good age.'

'I know he was past eighty but he seemed so much younger to me.' Ellie's voice quivered and on an impulse, Daniel rested his hand on her shoulder.

'Excuse me!' The voice was sharp with scarcely concealed anger and Daniel looked towards the doorway in surprise. A man a little older than himself stood, hands bunched menacingly, staring at him as though he would like to stuff his fist down Daniel's throat.

'Yes?' Daniel's voice was equally sharp, this man stank of the tan pits, he was clearly a working man, someone of no account. Daniel didn't consider himself snobbish in any way but it was impertinent for a rough labourer to intrude on a private discussion and to so address himself to a visitor invited in by the mistress of the house.

'Matthew,' Ellie spoke clearly, 'when I want you to come into my front parlour I will invite you. What is it?'

'I just wondered if you were going to work in the grinding house today, that's all,' the man's tone had become sullen. 'I don't know if I should put one of the men in there with Boyo, I haven't had any instructions from you.'

Daniel forced himself to remain calm, how dare this upstart address the lady of the house in such familiar terms?

'Perhaps you should know your place,' he found himself saying. 'Mrs Hopkins is in no mood to work anywhere, her husband is not yet buried, have some respect man.'

Matthew's face grew red, he recognized a man of quality when he saw one, knew a tone of authority when he heard it and yet his pride had taken a knock and that was something he couldn't permit.

'I'm Matthew Hewson, shareholder in this business, I have a say in how the place runs.' Why was he explaining himself to this young sprog? Yet Matthew felt compelled to make his position clear.

'In that case you should take decisions yourself and spare Mrs Hopkins any worries.' This was stating an incontrovertible fact and Matthew knew it. He twisted his cap in his hands and backed towards the door.

'I'll speak to you later,' Ellie said, her voice giving nothing away. 'For now, put someone else in with Boyo, we'll sort it out when I've had time to think.'

With one last glare in Daniel's direction, the man left the room and Ellie's shoulders sagged.

'You do not care for that man, shareholder or not,' Daniel spoke before he had time to think and Ellie looked at him, her expression telling him that he was right. She shrugged.

'My husband liked Matthew, he thought I'd be cared for by him, thought he would be married before long. Jubilee imagined that what he was doing was for the best.' She sank into a chair. 'But Matthew is a single man, it seems he has no intention of getting married in the foreseeable future. It's not right he and I should be thrown into close proximity, people are bound to talk, to draw the wrong conclusions.'

Daniel sat opposite her, his writing forgotten. 'Surely that thought would have occurred to your husband, too?'

Ellie shook her head. 'I think Jubilee felt he was invincible. In any case, Matthew lied to him, told him he was about to be married. Jubilee did his best for me.'

'Well you shouldn't be alone with the man. You have a maid?' Daniel said though looking round at the sparsely furnished room, he could scarcely believe a maid had worked here for some time, the dust lay thickly on the good furniture, the whole room held an air of neglect as though the occupants of the house barely used it.

'No,' Ellie looked at her hands, 'we have no money for such luxuries as maids.'

'Surely the business must be profitable,' Daniel felt obliged to go on, 'from what I understand, Mr Hopkins had a substantial amount of capital.'

'I think you have been misinformed. Though Jubilee will have left me well provided for, he didn't have a fortune, I'm sure.'

'My editor . . .' Daniel stopped speaking, this really was none of his business. There was one thing, however, he felt he must say. 'Employ a companion, a lady who will stay here with you, a needy but respectable widow who like yourself has been left alone unprotected. I think you'll find you have more money than you realize.'

'Perhaps,' Ellie said doubtfully, 'and I see that it would preserve my husband's good name but . . .' She shrugged.

'Your own good name needs protecting, I think you'll find people are only too ready to talk about a woman alone, especially a young and beautiful one like you.'

Ellie rose suddenly and moved to the door. 'Thank you for your interest but if I can't help you any further then I'll say good day to you.'

He looked at her steadily for a moment, she spoke like a lady, she had clearly been well brought up and yet her husband had allowed her to work like a common labourer, it was all very strange.

He picked up his hat. 'I think it will suffice for now,' he said but there was regret in his voice. 'I offer my condolences on your loss, Mrs Hopkins, and my sincere hope that you will find a suitable companion as soon as possible.'

As Daniel left the house, the stench from the tannery seemed to permeate the very clothes he was wearing. How people and especially a lady as delicate as Mrs Hopkins could live in such an environment, he failed to comprehend.

As he walked away from the tan yard, he was aware of Hewson watching him, every line of his body suggesting aggression. That was the way all labourers handled matters, with brute force. Daniel was surprised that the man had been given any part of the business let alone been made a shareholder.

Whatever Ellie believed to the contrary, there was a substantial amount of money coming to her. Arian Smale had her contacts and they were all a hundred per cent solid, if she said Jubilee Hopkins was a man of wealth then it was so.

Still, he must remind himself it was none of his business, he'd come here to do a job, that was all. Yet he couldn't rid himself of the vision of young Mrs Hopkins, her pale face looking up into his as though, silently, she was asking for his help.

Paul's behaviour, since the scene on the docks, had improved somewhat. He sat now in the chair at the opposite side of the fire from Bridie, ostensibly reading his charts, though Bridie doubted his attention was fully on them because the light from the window had grown rather too dim to read by.

A coal shifted in the grate and Paul looked up and caught Bridie's eye. He smiled and rolled the charts neatly before tying them with a ribbon.

'I'm neglecting my lovely wife,' he said. 'Come here and sit on my knee, let me make a fuss of you.'

Even as she wondered what he was up to, she obeyed him. She found her husband as fascinating as the day she first met him. It seemed a long time ago and yet she remembered every detail of it.

'It was Sarah Frogmore who brought us together, do you remember, Paul?' She smoothed back his hair. 'I fell in love with you the moment I saw you, at her supper party, did you realize that?'

Paul kissed her lightly. 'Of course and for my part I fell in love with your glorious red hair.'

Bridie felt inordinately pleased, she and Paul had become like any other married couple, she supposed, taking each other for granted. Well she had learned her lesson, she would make sure she looked after her husband in future. She was well aware of his need for flattery. In that he was like a small boy, desiring approbation. And, as a precaution against any more temptations, she would take pains to see that women the like of Ellie Hopkins didn't get their claws into Paul. Even if she came to the office, Elias had instructions to turn her away. Paul was her husband, the father of her sons and she would guard what was hers with her life if need be.

For a moment hate filled her as she thought of Paul walking along the docks side by side with that girl in her rough working clothes, with her red, chapped hands. Oh, she might speak very nicely but she quite clearly was no lady, hadn't she been cast out by her own family? But then, that was the sort men went for. Oh, they wouldn't want her in their homes, rearing their children, decidedly not, but in between the sheets was a different

86

matter entirely. Men were ruled by their sexual needs and it was as well for a wife to recognize it.

'You're very silent, suddenly, what are you thinking?' Paul nuzzled her neck, his lips warm. Bridie was too clever to reveal her true thoughts.

'Remembering happy times when we were in the first flush of our love.' Then she hadn't really known him, hadn't realized that he would be tempted to stray. And yet, there had been something that cautioned her, an innate feeling that she must keep the reins of the business her father had left her firmly in her own hands.

'We are still in the first flush of love, my sweet, don't be such an old cynic.'

Was she cynical? Perhaps so, and perhaps it was just as well, that way there wouldn't be any more nasty surprises coming her way. But for now she would bask in the warmth of his attention, there weren't many such moments any more and it was just as well to make the most of them when they came.

The following week, Paul shipped out with the *Marie Clare* on a trip across to Ireland. He would be away only a few days and Bridie intended to make the most of the time at her disposal. She had loads to oversee, cargos to direct to the Indies and to China, she must build up her fortune for her own sake and for that of her sons.

She missed the usual contact with her sons, they were in the hands of their strict tutor now and she scarcely ever saw them. They were being prepared for boarding school and, though it would hurt her to send them away, it was something she recognized needed to be done.

She took up *The Swansea Times*, studied the tide tables and saw to her relief that by now the tide would be out and any shipping would be well out into the channel. That distanced Paul from any tempting entanglements, at least for a time.

Bridie turned the pages of the broadsheet and stopped at the obituaries. There, plainly written was an account of the unremarkable life of one Jubilee Hopkins. The name was enough to make Bridie feel sick. So the whore was widowed now. Bridie read on and suddenly whistled inelegantly through her teeth as she read the amount of the estate left by Hopkins. It was sizeable indeed, who would think that a tannery, however successful would yield such an income?

But wait, the man had been endowed with a huge inheritance by his father, left a fortune which he had, apparently, salted away. And now Jubilee Hopkins was dead and that hussy, that fancy piece he'd married in his dotage was a very rich widow.

Bridie resisted the urge to crush the paper between her hands, she hated Ellie Hopkins with every fibre of her being. She had sold herself to an old man and now she had designs on a younger man, on Bridie's husband. Why else would the whore have been down at the docks that day, walking side by side as bold as a new penny piece with Paul?

Bridie clenched her hands into tight fists. She knew the type, mealy-mouthed, innocent-eyed monsters who prayed on decent men. Well Ellie Hopkins had made an enemy, and one day, she would regret it.

'But I can't be rich.' Ellie looked at the lawyer as he sat in her sun-filled parlour. 'Jubilee has never said anything about owning a fortune.'

'I expect he had his reasons.' Mr Telforth had been a contemporary of Jubilee Hopkins, had known him since childhood, knew a great deal about him, perhaps too much. He coughed and returned his attention to the matter in hand.

'You may sell the tannery but only when you have worked it for a year after Jubilee's death. In the meantime, might I suggest you employ the services of a housekeeper and a maid.' He looked round him with some distaste. 'Perhaps you could refurbish the house, I can release you enough funds for anything you might require.'

88

'Yes, I should have someone, here, it's been suggested to me already.' Ellie spoke almost absently and Bernard Telforth thought he recognized the signs of real grief in the young lady. Perhaps Jubilee had not been such a foolish old man after all.

'You will naturally observe the usual year of mourning.' He smiled at her and she gave him the full blast of her beautiful eyes; she was a sweet, innocent young thing, no wonder Jubilee thought so highly of her.

'You must beware of fortune hunters and the like.' He realized he sounded grave. 'Jubilee asked me to keep an eye on you, he had your interests at heart my dear.'

'Yes, I can see that.' Ellie bit her lip and her eyes filled with tears and old as he was, Bernard Telforth could feel the attraction old Jubilee must have felt. What a great pity his friend could not get heirs by this girl, just think what children would have been spawned from this delicious creature.

'Yes, well,' he shuffled the papers together, 'if there's anything you would like to ask me, please do not hesitate.'

'No, it's all quite clear,' Ellie attempted to smile. 'What you could do, if you're willing, is to take me in your carriage as far as the cemetery. I would like to put some early roses on Jubilee's grave. He always liked roses.'

Bernard Telforth resisted the temptation to utter the thought that Jubilee's widow was the fairest rose anyone could wish to see and pushed back his chair.

'Certainly, Mrs Hopkins, it would be my pleasure. Indeed, I will accompany you, if I may; it's not safe for you to be in such a place alone.'

'Don't worry, I've already begun to look for a housekeeper who, hopefully, will be a companion also.' Ellie smiled, 'I'm quite aware that as a woman alone here, I will be open to gossip and scandal.'

'I'm glad to hear that the matter is in hand, my dear.' Bernard Telforth held the door open for her and stepped outside into the sunshine in time to see the bulk of a young, bare-armed man barring his way.

'Am I to be let in on the secrets of my shareholder's will then, Ellie?' The man was rough, his voice, his bearing, even his apparel gave lie to the words he'd spoken, the claim he'd made of being a shareholder with Jubilee Hopkins.

'Who are you? Come on my man speak up.' Bernard Telforth knew he sounded testy, his words rushed from his lips on a flood of anger, how dare this labourer be so familiar with Jubilee's widow?

'I am Matthew Hewson, Jubilee, Mr Hopkins offered me shares in the business, isn't that right, Ellie?'

'It's true, Jubilee intended to give Matthew a share of the profit in the tannery in return for his greater responsibilities.'

Telforth studied the man for a long moment, he didn't need to be the clever lawyer he was to size up the situation. Ellie Hopkins didn't like the man, it was only her fair-mindedness that forced her to speak up for him.

'You signed no papers to my knowledge,' Bernard Telforth said, thrusting his hand into his pocket and taking out his watch, making a point of the fact that he had little time for this sort of nonsense.

'We had an agreement, me and Jubilee, it was in words not on paper and it would have been made all legal-like if Jubilee had lived a bit longer.'

The man was insensitive as well as self-seeking. 'A verbal agreement might have been reached, it might not,' Bernard Telforth said slowly, heavily, 'but unless Mrs Hopkins chooses to increase your wages, I'm afraid there's nothing you can do about bettering yourself.'

'I'll not put up with this!' The man moved forward menacingly and Bernard Telforth held his ground.

'Please, Matthew,' Ellie's voice small and uncertain filled the brooding silence, 'it will all be sorted out, don't make a fuss.'

'Stand aside,' Bernard Telforth lifted his chin, 'I have

business elsewhere, I've wasted quite enough time with you, my good man, I don't intend to waste even so much as another breath.'

He helped Ellie into the cab and the horse moved restlessly between the shafts seemingly in agreement with Telforth that the sooner he left behind the stench of the tannery the better he'd be pleased.

'Don't, on any account, allow that man to bully you.' Telforth took the liberty of covering Ellie's hand with his own. 'And for heaven's sake get more workers into the yard, I don't know what my old friend was thinking about allowing you to do menial work like a common woman.'

'Jubilee knew I wanted to earn my keep,' she said softly. 'I failed him once, I couldn't fail him again.'

Telforth knew the whole story, knew about the twins Ellie had been carrying, the offspring of Lord Calvin Temple, by all accounts. Knew too that Jubilee couldn't be a father, not since his sickness, though what had gone before was a secret Bernard Telforth had kept for many a year.

'Poor child, you've not had an easy passage in life so far.'

'I'm all right, really,' she protested. 'I can look after myself, I can.'

'Well, you won't have to, I'll be there, at least for the rest of the time the good Lord spares me, I'll look after you.'

He accompanied her to Dan y Graig cemetery and stood with her in the soft air, breathing in the scents blowing in from the docklands with a sense of relief, the tannery really was no place for a lady of Ellie Hopkins' delicate nature.

'I miss him already.' Ellie bit her lip, a tear rolled along her cheek and Bernard Telforth, hardened lawyer, wanted to hug her and protect her. What was there about some women that made men feel ten feet tall, he wondered.

91

'I had hoped that once the funeral was over I could come to terms with being alone but it's not so, I expect to see him at every turn, expect to smell his pipe, hear his voice. Will it ever get better?'

He rested his hand on her shoulder. 'I don't know, I'm a crusty old man who never had a wife or a sweetheart, what do I know about feelings? Facts, I understand, wills and testaments, legal matters, these are in my blood, dry old blood, my dear, I'm afraid I'm of little help to you at a time like this.'

She reached out and caught his hand. 'You've been a wonderful help to me, you give me confidence, you make me feel I'm not completely alone.'

'Then I have done something worthwhile.' Telforth moved away from the fresh grave, leaving Ellie to take the roses she had picked from the bushes at the back of the house she had shared with Jubilee and place them on his final resting place.

CHAPTER SEVEN

Bridie had searched diligently through her husband's possessions, hating her actions but unable to rid herself of the terrible suspicions that gripped her. He was being unfaithful, she was growing more sure of it with every passing day. If only she could find some evidence, something to prove or disprove her theories, perhaps then she could take control of her life.

Her mind, as it was, was in constant torment and it would almost be a relief to learn that her jealousy was founded on substance and not the fevered imaginings of a disturbed wife.

His notebook was not in the house, the grand house, bought with her money, the house they had both christened Sea Mistress when their love was new. Bridie slammed the drawers shut with tight-lipped anger. The book was invariably missing when he was away, the first time she had seen it he must have left it behind by mistake. She tried to remember what was in it, nothing of significance, she was sure. Why then, was it always in his possession when he travelled?

She tried to be calm, he needed his notes, she told herself, whatever they meant, he obviously understood them. And yet it irked her, like an itch she couldn't scratch, that there was little of a personal nature to show that Paul lived in the house. His toiletries he naturally took with him on his travels; his favourite clothes were more often on board ship than hanging in the wardrobe in his room. It was as though, when he went to sea, Paul ceased to exist for her.

In despair, she sank into a chair. Her thoughts raced

in a confusion of questions that could not be answered. She had no evidence that her husband was being unfaithful, nothing tangible she could examine at will. There was only the feeling that all was not well between them which continued to plague her.

She left the room and walked out onto the broad landing, resting her hand on the gallery rail as she looked down into the hallway below. The house was strangely quiet but then it would be at this time of day with the servants busy below stairs.

The boys had been taken, in the charge of their nurse and their tutor, on an educational trip to the galleries of Florence. It had been arranged for the children of Swansea gentry by the members of the town's most prominent businessmen and Paul had insisted his sons should go. Bridie had agreed but she missed their noisy presence in the house. Also, she recognized, his sons had been a solid factor which had drawn Paul home from his travels, now there was only her. The thought, in itself, held a mixture of fear and insecurity for Bridie.

Paul, since their marriage, perhaps even before, harboured ideas above his station. He was a small-time ship owner, his wealthy lifestyle courtesy of his wife's fortune. Over the years it had been Bridie's wit and acumen, her gift for employing the best people, that had made the firm of Marchant and James into the force it was today, something Paul should remember.

Lately, she had bought into a Cornish firm of steam packet owners; steamships represented the future, she was sure of it in spite of Paul's energetic denials, and Bridie meant to go with her instincts, they had not let her down in the past.

Marchant and James were among the most profitable shipping owners in the town of Swansea; the family, though comparative newcomers to Swansea, were well regarded. But even so when Bridie sought to put her boys on the list of prospective pupils at one of the best local schools, she had met with resistance. It was only when she had thought of endowing a large amount of money to the school that her sons had been accepted for admittance when they were older. Now she wondered if she had done what was best for them. Perhaps she should have heeded Paul and had the children enrolled in a much better public school, away from the area.

Paul was a self-made man who had been lucky to attend the grammar school in Swansea. He had seemed at first to be delighted by the fact that Bridie had been given the benefit of a good convent education in Ireland. Later, he had grown to resent what he saw as her superior attitude.

Bridie had learned Latin, had been taught to speak both French and German, indeed, she far outstripped her husband in knowledge of subjects learned from books. And, too, she had a sound business sense and a flair for looking to the future with a certain insight which Paul lacked.

On the other hand, Paul had taken to the sea in all its moods, he knew the tides, knew the sandbanks, knew instinctively what was right for his ship. Pity he did not study his wife the way he studied his charts.

Paul had not yet made any protest at the way Bridie manipulated the trips. Why should he? He believed unquestioningly that the money accrued from Bridie's ships as well as the few he owned was going into a joint fund. But there, he was wrong.

Bridie sighed heavily, she felt frustrated that she was no wiser about Paul's activities. Perhaps she should get out into the fresh spring air, take a walk, try to clear her mind. These days she didn't seem to be thinking straight. Perhaps she was allowing her imagination to run away with her. But then, she had not imagined the scene on the docks with Paul side by side with that whore Ellie Hopkins.

It came to her that perhaps she would learn more about Paul at the office than she did at home. She would give Elias the day off, send him away and be free to search through Paul's desk.

She hurried downstairs and rang for one of the servants to fetch her coat and hat. She was impatient now to put her thoughts into action. It was like a fever, this need to find something to set her mind at rest one way or the other.

'Collins, where's that damn carriage?' She didn't look at the butler as he crossed the hall, she was aware of his tallness, had been surprised by his youth when, some years before, she had interviewed him for the position. Butlers had always been old men; in her childhood days butlers were seen and not heard for her father had treated the servants with the same hard indifference with which he'd treated his daughter.

Her carriage was a long time coming, old Masters was growing slow and when at last he stood at the front door, Bridie issued orders to him in a sharp voice. In turn, he angrily chivvied the stable boy who had been sorting out the tack preparing the horses for the journey. At last, after what seemed an interminable wait, she was on her way towards the docklands.

The salt of the sea air drifted towards her as the carriage turned towards the lower part of the town. The offices were situated in Gloucester Place, in a pleasant street a short distance from the elegant Guildhall.

Bridie could hardly wait for her driver to rein the animals to a standstill before she was climbing down onto the roadside. There she was standing before the large building, the building that housed the offices of Marchant and James. It looked innocent enough behind the shining windows and elegant doors but within its walls the records of the company held a wealth of information.

The profits made by the business last year alone were enough to keep Bridie and her boys in comfort for a very long time. She stared up at the sign above the door bearing her name and felt a sense of triumph that most of it was hers. Paul would find himself in very diminished circumstances if he were ever to leave her.

'Morning Mrs Marchant, what a pleasant surprise, are you well?' Elias rose from his chair with difficulty and moved around the desk to take her hand politely.

'I have an even more pleasant surprise for you, Elias,' Bridie peeled off her gloves with an impatient gesture. 'If there's nothing pressing to do here, you may have the rest of the day to yourself.'

If Elias thought this strange, he chose not to comment. He moved to the coat stand and took up his hat and jacket and turned towards the door.

'If you're sure, Mrs Marchant, then I'll be off, Mrs Elias is rather poorly so I'm grateful to you.'

'You should have said,' Bridie looked at the old man, he was a faithful employee, she really should have more consideration for his age. 'Please go home at once and take tomorrow off too. I'll manage here just fine.'

'If you're sure . . .' he repeated and Bridie waved her hand at him impatiently.

'Go on, you know I've got as good a business head as any man. My coachman is outside, I'll come to no harm.'

She took the pins from her hat and turned her attention to the open books on the desk. 'Just a minute, Elias,' her voice was suddenly sharp, 'what's this entry for leather cargo all about?'

'Oh, that was Mr Marchant's doing, miss. Small load, I thought and only going as far as Ireland, not really worth the trip. Mind, he did take on board some fuel blocks as well, so the venture might be profitable in the end.' By his tone, Elias took leave to doubt it and so did Bridie.

'I see the load of skins was purchased from the Glyn Hir Tannery, that's Mrs Hopkin's place, isn't she a new customer?'

'Well we have bought one or two loads from her tannery over the past months, is anything wrong?' Elias hovered in the doorway and Bridie shook her head.

'No off you go, give my best wishes to your wife.'

She sank into the wide-armed captain's chair and tried to control her fury. So Paul was doing business with the woman was he? No doubt after the excuses Ellie Hopkins had made for being with Paul, the pair thought it best to regulate matters, put their affair on a business footing, at least to all outward appearances.

It was quite clear to Bridie, however, that it was all just a sham, Paul was taking the leather and transporting it to Ireland as a cover up for his other activities. Bridie saw a picture of Ellie Hopkins in her mind's eye, as she had been that day at the entrance to the dock, small, fair, and doubtless quite predatory. She was just Paul's sort, rich, young, pretty in a washed-out kind of way and probably only too available.

Bridie bit her lip so hard she tasted blood. She forced herself to think calmly, they wouldn't get away with it, she would put a stop to it right away. Her mind was suddenly clear, she would forbid Paul to take any more orders from Glyn Hir, he would have to tell the widow that this trip had turned out to be a most unprofitable one. Ellie Hopkins would find that it was Bridie who wielded the power and that Paul's little schemes were easily nipped in the bud.

It would make little difference financially to the brazen widow, of course, she was so rich, a little loss on leather wouldn't matter. Which made the entire transaction almost laughable if Bridie wasn't so incensed by the pitiful attempt to deceive her. Perhaps, even now, they were together in Ireland, perhaps Ellie Hopkins was the reason Paul had accepted the shorter runs with such good grace.

Well it wouldn't work, they would both see that, Ellie Hopkins and Paul. Later, she would think of other ways of undermining Ellie Hopkins, smearing her name so that she would be unable to hold her head up in Swansea ever again. But for now, at least she had somewhere to start.

She rose from her chair in a burst of determined energy, she would act now. Excitement rose within her, she would go over to Ireland on the next tide, she would foil Paul's plans, surprise him into an admission of his guilt, then, by God, he would have to come to heel or else.

She moved to the cabinet and looked through the list of sailings, there were three of her ships in dock at the moment, she saw with satisfaction. Good, she would just have time to make her arrangements with the master of one of them and then go home and pack a few necessities.

She clenched her hands into fists. 'I knew it,' she breathed, 'I just knew he was up to something. And by damn I'll find out what it is if it kills me.'

'I've been invited to this soirée at Sarah Frogmore's house,' Calvin was stretched out beside Arian on the bed in his luxurious house, his arms behind his head, 'is the woman entirely without sensitivity, I ask myself?'

'I know.' Arian sighed, 'She's so intent on being included in the social whirl of the town that she just doesn't stop to think what the effect on her husband might be. Parties, that's all she has to fill her life, I think.'

'Well, I will have a pressing engagement elsewhere, of course,' Calvin smiled, 'I don't think I could sit in the same room as poor Frogmore.'

'Well, you did make him a cuckold,' Arian ran her finger over Calvin's cheek, 'with a little help from Sarah, of course.'

'With a great deal of pressure from Sarah.' Calvin turned over and leaned on his elbow. 'I'm not excusing myself, I felt hurt and betrayed by the women in my life and I'm afraid I used Sarah as a sop to my damaged pride, not very noble of me, I'll grant you.'

'It's all in the past now.' Arian's voice trembled a little as she moved into the crook of his arm. 'We're together, that's all that counts, let's not waste a moment

99

of our time wallowing in unpleasant memories.'

'You've been to see Gerald?' There was concern in Calvin's voice and Arian closed her eyes against the unwelcome vision of her husband as she had last seen him, securely bound in straps, his eyes glaring at her with hatred.

'Two weeks ago but I need to pluck up the courage to face him again soon, I feel I owe him that much,' she sighed. 'It's awful, he becomes so agitated whenever I go to see him that he has to be subdued with sedatives.'

'You don't have to go,' Calvin kissed her forehead, 'the visits are not doing him any good and are certainly not helping you.'

'I feel I owe it to him,' she repeated doggedly, 'he's still my husband whatever he's done or become.'

'I know but you get so upset, Arian, look at you, trembling now at the very thought of going to that awful place.'

'Let's not talk about it.' Arian turned to him and put her arms around his neck, pressing herself against him as though to fuse her body with his.

He kissed her mouth, her throat, her breasts. 'I want you, Arian, I will always want you.' He took her sweetly, he was mindful of her needs as well as his own. He made love, as he did everything else, with finesse. He was all she could desire. If he was her husband instead of her lover, would she be so happy, she wondered?

She forgot everything then but this feeling between them. She moaned softly, arching against him as the flow of their passion swept away all other thoughts and sensations. She cried out his name and clung to him, tears of happiness and release flowing down her cheeks.

Later, they sat together in the dining room and took supper. Cook had prepared saddle of lamb in mint jelly for the main course with a rich plum duff in brandy to follow.

Arian felt aglow with the delight of being loved by such a man. How she had come to take it all for granted, her changed lifestyle, Arian mused. Such a long way to come from the girl who had ridden bareback over her father's land, defying anyone to try to tame her. How she had hated her father and yet here she was, successful at the very trade in which he had been engaged, that of newspaper proprietor.

The door closed behind the servants and Calvin leaned forward. 'You've gone far away from me,' his voice broke into her thoughts and Arian smiled up at him. 'I will never be far away from you, not while I have breath in my body.'

He took her hand. 'I wish we could be married. We *could* be married if only you would divorce Gerald Simples. You have every reason, he's criminally insane, no-one expects you to remain tied to such a man.'

'You know I won't divorce him.' Arian brushed back a stray wisp of hair from her eyes. 'I owe him some allegiance, I married him after all.' She smiled suddenly. 'In any case, you would be marrying a divorced woman, your reputation would be in shreds.'

'It is already,' Calvin's eyebrows were raised quizzically. 'Do you think people thought me a gentleman when I cast my wife and her child out into the street?'

'You had your reasons for that,' Arian protested. 'Eline had given birth to another man's child, you had the sympathy of most of the townspeople when you obtained *your* divorce.'

'I'm sure people speculate about our relationship, Arian,' Calvin's expression was grave, 'do you think I like it that *your* reputation is open to question?'

'Come now, who can prove anything except that we dine together at your home?'

'If one of the servants was to be indiscreet then everyone would know soon enough.'

'We'll have to risk that,' Arian said flatly. 'When you come to my home Mary is there at all times and though she hasn't been with me all that long, I think I can count on her loyalty.'

'I'll admit she makes an excellent chaperon,' Calvin's amusement was evident in the light in his eyes and the way his mouth turned upwards in a smile. 'She manages to interrupt us as often as she can.'

'Anyway,' Arian said softly, 'I don't suppose we are very often the subject of discussion, there's so much going on in Swansea and you and I are only a small part of it.'

'I hope you're right,' Calvin poured more coffee, 'but I doubt that much escapes the gossips of our fair town.'

'It seems that your popularity is not diminished,' Arian said dryly, 'at least you are still invited to soirées at the home of Sarah Frogmore.'

'An invitation I could well do without.' He put down his cup as Arian rose to her feet.

'I shall withdraw,' she said in mock severity, 'I shall wait for you in the drawing room. You enjoy your cigar and brandy in peace.'

As she left him, Arian paused for a moment in the hallway. This house of Calvin's was so different from her own home. She lived in an apartment above her business premises. She slept in a small bedroom at the top of the house while downstairs, far below her, was the lifeblood of her newspaper; the offices where the copy was written ready for the printers and even further down, in the basement, the machinery for printing. It would all be quiet now, empty and dark, shut up for the night this past hour. How she loved it all, she could never give it up, perhaps that was one reason why she could accept the role of lover rather than wife, as it was she had everything, well almost.

As she moved on towards the drawing room, she was unaware that Calvin was not so content, he sat in the dining room, staring up at the high ceiling, knowing what was lacking in his life, what he desperately wanted was an heir, a son to take over his title, his great wealth. That heir must be legitimate, there could be no other way. The uncertainties in his life must be resolved, he needed to settle his affairs one way or another. Arian must divorce Gerald Simples before it was too late, too late for her to bear Calvin the son he so desired.

The land was lush and verdant, the skies above her reflected the blue of the water lapping the edge of the dock. Ireland was a beautiful country but Bridie Marchant was in no mood to appreciate it.

'So the load of leather from Glyn Hir is sold then?' She spoke harshly to the master of the *Marie Clare*, he was unfamiliar to her, probably employed recently by Paul. He stared ahead of him obtusely, determined to give nothing away.

'It's sold, Mrs Marchant.'

'To whom?'

'It is in the records, Mrs Marchant. Shall I fetch them for you?' She ignored this. 'Where is my husband?'

'Mr Marchant went ashore.'

'I gathered that but where has he gone?' Bridie spoke the last four words with emphasis but they evoked no further response from the man who simply shrugged.

'Call me a cab,' she ordered and the man looked at her then in some surprise.

'No cabs around these parts, missus, only pony carts and such.'

'Where is the nearest hotel then, can you tell me that?' It was like wheedling a winkle from a shell but Bridie persisted. 'I'm not familiar with this part of Ireland but you must have been here before, man.'

'Aye, I have that.'

'Well then, where is Mr Marchant likely to stay?'

'The best place is Ma Murphy's ale house.' He stopped speaking as though he'd said too much and Bridie smiled triumphantly. 'There, that wasn't so difficult was it?' A gust of wind in from the sea lifted her hat and she fastened it more securely, replacing the pins.

'Now, you will take me to this ale house.' She held

out her bag and the man took it grudgingly. 'Be careful, you are newly in my employ and you will not remain with us for long if you do not serve me well, understood? What is your name?'

'Charlesworth, Richard Charlesworth.' His tone indicated he was not used to being spoken to in such a way even by the ship's owner but Bridie didn't give a fig for him. He could go or stay with the line, it was a matter of complete indifference to her. There were masters aplenty to be had and Charlesworth knew it.

'I must give my men some instructions, please give me a minute.' The master disappeared up the gangway and Bridie fumed impatiently on the dock, tapping her foot, torturing herself with the image of Paul in the arms of some hussy.

Soon, she was sitting beside a silent Charlesworth, taking the short journey towards the small group of buildings that sprawled around the docklands near Cork. A church spire rose into the sky and a huddle of houses seemed to crouch close to the cobbled streets.

Cork itself, as Bridie knew, was a flourishing township but Paul had, apparently, chosen a modest abode near the docks rather than take the trouble to select a good hotel in the town. Her spirits lifted, he could hardly be planning an assignation or he would certainly have been out to impress Ellie Hopkins.

They stopped outside a modest ale house and Charlesworth helped her alight from the cart. 'I don't know if he's here, missus.' He sounded surly but she saw his eyes flash to an upstairs room.

She went inside and immediately saw that the place was far from respectable. In the room to the left of the hallway, men sat around tables drinking dark beer and the floor of the bar was covered in sawdust.

A woman came forward dressed in a rough calico skirt and a freshly laundered blouse, her hair was twisted into a severe bun and a shawl was draped around her plump shoulders. This then was Mrs Murphy, hardly the type to interest Paul, Bridie decided with a sudden springing of hope.

'Can I help you, then, madam?' She spoke with a distinctive Irish accent and in spite of her polite manner, her eyes as they rested on Bridie's well-dressed figure were hostile.

'I am Mrs Marchant.' Bridie saw the woman's eyes narrow, 'I'm simply enquiring if my husband is lodged here.'

The woman glanced over her shoulder and Bridie felt, rather than saw, the master's almost imperceptible nod.

'Sure, your man lodges here but he's not in, not right at this moment. Sorry.'

'Then oblige me by taking me to his quarters, I shall wait for him there.' Bridie turned to look back at Richard Charlesworth, he was already walking into the ale-sodden bar, nodding to the locals and taking the corner seat as though he was a regular customer.

Mrs Murphy hesitated but clearly Bridie's imperious manner overawed her and with a bob, she led the way up the uncarpeted stairs.

Bridie wondered why on earth Paul should stay in a place like this when he had the means to reside in comfort in a much higher class establishment.

In his rooms Bridie looked around her disdainfully. The furniture was old but good, that much she conceded and the smell of beeswax indicated that the rooms were well cared for. She tugged back the patchwork quilt and saw that the bed linen was spotless. Perhaps, in this area of docklands, Murphy's was the best that Ireland could offer the casual visitor.

She dragged a rattan chair close to the small deep-set window and stared out into the gathering gloom of the evening. She felt weary, wondering if she had been foolish to come here, what if Paul was truly here only on business? How would he react to finding her spying upon him?

She was almost asleep, her head fell back onto the

hard cane of the chair and the contact jerked her into wakefulness. She forced herself to concentrate, the street outside seemed to be darker. Two people were coming out of the gloom into the splash of light from the open doorway of the ale house.

Bridie rose to her feet and with a beat of her pulse saw the stocky figure of her husband, his dark hair glinting with the fine rain that had begun to fall. Standing looking up at him was a woman, Bridie could see she was small and well-formed even though a coarse shawl was wrapped around her head and shoulders.

Anger filled her, she put her hand to her throat and leaned closer to the cold glass, straining to see if any scene of tender intimacy would be enacted between her husband and this whore he was with.

Was the woman Ellie Hopkins? The figure was small enough but it was too dark to see any detail. Paul put his hand on the woman's shoulder and for a moment, as he bent forward, Bridie thought he would actually kiss the upturned face. Then a third figure joined the pair, a man, it was Richard Charlesworth, Bridie would stake her life on it. Charlesworth spoke for a moment and then took the woman's arm and led her within the building and out of Bridie's sight.

Paul glanced up, his face a mere blur. She clenched her hands together and drew herself to her full height, her husband was betraying her. She turned into the room, perhaps they slept in this very bed together. Anger burned in her skull, she knew that if, in that instant, she had a weapon she would be capable of killing anyone who stood in her way.

She heard footsteps on the stairs and then Paul was in the room, the scent of the cold rain mingling with the clean fresh smell of his skin. She loved him so much she ached. And yet she hated him too.

'What are you doing here?' He sounded cold. He closed the door behind him and came further into the room. 'And why are you sitting in the dark?'

106

He lit the oil lamp and turned to look at her, there was no smile of welcome. 'Well?'

Bridie found she was at a loss to reply, she was afraid to accuse him outright of being unfaithful and yet what other reason could she have for coming to Ireland?

'You have been spying on me, is that it?' He was not playing the loving husband now, he was angry with her and Bridie knew that she had nothing to lose. She might just as well give voice to her suspicions and see if he could answer them.

'You are having an affair, aren't you, Paul?' She sounded as angry as he appeared to be.

'What nonsense is this?' he stood staring at her, his whole body tense. 'What on earth has put such a foolish notion into your head?' In spite of his words, he sounded uncertain.

'I know you're being unfaithful to me, so don't try to deny it,' she flung at him and he sank down heavily on the bed. There was a strange look on his face and for a moment Bridie thought he was going to confess everything but he remained silent.

'It's that hussy Ellie Hopkins, isn't it?' She was incensed by his silence, the swine was guilty, it was plain as the nose on his face.

His reaction startled her, he burst into loud laughter, leaning back against the pillows, uncaring that his booted foot was resting on the clean quilt. 'What rubbish!'

Was she wrong or was that relief she could hear in his voice? She stared at him closely. 'Tell me then, why did you bother to come to Ireland with such a pathetic load of leather? You know and I know that carrying a few boxes of skins, even supplemented with fuel blocks, can not be profitable.'

'Glyn Hir gives better service than some of the bigger tanneries. The skins are delivered to the saddler for me and then collected and brought to the docks as part of the bargain. I did it as a favour, if you must know.'

Now she had him. 'A favour for Ellie Hopkins, is that it?'

'No, that isn't it at all.'

'Then give me a rational explanation.' Bridie's words fell like stones and she saw Paul's mouth tighten in anger.

'I do not like your tone of voice,' he said. Bridie was taken aback by his air of confidence, for a moment, she didn't know how to react, had she been wrong?

From the ale room below came the sound of ribald laughter, the voices of men raised in the high spirits engendered by strong drink. She thought then of the pair of them standing outside in the rain, the woman looking up at Paul, the tilt of her face indicating a closeness that was not that of a casual acquaintance.

'Charlesworth, he warned you I was here, didn't he?' She resumed her attack. 'You were outside with your doxy, I saw you with my own two eyes and the ship's master warned you, don't take me for a fool, Paul.'

He came to her then and took her hands in his. 'You *are* being a fool, my darling,' his voice was suddenly soft. 'I was walking along with the landlady's daughter, that was all. She does my laundry while I'm in dock, there is nothing else to it, I assure you.'

He took her in his arms and she allowed her head to rest against the broadness of his shoulder. He was not a tall man but Paul had the whipcord strength of a man who lived his life battling against the sea.

'If only I could believe you, Paul, I want to believe you, God alone knows I do.'

'Then believe me, I'm not having an affair with Ellie Hopkins.'

She so wanted to believe him. He lifted her chin and kissed her lips warmly and as she clung to him, he kissed her neck, his hands caressing her shoulders so that she leaned against him weak with desire.

'Come on, let's eat a little supper and then go to bed.

As you're here, we might as well make the most of the occasion.'

She raised her mouth to his and he kissed her and if she sensed relief more than passion in his embrace, she was too grateful to question it.

It was only later, lying beside him, wakeful in the unfamiliar room clothed in darkness that the questions began to creep into her mind. For whom was Paul doing the favour of carrying the leather to Ireland if not for Ellie Hopkins? Paul had spoken of the landlady's daughter doing his laundry as though it was a task she undertook regularly. That meant he was in Ireland a great deal more often than she supposed. Was this the couple's trysting place? Did Ellie Hopkins travel out here on the *Marie Clare* with him, was she even now lying snug aboard ship?

She turned over on her back. What if she was? Surely Bridie could overlook a small indiscretion with a woman of no social standing. But Ellie Hopkins did have some standing in the town now that she was a rich widow. Bridie must make a point of monitoring Paul's trips more closely in the future, it seemed her husband must be kept on a tight rein. For now, she must get some sleep, it had been a long day.

Morning was creeping through the chink in the curtains by the time Bridie managed to sleep. When she awoke, it was to find the bed beside her was cold and empty. Paul had gone.

CHAPTER EIGHT

'Look, Ellie, you know as well as I do what Jubilee intended and that was for me to have a share in the business, it's only fair that you carry out Jubilee's wishes.'

Ellie was seated in the shabby parlour, the fire glimmered in the grate, the embers sending up sparks as the coal shifted. It had been a hot summer's day but now, in the evening, it had turned quite chill.

Ellie looked up at Matthew, she felt weary, weary and sick at heart, all she longed for was some peace. 'I told you it will be sorted out, Matthew,' she pushed back her hair. 'I won't cheat you of anything, you know that but I can't do this thing alone, I have to have Mr Telforth's help. You'll just have to be patient.'

'He won't lift a finger to help! He didn't like me and he made that obvious. It's a few months now since we put Jubilee in the ground, I think I've been patient enough and no-one can say I haven't.'

'I've given you a rise in your wages, made you chief hand, I don't see what else I can do.'

'You can honour your husband's wishes, that's what you can do. Had I been made a shareholder, I'd be a rich man now and it is what Jubilee wanted, isn't it?'

She could see he was going to persist in the matter. 'I'll see the lawyer about it, don't keep on, Matthew, I just can't cope with it all at a time like this,' she attempted to divert him. 'Are you getting married soon, Matthew? Isn't that what you led Jubilee to believe?'

'He assumed that was the case, aye, not that I said anything was certain, mind.'

Ellie's patience was growing thin. 'Are you getting married or not, give me a straight answer for once in your life?'

He smiled as though amused by her irritation. 'Maybe and maybe not.' Matthew thrust his hands into his pockets. 'I have been giving my future prospects some thought. You know I've always been fond of *you*, Ellie, perhaps it would be a good idea if I stayed free for the time being, you never know what could come out of our friendship.'

Ellie felt her skin crawl with revulsion, she rose to her feet, clenching her hands together resisting the temptation to slap Matthew hard across his smug face.

'There could never be anything between us,' she said, 'put that right out of your mind, Matthew.'

'Why not? I'm young and strong, Ellie, I could give you children, heirs, strong healthy sons. I'm not a seedless grape like old Jubilee was.'

'That's enough!' Ellie felt anger burn inside her. 'I won't have such coarse talk in my house, I never heard the like from my father or from Jubilee and I won't listen to it from you.'

Matthew lifted his chin and swaggered to the door. 'Don't pretend to be so holy and good, Ellie, I know too much about your past for you to try to pull the wool over my eyes.'

'How dare you?' Ellie walked past him into the hallway and drew the door wider letting in the late evening sunshine. 'If you think that sort of threat will endear you to me then you're very wrong.'

'Aw come on, you know I'm only joshing.' Matthew realized he'd overstepped the line. 'I wouldn't hear a word against you, Ellie, I'd kill any man who went over your name in public and you know it.'

Ellie's shoulders sagged. 'Look, Matthew, put any ideas of a romance between us out of your mind. In any case, it wouldn't pay you, don't you realize I'd lose respect if I married within a year of Jubilee's death.' She saw his look of surprise with a sense of triumph. 'I fully intend to observe a year of mourning, it's only proper, so you must see that marriage to anyone is out of the question.'

'Oh, I do see, I agree that's only right and proper.' Matthew's words came out in a rush. 'But I'll be here, helping you, I'll protect you from the other men, I'll look after you.'

To her relief, Matthew left her then and strode out into the roadway leading to the tannery yard. The shadows were long over the wooden buildings, it was high time the men finished work but Ellie was too tired to follow Matthew and give instructions for them to leave.

Luke and Harry were faithful workers, good men, and Boyo would do anything he could to help her but as Ellie returned to the sitting room, she faced the fact that none of them could protect her from Matthew Hewson.

'I can't marry you now, you must see that.' Matthew was lying on the grass, the sun warm on his naked back. 'I must get this thing sorted out with Jubilee's widow.'

Rosie turned to him, her bodice still open to reveal her full breasts, her skirt riding up above her dimpled knees. Her rosy lips were pressed together in a pout.

'We'll get married when I can give you a good living,' he continued, stretching his arms behind his head. 'I need to wheedle the shares Jubilee promised me from Ellie before I make any commitment.'

'*Duw*, there's long words then, the poet in you coming out is it, Mat Hewson?' Rosie slid her hand between his legs, 'But this is where you keep your brains, man, don't try to fool me.' She giggled as she felt him harden, 'Led by their urges, men are, see, and a sensible woman knows that only too well.'

He swiftly unbuttoned his trousers and then he was above her, poised for a moment before thrusting downwards. She cried out at his roughness but as his hands found her naked breasts, she began to moan softly.

Matthew paused and Rosie's eyes flew open question-ingly.

'Who is ruled by what?' he laughed, his teeth white, his head bent towards her. 'I could resist you, my dear Rosie but I don't think you would like that one little bit.' He thrust into her so deeply that she squirmed beneath him. And then Matthew paused once more, a restraint that in his present frame of mind was easy to achieve, besides, he needed to teach Rosie a lesson.

'Please, Mat, don't tease, come on, I need you, I really need you right now.'

'Beg,' he ordered, still holding back.

'All right, I beg you, Mat, make love to me, I want you so badly I'll die if you stop now.' Rosie was gasping, she arched herself upwards to accommodate him and he took her then with an almost disdainful lack of passion, watching her writhe, failing to climax until he closed his eyes and imagined it was Ellie with her enticing fortune who was lying beneath him.

Later, he sat in the Ship Inn enjoying a pint of ale, and slowly his thoughts crystallized into a workable plan. He would stop harassing Ellie for shares in the fortune that Jubilee had left, he would work his way into her life, into her heart, he would eventually marry her and then all of it would be his.

He wiped the froth of ale from his mouth with the back of his hand. It would be no hardship, Ellie was a delectable creature, a little too thin perhaps and lacking the full-breasted beauty that Rosie possessed but, all the same, a brood of kids around her skirts would take care of that. She would doubtless fill out in time.

She would see he would be good to her, he wouldn't allow her to work in the tannery, he'd want his wife in the home, waiting on his needs. He would be doing her a favour really, she didn't know how lucky she was to have him but she would learn, in time she would learn.

★　　★　　★

Ellie sat in the coolness of the chapel and bowed her head for a moment in respectful prayer. The sun spilled in through the windows, falling onto the lectern and the young man who stood there, waiting to preach his message to the expectant congregation.

Evan Roberts had, over the past months, made an impact on both the church-going population and those who never bowed the knee in prayer. The name of Evan Roberts had become synonymous with the joy of the renewed spirituality that was sweeping through the country and reaching far out beyond the borders of Wales.

Seated beside Ellie was her new friend. Martha Greenacre had come to Ellie's door several weeks before in response to the advertisement in *The Swansea Times*. She was a plump motherly woman who was seeking a post as companion in some respectable house and even though she held a spotless handkerchief to her nose, offended at the smell of the tannery, she had liked Ellie on sight and had been delighted when the liking was reciprocated.

'He's a fine man, all right,' Martha whispered, her Bible clutched in her gloved hands. 'I think the Lord has truly blessed him that he can bring such joy to the faces of his congregation even before he begins to speak.'

Ellie was aware of someone taking the seat at her other side and as she glanced around, her face lit up in welcome.

'Mr Bennett how nice to see you,' she whispered. He took her hand and shook it awkwardly. 'Please, call me Daniel won't you?' he whispered back. 'I spotted the empty seat when I came in, there aren't many left.' He smiled and a dimple creased his cheek. 'I was doubly pleased when I saw who it was I'd be sitting next to.'

Ellie felt her colour rise, it was clear that the young reporter was paying her a compliment, something she had been unused to. Jubilee's love had been solid and reliable but hardly romantic. She suppressed the thought as unworthy and bowed her head once more.

'I'm here for the paper,' Daniel whispered, bending close to Ellie, 'seems the *Cardiff Western Mail* carried an article headed, "Great crowds of people drawn to Loughor".' He smiled a little ruefully. 'Arian Smale is a fine editor, she's already published one article about the great man but she feels I should follow it up.'

Someone hushed him from behind and Ellie saw that Evan Roberts was about to begin.

'Let us pray.' The muted sound of conversation was stilled, the sunlit motes of dust caught in falling patterns from high windows to floor. Ellie felt herself tense, as though awaiting the opening of a great play.

'Lord Jesus, help us now through the Holy Spirit to come face to face with the cross. Whatever the hindrances may be, we commit the service to thee.'

Ellie recognized the power of the preacher, his words were ordinary but imbued with such feeling that tears rose to her eyes. Beside her, she heard Martha's slight sniff as she raised her spotless handkerchief to her eyes. On her left, she heard the scratch of Daniel's fountain pen, otherwise the silence was complete.

Evan Roberts was finishing his prayer. 'Speak thy word in power for thy name's sake. Amen and amen!'

The silence was broken by murmurs of amen from the congregation and then, a deacon rose from the *Set Fawr* and began to sing. His tenor voice filled the church, echoing from the rafters, sweet and pure. He was joined by other singers, tenor and bass in harmony.

Ellie felt tears come to her eyes, how Jubilee would have loved the magic of the sound. Daniel put his hand over hers, in a gesture of understanding.

Later, outside in the soft summer sunshine, Ellie paused breathing in the sweetness of the day.

'Wasn't he wonderful!' Martha was still drying her eyes, 'such *hwyl* I've never heard before.'

Daniel leaned towards Ellie. 'What's "*hwyl*" when it's at home?'

'Enthusiasm, I suppose that's the nearest I can get to it in English,' Ellie said quietly. 'One thing I know, he makes me ashamed of myself, I haven't lived a very worthy life.'

'I can't believe that.' Daniel looked down at her, his eyes warm. 'Someone as young and beautiful as you has surely enjoyed an exemplary past.'

'We'd better get off home.' Ellie took Martha's arm. 'Nice to see you, Mr Bennett.'

'Daniel, please.' He fell into step beside her, 'I have to get back to town, too, may I have the pleasure of your company on the journey?'

'Yes, of course.' Ellie didn't know why she was reluctant to share her time with Daniel, perhaps it was because he was so young and innocent and knew nothing of her past. He believed her to be simply an old man's widow, she wouldn't like him to be disillusioned by the truth. If she gave him a wide berth there was no reason why he should find out that she had been a mistress once.

Martha took to the young reporter and it was she who kept up a running conversation with him during the journey. He walked at Ellie's side, keeping a respectful distance and she knew he was covertly watching her every move.

A sharp regret filled her for lost innocence. If she had never become Calvin's mistress she would never have born twins, never have suffered the anguish of losing them, never, in all probability, settled for the life of wife to an old man. Yet she had come to love Jubilee, to respect him. He had been wise and good and she missed him so much it hurt.

'How sad you look,' Daniel spoke his thoughts aloud and then immediately apologized.

'Forgive me for being rude,' his colour had risen. 'I didn't mean to insult or hurt you, it's just that . . . ' He stopped aware that if he continued speaking he would be digging himself further into indiscretions.

'I suppose I feel sad,' Ellie replied. 'I'm missing my husband, I wish he could have been with me to hear Evan Roberts today.' She paused, knowing she was building a wall between Daniel and herself. 'He liked the preacher very much, respected him though Jubilee always stayed loyal to his own Church of England code, mind, nothing would have turned him from that.'

Daniel looked down at his feet, suitably subdued by Ellie's reminder that she had recently been widowed.

'What did you make of Evan Roberts, Martha?'

Martha Greenacre placed a hand on Ellie's arm. 'I thought him the finest man who ever walked on God's earth,' she said with heartfelt sincerity. 'I would follow him to the ends of the world if that's what he wished, he's the most holy person I could hope to meet in this world.'

Daniel drew out his book and began to scan his notes, adding a little it seemed of what Martha had said. He put the cap on his pen and returned it to his pocket. 'Do you mind if I quote you on that?' He looked at Martha and she flushed with pleasure.

'I would be most flattered. Martha L. Greenacre is the name, shall I spell it for you?'

'That's all right,' Daniel smiled. 'I'm quite familiar with the name, aren't you from the Uplands, at least your family is?'

Martha's face warmed. 'That's quite right, I was married to a pharmacist, Donald Greenacre, we had a fine big house high up on the hill.' She sighed, 'But when Donald died, I found the house was not solely his, it belonged in part to his brother and he made my life quite uncomfortable until I moved out, I can tell you.'

Ellie hid a smile, it was obvious that Daniel hadn't known what he was letting himself in for when he'd started the conversation. She put her arm around Martha's shoulder and hugged her. 'Well some good came out of it all,' she said encouragingly, 'you came to me and I'm so glad you did.'

'I wasn't sure at first, mind,' Martha admitted, 'that awful stink of the tannery, I thought I'd never get used to it but now I hardly notice it at all.'

'Perhaps later on we'll move house,' Ellie said pensively, 'buy something near the seashore, I'd like that, would you, Martha?'

'I'd love it,' Martha said decidedly. 'But one day you'll marry again, you won't want old Martha then.'

Ellie shook her head. 'No, I won't get married, I have no intention of tying myself to another man. I've learned to be wary of them,' she glanced quickly at Daniel, 'present company excepted of course.'

'Of course.' Daniel smiled. 'I'm glad to hear it, I've a long way to go yet, I plan to make a fine career out of the newspaper business. When I do, I'll be in a position to take a wife.' His meaning was clear and Ellie sighed, she had not, as she hoped deterred him from thinking of her romantically, she had merely afforded him some hope that she would be waiting for him.

'Ah, here we are, almost home, come along Martha, I want to get changed into my working clothes, do some cleaning in the house, it's like a tip in there.'

'When are you going to get a housemaid?' Daniel sounded concerned. 'It's not right you should work on such menial tasks as cleaning out the fire grate and washing clothes, it's not fitting for a well brought up lady like you.'

'That's exactly what I keep telling her,' Martha said looking approvingly at Daniel.

'All right, I will put an advertisement in *The Times*,' Ellie said, knowing she would have no peace until she did.

'Perhaps you'll allow me to do that for you?' Daniel suggested. 'Tell me what your requirements are and I'll scribble it down here.'

'There now,' Martha's tone held an unmistakable degree of satisfaction, 'you can't get out of it any longer, let the dear young man handle it for you, Ellie, he knows how to frame such an advertisement, I'm sure.'

'Thank you, Daniel,' Ellie gave in, 'it would be very kind of you. Have the bill sent to Glyn Hir, of course.'

Daniel allowed his hand to rest above her gloved fingers for a moment. 'Don't you worry about a thing, it will be my pleasure to attend to it for you.'

He was almost like a young puppy in his displays of willingness and Ellie found it rather endearing. She was relieved when he turned and raised his hat in farewell and strode away in the direction of the offices of *The Times*. Martha coughed, Ellie turned to look at her questioningly.

'He's a very kind young man that Mr Bennett. I'm pleased you are taking his advice to get in a maid to help you with the rough work.' She paused for breath. 'Believe me, I'm not urging you to be a spendthrift, far from it. You miss having enough funds of your own, I can tell you that from experience. I only wish I'd been more careful with my income while my husband was alive.'

Ellie took her arm. 'Well you're all right now, you coming to live at Glyn Hir has been the making of me, I feel much better able to cope with the men now you are there to keep them in order.'

Martha sniffed. 'There's only one needs slapping down and that's Matthew Hewson, bad lot, him, seen his sort before, motivated by sheer greed, his is, mind.' Her eyes sparkled for a moment with humour. 'He would quite like having you along with the Glyn Hir profits, I dare say but failing that, he'll settle for the money. Watch him, Ellie, that's all I'm saying.'

'I know, you've no need to warn me.' Ellie looked with fresh eyes at the blue sky above the hills of Kilvey and the Town Hill. The valley formed between them ran into mostly flat lands with crowded streets filled with elegant stores side by side with tiny shops whose goods hung in doorways and sprawled onto the pavements. Towards the edge of town, small houses crouched close together, fringed by the five mile curve of the sand dunes rising above the waters of the bay. Beyond the hills to the east hung the smoke from the industries crowding the banks of the river Tawe, blotting out that section of the summer sky with green smoke. Ellie was so used to it, the beauty and the ugliness of Swansea, that it was only at times like this she really saw it.

'*Duw* I can smell it already, can you, Ellie?' Martha's wrinkled nose confirmed that they were drawing near to the tanneries. Ellie could see the walls of old stone that shielded the yards from view but did little to contain the stink of leather freshly taken from the animal.

'Why does my heart sink?' She spoke without thinking and quickly, lest she should seem ungrateful to her dead husband, qualified her statement. 'Well, my heart doesn't sink, not exactly but I do feel as though I'm coming back after a pleasant outing to work I would rather not do.'

'Don't do it then.' Martha looked her straight in the eye as Ellie paused at the gates to Glyn Hir. 'Nothing your husband said in his last wishes indicated you should continue to work here, did it?'

'No, I suppose not. Jubilee did want me to live here, to keep an eye on the tannery but I suppose I don't really need to go to work in the grinding house any more.'

'Well then?'

'Well, I suppose it's what you said earlier, I don't want to squander Jubilee's hard earned profits.'

'It's not squandering if you delegate the tasks to one more fitted to do them, another boy perhaps or even a young girl if you like. Why not think about it?'

Ellie smiled, the frown of worry on her brow fading. 'I promise I'll think about it but remember, I've already come a long way, I've got you and now it seems I'm going to have a housemaid too, that will do for a start.'

It was almost two weeks later when Ellie sat in the kitchen and began to sift through the letters she had received as a result of the advertisement in *The Times*.

Some could be discarded at once, the applicants were either too old or too young, in Ellie's judgement. Finally, she was left with a choice of two suitable candidates, one was from a Rosemary Prosser of the Sandfields area of the town and the other from April Thomas of Honey's Farm up on the hill.

Both letters were well written with neat handwriting and couched in just the right terms and Ellie found it difficult to choose between them except that at fifteen, she thought April too young for the job.

A knock on the door startled her and she looked up to see Matthew framed in the doorway.

'Could I have a word, Ellie?' For once he sounded respectful and hope blossomed that he was not going to harp on about the shares again.

'You're looking for a girl to take on a cleaning job here?' he asked without further preamble. Ellie nodded wondering why Matthew could possibly be interested in who she chose to help her in the house.

'Could I just ask you a favour, to give the job to a friend of mine? Rosie Prosser, I can vouch for her honesty, Ellie.'

For once his arrogance was missing and Ellie looked at him sharply wondering if this Rosie was his young lady. If so, it would serve to keep him in check if she was around the house all the time.

'I'll certainly think about it.' Ellie smiled. 'I see she's willing to live in, you would be seeing a great deal of her, is that what you want?'

Matthew smiled. 'Rosie's a pretty girl, she would brighten the place up. She's experienced too, been cleaning the offices down near the docks she has, and that Bridie Marchant is a real stickler.' He was giving nothing away about his own feelings for the girl. Ellie paused for a moment, this Rosemary was probably the most suitable applicant of the two when she thought about it.

April Thomas had been adopted by Fon O'Conner

and would have a good living up on the farm. It was possible she was merely making the application out of a sense of bravado, of wanting to be independent, in which case she might not last very long in the job. And if this Rosie turned out to be Matthew's lady friend, her presence would solve a lot of problems. She made up her mind.

'Right, if she meets my requirements at the interview, she shall have the job,' she smiled. 'I'll write to her at once.'

'That's good then,' Matthew said. 'Have you thought any more about those shares Jubilee promised?'

Ellie hesitated and Matthew pressed home his advantage. 'I know there's nothing I can do in law, no papers had been signed and all that but you know and I know what Jubilee wanted, don't we?' He was speaking reasonably without his usual air of aggression.

Ellie nodded slowly, morally Matthew was within his rights to insist on having the shares. 'I am giving it some thought, it's just that I'm still in a muddle as yet, there's so much to sort out, so many matters to attend to.' She looked up at Matthew, 'You know Jubilee did everything himself, I have to learn from scratch how the business is run.'

'But don't you see what a help I could be to you, Ellie?' He spoke earnestly, 'I could at least take some of the burden off your shoulders.'

'You're doing that already,' Ellie said and Matthew lifted his hands in exasperation.

'I'm doing the work, taking the responsibility but not reaping the rewards, is that what you call fair play Ellie?'

'No. I will try my best to get something done soon, it's a promise.' She rose to her feet and moved towards Matthew hoping to edge him from the room, he stood his ground.

'I'm counting on you, Ellie,' he said, 'to see that Jubilee's last wishes are carried out to the letter.'

That touched her on the raw. 'I know what my

husband's last wishes were better than anyone, even you, Matthew.' Her tone was sharp. 'Please, go, leave me alone, can't you even allow me time to mourn?'

He rested his hand on her shoulder. 'I'm sorry.' He sounded sincere. 'I'm a thoughtless lout, of course I'll be patient, I know you'll do what's right.'

She was relieved when he turned and left the kitchen, disappearing along the path towards the yards. She sank into a chair, she couldn't blame him for wanting what was rightfully his she supposed, and perhaps with the added resources the shares would bring he would find himself in a position to get married. That would take a great burden from her mind, somehow Matthew's presence posed a threat. Not that she believed him capable of violence, it was just she continually felt the need to fend off his advances.

Ellie took to Rosemary Prosser on sight. She was about nineteen years old, well-built and with a healthy complexion that spoke of a life lived out of doors. Ellie looked down at Rosemary's letter to remind herself of the girl's background.

'I see you've been working near the docks, cleaning the offices for the shipping agents wasn't it?'

'That's right, miss, liked it too, better than being the daughter of a farm labourer, believe me.'

'You think you could stand the smell of the tannery Rosemary? It's not very pleasant but you do get used to it.'

'*Duw*,' that's nothing, you ought to catch a stink of the fuel works of a morning, it's enough to put you off your grub.'

'And you think you'd be happy here, cleaning and perhaps doing some cooking?'

Rosemary smiled, 'I love cooking, that's what I'm best at, mind. I do a fine beef stew with dumplings as well as making the best apple tart for miles around.'

Ellie concealed her amusement, Rosemary was no shrinking violet, certainly not a girl to hide her light under a bushel. 'I'm paying what I understand is the usual rate as well as your bed and board, will that suit you?'

'Suit me fine, miss, and please call me Rosie, everyone else does and I'm used to it, like.'

'When can you start, Rosie?' Ellie warmed to the girl's friendly nature, 'I'm sure we'll get on very well.'

'I can fetch my things up in the morning, miss, will that be all right?'

'That will be just fine.' Ellie rose to her feet, 'I'll show you your room. If I'm not here when you arrive, just settle in, make yourself at home.'

'*Duw*, a room of my own, I can't believe it. At home I sleep with my two sisters in the same bed, little pests they are as well wriggling all night, having nightmares. Don't think I'll ever have kids, they're too much trouble.'

Ellie led the way up the stairs aware of the shabbiness of the carpet. Rosie appeared not to notice, she was too busy admiring the large landing and the big, stained-glass window at the top of the staircase.

'Just here, along the passage,' Ellie said, 'Martha, Mrs Greenacre, is in the room next to you. You'll meet her tomorrow, I think you two will like each other.'

'I'm easy enough to get on with,' Rosie said, 'not many as don't like Rosie Prosser, especially Mat Hewson, I'm his girl.'

Ellie was pleased to hear it, the girl might just keep Matthew in line. Rosie generated a feeling of dependability and good humour, she would be good to have around.

'This is a lovely room.' Rosie stood in the centre of the floor looking around her. The large window facing south spilled sunlight across the worn carpet, warming the faded quilt on the bed and lending it a sense of colour.

'The furniture is good,' Ellie said, 'it could all do with a bit of beeswax and a great deal of elbow-grease I'm afraid.'

124

'I'll get it up a treat, don't you worry about that.' Rosie placed a hand on each hip and her breasts strained against the bodice of her blouse. A dark strand of hair had escaped from the restraining pins and hung down over one rounded cheek. Ellie could see why Matthew would be attracted to such a girl, she exuded a wholesomeness that was most appealing.

'Right, then you'll start tomorrow, it's agreed.' Ellie led the way from the room and saw Rosie glance back almost longingly.

'I'm going to work my fingers to the bone here mind, this is just the sort of job I've been dreaming about.'

Ellie smiled. 'I'm glad you're pleased. Hopefully over the next few months we'll be able to buy new curtains and carpets, brighten the place up a bit.'

'Well, it's like a palace to me after the little house my dad rents. Talk about cramped, couldn't swing a cat in there, see, not even a little one.'

Ellie let her out through the front door and watched as Rosie walked along the path, the sun glinting on her hair, her full hips swinging as though in time to some unheard music.

Boyo was just coming up towards the house, ready no doubt for his midday grub and he stopped, open-mouthed looking as if he'd seen a vision.

Ellie paused in the doorway as Rosie stopped and conversed with the boy who stood tall and thin as a willow in contrast to the girl's rounded figure.

Boyo's face had turned a fiery red, he shuffled his feet and looked down at them in what appeared to be an agony of embarrassment. Rosie laughed, tossing back her head before lightly tapping Boyo's cheek with her finger. Then she was away, swinging toward the roadway, her long skirt flaring behind her.

Ellie turned from the doorway wondering for the first time if she had not been a little hasty in employing Rosie. If her effect on Boyo was anything to go by, she would be setting the men in the yards back on their heels with desire.

Ah well, hopefully she would be married to Matthew before too long. Perhaps quite soon if Ellie arranged the transfer of some shares into Matthew's name. With Matthew safely married, it would be better for everyone.

CHAPTER NINE

Paul Marchant sat with Richard Charlesworth in the bar of Murphy's guest house, 'Suspicious woman, my wife, I hope she doesn't see fit to visit again. Yes, very suspicious.'

'Not without cause.' Richard raised an eyebrow quizzically. 'Very nearly got caught out then and not only with your little paramour. Thank your lucky stars your wife didn't enquire too deeply into the sale of the horse-collars or she would have been onto your little scheme.'

Paul laughed. 'My wife is only interested in one thing, my fidelity. The worst she could have discovered was my dalliance with little Carmella, she wasn't looking for anything else. She is just too stupid to realize that the affair, if you can call it that, is simply a side issue; I have bigger fish to fry.'

Paul subsided in his chair, his eyes narrowed. Bridie thought she was so clever, thought she was manipulating the loads to her own advantage, sending him on the short runs. What she didn't know was that he was well aware of her activities and went along with her plans because they made it easier for him to feather his own nest. His 'little scheme' as Charlesworth called it, was insurance against the rainy days that would surely come if Bridie continued to be so suspicious of him.

In Ireland, he was free to meet his accomplices in the knowledge that the Irish government was traditionally lenient with smugglers. Those whom Paul called business partners could come from foreign countries into Ireland with ease, buying the contraband cargos freely.

Cork was a fine meeting place, a place which saw ships travel to every part of the high seas.

'I'll have to be more careful for a time but only in the matters of the heart,' he smiled dryly. 'I'm not ready for an open split with my wife, not until I am a very rich man.'

'I should think not,' Richard looked knowing, 'your method of exporting opium without paying the very high duty involved has proved singularly profitable.'

'I sometimes wonder if I'm allowing you to know too much about my affairs, my dear chap.' Paul's voice revealed his irritation and it was not lost on Charlesworth.

'Don't worry about me,' he said, 'meeting your wife for the first time didn't exactly make me feel obligated to her in any way.'

'Imperious, was she?' Paul's voice held an edge of admiration. There were some things about Bridie that he rather liked, one of them was the regal air she could adopt whenever she chose.

'You could say that.' Richard was wise enough not to offer too forceful a criticism of his boss's wife. 'Fine handsome woman though.'

Yes, on reflection, she was. Bridie had changed over the last few years, had grown more positive and with her new air of assertiveness had come a sort of bloom. Her hair was thick and lustrous, darkly red, emphasizing her creamy skin. And no-one could deny she was a fine mother to his sons. He would be a fool, he decided, to openly cross Bridie at this point in his life.

He was quite confident that Bridie had no idea about his double-dealings either in business or in his private life. When she had accused him of having another woman, she had imagined he was bedding Ellie Hopkins, a rich and beautiful widow. Indeed, he would have grasped the opportunity had it arisen but Paul knew women, he could read them well, and Ellie was not a woman to be trifled with.

He sighed and picked up his ale, he was quite content to have Carmella as his little bedmate. She was sweet and young and until he'd come along she had been an innocent. He'd soon taught her the joys of the flesh which she had taken to with a gusto surprising in a good Catholic girl. But then she had Ma Murphy for a mother.

Mrs Murphy was a woman who had an eye for profit at all times. She liked the extra purse of money that Paul left her before he took to sea again. Liked the fine gifts he bought for her daughter and probably hoped that the affair would last, bringing her daughter the riches she could never expect to attain unaided.

'You're very quiet,' Richard's voice broke into his thoughts. 'By your smug expression I'd say you were counting your many blessings.'

'You'd be right.' Paul put down his ale. 'And those blessings are about to increase a hundred fold. It's about time Monkton was here, isn't it?'

Richard took out his pocket watch. 'He'll be here,' he spoke laconically, 'he'll be as eager to sell the goods on at a greatly inflated price, as he always is.'

'You're right,' Paul agreed. 'Well, we might as well have another drink while we're waiting, call the landlord, will you Richard?'

He didn't see the tightening of Charlesworth's mouth or hear the irritation in the man's voice when he complied with his order. And if he had, he wouldn't have cared one jot.

'Well Boyo, you're a fine set up young man, aren't you?' Rosie stared at the fifteen year old boy who was standing at the pump. He was stripped to the waist, his hair dripping. Beneath the rivulets of water, his cheeks were a fiery red and Rosie moved closer, enjoying the effect she was having on him. She leaned forward and pinched the pinkness of his nipple.

'Lovely lad. Had a woman yet?'

'Don't talk that way, it's not nice.' Boyo pulled on his

rough flannel shirt and backed away from her. So, he was shy, all the better.

'A virgin are you, love?' She smiled putting her hands on her hips aware of his eyes moving instinctively to her straining bodice. 'Never mind, you'll find out what it's all about one day. If you're lucky you'll have some fun before you're made a fool of by some pretty wench who you'll get full with your child. Once you're married you'll live a life of boredom, is that what you want, Boyo?'

'Dunno,' he shuffled his feet awkwardly, embarrassed but intrigued in spite of himself.

With slow, deliberate movements, Rosie undid her bodice pretending to fan herself. '*Duw*, it's hot today, isn't it, Boyo?' Beneath the calico bodice she was naked, her full breasts swinging free, the brown tinted nipples springing forth in the cool breeze.

Boyo stood as though entranced, his eyes riveted to the alabaster skin. He moved his hands to cover himself and Rosemary saw, with amused triumph, that the boy was aroused.

She closed her blouse deliberately. 'There, see, Boyo, that's a taste of what you got coming one day, let's hope that day comes before you burst is it? Here, fill my bucket for me, lad.'

He did as he was told, his hands trembling. Without effort, Rosie hoisted the bucket onto her hip and with a laugh, turned and waved to Harry who, being an old married man, had been watching her with amusement.

'You'll do that boy a mischief,' he called, 'why don't you take him out one fine night and show him what it's all about, put him out of his misery?'

'I might just do that,' she murmured quietly, 'I just might do that.'

In the house, she put the bucket of water down on the floor. She stood for a moment looking around the kitchen, it was already spotless, a tribute to her industry. Whatever else she was, Rosie was a good worker and there was none who could say different.

The door opened and the old woman came into the kitchen, looking round her disdainfully. Rosie had disliked Martha on sight and as far as she could see, the feeling was mutual.

'Can I get you anything, missus?' Her tone was respectful and yet carried an undertone that made Martha look at her sharply.

'I want some light refreshments brought into the parlour at once.'

'Oh, for you or for Mrs Hopkins?' Rosie asked.

'Why, does it make any difference who it's for?' Martha was trying to keep her temper.

'I know what Mrs Hopkins likes but then she scarcely ever eats anything between her regular meals.'

'Do you have to be so exasperating?' Martha shook her head, 'I know we are never going to be great friends but at least let us not be hostile to each other.'

'I'm sure I don't know what you mean, missus.' Rosie was determined not to be drawn.

'Just get on with it for goodness sake and please don't waste any more time arguing the toss.'

As Martha left the room in a huff Rosie smiled, she had succeeded in ruffling the old bat's feathers, she could always do that if she really tried and if she was in the mood to be amused.

Still, she liked working for Ellie, there was a sense of pride in being good at her job. Rosie had turned Glyn Hir House from a dingy, neglected building into a bright, clean home in the space of only a few weeks. The furniture shone with polishing, the floors were swept clean and if Mrs Hopkins would take her advice and invest in bright coverings and curtains the place would look almost respectable.

In the sitting room three women were seated and Rosie felt she could have cut the atmosphere with her sharp kitchen knife. Ellie sat near the window with Martha on the other side of the fireplace and the third woman, still in her coat and hat, had her back to Rosie.

'Some cordial Mrs Hopkins, shall I pour for you?'
Rosie had the jug in her hand just as the visitor turned
to face her.

'What are you doing here?' The voice was sharp, the
tone inferring all sorts of things that Rosie didn't much
like.

'Mrs Marchant, there's a surprise.' Rosie spoke
quietly, 'I'm working here now, see, I was only taken on
by Marchant and James as a temporary office cleaner,
the job finished when the old cleaner came back.'

'How remarkable that you should come here, whose
idea was that, might I ask?'

Rosie was puzzled by the woman's attitude, what did
Mrs Marchant care about where she worked?

'That's all right, Rosie,' Ellie smiled placatingly, 'you
may go.'

Outside the door, Rosie paused to listen, her curiosity
was aroused more by the strange attitude shown by Mrs
Marchant than by anything else. She wouldn't normally
eavesdrop but it seemed she was being blamed for
something.

'I know my husband is continuing to buy Glyn Hir
leather, much against my wishes, and yet you deny any
involvement with him. I've thought it over very carefully
and I believe you and he are hiding something from me.'
Mrs Marchant's voice was harsh. 'And now I find that
girl working here when she used to be in my husband's
employ, I find that rather too much of a coincidence.
Something is going on here, are you getting more than
money out of the arrangement with my husband, I
wonder?'

'I don't really know why you have come here Mrs
Marchant, but I can see you are upset so I will overlook
your foolish accusations.'

Ellie was dignified, Rosie granted her that, had she
been the one unjustly accused of having a roll in the hay
with a married man she would have slapped the woman.

'How *very* gracious of you. I saw you with my husband

132

at the docks or have you forgotten that? I saw you and him together, I know how he looked at you, do you take me for a fool?'

'I take you for an unhappy woman who harbours unfounded suspicions,' Ellie replied. 'You have my word of honour that there is nothing between your husband and myself.'

'I don't give a fig for your word of honour.' By the sound of it, Mrs Marchant had risen and moved to the door. Rosie stepped back sharply.

'I know about your past association with Calvin Temple, about the disgraceful way you got rid of the twins you were carrying. Do you blame me if I don't have any faith in your word of honour?' Mrs Marchant was shouting out loud in her anger and Rosie's eyes widened, this was the first she had heard of Mrs Hopkins' past.

Mrs Hopkins spoke again but her voice was so low that Rosemary failed to hear what she said. The door sprung open and Mrs Marchant sailed from the room, her head high, her cheeks flushed. She took no notice of Rosie, indeed, she scarcely seemed to see her. She left the house slamming the door behind her and Rosie made her way back to the kitchen musing on the strange ways of the upper classes.

'Monkton is late,' Paul was looking irritably at his watch. 'I don't like a fellow who can't keep to time.'

'He'll be here,' Richard spoke easily. 'I told you, he has too much to lose if he doesn't turn up.'

Paul frowned and lifted his hand impatiently and the landlord came to his side at once.

'More ale, sir?' He spoke unctuously, rubbing his hands on his stained apron.

'That's right, Murphy.' Paul's eyes went past the man to where a thin figure was hovering in the doorway. At last Monkton had arrived and Paul felt himself relax. 'Fetch another mug,' he said more affably and the landlord disappeared to do his bidding with alacrity, trade was not brisk in the small ale house at this time of the day.

'Have you got the goods?' Monkton asked without preamble.

'Of course, have I ever failed you?'

'Not up until now.' Monkton was a dry stick, he was not a man to warm to but Paul concealed his feelings well as he spoke in a low voice.

'I think you'll be more than pleased when I tell you that I have on offer some of the finest Bengal opium going at a very good price.'

'How have you concealed the cargo?' Monkton's voice was scarcely audible, he hardly sat on his chair perching on the very edge, his elbows on the table, seemingly unaware that the sleeves of his fine jacket were soaking up the pools of ale that had been spilt.

'The opium is concealed in leather horse-collars, packed tightly in the rye grass. It's surprising how many pounds of the stuff can be exported and imported that way without arousing suspicion. Makes a change from the boxes of candles I used last time. Ingenious, what?'

'If you say so.' Monkton was not easily impressed. 'I don't want the customs men chasing me. Can you get me the stuff in greater quantities for the next load?'

'Possibly, and don't worry about being caught, the cargo is as safe as houses. I bought the leather goods from a small tannery, no-one is going to suspect anything.' Paul wished the man would show a little enthusiasm. Perhaps he should announce that his prices had risen, give Monkton something to think about.

He was too late, Monkton had taken a brown package from his inside pocket and handed it across the table. 'I'll expect the cargo to be loaded on my waggons by first light.'

'Smug bastard,' Paul uttered the expletive from between his teeth as he watched the man disappear through the door.

'That's business,' Richard shrugged his shoulders. 'Where does he sell the stuff do you think?'

'I don't know, it could be moved anywhere from here. But that's his worry, the ungrateful wretch.'

'Well old chap, you should know better than to expect gratitude. Talking of gratitude, I should be abjectly grateful for a little taste of the goods before you hand them over.'

'That stuff is worse than spirits for clouding the brain.' Paul was beginning to be irritated by Richard's attitude.

'But much safer, old boy, doesn't leave any ill effects, not like drinking too much brandy.'

'In moderation, everything is all right but if you will indulge in excesses you can't blame anyone but yourself if you feel under the weather.'

Richard slumped back in his chair, his mouth closed into a thin line, he was quite obviously sulking.

'You're worse than my sons for having your own way, man,' Paul said.

'I do a hell of a lot for you,' Richard replied, 'unpaid lackey, that's what I am, is it too much to ask for a small recompense now and again?'

'All right, pick up one of the packets when you supervise the unloading.'

'Sterling work.' Richard brightened at once, his good humour restored.

'You want to be careful,' Paul said, 'that stuff can be addictive, you know.'

'Nonsense,' Richard dismissed the idea, 'that's a fairy story, told to keep the prices high. You know as well as I do that opium and some of its extracts are used in medicine every day.'

'Well, it's your life,' Paul gave up. He knew that taking opium brought about a sort of euphoric feeling, something like a happy dream, Richard had described it once but Paul had never indulged. Opium, as far as he was concerned was merely a cargo. It was smuggling sure enough but harmless, it was simply evasion of the duty

135

imposed by the government, it was not like moving arms and liquor to the ignorant natives of underdeveloped countries.

Richard rose to his feet. 'I'm going up to take a rest. We'll be sailing with the first tide, I take it?'

'If the cargo is shifted tonight, which is your responsibility, yes we will. In the meantime, I think perhaps you're right, bed calls to me, too.'

'But not quite in the same way?' Richard's voice held a note of derision which Paul didn't much like.

'I can't help it if I've got red blood flowing in my veins,' he snapped. It was a veiled reference to one of Richard's other odd habits but the man ignored it.

As Paul passed the bar, he nodded to the landlord. 'Tell Carmella to bring me some tea, there's a good chap.'

He made his way up the rickety stairs and paused for a moment on the small landing thinking about Richard Charlesworth. The man was becoming more than an irritating thorn in the flesh, he was becoming dangerous. In his own room, Paul threw off his jacket and sank onto the bed. He was always given the best room in the house which wasn't saying a great deal, the mattress was lumpy and the bedclothes shabby but at least the place was clean and smelled of much scrubbing.

He felt quietly satisfied as he withdrew the envelope Monkton had given him from his pocket, it was thick with notes and he ran his thumb through them counting rapidly. It added up to a nice little sum which he would put in his own secret bank account. Bridie who believed she owned him body and soul knew nothing about it and perversely, for a moment, Paul almost wished she did, then perhaps she would see him in a different light, treat him with more respect. As it was, she never forgot that she had come from a wealthy background and had been given the benefit of a fine education while Paul was a self-made man.

A small tapping on the door snapped him out of his

reverie and without haste, he tucked the notes away. 'Come in,' he said and the door opened to admit Carmella, her young face flushed, her dark hair falling to her shoulders. She had an innocence about her that he found irresistible. He held out his hand and she took it willingly, her mouth slightly open, her eyes alight.

She was obedient in all things, sweetly compliant as he took off her clothes. She lay then, naked against the sheets, her fair skin flushed from her breasts to the fine-structured bones of her face.

Carmella was still shy of her nakedness but not in the prim way his wife was; Carmella enjoyed his delight in her body while Bridie concealed herself from him whenever she could. She claimed that child bearing had robbed her of her charms. In a way, it was true, her breasts had slackened, her belly was scarred, she had grown heavy about the thighs. Perhaps that was why he sought solace with other, more virginal women.

He gently lowered himself onto the lithe body waiting for him. Carmella gasped as he entered her but she was as roused as he was and his progress was easy. He moved against her teasingly and she put her hand over her mouth to prevent herself from crying out in joy.

His head was pounding with blood, he felt triumphantly in charge, he had made a great deal of money today and now, he was the conquering hero, claiming the spoils of victory. Carmella was writhing with fulfilment beneath him, lifting herself upwards the better to encompass him. And then the sweet passion was flowing from him, fire burned exquisitely in his loins before he fell, replete, onto his side.

Carmella was sobbing gently, overwhelmed by her feelings. 'I love you Paul,' she touched his cheek, 'you bring me such joy, don't ever leave me, will you?'

He turned and kissed her shoulder. 'I won't leave you, my sweet darling, because I love you too.'

To Paul's surprise, he knew quite suddenly that he meant what he said. He who had enjoyed many women from dusky skin to alabaster white, had lain with exotic women from the east and had bought the favours of the ladies of the night who frequented British ports, he was in love with the little innocent Irish colleen who lay beside him.

He examined his feelings, was it Carmella's unconditional love for him that drew him to her or was it her clean, fresh beauty? He didn't know. All he did know was that he must be with her as often as his other commitments would allow.

'I will have a present for you next time I come here,' he said softly, 'something to show how special you are to me.'

'I don't want your presents, Paul.' She put her hand on his cheek and kissed his mouth. 'You know all I want is you.'

'I know and that's what makes you so wonderful,' he sighed and rolled away from her. 'But now, I have things to do, my love. I have a business to run and I can't rely on Richard to work without my supervision.'

She rose and washed her delicate body at the basin on the heavy washstand, every action was that of a dancer, balanced and fine and he wished that he could stay with her. But all too soon now, he would be heading for home and Bridie.

He was definitely colder towards her, angry that she had followed him to Ireland and thrown accusations at him. Bridie was lying awake, staring up at the dappled reflection of early sun on the white ceiling above her. And her trip up to Glyn Hir had been fruitless. She had found the woman at home and not secreted away on the *Marie Clare* as she'd suspected. Yet the feeling persisted that the woman and Paul were indulging in some sort of illicit relationship. The thought was beginning to obsess her.

Paul had returned home yesterday and he seemed to glow with an inner satisfaction that she failed to

138

understand. It wasn't only that he was indulging in an affair and was returning from his lady love, no, there was something more going on in his life, something that was making him less dependent on her but what was it?

She looked over to the side of the bed where he'd lain, cold and unresponsive, the night before. It was now empty, his pillow still marked with the line of his head. Bitter fury flowed through her as she recalled her humiliating failure to arouse him. She had tried, how she had tried with every trick she knew to make him want her. At last he had pushed her away, telling her he was tired, he'd hardly slept for the preparations he'd needed to make for the return journey. Anyone would think he was running an enormous fleet of ships the way he went on. It was she who kept the organization of the exports and imports in check, she who made the real money in this family and all for Paul to indulge himself on wasted trips transporting leather goods and fuel blocks.

It was true he'd made a little money on the cargo but not enough to warrant the time he'd spent over in Ireland. She, on the other hand, had seen to it that large stocks of coal and steel had been safely dealt with and went on their way across deep water.

Perhaps she had allowed her jealousy of other women to cloud the issue, it was just possible that Paul was up to other sorts of mischief like lining his own pockets. But how? She really couldn't see any way he could make extra money, especially not on the trifling loads he was exporting across the Irish channel. And yet were these cargos simply a cover for something else? It might be a good idea if she was to check up on her husband's business activities.

In the meantime, she would be sweetness and light, pretend there was nothing wrong, allow him to lower his guard. He was a careful man, she had learned that since she had taken to searching through his possessions. He left nothing around by way of paperwork that she could make any use of but there was always his sailing table, that he couldn't conceal.

Paul had eaten breakfast, the maid was just clearing his empty plates from the dining table when Bridie let herself into the room.

'Bring me a pot of tea and a little dry toast,' Bridie ordered, scarcely looking at the girl as she moved to the long windows and stared out into the garden.

He was there, her husband, strong and handsome in the bright sunshine, his hair curling around his forehead as he bent to talk to the gardener.

Suddenly, Bridie felt faint, she clutched the back of one of the heavy dining chairs and sank down, her face in her hands.

'Are you all right, Mrs Marchant?' The maid's anxious voice penetrated the haze that was settling over Bridie's mind.

'Water, bring me some water.' She fought to control the darkness that was flooding over her. The maid took an eternity to return and when she did she had Collins with her. The butler bent over Bridie holding the glass to her lips, coaxing her to drink. 'Come along, Mrs Marchant, you are going to be all right. Just a little fainting spell, natural enough in this heat.'

The mists cleared a little and Bridie sank back in her chair in relief. 'I'm all right now,' she opened her eyes, 'thank you Collins. Send someone to fetch the master in from the garden will you?'

Bridie felt her stomach turn over at the sight of the greasy kidney dish on the sideboard. The queasiness was familiar enough to her and she bit her lip in consternation.

Paul came into the room, his face showing concern and she was warmed for a moment. Perhaps this might, just might, be a good thing to have happened, it could be the means of bringing them closer again.

'Paul,' she said, 'sit down and hold my hand.'

He obediently sat and took her hand, leaning forward

in his chair. 'The servant said you were unwell, what is it, Bridie, tell me?'

'It's nothing to worry about, Paul, indeed, I think it might well be cause for celebrating. I believe I'm going to have another baby.'

A mixture of emotions chased across his face, Paul seemed to be assessing the situation, considering just what it might mean for himself. He smiled.

'I'm happy, my clever girl,' he said softly, 'but you must promise me that you will take things easy now, look after yourself, I insist on it.' He paused but only for a fraction of a moment. 'You must take care of yourself, no more travelling, understand me?'

Oh, she understood, she knew then what her condition meant to Paul and a bitterness filled her mouth. What she was holding out to her husband was not a concrete reason for them to be together, what she had given him unreservedly was his freedom.

CHAPTER TEN

'You are seeing a great deal of this Daniel Bennett aren't you?' The voice, harsh, condemning, broke the hushed silence of the parlour where Ellie had been ensconced since breakfast time trying to make sense of Jubilee's books. She looked up sharply to see Matthew Hewson standing in the doorway, his apron slung low around his hips, his cap pushed to the back of his head so that the black hair sprung upwards in waves.

'I beg your pardon?' She spoke as calmly as her sense of outrage would allow. 'What did you say?'

'This man, this pup reporter, he's been here again today, hasn't he?'

Ellie put down her pen and rose to her feet trying to appear much stronger than she felt. She could not allow Matthew to dictate to her, who did he think he was?

'And do I have to answer to you then, Matthew?' She spoke in deceptively soft tones and Matthew emboldened by her apparent docility was encouraged.

'It's not good enough. You see Ellie, you are encouraging this little snob of a reporter, he'll think he can get a foot in here if you don't watch him.'

He stared down at her so sure of himself that Ellie realized she would have to take strong steps to put him in his place. She took a deep breath but Matthew continued speaking almost at once. 'People will start to gossip about you, you don't want to besmirch old Jubilee's good name do you?'

Ellie clenched her hands together feeling the nails bite into the flesh of her palms. 'Be silent, Matthew, are you my keeper suddenly?' The sharpness of her anger penetrated Matthew's consciousness and he lifted his head defensively.

'I'm only thinking of you, what will people make of you, a widow, entertaining a caller?'

Ellie was so angry she felt like dismissing him on the spot. She told herself to be calm, knowing her own guilt was telling her that he had a point. Still, it was high time she put a stop to his proprietary attitude towards her, she wanted nothing to do with him. He was alienating her so much that she was past feeling guilty about the shares Jubilee had promised him. She was also past exercising tact, it was time Matthew was put firmly in his place.

'Do you wish to continue working here?' The question caught him off guard.

'What do you mean?'

'I mean what I say, do you wish to keep your position at Glyn Hir, your generous wages, your position as chief hand? I think you'll admit that you are better off now than you've ever been.'

'Aye, well not so well off as I'd expected to be.' Matthew's brows were drawn together in an angry line.

'Nevertheless, you are making a very good living, I assume it's one you value. If so, you had better watch your manners, I'm quickly coming to the point of losing all patience with you. For two pins I'd dispense with your services, get rid of you once and for all, I can do without this constant battling with you, listening to you whine about your lot, what makes you think that I owe you anything? It was Jubilee who spoke to you of shares, it was nothing to do with me, if you remember?' She saw him struggle with his anger, a mixture of emotions shadowed his face and then, common sense asserted itself.

'I'm only thinking of you, Ellie,' he was smiling now, his eyes, though, were hooded. 'I know Jubilee wanted me to look out for you, watch no-one moved in his carpet slippers and pipe to take his place.'

'No-one will ever take Jubilee's place so you can just stop thinking about me,' Ellie said. 'I am a sensible woman, I've had to be. You forget, I have expert advisers so I don't need your interference.'

She had launched into a tirade now that seemed impossible to stop. 'I am more than adequately chaperoned whenever I go out, more so than most women these days so who is going to talk about me? It is you who are jeopardizing my reputation by your habit of barging into my house whenever you see fit. You are a workman here, nothing more, have I made myself clear?'

Matthew was less sure of himself now and Ellie made the fatal mistake of softening towards him. She held out her hand in a gesture of reconciliation. 'Can't we just be friends, Matthew?' she said. 'There's no need for us to fight, is there?'

He came towards her and took her hand and Ellie smiled up at him. Before she had time to think, he had pulled her roughly into his arms and was kissing her mouth, his tongue probing, his hands gripping her waist. She felt his teeth against hers, felt his hands move upwards towards her breasts. She felt only revulsion at his brash approach.

She pushed him away, her eyes hot with anger. 'How could you insult me and the memory of Jubilee by doing such a vile thing?' She was shaking with distaste. 'Must I spell it out for you, Matthew? I don't even like you, try to get that through your thick skull, will you?'

'It's early days yet, you could grow to like me,' Matthew said quickly. 'I think you are a wonderful woman and I apologize for being so hasty, I just couldn't help it, seeing you standing there so pretty and sweet and helpless, like.'

'I am not helpless,' Ellie was exasperated. 'Let me tell you this, if you come into my house again without an invitation I'll have you sacked, I'll have the constables up here if necessary and you'll be out of here so fast your feet won't touch the ground.'

'Nice talk for a lady,' Matthew was growing angry again, asserting the manly authority he believed was his prerogative. In any event, he wasn't used to being rebuffed. 'You are turning into a shrew, Ellie, do you know that? You are a woman alone, I was only trying to be kind.'

'I'm too much of a lady to want your brand of kindness, I don't want you to touch me, I don't want you to even come near me again.'

Matthew's eyes narrowed to slits. 'You might act the fine lady but we both know different don't we? You are far from being a lady. Oh, you think you're the high and mighty mistress of the Glyn Hir now but I remember you was the talk of Swansea before Jubilee made a respectable wife of you. Brought bastard children into the world, you did, so don't come all holy and good with me because it won't wash, some men wouldn't touch you with a bargepole, wouldn't want shop-soiled goods at any price.'

Ellie was stung. 'I might be all you say I am but I still have some taste. I find you repellant, I would remain a widow all my life if you were the only alternative.'

'You bitch!' his voice was low, 'Well don't you try to get rid of me, I'm warning you, you'd regret it.' He turned and left the room and Ellie sank into her chair, her hands trembling, she clasped them together in an effort to control them. She wished she could have avoided an out and out confrontation with Matthew, he would not make a good enemy. Still, it was too late to think of that now.

She sat for a long time, staring unseeingly into the cold fireplace. How she missed Jubilee, his sound common sense, his unconditional love. If he had foreseen the trouble Matthew would cause, he would have thrown the man out himself.

After a time, she composed herself and looked down at the books on the table beside her, the figures swam together making no sense, it was useless trying to

145

concentrate. But profits were good, Caradoc Jones had assured her of that, she had no need to worry on that score.

She was glad she had asked Caradoc to recommend a manager for the mill; once someone suitable was found, she would be able to take a back seat in the day to day affairs of the tannery. She would be able to keep right away from Matthew and his venomous words. Words he would soon be spreading around Swansea, reviving old scandals, raking up the past. Perhaps she should go to see Calvin Temple, warn him of what might happen, perhaps he could find a way of keeping Matthew's mouth firmly shut. If it was money Matthew desired, Calvin certainly had enough of that, more than he would ever spend in a lifetime. If even Calvin failed to stop Matthew's tongue then she would just have to face the consequences, face the sneers, the cold-shouldering of the townspeople. Not even Daniel, kind and loyal as he was, not even he would wish to be seen out with her if he should learn the truth.

Unhappiness swept over her, she put her hands to her face and felt the tears' salt in her mouth. It seemed she was destined never to love again. But this was a foolishness, she must stop feeling sorry for herself, she should count her blessings, she had Martha's company and Rosie was a more than willing worker. Still, Ellie needed a change, to get right away from Glyn Hir at least for a time.

It might do her good to take a room down near the sea front for a few weeks, at least it would give her a breathing space. And she would be distanced from Matthew Hewson, allowing him to cool down, perhaps he would even come to see where his best interests lay. She remembered then the harshness in his face as he'd looked at her and quite suddenly she felt cold.

'Come on, give me a roll in the hay,' Rosie smiled up into Matthew's glowering face, 'might improve your temper, you look as if you've swallowed a whole cut-throat razor handle an' all.' They were walking along the lane at the back of Glyn Hir, a short way from the stink of the tannery. Rosie should have been down at the market buying fresh meat and cheese but she hadn't been able to resist spending some time with Matthew.

'Leave me alone,' he said and then, as though changing his mind, he turned to her and took her in his arms. 'I'll see you tonight, we'll have a good time, go down the public for a mug of ale and a singsong. Afterwards, we'll roll in the hay as much as you like.'

Happiness flared through Rosie, singing in her blood; she had succeeded in breaking the foul mood that had gripped him lately, made him aware of her again. All he seemed to think about these days was those damned shares that Jubilee had promised him.

'Look love,' she said touching his lips with her finger-tips, 'I know you want to get some of old Jubilee's money, well there's more than one way of skinning a cat, mind.'

She had his interest then and she smiled, catching his arm, hugging it to herself.

'How do you mean?' He was frowning, poor lad, he really wasn't very bright.

'Watch and wait, my boy, what you can't have by coaxing, you might be able to get by other means.'

He stopped walking. 'There's no way of fiddling the books, there's too many hands on them for that.'

'Not talking about fiddling, Mat, I'm talking about getting what you want in exchange for keeping your mouth shut.'

'My mouth shut about what? Everyone in town knows Ellie's past; she wouldn't want it raked up again, wouldn't want that poncy reporter to learn of it but on the other hand, I can't hold no threats of that over her can I?

'But there might be other things you *can* use and I'm in the house aren't I, I'm the one to see all that goes on.

She's nice enough telling me to call her Ellie and that but she's a bit uppity. And she takes too much of your time for my liking.' Rosie's tone was dry, 'She's the type who likes to get a ring on her finger before she gives anything away, holding out for marriage she is, learnt her lesson well that it don't do to be a mistress. Well she can't have you, I'm not willing, see.'

It had crossed Matthew's mind that Ellie wanted marriage and even though she'd protested otherwise, Ellie *was* the sort to want a ring on her finger. What couldn't be got by coaxing might be managed by persuasion. It wouldn't do any harm to encourage Rosie to spy on Ellie, though he doubted she'd find out anything.

'You won't catch her playing around,' he said. 'Miss Iron Drawers, Miss Icicle, that's Ellie Hopkins. Hasn't she lived long enough without a man? Dried up she has, don't need a man between her legs, not like some.'

'Ah, say you don't know, I've seen the way she looks at that young reporter chap, makes cow's eyes at him she does and him at her, too. They'll be in the sheets before long, mark my words.'

Matthew suddenly had a bad taste in his mouth, he didn't like another man to succeed where he had failed. 'How do you make that out?' His tone was abrupt.

'As you said, she's been without a long time and her only human, she's proved that. *Duw*, wasn't she put up the spout by that posh lover of hers, had two poor little by-blows that died, didn't she? Not exactly made for going without I'd say.'

Anger filled Matthew as he imagined Daniel Bennett stealing his prize; getting Ellie into bed and getting his hands on her money at the same time. Not that Matthew really wanted Ellie for a wife but marriage to her had its compensations. She would provide him with money and control of the tannery and he would teach her how to have a good time. Ellie Hopkins didn't seem the sort to give a man a good time in bed, too thin in the breast, nothing to get your hands around there. He glanced

148

down at Rosie's straining blouse and he wanted her. Then.

He thrust her against the hedge and pushed up her skirts. She moaned and shifted herself to accommodate him and he took her without preliminary, thrusting into her, feeling the hotness of her nipple between his lips as he toiled against her.

The sun was hot on his back, explosions of sensation rocked through him and then it was over.

Rosie slipped to the ground as he released her, she caught his trousers which were around his ankles. 'Come down here, boy, let me show you how to do it properly.'

Nothing loath, he slumped down beside her. Her experienced hands were rousing him to fresh delights. He stretched out his strong legs and then Rosie was astride him.

Her cries rent the air and he laughed out loud, he knew how to give a woman a good time if anybody did. She reached her climax as quickly as he did and together they lay, laughing up into the face of the sun with the fresh scent of the grass around them and the birdsong echoing sweetly between the trees.

'We're meant to be together me and you.' Rosie turned and curled against him, her arms around his chest, her leg draped over his groin. She was a good roll in the hay, that much he would grant but not the one who would ever have his ring on her finger. His ideal future would be to have a lady to run his house, have his children, a lady with nice manners, one who would be virginal until he deflowered her. It mattered not if his wife should be reluctant in bed, that was only proper, it was whores like Rosie who pleasured a man, a wife only did her duty.

Ellie could only fulfil part of that dream but if he couldn't get it all, he'd settle for second best, take on a woman who was no virgin but who acted like one.

He kept his thoughts to himself, he needed Rosie on

his side right now, he wanted to take his fill of her whenever he felt the need for release. In any case, she might just have something good up her sleeve if she was right and Ellie was smitten by this reporter chap then anything could happen and if it did, he would be around to cast the first stone.

'Will you allow me to accompany you to church on Sunday evening?' Daniel's voice was soft, coaxing and Ellie couldn't help but feel flattered by his attention. She had come to town with Martha who had gone into one of the shops while Ellie had waited outside enjoying the fresh early autumn air.

'You can bring Martha and you needn't fear for your reputation, who on earth could gossip about us when all we'd be doing is sitting in the house of God listening to the vicar preach?'

'I'm still in mourning,' Ellie said doubtfully. 'I know it seems a lifetime ago when I had Jubilee by my side but it really isn't that long. Perhaps we should be more discreet than to be seen in public together so soon.'

Daniel nodded. 'You're right, as always.'

'There's nothing stopping you arriving a little later and then coming to sit next to Martha and me,' Ellie suggested and she was touched to see how Daniel's face lit up.

'Sunday it is then.' He tipped his hat and moved away towards the offices of *The Swansea Times*, his step light, his shoulders swinging with the ease of a healthy young animal. And how young he seemed to her, Ellie mused, an untried boy while she . . . well she was an experienced woman. What was it Matthew had called her? A shop-soiled woman, an unpleasant but in her case accurate description.

She felt she owed it to Daniel to tell him about her past, explain to him that she wasn't always a respectable wife but she felt it would be a shock to him. In any case, they were never alone so how could she talk so intimately to him? Or was that just an excuse to preserve the magic between them?

She saw Martha coming towards her waving her hand energetically. 'I've been into Ben Evans and bought the most beautiful winter coat you've ever seen.' She scarcely paused for breath, 'Why didn't you wait inside for me, I wondered where you'd gone?'

'I wanted some fresh air and then I met Daniel and we were talking,' Ellie explained.

'You're getting quite fond of that handsome young man,' there was no hint of censure in Martha's voice. 'Good thing too, can't mourn for ever more.'

Ellie felt suddenly grateful to her, 'You've got a very nice nature, Martha, there's many would call me fast, standing in the street talking openly to a handsome young man and me a widow.'

'There's many ready to judge, I know that as well as you but you've got your head screwed on the right way, you'll not do anything to encourage gossip.'

Ellie wasn't so sure, she had felt a reawakening of her senses just lately, the blood cool for so long flowed hotly when she was near Daniel Bennett. Love, that was another matter, Ellie was afraid to think of love, she had loved once and it had been a disaster. Yet Daniel roused in her a tenderness as well as a desire; dangerous signs, perhaps she should keep away from him for both their sakes.

Yet when Sunday came, Ellie sat with Martha near the back of the small church nestling on the edges of Kilvey Hill and fidgeted impatiently, anxious that Daniel might forget the appointment or might be unable to keep it.

There was the muted sound of voices around her, some murmuring in prayer others simply gossiping as they all waited for the preacher to put in an appearance at the lectern.

There was a movement at her side and Ellie felt an arm rest against hers. The scent of cleanliness, of soap

151

and hair cream, drifted towards her and she knew without needing to look that Daniel was there at her side.

She was surprised and alarmed at the joy that filled her, she was behaving like a young girl in love for the first time. The colour rose to her cheeks and she bowed her head, afraid that if she looked into Daniel's eyes he would read her thoughts.

The congregation was rising to its feet, the stirring music flowed majestically from the organ, soaring to the rafters and she was unaccountably happy. The evening sun streamed in through the windows, motes of dust danced in the incandescent shafts, her senses were heightened and it was because Daniel was there.

He stood tall beside her, his arm pressing deliberately against hers, he was willing her to look up and at last, she did, unable to resist seeing his face. He smiled and her heart caught as though in pain as she realized how young he was, not only in years but in the ways of the world. If he knew the truth about her his illusions would be shattered, surely she should pray for strength to end it all now before it had even begun.

She listened to the reading from the New Testament trying to concentrate on the beautiful words the preacher was uttering but aware all the time of a gladness that, for this moment at least, Daniel was with her.

Later, outside in the dying sunshine, he asked politely if he might walk the ladies home. Before Ellie could frame a refusal, Martha had slipped her arm through Daniel's and was nodding so vehemently that the feathers on her hat lifted and dipped with a life of their own.

Ellie fell into step beside Martha, separated from Daniel but still aware of his presence with every nerve in her body.

'I propose, ladies, that we go for a picnic, say next Saturday if the weather permits.' He didn't wait for a refusal. 'I have taken the liberty of borrowing a carriage

152

and pair and I thought I'd drive us as far as Crawley Woods. We can picnic on the slopes and then walk down to the beach if we feel inclined. It will be very private,' he emphasized the word private and Ellie smiled knowing he had forestalled any argument.

'That would be lovely, wouldn't that be lovely, Ellie?' Martha sounded pleased and Ellie caught her careful wink. Crawley Woods was a favourite spot with lovers, the woods led steeply down to a large curving beach that was populated only by the determined few who were fit enough to face the return climb up sandy pathways through the trees.

'Yes, I suppose it will be all right.' Ellie knew she was being weak, she should refuse, she should be listening to the voice of common sense that at the back of her mind was disapproving of any such arrangement. She, alone on a beach with Daniel, it was such a temptation. She said nothing.

At the foot of the slope leading towards the tannery, Daniel lifted his hat and bid them good day. 'See you Saturday.' His gaze was on Ellie, his eyes were warm, his mouth curving into a smile that was for her alone.

'We'll be looking forward to it.' It was Martha who replied and then Daniel was striding away, his step buoyant.

Inside the house, Ellie took off her hat and handed it to Rosie who smelled of freshly baked bread.

'What am I doing, Martha?' Ellie led the way into the drawing room, 'I shouldn't be agreeing to such an outing, you know as well as I do that you won't make it down to the beach, Crawley Woods is far too steep.'

'I can share the picnic with you and then I can wait at the top of the hill. I might seem a dried up old lady to you, Ellie, but I sometimes need a little hour to myself, have you thought of that?'

'No,' Ellie admitted, 'I suppose I've been a bit selfish.'

'No, not selfish, just cautious, afraid you'll get hurt. That Daniel is a very nice young man.'

153

'Yes, and I'm a widow.' Ellie could have added that she was more than that, she had a past that was still lurking in the shadows waiting to pounce. What would Daniel feel about her if he knew the truth?

'*Duw*, it's only a trip out to the beach, a little picnic, nothing to stew over, mind,' Martha argued with unshakable common sense.

'I suppose you're right, I am making a fuss about nothing.' Ellie felt herself relax, why not go with the flow, enjoy what little she might have of Daniel while she could?

'They're going on a picnic,' Rosie's eyes were round with triumph, 'Miss Ellie and that reporter chap, down to Crawley Woods and you know how deserted that place is.'

Matthew wasn't sure whether he was pleased or angry at Rosie's revelations. 'How do you know?'

'Cos I'm putting up the picnic basket of course, a bit of cold rabbit and some game pie as well as lovely fresh bread and a bit of cheese, eating well, they'll be.'

'They are surely not going alone?'

'No, silly,' Rosie smiled, 'Martha's going too but can you see her with her bone ache getting up and down that steep hill? I can't.'

She was right, Martha would probably sleep a little under a tree, perhaps take a walk along the lanes that fringed the bay but it would be Ellie and Bennett who would walk alone down to the broad, sweeping beach. What they would do there was anyone's guess.

'You've done well, my little flower,' Matthew said, 'I'm glad you've got your wits about you.'

'Someone's got to have,' Rosie said cheekily, looking up at him with promise ripe in her eyes.

'You'll have your reward later,' he said abruptly. He wished just for once she would show a little restraint, she was like a bitch on heat with her constant demands. Well, as soon as she had served her purpose, he'd have done with her, give her marching orders, women like her were ten a penny.

'What about now?' She leaned against him, her breasts prodding his chest. He held her away. 'Not now, now I've got something far more important to do.'

As he swaggered away, he was marshalling his thoughts, he would need a horse, one of the young farm animals would do, Crawley Woods was too far away to make the journey on foot. He would get there before Ellie's little party and wait and watch and then, if he was lucky, he would have something he could use as a weapon in his fight for what was, after all, only his right. It looked as if Ellie Hopkins would have her comeuppance and sooner than any of them had believed possible.

CHAPTER ELEVEN

Bridie rose from the table unable to face the rich assortment of foods cook had sent up from the kitchens. In her delicate condition, the very sight of devilled kidneys, or even her usual favourite breakfast of haddock poached with an egg was enough to bring back the feelings of nausea which had plagued her since the beginning of her pregnancy. She pushed away her cup of tea and dabbed her lips with the pristine white napkin from beside her plate. Perhaps a turn in the garden, a little fresh air might clear the clouds from her mind.

Was there something wrong, she wondered? She had never felt like this when she was carrying the boys. Of course she was a little older now but not too old she assured herself quickly.

The air in the garden was sweet with the fragrance of late roses and the feeling of nausea abated a little. Bridie dabbed her brow with her handkerchief, here she would interview Daniel Bennett, here in the softness of her garden.

A feeling of anger and renewed jealousy gripped her, she would tell him all about Ellie Hopkins and the games she played with men, men who had titles and riches or men who simply had rich wives. Ellie Hopkins wasn't choosey which, so long as she was able to further her own interests.

Ostensibly, he was interviewing her about the new steam packet she had bought to add to her fleet. The *Gloriana* was splendid, with rich brass fittings and polished wood and an engine that took most of the hardship out of sailing. All this she would talk of to the reporter but he would learn more than he'd bargained for, she would see to that.

Bridie had seen them together in church, seen the way they looked at each other, Daniel Bennett and Ellie Hopkins. Men were fools, susceptible to a little flattery and a pretty face. The certainty, in the face of all her denials, that Ellie Hopkins was involved with Paul at the same time as she was encouraging this other man was more than Bridie could bear.

When Daniel Bennett arrived a few moments later, Bridie felt almost sorry for him, she was after all about to destroy his illusions. He was a handsome young man, well-set and with a charming manner, he smiled down at her as he lifted his hat in greeting.

'I am a great admirer, Mrs Marchant,' his opening words threw her temporarily off course. 'I know that you have a gift for business which has made you one of the wealthiest women in Swansea, I'm honoured to be allowed to interview you.'

He was right, she did have a gift for business, she hadn't thought about it like that before. In some strange way, that made Paul's little games with other women all the more insulting. She smiled and sat back in her seat, prepared to bide her time, she would have to be careful how she broached the subject of Ellie Hopkins, she didn't want to be too obviously hostile.

'Thank you for your pretty compliments,' she smiled, 'and I think it might be advantageous if you take a closer look at the *Gloriana*, go on board, see her for yourself, you might find she is the smartest vessel in the entire docks.'

He uncapped his pen and as Bridie talked, he wrote swiftly in his notebook, a lock of dark hair fell across his forehead reminding her of Paul and she felt a momentary sense of loss. Why couldn't she be enough for her husband, wasn't she good to him?

She had provided him with sons, with a fine house

and a secure future and to her knowledge she had never failed him in the marriage bed.

'You look sad, Mrs Marchant,' Daniel's voice intruded into her thoughts, 'is anything wrong?'

She shook her head, 'No, not at all, it's just that this morning I'm a little under the weather.' She paused, perhaps it would be a good time to launch the news of her pregnancy, let the whole town know, especially that whore Ellie Hopkins that Bridie's husband still found her desirable.

'Perhaps you would like a nice gossipy item for your paper,' she said almost coyly. Daniel looked up at once, his eyes full of interest.

'I certainly would; Miss Smale prides herself on being first with any news about the prominent citizens of Swansea.'

She recognized the flattery but was, nonetheless, pleased by it. 'I'm expecting another child,' she said. 'My husband and I are both very thrilled about it, naturally.'

'Might I offer my congratulations?' If Daniel was disappointed that her news was domestic rather than of moment to the business world, he wasn't tactless enough to let it show.

'That's kind of you, indeed.' Bridie sought for a way to introduce Ellie Hopkins into the conversation. 'I do realize how lucky I am, of course, some women are not so fortunate, take Ellie Hopkins for instance.'

The look in the young reporter's eyes changed, became guarded. 'Mrs Hopkins?'

'Poor girl, lost her twins, you know, stillborn, so sad.' She watched him closely, his shoulders were tense but otherwise, his expression revealed nothing. 'It didn't help that she had no husband to protect her, being merely a mistress of a rich man she was alone against the world until Jubilee Hopkins took her in out of the goodness of his heart.'

Daniel closed his notebook, he was suddenly pale

or was the brightness of the sun deceiving her eyes?

'You did know that Ellie was carrying illegitimate twins when Jubilee married her didn't you?' She didn't wait for a reply. 'I imagined that on *The Times* you reporters knew everything about we inhabitants of Swansea.' She couldn't resist the small barb.

He rose and bowed. 'Thank you so much for your time. If you don't mind, I'll take your advice and walk down to the docks, have a look first hand at the *Gloriana*.'

'I haven't upset you, have I?' She couldn't help but probe, somehow her revelation seemed to have had little effect on the reporter.

'Upset, why should I be upset?' His smile was somewhat forced. 'I've ceased to be surprised by human nature.'

He left her then and she watched him walk away through her large gardens. Was his step less jaunty, his shoulders a little hunched? It was a pity to hurt him but the sooner he learnt the truth about that hussy the better.

Quite suddenly, Bridie felt very sick, she rose to her feet and stood there swaying for a moment, her senses swirling around her like a fog. And then, blackness thick and dark closed in on her and she knew nothing.

When she opened her eyes, she was in her room, the doctor was standing over her and behind him was the shadowy figure of her husband.

'Paul, you've come home,' her voice sounded weak and Paul with concern etched on his face came towards her quickly.

'My darling,' he kissed her fingers, 'you are going to have to be brave.'

'What do you mean?' she heard her voice trembling. She stared from her husband to the doctor and waited for one of them to speak.

'I'm sorry, Mrs Marchant, you are most certainly miscarrying of your child.' It was the voice of the doctor which penetrated the silence like a death knell.

But she felt no pain, no sensation. What was she supposed to feel? She didn't know, she had not suffered a miscarriage before.

'Paul,' she looked into her husband's face, 'Paul tell me this isn't happening to me, I can't lose my baby.'

The doctor intervened. 'Sometimes it's nature's way of ensuring that a defective child will not be brought into the world.'

A defective child. The words struck terror into Bridie's very soul. She imagined herself with a crippled baby and knew she could not face such a prospect. She wanted, quite suddenly, to be free of her burden, she wished the miscarriage was over and done with, how could she live with a child that was not perfect?

'You have already bled quite profusely,' the doctor continued. 'We shall have to take care that the miscarriage is complete, we don't want you suffering complications, do we?'

The pain came quite suddenly, rocketing through her, contracting her muscles. She bit her lip to silence the scream but it was no use, she heard her own voice crying out in agony.

Paul leaned closer, his eyes anxious. 'Doctor,' he said, over his shoulder, 'can you give her something for the pain?'

'It will be over all the sooner if I don't sedate her.' The doctor's voice was low but Bridie caught what he said.

'I don't want anything, do you understand?' Her words were taut with the effort she was making to control her pain. 'I want this sorry business over and done with as soon as possible.'

It was not an easy matter to accomplish, this rejection by her body of her child. The agony seemed interminable. Bridie began to fear for her very life, she was weak, she knew she could fight no longer, her life's blood was flowing away. Paul, the doctor, the solid walls of the

160

room were fading from her sight and she gave herself up to the welcome darkness.

The beach was silent except for the sound of gulls wheeling overhead. A cormorant stood poised on a rocky promontory, indistinct, a shadowy blur in the autumn haze.

Ellie felt young again, she had taken off her shoes and stockings and her bare toes dug into the warm softness of the sand. Her fair hair was lifted away from her face by the salt breeze, by her side was Daniel and she was rapidly falling in love with him.

Ellie leaned back against the warm ruggedness of a rock and turned, allowing herself to meet his eyes. His expression was warm, admiring and yet there was a sort of sadness about him today that worried her.

'How's work at the newspaper going?' She wanted to reach out and touch him, to feel his mouth on hers but here she was making polite conversation.

'It's fine,' Daniel looked down at her and shifted his position so that he was closer to her. 'Miss Smale is a great boss, I'm lucky to be working for her. I even had a childish fancy for her once but that was before I met you.'

A shadow of guilt fell on Ellie's happiness. 'Arian is a very clever lady.' She meant the words but they rang hollowly on the salty air. Arian knew all about Ellie's past, all about her affair with Calvin, would she have spoken of it to Daniel? But no, that was not Arian's style, she did not indulge in gossip herself even though she allowed it in the pages of her newspaper. And yet, Daniel would have to know, he deserved the truth.

Ellie sighed, looking up at the cloudless sky, not wanting to spoil the moment, uttering a prayer to God for forgiveness for holding her happiness to her for a little while longer.

'Why the sigh?' Daniel took her hand in his and held her fingers as though he was examining each one in detail. Ellie was ashamed, her hands were still calloused even though she had not worked in the grinding house since some time after Jubilee's funeral. She tried to draw away but he held her fast.

'There's such a lot you don't know about me.' The words fell softly in contrast to the harsh screaming of the birds but Daniel heard them.

'I know all I want to know,' he said, 'I know that you are good and kind, the sort of girl I would be honoured to have as a wife.'

'No.' She must speak, it wasn't fair to Daniel to let him labour under a misapprehension about her. 'I'm not good at all, I've been foolish and wrong in the past and I've kept the truth from you, may God forgive me.'

'You needn't say anything,' Daniel's voice was firm, 'nothing would make me change my mind about you, Ellie.'

Realization dawned on her. 'You know. You know all about me.'

He nodded. 'Of course I know, Ellie, but you need make no excuses, the past is over and done with. I can see with my own eyes what you are really like.' He leaned closer. 'I know this isn't the time, you are still in mourning but what I said just now, I meant, I would be honoured to have you for my wife.'

A warmth flooded through Ellie's limbs and rose to her face, she knew she was blushing with pleasure and happiness. She clung to his hand and fought back the tears. 'You are wonderful, Daniel, I don't deserve the friendship of anyone so fine as you.'

'Nonsense!' He was embarrassed and pleased at the same time and he was very young, did he really understand everything she wondered uneasily?

'Daniel, you do know that I was . . .' her words were silenced by the finger he placed over her lips.

'It makes no difference what you *were*,' he said evenly. 'You are now what life's experiences have made you, a loving and generous spirit.'

The tears came fast then, rolling hugely down her cheeks and into her mouth. She covered her face with her hands like a child and, as though she was a child, Daniel took out his handkerchief and dried the tears.

'I love you, Ellie,' his voice was little more than a whisper, 'I love you so very much.'

They sat together until the sun's warmth was cooled by the evening breeze and the birds cried on the outgoing tide as they searched for food. Then Daniel took her hand, helped her to rise, watching as she brushed the sand from her feet. He took up her shoes and put them on for her and hand in hand they set back up the steep slope to where Martha was waiting for them.

In the distance, a figure hovered, waiting, watching. Matthew Hewson stood on the slope of sand, his hands clenched in fury, the couple had done nothing more than talk together. And yet, he would store the touching little scene away in his mind, some day, some time, it might just come in useful.

Bridie came awake slowly, the brightness of the day hurt her eyes and she closed them against the glare, hardly daring to move in case she found herself in the grip of unbearable pain. But there was no sensation in her lower limbs at all. She tried to sit up but found she couldn't move. In panic, she opened her eyes and saw that the dazzling white sensation she had experienced was caused by the sun on the pristine white walls of an unfamiliar room. She was in hospital.

Cautiously she turned her head, on the chest at her side stood a brass bell. Tentatively, she reached out her hand towards the chest. The ringing of the bell hurt her ears, she dropped it quickly and it rolled along the floor like a wounded bird.

'Mrs Marchant, you're awake, that's very good, very good indeed.' The nurse was tall and clad in a voluminous white apron that crackled starchily as she moved. 'Pulse is stronger, good sign, good sign.' She jerked at the sheets and straightened them even though they weren't creased.

'I'm Sister Michaels, Dr Carpenter will be here in a little while, he's a very clever man, just come to us from another hospital and we are very fortunate to have him. He'll put your mind at rest, you'll see,' she smiled in what she hoped was a reassuring manner. 'I'll just go and tell him you're awake.'

'Nurse, wait,' Bridie scarcely recognized her own voice, 'what's happening to me, why can't I move my legs?'

'Doctor will tell you all about it in just a moment, no need to worry, no need at all.' The woman had an irritating habit of repeating herself and Bridie wished she was strong enough to give her the sharp edge of her tongue. As it was, she watched helplessly as the nurse left the room and closed the door behind her.

Impotently, Bridie stared at the closed door, how dare the woman treat her so cavalierly, didn't she know that Bridie owned the biggest shipping fleet this side of the Bristol channel?

Her mouth was dry, she was desperate for a drink of water. Her tongue darted over her lips, they felt cracked and sore and even such a small effort wearied her. She closed her eyes, hoping that sleep would come, would take away the doubts and the frightening questions that ran through her mind. But she didn't sleep, instead, she lay quiet, waiting, trying to summon some inner strength she felt instinctively that she would need.

It was a relief when the door opened and Dr Carpenter entered the room. Eddie Carpenter was a big man with an air about him that inspired confidence. The hair of his sideburns was silver, his kindly eyes were prematurely furrowed with lines, he was a man who knew suffering intimately.

Bridie suddenly brought to mind the awful scandal that had swept Swansea when the doctor's daughter, his only child, had been found murdered in an hotel room,

164

killed by the maniac Gerald Simples. She knew she was putting off the moment when the questions and answers would begin but she was so frightened. And where was Paul? She needed him here, now.

'Mrs Marchant,' the doctor seated himself on the chair beside her bed, he looked grave. 'Had I known you would regain consciousness this morning I'd have asked your husband to be present, as it is, it might be just as well for me to tell you about my findings now, do you agree?'

For a moment, Bridie hesitated, what was worse, knowing the truth or waiting in an agony of the unknown? She made up her mind.

'Tell me your findings by all means, Doctor, it *is* bad news, isn't it?'

He paused for a moment, head bowed, it was as if he was selecting his words with care. 'You know you suffered a miscarriage, you lost your child, a grievous thing to happen to any parent.' He swallowed and then took a deep breath. 'What you don't know is that there have been some complications.'

Bridie forced herself to speak. 'What sort of complications? I need to know, Dr Carpenter.'

'A small operation was performed, not by me of course but by one of our surgeons, a very eminent man. You came out of that very well indeed, nothing wrong with your health that a little rest and recuperation won't cure.'

'But?' Bridie's voice was a little stronger now, 'And there is a but. Don't beat about the bush, please tell me what's happened.' Small wings of fear beat at her brain. She knew what had happened.

'I'm paralysed.' The words fell dully, like stones into the silence. 'That's it isn't it?' She closed her eyes and tried to calm herself. 'Is it a permanent condition?'

Eddie Carpenter took a deep breath. 'I don't know. There is nothing physically wrong that we can discover, this is a nervous disease. Hopefully, with rest and gentle exercise you will find the use of your limbs

165

returning but at this stage it's impossible to make any firm prognosis.'

'This thing is all in my mind, then, is that what you are saying? In that case, surely there is the possibility that I might walk again?'

'There can be no guarantees in medicine,' he was prevaricating, 'but you are a normally fit and healthy lady, there is no reason why, in time you can't live a full and useful life.'

'But I won't be able to walk,' Bridie said coldly, 'at least not unless a miracle should occur and miracles are hard to come by aren't they Doctor?'

She wanted to lash out and hurt him as his words had hurt her. 'You couldn't save your own child, could you, so why should I expect you to put yourself out to save me?'

He rose abruptly, his colour ebbing. Bridie could see him struggling for composure and the thought gave her a feeling of release. Let him hurt, just as she was hurting at this moment. Why should she be the one to suffer alone? What had she ever done to deserve such a punishment?

'I'll leave you now to rest,' his tone was measured. 'I hope to contact your husband soon, I've left a message for him both at home and at the shipping office though I believe he is at sea at this precise moment.'

So Paul had gone and left her when she had most needed him, how she hated him, how she hated everyone in that bitter moment.

'Very kind of you to concern yourself,' her voice was edged with sarcasm. 'But then it's quite easy to do things when you are not confined to a bed for ever more isn't it?'

'Mrs Marchant, Bridie, I know you feel dreadful just now, it's only natural but you will come to terms with your condition, I promise you. In time, you will learn to make the best of it, after all you have a good constitution, you have a comfortable home, enough money to ensure

166

that you need never work again, please, try to count your blessings.'

'Don't patronize me.' Bridie was outraged. 'How dare you offer me platitudes which wouldn't convince a five year old child. I'm young, I want to live my life normally not as a cripple, can't you even begin to understand that?'

His shoulders sagged, he shook his head in defeat. 'I'll leave you now, give you a chance to think and be quiet. A prayer or two might not go amiss if that is your way.'

'A prayer! You must be mad. What have I got to pray about, should I thank God for making me a cripple then? Oh, go away and leave me alone.'

The door closed quietly behind him and Bridie stared up at the cracks in the white-washed ceiling. What hope did she have of holding Paul's interest now? Oh, he would pretend of course, on the surface he would be a loving, caring husband but when he was away from her, he would behave just like the ram he was. She stared at the surface cracks on the ceiling, at the small panes of glass in the window, concentrating on anything in an effort to take her mind off the dreadful picture of the future that stretched before her.

'Oh God!' She clenched her hands into fists and waved them above her head. 'Why me? I'm so young, I have children who need me, I can't live as a cripple for the rest of my life, I just can't.' She turned her face to the wall and wept.

It was two weeks later when Bridie was able to return to her own home. Paul had returned from sea and was there to lift her into the carriage, carefully covering her legs with a warm rug because she was shivering in spite of the warmth of the late slant of sun.

She felt ashamed of her weakness, marked out from the rest of humanity, someone to be looked at as an object of pity. She bit her lip as Paul seated himself beside her, she would show them, show them all that Bridie Marchant was still a force to be reckoned with.

'I want a detailed list of all your sailings.' She spoke

to Paul as though he was a stranger in her employ and he turned his head to look at her in surprise.

'What?' His voice had an edge to it, his patience and consideration had apparently vanished.

'I intend to be in control of everything.' She didn't look at him. 'I can't stop you whoring around with other women, oh, don't protest your innocence, I know you too well Paul, but what I can stop is the expenditure of my money on your doxies.'

'You are mistaken, Bridie, there's no-one.' Paul attempted to be firm but his voice lacked conviction.

She sighed heavily. 'Don't insult my intelligence, Paul.' She paused listening to his breathing, loving him and hating him at the same time. 'I know you are having some sort of liaison with that trollop Ellie Hopkins, I know you had meetings with her in Ireland so don't lie. You are in love with her, you wish you were free to marry her, especially now that she's a rich widow. But I'll never let you go, Paul, never.'

Paul took her hand. 'You are obsessed with this woman and you couldn't be more wrong about her, she is not the sort to indulge in a casual liaison.'

'Oh, I see, you are defending her now. Well you don't fool me, not for one moment.'

'Bridie, I've sworn to you that I have never touched Ellie Hopkins, not in that way.'

'And yet you bought leather from her, a pitifully small supply of it at that, how do you explain that?'

For a moment, Paul seemed at a loss, he shook his head and sank back into the shadows of the coach. 'I promise you, Bridie, on my sacred oath that I am not involved with Ellie Hopkins in any way except that of doing business with her company.'

'You would say anything to prove me wrong,' Bridie said harshly. 'What profit is there in transporting such a small load, answer me that?' Bridie was determined to pursue the point. She clenched her hands into her lap and waited to hear Paul's lies.

'It was a favour for a colleague in Ireland,' he spoke at last, his voice heavy. 'He needed some tack, I don't know why he wanted it from me but I wished to oblige him.'

'And you repeated this favour, several times over the past months. Who is this colleague? It all sounds very thin to me.' Her voice was scathing and she felt Paul recoil.

'Bridie, I will not have you speaking to me in that tone of voice.' He spoke quietly so that his words carried even more weight. 'I am not a child and even though I am making allowances for your illness I cannot endure such an attitude. I ran my own shipping fleet very successfully for many years alone before I met you, I can run it alone again, if needs be.' He paused for breath, obviously he was choosing his words carefully. 'I cannot and will not have you questioning my every move in this way, I cannot allow you to undermine my authority with the men of my fleet, do you understand?'

Bridie felt a trickle of fear at his words, Paul's meaning was clear, they could work together or each go their separate ways, it was up to her. She decided for the moment to capitulate.

'Of course you must run your own business as you see fit,' she said, 'I'm only thinking of you, such small loads are scarcely worth dealing with, are they?'

'Not in immediate financial terms, I suppose,' Paul agreed, 'but what you must take into consideration, Bridie, is the good will of the customer. A little bit of co-operation oils the wheels. Perhaps that's something you should think about.'

The carriage jolted to a halt and Bridie realized she was home. She made to rise, forgetting in that instant that she was unable to move without help. Her leaden limbs refused to function and she put her hands over her face in sudden despair, hating herself for the weakness of tears.

'It's all right, my love,' Paul was all concern, it was

rarely he saw her like this, soft and vulnerable. He put his arms around her and held her close.

'You are my wife, mother of my sons, you will always be my first consideration, remember that. Of course I have a part of my life in which you have no share, that is inevitable, but it is you I come home to from the sea, that will never change.'

But other things would change, Bridie thought helplessly, Paul had made it clear that he would go his own way and brook no interference from her.

The threat was there, he could leave her if he chose. But if she accepted his 'separate life' their marriage would survive, at least on the surface. She knew she had no choice in the matter, not at this very moment. She held out her arms to her husband.

'Take me home, Paul,' she said softly, knowing that her words were acceptance of his terms. He lifted her out of the coach and carried her into the house.

Collins opened the door wide in welcome. The sun filled the hallway and the gallery above with jewelled light, the servants were assembled near the doorway, waiting for her. Bridie suddenly felt very humble and then the overwhelming need to hide herself away swept over her. She felt flawed, imperfect, from henceforth she was destined to be a useless onlooker in life.

As Paul carried her through to the sitting room where a fire flickered cheerfully beneath the ornate mantleshelf, she was aware of the servants bobbing and murmuring their welcome.

'You know I envy them, all of them,' she said as Paul set her into an armchair. 'All healthy and vigorous. None of them like me, if I wasn't paying their wages they wouldn't give me the time of day.'

'You are too hard on them, sometimes.' Paul adjusted the wrap around her legs, 'They would like you well enough if you gave them the chance.'

'What do I care for them?' Bridie waved her hand in

a sudden gesture of defiance. 'They are there only to do my bidding.'

'That's where you're wrong, Bridie, they are servants not slaves, they have rights and they have feelings just like you and me.'

'Oh, turning into a philanthropist now are we?' Sarcasm edged her voice. 'Well, will you tell one of those feeling servants to bring me a glass of port and quickly?'

Paul looked at her and shook his head and after a moment, walked towards the door.

'Where are you going?' Bridie demanded and he paused at the door to look at her.

'I'm going out into the garden,' he said 'to get a breath of fresh air. In the meantime, I trust you'll think over your ill humour and try to moderate your speech, otherwise I shall find it necessary to curtail my shore leave and return to sea as soon as possible.'

'I'm sorry,' Bridie held out her hand in supplication, 'don't leave me, Paul, I need you so much.'

He returned to her side and took her hands in his, she read compassion in his eyes and suddenly felt she had the key to him.

'I feel so helpless, so alone, I can't bear to be dependent on other people. I'm frightened for our future, Paul, hold me close, please hold me.'

As he took her in his arms, a smile of triumph curved Bridie's lips, she saw it all now, she must play the weak woman, in need of protection and Paul would do anything for her. She pressed her face into his neck, breathing in the scent of him, loving him so much that it hurt. What was it about him that roused in her these feelings? She would do anything to hold him, anything at all.

CHAPTER TWELVE

Boyo took the mug of ale from Harry and sipped it gingerly, it tasted bitter and yet nutty, he found he liked it. He was seated with the other men around the fire in the yard. The week was ended, another load of skins had left the tannery, the wagons, piled to the brim, were bound for Mikefords the wholesale merchant in town. Tomorrow was Sunday, a day of rest and of going to church, it was something the men celebrated each week without fail. And it was Boyo's birthday.

Harry took up his fiddle and began to play, the notes haunting on the quiet air. The sound drew Rosie from the kitchen, her sleeves rolled above her elbows, her face smeared with flour. She stood for a moment, lifting her skirts and tapping her slim foot in time to the melody. It was growing dusk, the fire glowed, the ale was being passed and a sense of well-being washed over Boyo; he felt at one with the other men, they had become the family he had never known.

Rosie suddenly took his hand and dragged him, protesting to his feet. 'Come on, my lad, time you learned to dance.' She held him close and Boyo smelled the essence of her, the sweetness of her hair, coming loose from its ribbons, the yeasty tang of new baked bread that clung to her and a strange longing for he knew not what gripped him.

'Enjoying yourself, lad?' Rosie said breathlessly. She was against him one moment, then flinging apart from him the next. He relaxed, he might as well enjoy himself, here he was the focus of attention for once in his young life.

He shook back the hair that had fallen over his eyes, giving himself up to the intoxication of the music and Rosie's nearness.

'He's a fast learner,' Rosie called to the men and Harry waved his hand at her.

'Time he learned other things beside dancing, mind,' he said. 'Matthew's away with the wagons, what a fine chance will you have then to make the boy, this night, into a man?'

A strange feeling, half fear, half exhilaration filled Boyo as Rosie nodded. 'Perhaps, if he's lucky, he might learn the sins of the flesh before the morning light.'

'Take him off now before he gets too fuddled with ale to be any good.' Harry advised and Rosie drew Boyo close to her.

'Want to learn the delights of flesh, Boyo?' she whispered in his ear. She threw back her head laughing, the white of her throat a gracious column leading the eye to the swell of her breasts.

He was confused, he was a good church-going boy, the sins of the flesh were forbidden and yet his body was filled with desire to taste of the forbidden fruit of Rosie's ripeness. Sensing his hesitation, she took his arm and led him away from the flames, into the darkness of the currying house. He scented the aroma of the skins, so familiar, so much part of his life. The scent mingled with Rosie's clean-washed smell and he knew he was lost. He would learn tonight to be a man, it was his fate, no good fighting against it.

Rosie drew him down onto the floor and as her hands moved purposefully to his buttons, a great excitement filled him. It washed away any doubts he had harboured; he was being offered a priceless gift, how many boys of his age could boast knowing a full-grown woman? One of his friends claimed to have deflowered an untried girl but Boyo took leave to doubt the truth of it. The boy's description of the act was scrappy, he had seemed uncertain about his feelings as he'd recounted the event

173

boastingly to Boyo. Now, Boyo was about to learn the truth.

His buttons open, his manhood exploded from the confines of the rough cloth of his trousers. Rosie clucked her tongue. 'There's a fine big boy you are then, it's going to be a pleasure to teach you how to love.' She drew him to her but no sooner had he touched the fullness of her breasts than he felt a surging of hotness in his loins. It was as though a thousand stars were bursting inside his body. He pressed his lips together to prevent crying out into the night, his eyes were clamped shut. He knew it was too soon, much too soon, Rosie needed pleasuring as much as he did. He fell onto his back, tears of failure rising to his eyes.

Rosie leaned over him. 'It's not the end of the world, Boyo, my darling,' she said breathlessly, 'Rosie said she'd teach you to be a man and she will. Rest a minute and then we'll try again. You'll see, it will be all the better for it, I know, I'm an experienced woman, mind.'

It might have been her words of encouragement, it might have been something deep within himself, but Boyo quickly found that she was right. He carefully eased himself into her and she gasped with the delight of it.

'That's right, gentle now, no pushing, no need for roughness; after tonight, my darling, you will want to pleasure many girls but don't throw away your precious gems, keep them for the girl you will love.'

The experience was all that he could have wished for, he heard Rosie moan beneath him with a sense of joy and accomplishment, he was pleasing her and it made him feel good. He touched her swelling breasts with reverence; he would remember this, his first coupling, always. The smell of the tannery, the burning of the wood fire and the sound of Harry's music reaching fingers in the darkness to heighten his pleasure would be a precious experience, one he would thank God for all his life, or was that a blasphemy?

When it was finally over, Rosie took him to the pump,

174

helped him strip off his clothes, washed him as carefully as though he was her child. It was difficult to believe that a few minutes before, she had been clinging to him and sighing with the satisfaction of the fulfilled woman.

'One last thing, Boyo,' she rested her hand against his cheek. 'A real man doesn't need to boast, see, he lets his actions speak for him, remember that. I've found in my lifetime that the more a man talks about his prowess, the less of it he has.'

He kissed her fingers, 'I won't do any boasting, Rosie, I'm grateful to you, I think I love you.'

She smiled. 'Aye, well you'll think yourself in love many a time yet but wait for the real thing, Boyo, the waiting is worth it.'

When they returned to the glow of the dying fireside, Harry's eyebrows lifted, a smile curved his mouth. 'I see the flush of happiness, if I'm not mistaken,' he spoke softly, approvingly. Rosie rested her hand on his shoulder for a moment. 'Harry, this boy didn't need no teaching from me, he's a natural lover, whichever girl gets him, she's going to be one satisfied customer, believe me.'

The blood beat in Boyo's temples, he felt he would burst with pride. He knew what it was all about now, this thing between a man and a woman. The mystery was no more. With a feeling of happiness, he knew he need not boast, or preen, he fully accepted what Rosie had said; a real man has no need to talk about his conquests, he could hold the knowledge to him, his own special secret for ever.

'Have another drink, lad,' Harry said gently, 'I reckon you're one of us now.' Boyo crouched beside Harry and touched the gleaming curve of the fiddle.

'Will you teach me to play, Harry?' he asked humbly. Harry smiled. 'Aye, I will that, Boyo, you are eager to grasp life but remember there will be nettles as well as Rosies.' He laughed at his own joke and punched Boyo lightly on his arm. 'Enjoy life, don't hurt anybody, if you can help it, and you won't go far wrong.'

Boyo sighed luxuriously, stretching his arms up to the stars. He had a mug of ale in front of him and Rosie at his side. He felt good, he felt he was no longer a green lad.

On Sunday morning, instead of attending his own church in the centre of town, he went to Cwmbwrla to hear Evan Roberts preach. Boyo sat alongside a group of other boys of his own age, they seemed juvenile and silly as they folded up pieces of paper and flicked them surreptitiously at the congregation.

Boyo wondered if Evan Roberts had ever enjoyed the sins of the flesh but the thought seemed blasphemous and he thrust it away. The hymns were the ones he knew and he sang cheerfully, his light voice lifting to the rafters along with the deep bass of some of the older men. Boyo liked going to church, it had been forced upon him in the workhouse where he spent his childhood but he had always found it an escape from his unhappiness. It was a place where voices were never raised in anger, where brows were clear and people spoke kindly to each other.

Boyo wondered if his sin was unpardonable, he had taken a woman outside the marriage bed, that was wrong, he knew it. He felt uncomfortable for a moment but then Evan Roberts began to speak. His fervour was unmistakable, his face shone with conviction, he told them in plain terms that God would forgive them all their sins, that he had sent his son Jesus into the world to save sinners.

Boyo felt better. He was not going to be doomed for ever because he had tasted Rosie's sweet sinfulness. He shifted uneasily in his seat, embarrassed to be remembering such a lustful scene in the holiness of the chapel. He ran his finger around his collar and eased the stiffness away from the newly shaved skin of his neck. He glanced down at his wrists, they were protruding from the sleeves of his best, his only, suit which he was fast outgrowing.

He thought with warmth of the savings he had accumulated since he'd been working at the tannery, he had quite a bit of money put by in the bank in Wind Street in Swansea, perhaps it was time he bought himself some new clothes.

He tried to concentrate on the service but a group of ladies were standing beside the preacher singing sweetly, mouths opening and closing like those of the young birds in the spring. His attention was wandering, he glanced over his shoulder and suddenly sat up straighter, Ellie Hopkins was seated across the aisle from him. She felt his glance and turned, a smile lit up her face and she lifted her hand in greeting. She looked fresh and sweet and innocent. So different from Rosie. He immediately felt the thought was mean and unworthy.

At Ellie's side was the reporter from *The Swansea Times*, handsome enough but so sure of himself, so polished. Of course he was older than Boyo by at least three years and from a good family by the look of his clothes and from the sound of his voice. Posh he was, his accent only faintly noticeable. Boyo envied Daniel Bennett, his privileged background gave him the right to escort a lady like Ellie to church. Of course it was all very proper, their being in church together because Martha was there too, her face turned earnestly toward the pulpit where Evan Roberts was standing once more, the ladies having subsided like full-blown roses into their seats.

Still, there was something about the situation that Boyo didn't like, Ellie was Jubilee's widow, she was Boyo's idol, untouchable, on a pedestal and he could see by the way Daniel was leaning close, the way he was looking into Ellie's eyes that he wanted her. Boyo knew the signs and from experience he thought with a sense of shame. Who was he to judge another man, he wasn't exactly without sin, himself, was he?

Boyo tried to imagine Ellie, her breasts exposed, her legs akimbo, the way Rosie had been last night but the image was an impossible one to conjure into his mind and in any case, it was surely sinful to harbour such thoughts at a time like this when everyone's head was bowed in prayer.

'If we are to be fools, make us fools for thee.' The earnest voice rang out in the silence and Boyo looked down at his boots, good boots, made from leather from Glyn Hir. Was he a fool, he wondered? Perhaps he was, he had snatched at what Rosie offered him and though it had given him momentary gratification, he did not feel good inside himself. Perhaps it took love to make this sweetness between a man and a woman right.

The last hymn was being sung, Boyo stood and looked around him realizing he was taller than any of the boys standing beside him, taller than many of the men in the congregation, come to that. He was growing up. Perhaps he should give his mind a chance to catch up with his body, he thought moodily. The congregation was moving now, edging out towards the doors to where the sunlight poured in. Ellie smiled at Boyo and walked along beside him.

'Will you walk along with us, Boyo?' she asked and he felt a warmth flow through him. How many bosses would stoop to be seen with their most menial worker? But then, until Jubilee's death, Boyo and Ellie had worked side by side, she thrusting the plates into the grinder and he carrying the baskets of oak bark to the yard.

He fell into step beside her and to his satisfaction saw that Daniel was forced to walk with old Martha who was complaining bitterly at the sudden squall of rain which was making the feathers on her hat go limp. Boyo resisted the urge to laugh.

'What's amusing you?' Ellie was nothing if not perceptive.

'I'm sorry, I'm just looking at the way Martha's

178

feathers are giving up the ghost, slowly they're creeping down her forehead, they'll be touching her nose in a minute.'

Ellie's eyes lit up as she glanced over her shoulder at Martha. She squeezed Boyo's hand and pressed her lips together and he could see that she was bursting to laugh out loud. After a moment, she composed herself. 'How's work in the yard, Boyo, still managing without me, are you?'

'Aye, Ellie, managing but not liking it much. You were fair by me but some of the men seem to think I'm built like a mule and able to carry baskets of bark chippings at the double.'

'Well, you are grown up, now,' she said reasonably and he looked at her wondering how much she knew of last night's events. He saw her frown and rich colour flooded into his face. That Rosie, she never could keep her mouth shut, she was a fine one to be telling him not to boast.

'I suppose you think I should save myself for my wife.' The words were spoken before he had time to withdraw them and he regretted them at once. He should have remained silent, kept his dignity but now the subject of his initiation into manhood was open for discussion.

'I'm not the right person to tell anyone what to do with their life.' Ellie's voice was gentle. 'I've made mistakes, it often happens when you're very young.'

Boyo had heard of Ellie's past, who in Swansea hadn't? But she was an innocent, beautiful and trusting, she had doubtless been taken advantage of. 'But you thought you were in love, when you made your mistake, that's true, isn't it?'

'It's true but I shouldn't have allowed myself to settle for second best. I knew the love was one-sided, it couldn't ever have worked even if I'd been married to the man. Don't ever do that, Boyo, settle for second best.'

The rain had ceased, the sun was warming the

pavements, steam was rising from the cobbled streets. Suddenly, it was good to be alive and Boyo squared his shoulders as he walked along, side by side with Mrs Ellie Hopkins, owner of Glyn Hir Tannery.

'He's a little in love with you,' Daniel's voice was warm, good humoured and Ellie looked at him as he sat beside her in the garden. He had eaten roast dinner with her at Glyn Hir and now they were spending Sunday afternoon together, enjoying the wash of warm sunshine.

'It's just a fancy, he will forget it all when he meets a girl his own age.'

'You talk as if you're an ancient.'

'I suppose I am in terms of experience of life and the unhappiness it can bring.'

Daniel leaned forward and took her hand. 'You are wise and beautiful, a lovely woman. And before you chastise me again, yes, I know it's too soon to speak of my feelings to you but they are there, I can't deny them.' He sighed and drew away. 'In any case, there's something else I wish to talk to you about.'

She looked at him, his face was grave and she knew that he was going to speak to her of something very important to him. 'Is there a problem, if so, is there anything I can do to help?' As she waited for him to marshal his thoughts, she was uneasy, wondering if there was anything wrong in his life, he was usually most amiable, a man given to few swings of mood.

'I am thinking of giving up journalism.' The words fell into the silence of the bright afternoon. A lone bee droned among the late roses and Ellie felt herself grow tense.

'Are you going away?' The thought seemed unbearable, she knew in that instant how much she wanted Daniel at her side.

'Perhaps. I want to go into the church. I'm not sure yet how to go about it but I shall learn.'

'Were you influenced so much by Evan Roberts?'

'I think so and yet I know I don't want to work, like him, in the non-conformist chapels, I want a living in a proper parish, I want to put down roots, preferably in Swansea. But if my ministry took me away from here would you come with me?'

'Ask me again, Daniel,' she said, 'when the time is right. When the year of mourning for my husband is past, then ask me.'

Perhaps by then, she thought dismally, Daniel would have changed his mind, found someone more suitable, she was hardly the type to be the wife of a cleric, was she?

He gave a huge sigh of relief. 'I take heart from that. You would be with me all the way, I know, accepting the demands of being a vicar's wife with grace.' He paused, 'Am I asking too much, could you bear being at everyone's beck and call?'

Ellie flung back her head and laughed, not knowing how lovely she appeared to Daniel as he leaned towards her longing to kiss her white throat. 'Bless you, don't you think that's what I've always done here at the tannery? I've been the dogsbody, running everywhere trying to do everything at once, after this a life as a vicar's wife would be peaceful, believe me.'

He took her hand, 'We are betrothed then?' he kissed her fingertips. 'I wish now I'd brought you a ring.'

She shook her head. 'No, not yet, let me give Jubilee his due respects before anything is made official. This is just between you and me, you do understand that, don't you Daniel?'

'All right, Miss Cautious, we are promised to each other but only we will know it, does that suit you?'

'Come on,' she said, 'the sun is going behind the clouds, it's going to rain again, we'd better go inside.'

'But in there, I can't hold your hand, can't kiss your fingers, can't sit so close to you, don't be cruel to me, Ellie.'

'Behave yourself.' She rose to her feet and shook the

creases from her skirts and looked directly at him. 'One day we will be man and wife, for now let the thought be enough for both of us.'

Boyo was lying in his bed, stretched out like a starfish, his legs projecting over the sides of his narrow bed. He came awake slowly, someone else was in the room. He sat up quickly, his heart was in his throat. 'Who is it?'

'Hush, it's all right, it's me, Rosie, don't make a fuss.' She crept beneath the blankets and he felt her nakedness against him. Immediately he was roused.

He groaned, 'You shouldn't have come here, what about Matthew?'

'Matthew's not back yet from town, probably having his fill of pleasure with some wench from one of the taverns. Anyway, boy, don't look a gift-horse in the mouth, see?'

She took his head and drew it down onto her breasts, he had tasted the full, resilient sweetness and knew he could not resist. She was a witch, she knew what a man liked, her hands worked magic upon him, he wanted to take her, to possess her, he could wait no longer. But she made him wait, she made him learn how to please her and he learned eagerly, knowing that this was simply a preliminary to achieving his own splendid release. And as he touched her intimately, felt her move and moan, grip him tightly, arch herself upwards, waiting for him, he experienced a surge of power that exhilarated him. It was almost daylight before she allowed him to rest and he slept like a child, curved against Rosie's breast.

It was how Matthew found them. He stood at the end of the bed and stared down coldly at the two of them, his eyes half closed, the gleam in them hinting at retribution to come.

'Outside,' he jerked his thumb over his shoulder, 'I'll deal with you there.'

'Mat, he's only a lad . . .' Rosie began but Matthew withered her with a look.

182

'He's man enough to bed you and he's got to learn to be man enough to take his punishment.'

Boyo didn't protest, it would do no good. He pulled on his trews and then Matthew was leading the way down the stairs and out into the yard.

'Hey, what's going on by here then?' Harry was just putting down his box of grub, his canteen of tea still swung in his hand.

'Keep out of this.' Matthew didn't look at him, his gaze was still fixed on Boyo as though fearing he would run away.

Boyo looked at Matthew's jutting jaw, his big shoulders and he was afraid.

The first blow sent him reeling to the ground, he shook the stars from his head and tried to see through the blood that was running down from his temple.

'See boy, everything has to be paid for in this life. Pleasure has it's price, did Rosie fail to explain that to you?'

Boyo got to his feet, took stock of Matthew and moved in swiftly, catching the bigger man unawares. He landed a blow against Matthew's stomach, but Matthew was hard and strong, the muscles of his body well-formed and Boyo's fist made little impact. Matthew pushed him away and his fist caught Boyo's mouth, splitting his lip. He fell onto a pile of oak bark and the smell of it was in his mouth along with the bitter taste of blood.

'Come on, Mat,' Harry was calling, 'this isn't a fair fight now is it? Give the boy a chance, we was all in it, egging him on, like, it was only a bit of fun.'

Matthew turned and almost casually hit Harry on the point of the jaw sending him reeling, his head snapped back, his eyes glazed.

'Luke,' Matthew's voice was a warning, as the other man stepped forward, 'keep out of this, it's not your battle.'

'Come on then,' Boyo spoke defiantly, 'finish it, what are you waiting for, you don't need to play with me and we both know it.'

'Oh, no, you don't,' Matthew's voice was filled with scorn, 'you are not going to be let off that lightly.' His fist snaked out and caught Boyo in the ribs, he doubled up and before he could get his breath, the next blow sent him flying backwards so that he slammed into the wall of one of the sheds.

Already Boyo's eye was closing, he could hardly see for the blood that ran down his face. His body ached as though he had been fighting for hours rather than minutes. He was aware of Rosie running across the yard, her skirts flying.

'I'm going to call Ellie, she'll settle you.' She tried to dodge past Matthew but he caught her easily, holding her arm with one hand and slapping her across the face with the other.

She cried out and Boyo, enraged, rushed at Matthew, the force of his body carrying the bigger man to the ground. Boyo for a moment was in charge, he beat at Matthew's face with his fists, the flurry of blows hitting home, drawing blood.

'Go on, Boyo!' Harry was sitting up urging the boy on but even though he continued to hit Matthew's face, Boyo knew his strength was running out, he would not win in the end. Even as the thought ran into his mind, he felt Matthew thrust him aside and then the big man was on his feet, dragging Boyo upright by his hair. He held him away and took aim, punching mercilessly.

Boyo felt his senses reel, he tried feebly to hit out but there was no power left in his limbs. He was unaware that Matthew continued to hit his senseless body until between them, Harry and Luke, along with one of the casual labourers, managed to wrestle Matthew to the ground.

When Boyo regained consciousness he was lying in the parlour of Ellie's house. There was the softness of the sofa beneath him and a wet bandage was being held to his face. One eye refused to open at all and with the other, he saw Ellie, her face white, standing near the fireplace, her hands clasped together.

'I can't believe what's happened here,' she was saying and, turning his head with difficulty, Boyo saw that all the men from the yard including Matthew were standing near the doorway.

'Such an act of barbarism cannot be overlooked.' She gestured to where Boyo lay.

'You could have killed him, Matthew, and for what, what had he ever done to hurt you?'

'I'll tell you what the little runt has done,' Matthew said harshly, 'he's bedded my woman, that's what.'

Boyo felt shame creep through him that was worse than any pain he was suffering. Ellie's cheeks were suddenly red, she turned away for an instant and then she seemed to compose herself.

'I can understand your anger but to take it out on a defenceless boy is not the act of a man, now is it?'

'It's the only thing he'd understand.' Matthew was unrepentant. 'A good hiding never did anyone any harm, teach him not to fish in another man's pond again won't it?'

Ellie was silent for a moment. Then she sighed, 'So Rosie is betrothed to you, is she, you intend to marry her?'

It was a chance she was offering, Boyo saw it, a chance for Matthew to redeem himself, an opportunity for him to salvage some good from a bad situation. But Matthew failed to see the hand of compromise that was stretched towards him.

'I wouldn't marry that whore, not if she was the last woman on earth. God only knows how many others she has had between her legs.' He looked as though he wanted to spit but he contented himself with thrusting his hands into his pockets and drawing out his pipe.

'So you half killed Boyo on a point of pride not because you were in love with Rosie?' Ellie's words were

185

soft and Matthew was too angry to see the danger in them.

'He could have had her when I'd finished with her and not before.'

Rosie had been dumb until then, crouched against the wall, a stricken look on her face. She stood up straighter at his words, her colour high, the mark of his hand on her face already turning blue. 'I'm not a *thing* to be handed from man to man, cast aside like a used coat.' The words burst from her lips. 'I wouldn't stay with an animal like you if you paid me, not after today, I wouldn't, I could never trust you again, could I?'

'That's rich, I find you bedding a boy and you talk about trust. If it wasn't such an insult to my intelligence I could laugh at what you've just said.'

'I couldn't trust you not to kill me if the mood took you, that's what I mean.' Rosie thrust her chin forward. 'And if I should go into town, speak to the women who hang around Adelphi, what would I find out about your goings on, I wonder?'

Ellie's voice broke into the ensuing silence. 'Stop arguing, I've heard enough. I have no other choice but to dismiss you, Matthew, I don't want to see you around my yards ever again.'

'You've had it in for me ever since old Jubilee died,' Matthew shouted, 'wanted shot of me in case I asked for my rights, for my shares in the business. Well you think this is a perfect excuse but you'll live to regret it, my fine lady.' His mouth turned up in an unpleasant sneer. 'I saw you, down on the beach with that reporter, half undressed like a wanton, you are as bad as Rosie, no better than you ought to be. Well you'll regret the day you sacked Matthew Hewson like a dog.'

He stormed out of the room and the slam of the front door reverberated through the house.

'Go back to work, men,' Ellie said, 'not you, Boyo, we have to talk.'

He struggled to sit up wincing as his very bones

seemed to creak. His head hurt and his mouth felt the size of a mule's backside.

Ellie sat opposite him and leaned forward in her chair. 'I don't want to hear any more about why all this happened,' she began, 'but I want you to think very carefully about your behaviour. Matthew was wrong to beat you as he did but you were just as wrong in a different way. It's a hard lesson to learn but at least you'll understand from now on that it doesn't do to take what doesn't belong to you.'

'I've never stolen anything in my life.' Boyo protested through stiff lips.

'Well, you have now,' Ellie said, 'just think about it. Look, Boyo, you'll meet a fine girl one day, you'll fall in love and then you'll be sorry you didn't wait for her. I know what I'm talking about, it's how I feel now about Daniel.' She sighed and leaned back in her chair, her face in shadow. She was completely unaware of the effect of her words on Boyo, they hurt him more than any of Matthew's blows.

'If only I could be young and innocent again, be perfect for him which is what he deserves, I'd be so happy.'

'It's different for men, though,' Boyo said, 'men want to be in the know, not to look foolish when they . . . they go with the woman they love.'

'Is it different?' Ellie challenged him, 'What about this girl you'll one day meet, the girl you want to impress with your knowledge, will you expect her to be virtuous?'

'Of course!' Boyo's own indignation showed him more than any words could, just what Ellie had been trying to tell him.

'You'll want to be perfect for each other, to be the first with each other, to make the relationship really special,' she said.

'I see what you mean,' Boyo hung his head, ashamed to look at her. 'You're right, Ellie.' He looked up at her

187

then, 'But any man would be lucky to get you and I mean that.'

'Thank you, Boyo, I know you do and it makes me feel good. Now, you are not going back to the barn, you are going to sleep here in the back bedroom, I want to make sure you're all right.'

She rose and as she passed him, Ellie rested her hand on his brow. 'You're a good boy, I've great hopes of you and I know you won't disappoint me.'

He was alone then, nursing his bruises. There were tears in his eyes but he wasn't crying because of his injuries, he would be hard put to know why he *was* crying but the tears ran salt over his battered face and mingled with the blood drying on his lips.

CHAPTER THIRTEEN

'What have you been up to this trip?' Bridie's voice had a hard edge to it as she looked up from her chair at her husband. He dropped his bag on the floor and, without replying, came over to her, dutifully bending to kiss her cheek.

'Is that all I'm going to get?' She narrowed her eyes, 'I'm your wife, not your maiden aunt, or have you forgotten that?'

'For the moment,' Paul said evenly. 'For now, I want a bath and a change of clothing and then I'm going out on business.'

Bridie felt herself curl into a defensive ball, her hands were clenched together, her shoulders were tense, even her insides seem to tighten in anger. 'What business might that be?' she asked.

'I'm going down to the offices, if you must know.' He shrugged off his topcoat. 'I've got to take over the reins if you are going to be indoors for ever more.'

Panic filled her, he must not look too closely at the books, the private set of books that she kept locked away. One glance would be enough to tell him the profits from the deep sea trips far exceeded the moderate sums he was making on the coastal and short distance trips.

'No, please don't go.' She looked up at him and held out her hand, it was slim, her fingers long and white, delicate almost. Since her confinement to her bed or at best a chair, she had lost weight. But then, she hardly ate anything and her nervous energy was always at a level she found difficult to control.

He came to her and bent his head, kissing her lips.

Bridie felt herself warm to him. 'Paul, I am grateful to you,' she said softly, 'grateful for your care of me. You are always here when I need you most and I won't forget that.' It wasn't true but it didn't hurt to flatter her husband a little. Paul always took it in, hook line and sinker, she thought scornfully.

He moved to the door. 'I won't be long, I'll be back before you've had time to miss me.' His words were spoken as he left the room giving her no chance to try to coax him into changing his mind.

Bridie bit her lip, what did he want to go to the offices for? It wasn't as if he'd ever taken any notice of the paperwork before. Or had he? What did she really know about this man, her husband? She looked through the window and cursed her inability to move. She couldn't see very far, her vision was impeded by the huge plant that spread above the pot, glossy leaves reaching towards the light.

She really must get herself a chair with wheels, she thought with a sudden surge of energy. She would have one especially made, a comfortable chair with room to fit a tray over the arms so that she could work in comfort. She might be a cripple but she still had all her other faculties didn't she?

There was a diffident tapping on the door and Bridie ignored it at first knowing it would only be one of the servants. The tapping came a little louder and impatiently she called out, 'Come in for heaven's sake!'

'Sorry to disturb you, missus, the master thought you might like some refreshment.' The maid bobbed anxiously and stood awkwardly near the door.

'Well I wouldn't.' Bridie heard her voice shrew-like and hard. 'But you can do something useful, you can go to town and get me one of the coopers from the brewery buildings.'

The girl's eyebrows were raised but she knew better than to ask questions. She bobbed again as she left the room and Bridie was alone in the brooding silence.

Why hadn't she thought of it before? If she could get herself a chair with wheels, she could get out to the stables. With a specially adapted saddle, she could ride out alone instead of always taking the coach. She would be free, well almost.

Excitement washed over her. The first thing she would do would be to bring home her own set of books from the office. Hide them where Paul would not find them. The bedroom they used to share was the best place, she thought bitterly, he hardly ever came there any more.

She clenched her hands so hard that the nails bit into her flesh, he was getting his pleasure somewhere else, there was no way he had become celibate overnight, not her Paul. But he needn't think she was done for, no, not her.

She would get a new doctor. She would practice walking. Surely, in time, the strength would come back into her legs? In the meantime, she would just have to manage best she could and stop feeling sorry for herself. But even as the thought rose to her mind, a tear trickled along her cheek falling like a raindrop onto her useless legs.

The sound of seagulls wheeling overhead told Paul he was nearing the offices in Gloucester Place just a short distance from the docks.

'Afternoon, Elias,' he greeted the old man affably. 'How about you taking the rest of the day off?'

Elias lumbered awkwardly from the desk and took his hat from the stand near the door. 'I'm obliged to you, sir.' He paused for a moment. 'Could I just have a few minutes of your time, sir?'

Paul was impatient for the man to go but he concealed his feelings behind a smile. 'Of course, is there anything wrong?'

'Not really, sir, but me and the wife are not getting any younger and, well the truth is, sir, I'm thinking of retiring. Of course I'll wait until you are suited, I won't just walk out on you without proper notice.'

This was a turn up, Paul had imagined Elias to be a permanent fixture in the office. A small prickle of excitement filled him, he could put someone else in, a man more inclined to do his bidding rather than listen to Bridie's rantings. Not that she managed to get to town very often these days, it was all too much of an effort.

He couldn't be held responsible if her indisposition made life so much easier for him, it gave him a sense of power to know she was tied to the house most of the time, leaving him in charge of his own destiny for once. He had come to realize just how tight a rein Bridie had kept on him. Still, it hadn't prevented him going his own way in business had it?

'Well of course we'll be sorry to lose you, Elias, but I take your point and of course you will need to be home more, putting your feet up.'

'Thank you, sir, I knew you'd understand.'

Paul smiled, it was clear Elias was relieved to be breaking the news to Paul and not Bridie. She would most certainly have put up some argument, made the old man feel obligated, urged him to stay.

'Right, off you go then, I'll lock up here when I've finished.'

When he was alone, Paul went through the drawers one by one, moving papers and replacing them, his eyes sharp, his brows drawn in concentration. At last, he came upon a drawer that was locked and breathing a sigh of relief, he knew he'd found what he was looking for. Carefully, he picked the lock and the drawer sprung open. Inside was a set of ledgers, just as he'd expected. He had come to the conclusion since handling the loads for overseas that there must be a great deal that Bridie was hiding from him. He took out the books and began to look through them. After a time, he whistled through his teeth, slumping back into the seat old Elias had vacated. Bridie was a cunning business woman, she

192

had made herself rich, very rich indeed and it was time that Paul transferred some of the riches into his own bank. He was quite wealthy in his own right, the opium saw to that, but Paul was growing a little tired of being always on the alert for Customs and Excise men. He was getting wary of Charlesworth, too, the man was becoming obsessed by the opium, pushing more and more of it into himself until half the time, he couldn't function properly, he was becoming a liability.

Once he had his hands on Bridie's fortune, Paul could stop the smuggling racket at least for the time being. Get Charlesworth off his back. He smiled, he would bring his little Irish colleen home, set her up somewhere, have Carmella always on hand. Bridie could hardly check on him now could she?

As he studied the figures in more detail, anger began to build in him, Bridie had pretended to love him when all the time she was feathering her own nest, keeping the bulk of the money in her name. It didn't occur to him that he had been doing exactly the same thing. He scratched his chin, the only way he could get his hands on Bridie's fortune was to trick her into signing some of the vessels over to him. But she was shrewd, a good business woman, how could he fool her into signing a document without reading it? It wouldn't be easy but it would have to be done.

He remembered when she was sick, he'd asked her to sign a release to the bank enabling him to take out of the account enough money for the boys to extend their trip abroad. She had done it willingly, trusting him to take care of their sons' future. Could he use the same trick again? He must bide his time, wait until she was vulnerable. But that day might never come, Bridie had a hard edge to her especially when it came to money.

Paul replaced the books and closed the drawer, it clicked, the lock falling into place and he was satisfied that Bridie would never know he'd discovered her little scheme.

He'd better get home, give his wife a little attention, make sure she suspected nothing. If anyone could twist Bridie round his little finger it was Paul, she needed him, wanted him with her and for now, he would play the attentive husband till he dropped. The house seemed to bustle with people, Bridie was in the big sitting room with tradesmen standing around her, listening attentively to her every word.

'Ah Paul,' she smiled at him, she seemed in a good mood, 'I've had the most wonderful idea.'

He went forward to kiss her warmly, knowing somehow that this good idea was not going to suit him at all.

Bridie soon learned to negotiate the downstairs rooms with ease, her chair having been made exactly to her specifications. The wheels turned smoothly, propelled by the strength in her arms. At first she had to rest frequently but she soon improved, her shoulders becoming strong, her muscles hardening. She was nothing if not determined and she found that with something positive to occupy her mind, she was less frustrated, more able to deal with her life as a cripple.

She was still bitter, who wouldn't be? But at least she wasn't confined to one room, she could even go out into the garden if she chose, sit in the rose arbour, think her thoughts in peace. One of the downstairs rooms had been converted into a bedroom, she could retire when she chose, she felt in charge of her life once more.

Her renewed vigour seemed to affect Paul, he'd been far more attentive, spending much of his time with her. She wondered a little if he could be up to something but dismissed the idea as being unworthy and ungrateful. In any case, what harm could he do? He'd been to the office several times, hadn't mentioned her secret set of books so he couldn't have seen them. He wasn't the type to keep quiet about something if it aggrieved him.

And then the chill struck her, just when it seemed she was on top of things again and taking her life into her own hands, she fell sick. She realized she had spent too long outdoors, the days were growing cold as autumn was nearly over, and yet she had so enjoyed the feeling of freedom being in the garden had given her. Well, now she was paying for it.

Bridie lay in her bed, shivering, aching all over and even Dr Carpenter's assurances that it would pass didn't comfort her.

'Her temperature is bound to rise,' the doctor was telling Paul, 'she will almost certainly be feverish, perhaps talking nonsense but don't worry, just keep her cool, give her lots of liquid to drink and she'll be all right. Get a nurse in if it makes you feel any better.'

'No, I'll cope.' Paul was beside her, holding her hand, he seemed at his best when she was ill and defenceless, it was something she would do well to remember. Perhaps Paul was the sort of man who needed to be in charge. Had she been too confident, too independent? Was that the mistake she had been making all her married life?

She had heard the doctor tell Paul that the next few days would be the worst but she hadn't reckoned on being so low, so depleted. All she did was lie in her bed, unaware of the time passing, slipping in and out of a restless sleep. She was vaguely aware of Paul sitting beside her, talking to her softly, a paper in his hand, holding out a pen towards her.

'I wouldn't trouble you, my darling,' she scarcely understood his words, 'but it's the boys, their tutor is asking for more funds. It won't be much longer now before they come home, might as well let them enjoy their last few weeks abroad.'

She scrawled her signature willingly, she should really give Paul more say in the handling of the money. It was all well and good for her to hold the purse-strings but what if she became ill, really ill, how would Paul manage with all the expenses of the household and more importantly with caring for the boys? He would be quite lost. When she was well, she would hand some of the responsibility over to him. No wonder he acted like a child when she treated him like one.

At last, the haze began to clear from her mind. She still felt weak, even her bones ached but she was slowly regaining her strength. Paul was wonderful, he had the maid bring her some warming beef broth and he fed it to her himself, lovingly taking care of her. She fell back on the pillows and smiled up at him.

'Paul, I want you to take over handling the household expenditure,' she said. She was still unsure about her secret accounts, perhaps for now she should keep that card up her sleeve, ease Paul into the business slowly. His own income was modest in the extreme, indeed, the way he spent his money it was doubtful he had any resources at all to fall back on; it really wasn't the way to treat her husband.

She almost blurted out the whole story, how she had sent ships deep sea, how their profits far exceeded his expectations. She almost handed him the key to her drawer in the office and yet something kept her silent.

'I'll gladly take over the running of the house and the business, if you want me to. But I have to go back to sea in a day or two.' Paul took her hand, 'It's only a short trip and I'll be back before you know it. Shall I bring in a nurse while I'm away?'

Disappointed, Bridie shook her head. She had become used to having him with her, at her side, caring for her, loving her. It seemed her suspicious nature had led her in the wrong direction, Paul didn't seem to want to take over the finances, he certainly hadn't jumped at the idea as she had expected him to.

'Do you have to go?' She knew she sounded weak, defenceless but she couldn't help it.

'Yes, I have to, my darling but it won't be for long, I promise you.'

'Why do you have to go now, what's so urgent?' Bridie found all her old suspicions about him having an affair were returning. She tried to keep the edge from her voice but she didn't quite succeed.

'I want to rid myself of Charlesworth,' Paul said, 'the man is becoming more of a liability than a help.'

'Well, you're full of surprises,' Bridie said, 'what's Charlesworth done to upset you?'

'Nothing specific, it's just his way, he thinks he's the boss for a start, he thinks he doesn't need to work too hard. Well I can't afford to employ a man who doesn't carry his full weight.'

'All right, go if you must but don't be long, Paul, I don't know how I'm going to manage without you.'

Paul took her hand and kissed it. 'I'll be back before you know it.'

The days seemed empty without Paul, the house was only a place to live, it was no longer a home, a haven where she was safe.

Bridie found all her old fears returning, was Paul involved with Ellie Hopkins? But no, he'd spent all of the past weeks at her bedside, there couldn't be anyone else. Who would wait that patiently for him?

When she was feeling a little stronger, Bridie sent for the carriage, it was time she went to the office, sorted matters out. She was still inclined to tell Paul everything; if he kept his word and came home quickly, maybe she would show him her books, let him know how rich they really were.

The maid helped her to dress and Bridie saw with alarm how much weight she had lost. She wheeled her chair to the mirror and looked at her face, she was drawn and pale and yet somehow she looked more beautiful than she had ever done in her life. Perhaps being the delicate invalid was a role that suited her, on the surface at least.

It was undignified to have Collins carry her out of the house, though he stared straight ahead lest she accused him of being familiar. He clucked softly at the horses, urging them to be quiet and placed her carefully inside the carriage, wrapping a rug around her legs.

She smiled at him warmly, seeing him as if for the first time. He was young and quite handsome in a rugged sort of way. No gentleman, of course, but somehow he reminded her of her cousin Jono.

As the carriage jerked into motion and picked up speed between the overhanging trees, the wheels seemed to catch every stone, every rut in the driveway. Bridie winced, she still felt very weak, perhaps she was ill-advised to go to the office so soon after her illness. The cobbled streets of Swansea were little better, the carriage seemed to leap and buck with a life of its own. Bridie's head began to ache, she wished now that she had stayed at home. It was a relief when the elegantly painted front of the offices came into sight. She sighed and waited while Collins, who had been up top with the driver, came round to the doorway and carried her quickly indoors.

Bridie was still self-conscious about being seen in public; helpless, ineffectual, it offended her independent nature. At least Collins appreciated the fact and was tactful in his handling of her.

When Collins knocked at the inner door, Bridie's impatience returned. 'Go in, man, no need to knock, I do own the place after all.'

Collins obeyed and strode into the office, placing Bridie carefully in a chair. She took a deep breath staring in consternation at the man behind the desk, he was a stranger, a thin bespectacled, dour stranger.

'Where's Elias?' She asked abruptly.

'He's retired this past two weeks.' The man looked at her askance as she stared balefully up at him.

'And who are you?' Bridie said, hostility in every line of her body.

'I'm the new office manager, Brian Thomas. Who are *you*?'

'I'm Bridie Marchant, owner of the shipping line, that's who I am.'

'I think it's Mr Marchant who is the owner,' Brian Thomas said carefully, 'I handle the books you see, I know exactly the state of play in the business of Marchant Shipping line.'

'It's Marchant and James,' Bridie felt her anger rising. This stranger, this man with the superior attitude was daring to talk so insolently to her.

'Collins,' Bridie said, 'take this key and open the drawer over there, that's the one, second down. Bring me the books from inside.'

Brian Thomas stepped forward as if to protest but Collins brushed past him as if he wasn't there and she wanted to applaud him for putting the upstart in his place. She watched as Collins did her bidding, the books were still there and Bridie sighed with relief. For a moment she had been frightened, imagining that Paul had discovered her secret.

She opened them and placed them on the desk. 'Look at these, Mr Thomas, you'll soon see who owns the biggest share of the shipping line.'

He put on a pair of thick-rimmed glasses and took the books towards the window, running his finger along the columns of entries.

'Very interesting,' he said after what seemed an interminable length of time. He snapped the books shut. 'Not worth the paper they are written on, alas.'

'What do you mean?' Bridie heard the hoarseness in her voice and was impatient with her own weakness.

'I mean that these,' he threw the books down scornfully, 'are out of date, all these vessels and their cargos and so the profits too, have been transferred to Paul Marchant.'

'That can't be, not without my consent,' Bridie said quickly.

'Then I suggest you must have given your consent, Mrs Marchant.' The man was so sure of himself that Bridie knew he must be right.

'Have you not recently signed control over to your

husband? After all, you are not exactly fitted to running a shipping line, are you?'

She longed to smack his face but it was Collins who moved forward.

'You keep a civil tongue in your head when you're talking to Mrs Marchant,' he said and the man gawped at him from behind his spectacles.

'I have signed nothing,' Bridie said almost to herself. But a thin icicle of fear touched her spine. She had given Paul her signature. It was when she was sick, confused. Paul had brought her documents, told her she was releasing money for the benefit of their sons, could he have tricked her?

'I want you to get out of here this minute, Thomas.' Bridie suddenly felt in charge. 'I am going to go through the books myself, I'll soon find out what's been happening in my absence.'

'I can't do that,' Thomas said but his protest was weak, he glanced uncertainly at Collins who was still standing uncomfortably close to him.

'Out,' Collins said, 'otherwise I'll have to help you out, understand?'

Thomas went towards the door, his face was flushed as he took his hat from the stand. 'I'll take no responsibility for any of this,' he protested. 'When Mr Marchant returns I'm sure he'll have something to say to you, my good man.'

As the door slammed behind Thomas, Bridie looked directly at Collins. 'I don't know why you should be on my side in all this but I am very grateful to you.'

'You have always been fair,' Collins said carefully, 'you have paid good wages and always on time. In the beginning when I first worked for you—' He stopped speaking.

'You needn't go on, Collins, I know I've changed lately and for the worse. Go on out, go have a beer, I need to look over the books. You can come for me later.'

'If it's all the same to you,' Collins said quietly, 'just in case that . . . that person wants to come back.'

Bridie nodded her agreement and watched as Collins searched through the drawers and produced bright new accounts books. Her heart sank, it was clear that Paul had been up to something but was he capable of cheating her out of her inheritance?

It took her much less time than she had thought to go through the books; everything was quite clear, Paul had transferred the entire shipping fleet to himself, she owned nothing, not one single vessel. For a moment Bridie felt beaten, she poured over the books listing the shorter trips, many of them were to Ireland. It seemed Paul had been shipping various cargos across the Irish sea from candles to leather saddles and horse-collars, why, what was in it for him?

She rubbed at her eyes tiredly, perhaps Paul was shipping forbidden goods, tea, tobacco, or silks, contraband cargos of some kind. She remembered the notebook she had found in his bag, she hadn't understood it, the entries were in some sort of code.

She looked up, Collins was seated in the chair opposite her, his shoulders tense as he watched the door. 'Collins,' she said gently, 'I want you to take me to the bank.'

She would speak to Jake Simmons, he was an old friend of her father's, he would tell her all she wanted to know, none of this ethical nonsense with him. He knew full well who had made the largest part of the money that had gone into building up the shipping line of Marchant and James. Jake was just about to leave the bank but he smiled when he saw Bridie and ushered Collins, with Bridie in his arms, into his own private office.

'Bridie, so good to see you looking well again.'

'Thank you, Jake.' She bit her lip for a moment, 'I have to talk to you. This is serious.'

'I suspected it was.' Jake said softly and glanced at

Collins who had settled Bridie in a chair and stepped back self-effacingly.

'You can talk in front of Collins,' Bridie said, 'please Jake, what is going on here?'

'You tell me,' Jake sat down and played with the quill pen resting in the ink-pot on his desk. 'I can only say I was devastated when your husband withdrew all the moneys and closed the account.'

Bridie felt as if she had swallowed something bitter. 'When did Paul do all this?' It was an effort to speak normally.

Jake looked at her compassionately. 'About two weeks ago, no explanation, took the whole lot of it, not only the considerable amount of money he'd made himself but your fortune too, Bridie, he had all the right documentation, I assumed you were too sick to deal with matters yourself.'

'His own money, he had quite a lot, did he?'

'The profits Mr Marchant made on the short runs were greater than those you made from your deep sea cargos which I thought very strange.'

Not so strange if her suspicions were correct. Bridie tried to think clearly but muddled thoughts kept running round and round in her head until she thought she would go mad. 'Well then, Jake, I can only apologize and explain that I knew nothing about what my husband was planning.' Did she sound as desolate as she felt?

'I'm sure he did what he thought was best,' Jake leaned over and touched her shoulder, 'once he took charge it was a case of a new broom sweeps clean and all that, I suppose.'

'You're taking it really well,' Bridie said softly, 'but I do wish you'd come to me and talked it over, Jake.'

He shrugged, 'How could I? I knew of your illness, I believed you were too sick to see anyone.'

Bridie sighed, Jake was right and Paul could be most convincing if he wanted to be, she knew that better than most. 'Right then, it's home for us, Collins, nothing more I can do in town today.'

When she was settled in the carriage, Bridie closed her eyes wearily. What could she do? It seemed that Paul had cleaned her out, taken all her money, all her ships. She looked down at her useless legs, here she was, helpless, a cripple, unable to stand up to her husband and demand an explanation. She began to cry, sobs racked her thin frame. Bridie felt she had no weapons and no energy to fight for her future. She was defeated.

By the time the carriage drew up outside her home, she was composed and if her eyes were a little red, her cheeks a little blotchy, no-one among her staff was going to be indiscreet enough to mention it. In her room, Bridie lay for a long time, staring at the lengthening shadows that crept across the ceiling. She felt empty of all emotion, there wasn't even a glimmer of hope to give her cheer.

In the morning, she woke early, a pale sun was shining through the window and suddenly Bridie was filled with a sense of resolution, she was not beaten, not yet she wasn't. After she had eaten a light breakfast, she sent for Collins. 'I intend to walk again,' she told him. To her gratitude, he didn't appear surprised, he merely nodded.

'I don't want anyone to know about it,' she instructed, 'I want you to get me some walking sticks and, Collins, I'll need you to help me, will you do it?'

She was asking him humbly and he smiled at her. It was the first time she had seen him smile, he was a good man, a trustworthy man and Bridie's heart warmed a little. 'I know it's not going to be easy,' she said, 'I will fail lots of times but I will do it, you'll see.'

'I know you will, Mrs Marchant,' Collins nodded reassuringly. 'I know you will.'

'Now,' Bridie said, 'I want you to find me someone to board the *Marie Clare*, I want him to sail with my husband on his next trip.'

Collins never seemed to be surprised by anything she

said. Bridie smiled, 'This man must be more than a sailor, he must be a special sort of person, one not quite . . . honest. He must be able to keep his eyes and ears open, find out what exactly these trips to Ireland are all about.' Bridie paused. 'I needn't tell you, Collins, you will have gathered as much for yourself that I have no money, this man must sign on as crew like any other but I refuse to accept that I have been cheated out of my father's inheritance, I will put the matter right and when I do he will be well rewarded, you too Collins.'

'I need no reward,' Collins said simply. 'And if I might make a suggestion, I have a little money put aside with which I can pay for a man's services. A loan of course,' he said as Bridie made to protest, 'I'm sure it will all be put right when you regain control of your business.' His tense look eased a little. 'As I said, you were always fair and honest.'

Bridie felt tears come into her eyes. She was getting soft, she who had been feared in Swansea, Bridie Marchant of the sharp tongue, she was touched by this man's simple loyalty. Perhaps it was something to do with the fact that she was penniless, a cripple, dependent for the first time on others to help her. Well, she might be broke but she was not helpless and that was something Paul would shortly learn.

It was no chance encounter that led Collins to seek Matthew out at the bar of the Ship Inn. He had heard much of the man from one of the serving maids, knew he was the sort who would do anything for money. When he was face to face with Hewson, he saw a big man with a ruthless air about him and congratulated himself on choosing wisely.

'Mr Hewson,' he said quietly, 'I hear you are currently without a position. I think I might just have something to interest you.'

CHAPTER FOURTEEN

'I want to buy more of your fine leather, Mrs Hopkins.' Paul Marchant looked down at Ellie, his face close to hers, his eyes regarding her with far too much interest for her liking. 'I did look for your foreman in the yard but apparently there isn't one. I understand you dismissed him from your service?'

Ellie wondered just how he had come about that little piece of information. 'That's right, I need a replacement for Matthew Hewson as soon as possible. Please come indoors, Mr Marchant.'

Ellie led the way into the sitting room where Martha was busy embroidering a sampler. The older woman looked up and regarded Paul Marchant with shrewd eyes. She nodded her head in acknowledgment of his polite greeting but didn't speak.

'Of course you may buy all the leather you want from us,' Ellie said, 'please, sit down, but you will have to do business with me, for the time being.'

She knew her tone was businesslike but it was difficult to be friendly when she remembered the last time they had met when Bridie Marchant had behaved like a harridan. Later, she had come up to the tannery and accused Ellie of having an affair with her husband, it was all so embarrassing. Ellie knew she should not hold it against Paul, it was not his fault that his wife was so jealous. Or was it?

'That is fine by me.' Paul rested easily in one of the big chairs. 'I know your leather is of the finest made around these parts, the saddler who makes up the tack for me is delighted with the quality. I appreciate the extra

205

service you do me, delivering the leather, it's very kind of you.'

'It isn't something we would do for everyone. It takes a considerable amount of time and manpower to run the wagons down to the saddler and then, later, to bring the finished goods to the docks.' Ellie had no intention of being overly polite, Paul Marchant was not one of Glyn Hir's biggest buyers, indeed, his orders were comparatively modest. It was from the large warehouses that the real orders came, the furniture makers, the boot and shoe emporiums. The leather from Glyn Hir was shipped all over the country. Still, she reasoned, a customer was a customer and Ellie felt it necessary to show a degree of interest. She looked at him from under her lashes, Paul Marchant was a personable man, a charming man, why then, didn't she quite trust him?

'The leather I buy from you, is ideal for horse-collars, saddles, that sort of thing, it's so well treated.' He was sincere enough; Jubilee had always prided himself on quality. 'I ship the goods abroad to a customer of mine in Ireland.' Paul smiled. 'It's not a big order for me, as I'm sure you appreciate, but the goodwill of a business is so important.'

It was a reproof and Ellie recognized it as such. Paul smiled again as if to soften his words. 'I needn't remind you of that, of course. Later on, I'm hoping to increase the stock of leather I buy from you to a much bigger quantity.'

'I see.' Ellie didn't much care, one way or another, she would rather have as little as possible to do with Paul Marchant and his fiery wife.

It was as though he read her thoughts. 'I'm sorry for the way my wife acted that time,' he said quietly. 'I'm sure she would have apologized to you herself but she hasn't been well lately, indeed, she is a complete invalid these days, confined to a chair.'

Ellie had heard a little of Bridie's illness from Martha who seemed to pick up all the gossip being spread around the town but she hadn't realized how serious it was. 'I'm sorry to hear that. I don't suppose there is anything I can do to help?'

'That's very kind of you, especially in the circumstances, but no, I'm managing everything just fine, thank you.'

Ellie forbore to ask how his wife was managing; Bridie Marchant was not the most patient of women, it couldn't be easy for her to be dependent on other people. Paul rose to his feet and smiled down at Ellie as though entirely sure he could charm her. She looked at him without expression. 'Please feel free to choose any of the skins you want,' she said as pleasantly as she could, 'though we have no inferior goods on sale, I do assure you of that.'

'I am aware of the quality of your leather,' he replied, 'as I said, it is of the best, that's why I have returned to buy more.'

Ellie wished he would go and leave her alone, she really must get a good manager in, someone who would take the responsibility of running the tannery without her help. She moved impatiently towards the door, she was expecting Daniel and she wanted time to prepare herself. Her spirits lifted at the thought. All she had to do was to be patient and soon she would be with the man who had come to mean more than all the world to her.

'You can't mean it,' Arian Smale was looking at Daniel in disbelief and though he was flattered by her reluctance to accept his decision, he was not one bit influenced by it.

'I am grateful for my training here,' he said humbly, 'I've learned such a lot, things I should be able to put into use when I have a parish of my own.'

'You really mean to go into the church then?' Arian shook her head. 'I knew you were impressed by Evan Roberts, I just didn't realize how impressed.'

'I hope you've thought this over,' Mac was leaning across his desk, his long legs looped around his chair. 'Not much money in being a vicar, you know.'

'I don't mind that,' Daniel answered good naturedly, 'I'm not out to make myself a rich man. In any case, I've spoken to the bishop and he feels I will do very well in the church. So you see, it's all settled.'

'Doesn't have to be, keep on the job for a while, it wouldn't hurt to have a bit of cash by you, especially a young sprig like you who might want to get hitched one day.'

Daniel looked at Mac with affection. 'I won't be in a position to get married for a long time yet.'

'Not until Ellie Hopkins' year of mourning is over, at least.' Arian said.

Daniel felt his colour rise. 'I would be very honoured to marry Mrs Hopkins but I will respect her wish to give her husband's memory the respect it deserves.' He knew he sounded pompous but he couldn't seem to help it.

To their credit, neither Arian nor Mac mentioned Jubilee's will and the great fortune he had left his widow. They knew Daniel better than to believe him a golddigger.

'I'll work out the month's notice if that's suitable,' Daniel said, 'I don't have to go to college until the beginning of the next term.'

Arian smiled. 'As Mac said, why not keep on your job 'til then?' It really was generous of her, she could have begun looking for a junior reporter at once.

'I would be delighted to stay as long as I may,' Daniel smiled warmly. 'At the risk of sounding sentimental, I feel I belong here.'

'Right then, I have an assignment for you,' Arian said. 'I've heard a rumour, just a rumour, that Paul Marchant has somehow taken charge of his wife's shipping fleet, apparently she is left with no assets to her name at all. See what you can dig up about it, Daniel.'

This was part of the job he didn't like; the snooping,

the prying into the private affairs of others but it was all in a day's work in the life of a junior reporter and for now, he was still in Arian's employ.

'I don't know how you'll go about it,' Arian continued, 'you can hardly go and ask Paul or Bridie Marchant outright, can you?'

'Leave that to Daniel,' advised Mac, 'any reporter worth his salt knows how to winkle stories out of unsuspecting folk.'

It was easier said than done, Daniel mused as, later, he walked along the Strand. He knew his starting point, the shipping office in Gloucester Place, but how to make enquiries without seeming too inquisitive. Daniel knew he could write the stories well enough, it was the ferreting out of information he was no good at. Perhaps it was just as well he'd chosen to go into the church, there people would confide in him only so much as they wanted him to know.

Brian Thomas was uncommunicative. He sat in the offices of Marchant and James and stared stoically at a point somewhere above Daniel's head. 'I don't know what information you are seeking,' he said pompously, 'but remember, I only work here, if you want to know anything you must speak to the owner.'

'I thought there were *owners*, plural,' Daniel said quickly. 'But then,' Daniel continued, 'I don't suppose you would know, not being in the confidence of the owners.' Daniel tried playing on the man's sense of importance; Thomas was obviously puffed up with pride.

'Mr Marchant is the sole owner these days,' Thomas fell into the trap and then immediately regretted his words. 'I'm saying no more.' Daniel left the office knowing he would have to search elsewhere for his copy though it did seem as if Arian's sense of a story was working as well as ever.

Daniel walked up the hill to where the big houses sat in woody gardens. Sea Mistress, the house owned by

Paul and Bridie Marchant was set back from the roadway, the elegant gables reaching fingers skyward, the windows gleaming brightly against the old stonework.

Perhaps, Daniel thought, he could talk to one of the servants, there seemed no other line of enquiry open to him. He paused by the imposing front entrance, the old wood of the double doors, lovingly polished, opened up a way into a marbled outer hall. He would gain no entrance there. Daniel made his way round the large structure to the back. The gardens stretched away into the distance, trees and shrubs offering privacy to the neat walkways and pretty arbours. Stone statues were placed among the trees to charming effect and Daniel stood for a moment appreciating the scene before him.

'Can I help you?' A voice broke into Daniel's reverie and he turned to see a man a little older than he himself watching him with suspicion. This was one of the male servants, a man of position in the household and he was looking Daniel over with a practised eye, correctly assessing his status in the place of things and speaking respectfully.

'Excuse me,' Daniel smiled disarmingly, 'I'm afraid I'm trespassing.'

'Do you have any business here?' the man was cautious, overly polite and yet with a distinct air of one who would guard the privacy of the residents of the house with force if necessary.

'I'm afraid I am snooping,' Daniel liked the look of the man and decided he might as well be honest. 'My boss, Arian Smale, asked me to look into the rumour that Mrs Marchant has signed the business over to her husband.'

The man appeared startled. 'How in heaven's name . . .' he broke off and ran his hand over his brow. 'Wait here.'

Daniel stood in the garden wondering what on earth was going on behind the solid walls of the big house. Women, in the past had fought hard to retain control of their inheritance and now, Bridie Marchant, a woman renowned for her toughness in business was handing everything over to her husband on a plate, it was incredible. A sense of excitement filled Daniel, Arian could well be right, there could be more than a gossipy item here, there could be a big story.

The man reappeared. 'Come with me,' he led the way inside the house, through the dark corridors and out into the elegant front hallway. 'Mrs Marchant is in the blue drawing room, she'll see you right away.'

He opened the door and admitted Daniel into the sumptuous deeply carpeted room. Bridie Marchant was seated in a chair fitted with wheels, she looked well enough, Daniel thought flipping open his notebook.

'Thank you, Collins,' Bridie smiled and inclined her head and the servant withdrew, closing the door quietly behind him.

'So,' Bridie said, 'you have heard rumours then?'

'Well, yes,' Daniel was taken aback by her out-spokenness. He'd had little contact with Mrs Marchant previously but what he did know of her warned him she could be a dragon lady.

'Sit down,' Bridie said and Daniel obediently sat. 'So you've come to ask me if it's true?' Bridie said baldly.

'Yes. I suppose it's forward of me but if *The Times* doesn't run the story some other paper will and at least I'll handle it sympathetically and fairly.'

Bridie was lost in thought for a moment. 'Very well, then let's say that because of my indisposition I have given my husband free rein with the shipping business.'

'But it wouldn't be exactly the truth?' Daniel said shrewdly.

'The truth is that my husband took advantage of my illness to trick me into signing my business over to him. What's more, I believe he is doing something illegal, I found his notebook, saw that he'd been shipping cargos that weren't all they appeared to be. No-one would believe it, of course.' She looked at Daniel with large, tear-filled eyes and Daniel, instinctively, made a move towards her and then hesitated.

'I'm so sorry.' The words were out before he could prevent them. He must learn to curb his tongue, he needed to be objective, not only in his role as reporter but if he ever achieved his ambition in the church he'd need to be restrained.

'You can tell Arian Smale what I've said but she can't use it, not without evidence.' Bridie looked up at him. 'I know you must think me a bad wife, talking to you like this, but Paul has left me penniless.'

'Don't worry, I won't betray your confidence,' Daniel said. 'But what are you going to do?' It was beyond understanding that a man could rob his wife of all she possessed, he thought angrily.

'I won't let the matter rest here, I'll recover my inheritance one day then Paul can look out.'

Daniel snapped his notebook shut and bowed slightly. 'Until such a time, I'll leave you in peace.'

'Thank you for your concern and please give Miss Smale my regards when you see her.' Bridie Marchant was once more in control, her head high, her expression bland.

Daniel left her and walked back to town pondering on the ways of men. Paul Marchant had married Bridie when he had nothing but a small shipping fleet to his name. Well now he was rich enough but ill-gotten gains did no-one any good in the long run. For a moment he felt downhearted, it was a sad story, a sick woman betrayed by the man she loved. As for the hint that Marchant was dealing in contraband, it was all rather too far-fetched to be believed. He would tell Arian all he knew just as Mrs Marchant had suggested and then it was up to his boss to make of it what she would.

His spirits lifted, tonight he would see Ellie, he would be near her, would breathe in her perfume and one day, he would take great joy in making Ellie his wife.

*   *   *

Ellie looked across the room to where Daniel was seated and found it difficult to hide the pleasure in her eyes. In the corner Martha was busily sewing, bent towards the lamplight, her back to the room, Martha was the perfect chaperon, present and yet self-effacing.

'So you've found a new manager.' Daniel was leaning forward eagerly in his chair, wanting to be as near to Ellie as he could. 'Thank goodness for that, I've been worried in case Matthew decided to come back and cause trouble.'

'I'm as surprised as you are that he's gone so quietly,' Ellie said. 'I suppose he'll turn up again like a bad penny.'

'Not for a while he won't,' Martha spoke without turning her head. 'He's gone to be a sailor with one of the Marchants' ships, the *Marie Clare* or some such outlandish sounding name.'

Ellie's heart lifted. 'How do you know that, Martha?' she asked in surprise.

'Well Rosie told me, of course, there's not much passes her by where that man is concerned, still in love with him she is in spite of everything, if you ask me.'

'I thought you and Rosie didn't get on,' Ellie said, hiding a smile.

'We don't, well not particularly, but then the girl has to talk to someone and I'm here so I suppose I serve the purpose.'

'Well, I never thought Matthew was one to take to the sea.' Ellie mused, 'I wonder what on earth induced him to become a sailor.'

'A fat purse, I suppose,' Martha said flatly and bent her head over her sewing once more, her shoulders hunched, indicating that the conversation was over.

'Ellie, I think I'd better be going.' Daniel looked towards Martha who took no notice of him. 'Will you see me to the door?'

Ellie rose to her feet at once and suddenly Martha gave them her full attention. 'I've never known anyone take so long to say good night as you two.' Her tone was dry.

'Oh shut up,' Ellie said good naturedly. Together, she and Daniel left the room and crossed the large bare hall towards the front door. The night air was cold and damp, the wind was blowing towards the sea taking the smell of the tannery with it.

'I wish I could take you away with me.' Daniel stood next to her, not touching her. 'I love you so much, Ellie.'

'I love you too Dan and I hate to think of you leaving Swansea. When do you think you'll be going?' Her tone was anxious, they had had so little time together.

'I'll start college in the new term,' Daniel said. 'In January I expect but I haven't been accepted yet, not formally.'

'You will be,' Ellie spoke with confidence, Daniel was from a good family, he would have an excellent reference from Arian Smale, there was no doubt he'd be accepted into the church college.

She felt suddenly empty, how would she manage without him? Daniel had become such an integral part of her life, she loved him more than she had believed it possible to love anyone. Of course she had loved Jubilee, would always love him, but as a protector, a father-figure not a lover. Once she had believed herself in love with Calvin Temple but now she recognized that she had been fooled by what was a youthful infatuation. As yet she and Daniel had done nothing more than hold hands. He was diffident, a gentleman. He respected her which she found touching given the facts of her past. But Daniel was not one to judge, he would make an excellent cleric.

She looked up at him, she would very much like to be in his arms, to feel his lips probe hers with passion. She was glad it was dark otherwise he might read her desire in her face. She reached out and touched his hand and his fingers curled around hers, strong and reassuring.

214

'Even when I'm away, I will come to see you often, Ellie,' he spoke softly, 'I love you, nothing will ever change that so don't you go getting any doubts, mind.'

She smiled, 'You'd better go.' She moved away from him, 'Go before I forget I'm supposed to be a lady.'

He touched her shoulder lightly. 'One day it will be right for us, Ellie, then we will have the rest of our lives to enjoy each other.'

She closed her eyes, thanking God that Daniel was so sensitive, so honourable.

'Good night, Ellie.' She felt his lips touch her hair briefly and then he was striding away, his feet crunching against the gravel on the path leading towards the road.

She returned to the house and Martha was putting away her sewing, straightening her back, rubbing her eyes. 'Sooner you two can be wed the better,' she said softly, 'I know you are both good people but do you really have to wait before you can – well *be* together?'

'What are you suggesting, Martha?' Ellie said gently. 'That Dan and I have an affair? It wouldn't do, it really would be against his principles, you know that as well as I do.'

'And your principles, what of them?' Martha asked archly.

Ellie raised her arms above her head and stretched luxuriously. 'I would throw them aside tomorrow, if I could. I would tear off my clothes and fall into bed with Daniel like a wanton, if only it weren't for the debt of honour I owe to Jubie's memory.'

'Ah, well, such is life. I'm glad I'm past it all myself, not that I ever was great on passion and the sins of the flesh, mind.'

Ellie smiled, 'I don't believe that for one minute but anyway, you're right, it's time we were going up to bed, there's work to do tomorrow.'

★　　★　　★

The sea was running fast, lifting the *Marie Clare* as though she was a toy and then dropping her deep into the green troughs of water.

'God, I hate this life.' Matthew Hewson was soaked to the skin, he had lost weight, unable to eat the unappetizing meals dished up by the none too clean cook in the greasy galley. But more than anything, Matthew was missing having a woman beside him, a woman to make him feel good, to cater to his needs, to hold him in soft, scented arms. In short, he admitted to himself that he was missing Rosie. Perhaps he had been hasty in ditching her and he might have been better advised than to give that young cock Boyo a beating. Had he kept his temper he would still be leading a comfortable life at Glyn Hir bossing the men, having his fill of the good life with plenty of money in his pocket. Instead, he'd taken this job on board ship, a temporary situation, he had promised himself that at the start and now he was even more sure that a life at sea was not for him.

He'd been surprised when Collins had come up to him at the bar of the Ship Inn and struck up a conversation. He'd seen the man in the public several times, knew he was a servant up at one of the big houses on the hill and that was all he knew.

Collins had been impressed with Matthew's reputation as both a bard and a tough man, which admittedly was an unusual combination but then Matthew knew he was an unusual man, not the run-of-the-mill type at all which was why he'd been selected for this job. Collins had been aware that Matthew had worked at Glyn Hir; he explained that a load of leather goods originating at the tannery was being shipped to Ireland. He told him exactly what he must do, he must watch the owner of the *Marie Clare*, follow Paul Marchant when the ship docked in Ireland, find out as much about the man as he could.

The thought appealed to him as did the promise of a great deal of money when his job was over. Admittedly the sum Collins handed over initially was pretty paltry but Matthew knew that what he would find out would be of value. He sensed a bit of jiggery-pokery was going on; if he was being paid to follow Paul Marchant then the man was up to something not quite legal. If the information was not worth money to Collins then Matthew could always defect to the other side, come clean with Marchant or even go to one of the newspapers. *The Swansea Times* would be glad to pay for a good story.

It had been fortunate that the *Marie Clare* had been short of crewmen, he'd been taken on without a great deal of ceremony, after all, it was just a cross-channel trip, nothing to speak of. So here he was, praying that the ship would dock soon at one of the Irish ports.

Relieved from his duties, he went below and rubbed his face with a piece of dry cloth, his clothes he could do nothing about. He sat on the wooden bench that ran along the galley and watched the morose cook peeling potatoes.

'When are we going to dock?' he asked at last, anything to break the silence.

'Bout an hour.' The man's reply was terse but Matthew felt a sense of relief, soon he'd been on dry land again. Why anyone chose to live this sort of uncomfortable existence he couldn't comprehend. It was his idea of hell to be continually soaked and uncomfortable not to mention being isolated among a gang of men for hours on end. Perhaps he should take a little look at the cargo while he had the chance, he was supposed to learn as much as he could and that's exactly what he intended to do. Who knew what tasty piece of information he might pick up and find useful?

The hold was tightly packed with foul smelling fuel blocks and for a moment, in the darkness, that's all there seemed to be. But no, over to the side were stacked about forty boxes lashed together and Matthew felt his nerve ends tingle. He was about to find out something of moment, he just knew it, something that was going to be very profitable to him. He clambered over the top of the boxes and easily prized one of the tops open and the familiar tang of leather assailed his nostrils. Immediately he was back at Glyn Hir, currying, soaking, working the leather.

The load was not in the form of skins though by the feel of the leather it was of the best quality, Matthew would have known even if he hadn't already been told that the leather had come from Glyn Hir. The leather had been fashioned into tack, into fine saddles and horse-collars. Good stuff but not a very big load of it, not enough surely to make the cost of transporting it to Ireland worthwhile.

Matthew lifted one of the collars and examined it, the stitching wasn't particularly well done, it could easily be opened with the touch of a blade. Perhaps, he thought, excitement beginning to grip him, that was the whole point. He took out his knife and carefully cut through a few of the stitches. He slipped his fingers inside and they encountered the stiffness of rye grass, the usual padding for collars. He probed further and his fingers found a soft package.

So Marchant was smuggling something, that much was clear. The substance wasn't rough enough for tea, in any case, the smell of the leather would impregnate the tea, spoiling the taste. Neither was it tobacco. It could only be one thing. Opium. So that was Marchant's little game, avoiding the duty on the goods and no doubt selling them on at a fine profit. Matthew looked at the cases, stacked one on top of the other and calculated that an enormous amount of opium could be smuggled abroad by such a means. He doubted that all the leather goods had been tampered with, the contraband was probably in selected, marked boxes.

He climbed carefully over the boxes and made his way up on deck, the ship would be docking soon and he would be needed. No point in making anyone suspicious of him at this juncture. He hugged the knowledge of the contraband to himself, it was something he could use to his advantage, he was sure of it. The deck was rolling, it was slippery and wet but the shoreline was just coming into sight. Matthew heaved a sigh of relief, with what he knew, he would be making the return journey in style not as a common deck-hand.

Later, when he left the ship, he traced Paul Marchant to the small guest house a short distance from the docks, keeping well out of sight. In the warmth of the bar, he mingled with the other customers and found that his subterfuge had been unnecessary, most of the crew from the *Marie Clare* were there before him. He saw Paul Marchant standing near the foot of the rickety staircase, he said something to the landlord and then disappeared to an upper room. Shortly afterwards, a beautiful young girl came out of the kitchen with a tray and she too went upstairs.

Matthew grimaced, he should be getting some of that; he needed a pretty girl and it looked as if Paul Marchant was cut from the same cloth. When the girl didn't reappear, Matthew knew he was right, Paul Marchant was amusing himself with the young Irish girl, something that perhaps Collins would like to know. Collins after all was only acting for Mrs Marchant, any fool could work that out. What would interest Mrs Marchant was her husband's infidelities, women were like that. Well if she wanted to know the truth then let her have it. Not that Matthew was above playing both ends from the middle. If he could blackmail Marchant and at the same time take money from Collins, he would do it without a qualm.

He helped himself to more ale from the jug the landlord had placed on the table before him and settled back in his chair. He felt well satisfied with himself, he had found out a great deal more than anyone could have anticipated. Well, all he had to do now was to keep his eyes peeled and his ears open. Marchant must have a contact here in Ireland. Whoever was buying the goods, he must be more powerful than Marchant, have more clout, have plenty of contacts otherwise Marchant would be distributing the contraband himself.

The little Irish girl reappeared and Matthew waved his hand to her. She came over to him and he could see she was flushed, it was clear she had been well and truly bedded.

'I could do with a little company,' Matthew turned on his most charming smile but it cut no ice.

'Sorry, I only serve ale,' she said shortly. It was on the tip of Matthew's tongue to tell her that from his observations she was not telling the truth but he stopped himself in time. He must keep control of himself, not arouse suspicion.

He inclined his head in a mock bow. 'Forgive me then, it's a long time since I've seen such a beautiful woman.' It was true, she really was lovely with her cloud of dark hair, her fine skin and large, dark fringed eyes. Marchant was a lucky man but then, perhaps his luck was just about to run out.

CHAPTER FIFTEEN

'My husband's ship is due in port some time today.' Bridie was sitting near the window staring out at the ice-bound garden. In spite of the winter weather she felt well, she knew she had more colour in her cheeks, her hair had a new shine and her eyes were alive. Paul might have taken away all her possessions but he could not rob her of her spirit. 'You think this man Matthew Hewson will have done a good job?' Bridie looked anxiously up at Collins.

'I don't think he's altogether to be trusted but then we had little choice but to employ someone of his type.'

'You're right, no decent person would want to spy on others so I suppose I'm not a decent person.'

'You've been badly wronged, Mrs Marchant,' Collins said evenly. Bridie studied him for a moment, wondering at his loyalty. It seemed that these days he was always there at hand to offer comfort and support. When he had first come into her employ, Bridie had been coolly gracious to him as she was to all the servants but when unhappiness and suspicion had clouded her mind, Collins had known the sharp edge of her tongue on more than one occasion. Now, it seemed, he had become her staunchest ally in her fight to walk again. She did not deserve his friendship and she knew it.

As if reading her thoughts, he spoke, 'How about doing your walking exercises for the day? It wouldn't do to let your limbs grow weak again.'

Bridie smiled, 'How would I manage without you, Collins? Come along, then, help me out of my chair.'

She had been practicing walking for only a week, her

legs trembled whenever she tried to stand, her back ached and she feared her spine would not hold her upright but her own determination and Collins' strength lent her courage.

'Just one step at a time, now.' Collins talked to her as though she were a child, he chided and encouraged and Bridie, with her arm around his shoulder, realized she was becoming more than a little dependant on him. He was becoming important in her life, could she be falling a little in love with him?

How that would amuse the people of Swansea, toffee-nosed Bridie Marchant in love with a servant. So what? It had happened before, look at Emily Grenville and John Miller. They had set the town on its heels quite a few years ago by getting married, the rich heiress and the poor cobbler. It had been the talk of Swansea for a time and yet now the couple were accepted everywhere. Not that she could ever think of marrying Collins. She was of good Catholic stock, divorce was certainly not an option for her. In any case, Paul was the father of her sons and he now held the purse-strings. He had her just where he wanted her and even in her most optimistic moments, she could not see a clear way out of her dilemma.

While Paul was away, she had pondered on how she would react when he returned home. Should she accuse him outright of robbing her? Tell him that she believed he had turned smuggler into the bargain? That course of action appealed to her but some sixth sense warned her she would need to be as devious as he was.

'That's enough for now, Mrs Marchant, mustn't overdo it.' Collins led her towards her chair, easing her into it. Bridie looked gratefully up at him. 'Do you know, I'm not as tired as I usually am, perhaps I'm getting stronger.'

Collins gave one of his slow smiles, his face took on a new warmth and she saw with a feeling of tenderness that he was as happy for her as she was for herself.

'What's your name, Collins?' She laughed. 'I mean your Christian name, of course.'

'Simon Peter, my mother was a very religious woman,' Collins smiled, 'I think she had dreams of me becoming a lay preacher or something of the sort.'

Simon. Bridie turned the name over in her mind, it was ironic that a woman who had once had everything she could desire had found the only one to stand by her in adversity was a servant called Simon.

Collins looked through the open door at the clock in the hall. 'The *Marie Clare* will have docked by now, perhaps I should go down to the Ship Inn and meet our Mr Hewson.'

Bridie felt as nervous as a child at the thought of what she might learn from Hewson. What revelations would he make, would he have found Paul out in some illicit deal, perhaps? She swallowed hard, soon she would be face to face with Paul, what would he say, what would she say? She didn't know if it was possible to keep her tongue still, to keep her bitter thoughts to herself. Yet there was nothing to be gained by blurting out the truth, that she knew he had cheated her, tricked her into signing the papers that would give him everything. Should she tell him that she had covered his tracks, saved his face and her own by concealing the truth? The story published by the newspaper was the one she had asked Daniel to print, that being too sick to cope, she had willingly given her husband charge of all her assets. It would please him, of course it would, Paul was nothing if not a snob. He would not like to lose his standing in the community.

When Collins left the house, Bridie tried to occupy herself with the daily chores. She spoke to the cook and organized the evening meal, choosing deliberately to serve Paul's favourite dishes. Best by far to let him remain in ignorance, she decided bitterly, let him believe she was still his dupe. She bit her lip, how could he have been so grasping, so mercenary? And yet hadn't she been cheating him? Giving him the short trips, the less profitable trips, well if she had been wrong, her sins had found her out and she was paying for them a hundredfold one way or another.

It was about an hour later when Collins returned, his shoulders were slumped, he seemed dispirited. 'The man didn't turn up,' he said. 'I'm very much afraid he might have gone over to the other side.'

His words chilled Bridie, if Paul had been forewarned, he would have his defenses ready. Her one advantage now was that he didn't know she suspected him of smuggling. That was one ace she would keep up her sleeve.

'Well, if Hewson has told Paul everything, there is nothing we can do about it,' Bridie said softly. 'Paul will be on his guard from now on, we'd have no chance of spying on him. I might as well resign myself to the fact.'

Collins smiled. 'Excuse me, Mrs Marchant, but I can't see you ever being resigned to anything, you're a fighter, you've got spirit.'

His words warmed her, she held out her hand and caught Collins fingers in her own. 'Collins . . . Simon, I'm so grateful to you for all you've done, I wouldn't have got through all this without you.'

His colour rose as she squeezed his hand tightly. 'In the past I must have been a real bitch to work for,' she continued. 'I'm afraid I was brought up to judge people by what they had not what they were.' She paused still holding onto his hand. 'I've become very fond of you, you know that, don't you?'

Collins looked down at her gravely. 'I will always be your devoted servant, Mrs Marchant.'

Bridie sighed, he was a man who would always know his place, he would never be so forward as to give any indication of his own feelings.

It was late when Paul came home. He was smelling strongly of rum and there was a strange, gloating look

224

on his face. He entered Bridie's bedroom and sat beside her and she searched his face for any sign of the tenderness he'd shown her when she was sick.

In one of the upstairs rooms, there was the sound of activity, of maids shifting furniture, presumably stripping and remaking beds. Bridie looked up at her husband questioningly and he leaned over her and smiled. 'I've found out your little scheme, madam,' he said softly, 'I know you set a man to spy on me, a Matthew Hewson. Well, he was wise enough to see which side his bread was buttered, he knew who would pay him generously for his time. You insulted him by the pitiful advance payment you offered. Hewson isn't a stupid man, whatever you might think.' He paused, 'I worked it out and came to the conclusion that if you were spying on me, it could mean only one thing, you'd learned that I was now in control of the business.' He lifted his chin. 'And rightly so, in my opinion.'

He looked at her with something like triumph in his eyes. 'I'm glad everything is out in the open, it makes life so much easier for me.'

'I don't know what you are talking about and can you tell me just what is going on upstairs? The servants are making an awful lot of noise.' Bridie struggled to sit up against the pillows.

'I've brought home the woman I love,' Paul said. 'She is to live here, with us.'

'You can't mean it!' Bridie felt as though her heart had stopped beating. 'What of the scandal?'

'You, as the mother of my sons, may stay here for as long as you behave yourself and keep a civil tongue in your head. Carmella will be given the title of house-keeper but have no doubts about it, it is her bed I will be visiting and not yours.'

Bridie felt anger build up in her like a storm, she wanted to reach out and slap Paul's face, to slap and slap until the stupid smile was wiped away. Instead she looked at him silently, unbelievingly. He had the

225

audacity to sit there and tell her he had brought a mistress home, into her house, the property bought with her money. He meant to flaunt the woman before Bridie's very eyes, to humiliate her, his wife. Then, strangely, she was calm. Did she really care what woman Paul had this time? He was bad through and through, he was not worthy of her love.

He rose to his feet. 'Oh, by the way, I know what part Collins took in your little scheme so I've dismissed him,' he said. 'He packs up his things and leaves first thing in the morning.'

Bridie drew a ragged breath of disbelief. 'You've done what?' she could barely speak she was so angry, so frightened.

'You heard me, I'll teach you to spy on me, to cheat me, making money hand over fist from deep sea trade while I had the scraps.'

'I've cheated you?' she said incredulously, 'That's rich, it's you who made me sign the business over to you, you who took advantage of a sick woman, how dare you accuse me of cheating?'

'Well you'd better watch your mouth and you'd better learn to give me a little respect, something you've never done in all our married life.'

'But Collins is the only friend I have in the world,' Bridie protested. 'I can't manage without him, if Collins goes, I go, too.'

Paul looked down at her disdainfully. 'In love with a servant now, I see, well, we have come down in the world.' He regarded her almost cruelly for a long moment. 'But then you haven't very much to offer these days, have you?'

He left the room and Bridie fell back on her pillows dry-eyed, wondering how it was she had ever believed that Paul loved her. What was happening to her lately? Her world had come crashing down on her so suddenly and with such a devastating effect that she didn't know what to think any more, let alone what to feel. She closed her eyes wearily, she was too tired now to sort out the chaos in her mind, far too tired, she must sleep, she simply must sleep.

In the morning, she had one of the maids pack a bag for her, she had only the vaguest idea where she would go but she knew she couldn't stay in the same house as Paul and his woman.

'Get Collins for me,' she said to the maid and the girl bobbed a curtsey, her eyes pitying.

Bridie was desperate and she knew it. She had no money to go to an hotel, she had no close friends. The only place she could think of where she would be welcome was her cousin's house in Clydach. Jono would look after her; big, kind-hearted Jono would take her into his home and no questions asked. He would take Collins, too, she felt sure of it, she needed Collins, he would continue to help her walk again. Her health would improve and one day soon, when she was strong, she would see that Paul got his just deserts.

Paul entered the room as though drawn by the force of her anger, he stared down at her, his eyes narrowed. 'And where do you think you are going?'

'That's my business,' Bridie said coldly. 'I'm not staying here, that's for sure.'

'How do you expect to travel in your state?' Paul was frowning, doubtless he was wondering how her abrupt departure would reflect on him. His next words confirmed her suspicion. 'And what do you think people are going to say?'

Bridie glanced up at him, her lips were trembling. 'I hope you are proud of yourself, Paul, you've humiliated me, left me penniless, virtually forced me to leave my own home, what do you think people are going to say?' She shook her head.

'And what do you think your sons are going to do if you leave home?' Paul demanded. 'That's something you've failed to consider, they'll be home soon from their trip, they will want you to be here. Look, I'll make you

227

an allowance, you will be cared for, no need to worry about that.'

'Thank you!' Bridie felt like hitting him. 'How very generous of you to offer me the crumbs of my own fortune. Well you can keep your offer, I will not stay here and be humiliated any more. I'm leaving you Paul and you can tell people what you wish I no longer care. As for my sons, when they come home it will be their mother they will want, not the man who calls himself father but scarcely ever sees them.'

'If you leave this house now, you will never see the boys again, I'm warning you, Bridie.'

There was a light tapping on the door and Collins entered the room. He didn't look at Paul. 'You wanted me, Mrs Marchant.'

'Yes Collins, I'll need you to take me to the station.'

'Collins!' Paul's voice was sharp, 'Don't do any such thing, I'm ordering you to leave us alone.'

Collins looked at him steadily. 'You no longer employ me, sir, I accept orders from no-one but Mrs Marchant.'

Seeing the resolution in the man's face, Paul turned to Bridie, 'Where will you go, what will you do for money?'

'I always have some petty cash in the house, if you'd ever taken an interest in the running of the place you'd know that. As for where I'm going, that's my business.'

'I mean it, Bridie, you'll lose the boys, you'll lose everything if you walk out.'

Bridie ignored him. 'Collins will you carry me to the hallway please?'

Collins took her easily in his arms and Paul made one last attempt. 'Bridie, don't do this, you'll be sorry.'

'I'm sorry now,' she said over Collins' shoulder, 'sorry to learn what a fool I was to ever trust you.'

It was cold outside with an easterly wind blowing along the curving driveway but Bridie, seated in her chair, was warm and comfortable. Collins had thoughtfully provided a rug which he tucked snugly around her legs. Bridie looked up at him, gratitude to this man who had been no more than a servant washing over her.

'We'll go to my cousin's house,' she said over her shoulder as Collins wheeled her along the drive towards the huge double gates leading out of the estate, 'Jono will take care of everything. You will stay with me won't you, Collins?'

'Where else would I go, Mrs Marchant? My place is with you.' His tone was matter of fact and Bridie felt a smile curve the corners of her mouth. She might have lost everything she had once held dear but she had gained much too. She was learning to walk again, she was learning a new humility and most important, she was beginning to realize just how much Collins cared for her.

It was late afternoon by the time Bridie reached her cousin's house. The building was modest, made of warm stone it was situated on top of the hill, looking out over the small village spread along the line of the canal.

Collins knocked on the door and a young maid opened it almost as though she had been expecting them. Behind her, in the cheerfully lit hall, was Jono, a smile spreading across his face as he saw her.

'Bridie, my little love, you're looking better than when I saw you last in Swansea, bit more colour in your cheeks. You're not so thin, either. Come into the warm, I've got a lovely fire burning in the grate.' He looked at her bag. 'You come to stay then?'

'If you'll have me, Jono.' She held her breath as between them, Jono and Collins lifted her chair over the few steps leading into the main body of the house.

'My house is your house *cariad*, you know that.' Jono looked down from his great height and, tall though Collins was, Jono towered over him.

'This is Simon Collins,' Bridie explained, 'he's a very dear friend.'

229

'In that case, Collins, you are very welcome, too.' Jono pumped his hand and Bridie hid a smile knowing that Collins was more than a little embarrassed at being accepted as an equal.

'I have no money, Jono,' Bridie said when she was settled before the blazing fire. 'It's a long story, I'll tell you all about it later but right now I could do with a wash and a long rest.'

'Both those things are easy enough to provide,' Jono said in his slow voice. 'As for money, I've got enough for both of us.' He left the room for a moment and he could be heard issuing orders to the maid to prepare two of the spare rooms and then to fetch some hot water.

Bridie looked at Collins who was standing uneasily near the door as if wondering what to do next. She smiled, 'Sit down, for goodness sake, there's no use trying to stand on ceremony with Jono, he just won't have it.'

Her cousin returned to the room. 'You know I've done very well these last few years,' he said easily. 'There's more than enough to go around so you must stay with me just so long as it suits you, right?'

Bridie nodded, 'Right.' Jono had never been short of money but since he had invested in Arian Smale's newspaper business, he had become quite wealthy. Whatever he had, he had earned it. Jono put his back into the work he did for Arian Smale. Before the publication of *The Swansea Times* he had rescued the printing machines from the cellar where they had been rusting for years. He had renovated them, treated them lovingly until they were functioning effortlessly again. He had put funds into the enterprise too and Arian Smale had been generous in repaying her debt of gratitude to him.

Bridie settled back in her chair, waiting with a patience newly learned for her room to be prepared. Jono was seated on her right, his long legs stretched out before the fire. Opposite, on the other side of the fire sat

Collins. There was silence but it was an easy, comfortable silence and Bridie felt more at peace than she had done for a very long time.

Collins was covertly watching her and she was well aware of his scrutiny. He was so necessary to her she mused, and she would never have known the real man at all if it had not been for the events that had changed her life. Who would have thought that in so short a time she would have been cheated out of her dignity as a wife and out of her fortune? She was, in one stroke of the pen, worse off than any of her servants. And yet she was content, she was warm, she was welcomed and she was, she realized, almost happy.

Matthew felt inordinately pleased with himself. He'd been very clever fooling Bridie Marchant who had thought to buy him off with a paltry few pounds. Everyone in Swansea knew how rich Bridie Marchant was, or had been before her husband had outsmarted her, taken all her money. Paul Marchant was a man after Matthew's own heart. Not that he would have hesitated to expose him as a crook if it had been in his best interests but the more he spied, something he found he was very good at, the more he had learned about the man and his nefarious dealings. It had been a good day for him when he'd discovered the opium in the hold, safely secreted inside the leather tack.

At first he had intended to go to Bridie Marchant with his findings, figuring out that when she claimed back her empire he would be richly rewarded. But that would have taken a great deal of time so he had decided it was better to work out the true lie of the land and how wise he'd been.

It was when he was deliberately eavesdropping on Paul Marchant's conversation with his lady friend that the truth had become clear. Marchant had been bedding the girl, something Matthew would have liked to have done himself, she was a real Irish beauty. Marchant had

231

been boasting to her of his cleverness. He told her he'd managed to get a hold of all his wife's assets, she was in his power, she would be obliged to do just as she was told. He'd made plans to take his little whore home with him on his next trip and when she had protested that her parents wouldn't willingly let her go, he'd promised he'd see them all right. It was then that Matthew had decided which side he would take.

At first Marchant had tried to bluff him. He had blustered, bluffed and argued until, at last, Matthew had produced his ace, had shown him the small packet of opium he'd taken from inside one of the leather horse-collars.

'I can be of use to you, Mr Marchant,' Matthew had urged, 'a man like me can do a great many useful things.'

'Prove it,' Marchant had taken up the challenge, 'get rid of someone who has become a nuisance and you've got a job for life.'

Charlesworth was the master of the *Marie Clare* but it seemed he also had too much knowledge of the deals in which his boss was involved.

'He's become a threat,' Marchant said bleakly, 'I want to be rid of him.'

It was easy to arrange an unexpected ride for Charlesworth in a boat heading for Hong Kong; the man had never known what hit him, one moment he was returning to Ma Murphy's ale house, the next he was on board a foreign ship. It was doubtful if the man would survive the trip, he was travelling as part of the crew and the ship's master was one who believed in blows rather than reason. No, Charlesworth was well out of the picture. And Marchant had been suitably gratified.

Now Matthew was on his way towards Glyn Hir Tannery, he would be seeing Ellie again and this time, he would have the whip hand. He would be clever enough to make money out of her as well as out of Paul Marchant.

The yard was just the same, the stink of the leather,

the noise of the grinder were all familiar to him and for a moment, a wave of something like nostalgia swept over Matthew. He had enjoyed his life here, making up to Ellie while at the same time having a fine old time with Rosie. He saw the same men in the yard, Luke and Harry looked up and nodded as he passed but there was no welcome in their faces. Well to hell with them, he needed no-one. Boyo looked out of the grinding house, he was taller, bigger built now but Matthew could still beat the living daylights out of him if he chose to.

Ellie was not pleased to see him. She stared at him blankly for a moment and her small figure barred his entrance into the house.

'I must talk to you, in private,' he said bluntly, 'it's in your own best interests Ellie, I'm warning you, you're in deep trouble and I've come to help you out.'

'I don't know what you can possibly mean,' Ellie was adamant. 'Please go away, Matthew, I don't want you here.'

Matthew glanced around him and spoke in a low voice. 'Do you know you have been aiding and abetting Paul Marchant to smuggle opium out of the country and into Ireland?'

'Rubbish!' Ellie stepped back as though his words were a physical blow. 'If this is the truth why haven't you gone to the constabulary with this tale?'

'Because I wanted to protect your good name, Ellie,' Matthew said smoothly.

'I'm not such a fool as to believe that.' Ellie looked at him for a long moment. 'You'd better come in and tell me the whole story.' She reluctantly held the door wider and let him into the hall, 'Now either come to the point, tell me why you are really here or get out and leave me in peace.'

'The leather you sold Marchant, it was for tack, collars, saddles that sort of thing.'

'Yes?' Ellie stared at him, 'Our waggons delivered the skins to the saddler's and then to Marchant's ships, so

233

what?' Her head was high, her expression one of distaste and Matthew felt anger begin to burn inside him. He didn't fancy her, she was far too prissy for that but he'd love to bed her just to teach her who was boss.

'So, your leather was paid for very generously, wouldn't you say?'

'I sold it for the going rate.' Ellie was frowning, 'I don't see how you can accuse me of anything illegal. Get to the point, Matthew for heaven's sake.'

'You recommended the saddler, didn't you?' Matthew said with maddening slowness.

'Yes, I did and he's a good man.'

'Oh, he's a good man, all right,' Matthew laughed shortly. 'The saddler was the one who placed the opium inside the tack, that way there was no duty to pay on it, you see?' He looked at her shrewdly. 'Of course you will say you don't know anything about it, you'll put the blame on the saddler. He will say different, I've already spoken to him.' Matthew paused to let his words take effect.

'Even if folk think *you* are innocent, they will not believe Jubilee didn't know anything about it, this little scheme has been going on since before his death.'

In that moment, Ellie felt fury run through her like a torrent, she had never hated anyone in her life, but for Matthew Hewson she could make an exception. He would stop at nothing, he would stoop so low as to besmirch the good name of a man no longer able to speak up for himself.

'Now,' Matthew said, 'if you look at your books properly you will see that your payment for the leather was way above the going rate, why was that? Questions will be asked such as why buy from you when Marchant could buy good leather at any number of places much more cheaply.'

Ellie shook her head, trying to think clearly but her mind was clouded with anger and she couldn't marshall her thoughts into any sort of order.

Matthew spoke again, softly, insistently, 'People will think you were a willing accomplice. You see, Ellie, things are beginning to look bad for you.'

Ellie forced herself to be calm. 'We can settle this now, I'm sure you are wrong about the payment made to us by Paul Marchant.' Ellie led the way through the house to where the books were kept. 'Caradoc Jones, my accountant, he's not mentioned anything about all this extra money you say I've had.'

She thumbed through the books, and stopped when she came to the relevant sheets. She was not very good at figures but even she could see that the income from the leather sold to Paul Marchant was, as Matthew had claimed unusually high. 'I must talk to Caradoc,' she said almost to herself, 'ask him what this is all about.'

'I've told you what it's about,' Matthew was growing impatient, 'it's about you being an accomplice to smuggling, that's what it's about.' He paused. 'And what would that fancy boyfriend of yours think about it and him going into the church? Wouldn't look good for him, would it, consorting with criminals.'

Ellie put down the books. 'What's all this to you, anyway? What do you want, what do you really want, Matthew?'

Matthew felt himself relax. 'I want what I was promised by your husband, by Jubilee, but now my demands won't be so modest.' He looked at her with narrowed eyes, 'And as for talking to Caradoc or anyone else, if I were you, I'd keep my mouth shut, people don't understand this sort of thing, they have scruples, they do silly things like going to the police.'

Ellie felt trapped. 'I want proof that what you say is the truth,' she said desperately, 'I can't believe the Marchants would be mixed up in this sort of thing. Give me dates and times of sailing, I want to know who Paul Marchant's contact is in Ireland and I want to see the leather in which you say this opium was smuggled.'

'You don't want much, do you?' Matthew asked with

sarcasm. 'What makes you think I'd give you all that information?'

'I might just sign over to you half my inheritance from Jubilee if I think it's worth it.' She looked directly at Matthew, estimating the power of his greed. 'We could do it almost at once but I want proof of what you have told me before I take any action, wouldn't you do the same in my place?'

'How can I trust you?' Matthew said hesitantly.

Ellie shook back a curl of hair from her brow. 'You'll just have to, won't you, what choice have you got? If there's proof of what you've told me, I'll have to pay up, if not, you are wasting my time and yours.'

Matthew took a small packet out of his pocket. 'Here is some of the opium,' he said showing it to her.

She shook her head. 'Opium it may be but how do I know where you got it from? Oh no, Matthew, you are going to have to do better than that, it's only reasonable I'd want convincing, didn't you think of that?'

'Of course I did,' he said quickly but of course he hadn't. He'd imagined that Ellie would crack at once, would pay him anything not to have the good name of her dead husband besmirched. She had grown tougher since he'd last seen her, more resilient.

He moved closer and touched her hair lightly. She looked up at him. 'I might give you money,' she said, 'I just might but don't think you'll get anything else from me, I'd kill you first.'

He stepped away from her, he wasn't used to being spurned and Ellie had done it once too often. 'I don't want you, don't flatter yourself,' he said sulkily.

Ellie smiled but it didn't reach her eyes. 'We're even then,' she said, 'I wouldn't fancy you if you were the last man left alive on earth. Now please leave my house and don't come back until you have what I want.'

When Matthew left the yard, it was with mixed feelings; he'd expected to come out of all this on top, to add Ellie's contribution to the money Paul Marchant was already paying him but here he was sent away like a whipped dog. He ran his hands through his hair, she would pay and good, he'd bring her the proof she wanted, she wouldn't dare talk to anyone else about it. In the meantime, he would go to see the saddler, persuade him that it would be in his interest to do whatever Matthew wanted of him. It would not be difficult to get the man to implicate Ellie, to say it was all her idea that they hide the contraband inside the saddles and collars. It was the waggons from Glyn Hir that had delivered the leather to the saddler and had collected the finished articles of tack some time later. Oh, yes, it would appear to anyone interested that Ellie Hopkins, or at least her husband Jubilee, had been in on the scheme from the beginning. He would beat her yet, just let her wait and see.

After Matthew had gone, Ellie went into the kitchen and sank into one of the wooden chairs. She put her head in her hands and closed her eyes.

'What's up, missus, you look like death?' Rosie had come into the kitchen and was standing beside her.

'I've just had a visit from Matthew,' Ellie said with a sigh, 'he's after money again.' Ellie did not choose to go into too much detail, Rosie meant well but she was an incurable gossip.

'Still on about them shares, is he? Your husband should never have promised him anything.' Rosie was still bitter about the way Matthew had treated her. 'He's a no-good and he's a dangerous no-good, you look out for him.'

'Oh, I will.'

'Anyway, let me take your mind off things,' Rosie sat opposite her, plump arms on the scrubbed surface of the table, 'I've heard a bit of gossip.'

'No, really?' The irony was lost on Rosie, she leaned forward eagerly.

'Mrs Marchant has left her husband, been forced out

of her own home, so the gossips are saying. *He's* gone and brought in some fancy piece from Ireland, says she's a housekeeper, a bedwarmer more like it, and no woman is going to stand for that. Course the rich will turn a blind eye to it all, as they usually do when it comes to one of their own. So long as that man Marchant don't parade his lady love in public no-one will say a word against him. All at it, they are, if you ask me.'

Ellie looked up. 'Where on earth would Bridie go in her state of health?' she asked and Rosie shrugged.

'Blowed if I know but all she got with her is that funny chair she had made for herself and a change of clothes. Took one of the servants too so I heard. Suppose she had to have someone, her not being able to walk.'

Ellie sat up straighter, this needed looking into, there was something very strange going on and it seemed that what concerned the Marchants was going to concern her too if she was ever to get Matthew Hewson out of her life. But she knew where she might be able to learn more about Bridie, if anyone could make an educated guess it would be Arian Smale, she and her newspaper hounds seemed to know everything.

Ellie felt her spirits lift, Matthew believed he had the upper hand, well she wasn't so stupid as he thought, she would find out the truth herself, she would speak to Paul Marchant, it would be in his own best interests to refute Matthew's absurd claims. She rose to her feet, she had to be alone, she needed to think things through away from everyone, even Martha. 'I'll go through into the study,' she said, 'and Rosie, you'd better take some hot milk up to Martha, I know she went to bed early but she won't be sleeping yet.'

When she was seated in the big leather chair, in what had once been Jubilee's retreat, Ellie bit her lip trying to sort out her muddled thoughts. If what he claimed was anything like the truth, she might have to give Matthew half her money just to get him to leave her alone but she would have to make sure he didn't come back for more and keep coming back. The last thing she wanted was another scandal in her life, especially now that she had Daniel to consider. Matthew knew her weak spots, all right, Jubilee's good name and Daniel's too were more important than Ellie's own.

But she wouldn't give up without a fight, she would learn all she could about Paul Marchant's affairs, arm herself with every possible weapon of defence and perhaps, just perhaps, she might get the best of Matthew Hewson.

CHAPTER SIXTEEN

Paul Marchant looked at Ellie Hopkins as if she had taken leave of her senses, she had called this evening meeting claiming it was urgent and yet she was sitting there so calm and composed anyone would think they were here to discuss the weather.

He was seated in his ships offices behind his imposing desk, his brief Christmas holiday over and he was not feeling in very good spirits. His sons had come home from their trip abroad and far from being grateful for the fine time they'd had, they got on his nerves by whining for their mother throughout the festive season. They hated Carmella on sight and had driven the young Irish girl to distraction. In despair, Paul had arranged for the two boys to go to visit his aunt in Shrewsbury vowing that whatever happened, he would never allow Bridie the satisfaction of knowing she had been right about her sons' wishes all along.

'Mr Marchant, this is very difficult but there is no other way than to be blunt,' Ellie spoke firmly. 'I want Matthew Hewson to stop trying to blackmail me or I might be compelled to take further action.' Ellie's eyes were large in her pale face. Paul waited in silence for her to continue, he had no intention of revealing his hand, not until he knew what it was she had in hers. 'These illicit dealings you might or might not be involved in have nothing to do with me, I am not interested so long as I am left alone.' When Paul didn't reply she continued more urgently. 'You do know what he's saying about you, don't you?'

'Blackmail, that's a nasty word, Mrs Hopkins,' Paul

was prevaricating, wondering how much this woman really knew of his affairs. 'As for illicit dealings, I'm not sure I know what you are talking about.'

'The smuggling of opium in the leather you bought from me, that's what I'm talking about.' She sounded impatient and Paul realized there was no point in avoiding the issue, Hewson had really spilled all he knew, the fool.

'Unfortunately no-one is going to believe that *you* are not involved,' Paul was still confident. 'So I would just go home and keep your head down and your lips closed.'

'And allow Matthew Hewson to blackmail me?' Ellie leaned forward in her chair. 'Don't you understand?' Paul heard the tone of desperation in her voice. 'This man is a threat to me and to you, too.'

'Oh, I hardly think so.' Paul toyed with the silver paper knife on the polished surface of the desk, 'Who is going to say anything to the authorities without incriminating themselves?'

'So in other words you are hand in glove with Hewson, you are condoning what he is doing.' Ellie's shoulders sagged and Paul, watching her, felt a moment of triumph; good, the woman knew when she was beaten. He had admired her looks, had been nice to her in their past dealings but she had always seemed a bit above herself for the wife of a tannery owner.

Paul's first reaction to the fact that Hewson had told his little story to Ellie Hopkins had been one of anger but, on second thoughts, he saw clearly that the scheme to get a share of Ellie Hopkins' not inconsiderable fortune might benefit him too. From all accounts Ellie was now a very rich widow. If Hewson had a windfall coming, Paul wanted a share in it. As for the smuggling, he could give that up if it became too dangerous. At the moment, though he was getting richer by the minute and it was a feeling he very much liked.

He was on top of the world, he had rid himself of Bridie, not that he'd meant her to actually leave home, but now she had gone he was free to indulge himself as much as he liked with his little Irish colleen. He was very discreet when visiting her room but in any case the servants knew better than to gossip about him and what's more Carmella had won most of them over with her pale Irish beauty. His feelings softened, Carmella was the one woman he knew who loved him for himself, not for what she could get out of him. Take Bridie, his dear wife, she had spent years keeping secret books, making money to salt away in her own account, it was doubtful if she had ever loved him. It was madness at his age to fall in love when he had avoided it for so long but Carmella was irresistible, he wanted to hold her in his arms and make love to her whenever he saw her. Every other woman paled into insignificance when he looked into Carmella's lovely face.

He had never enjoyed his role as second in command to Bridie; to be accepted in society only because he was her husband had been a blow to his ego. Well now he was in charge of his own destiny and everyone would have to learn their place.

'I'm sorry,' he said calmly, 'it appears I am unable to help you.' He rose to his feet indicating the interview was at an end. Ellie rose too but she looked at him levelly, her eyes open and clear and for a moment, Paul felt uneasy.

'He's dangerous, make no mistake about it, Matthew Hewson is not to be trusted. He'll turn on you when it suits him. He thinks only of himself, so I'd advise you to watch your back when he's around.'

'It's you must watch your back, Mrs Hopkins,' Paul said quickly, a little too quickly.

She shook her head. 'I'll tell you one thing, if Matthew pushes me too hard I'll go the authorities, I don't care what the consequences might be, I won't be blackmailed by someone like him. And have you thought of what would happen to you if I did that? Action would have to be taken. Everything about your business would be scrutinized, I don't think you would like that one bit.'

For a moment Paul was uneasy but he forced a smile. 'I would claim I had no knowledge of any illicit dealings,' he said loudly. 'It was my wife's ships which brought in the contraband from abroad, I'd say that was the reason we separated.' He smiled more easily now, he was still on top of everything. 'I'd say I hadn't the heart to turn my wife, my poor sick wife, over to the Customs and Excise men but that on the other hand, I couldn't live with what she'd done.' He leaned forward and stared hard at Ellie and she flinched visibly. 'And if I did go down, believe me I'd drag a lot of other people with me.'

He knew she was convinced, he saw it by the set of her face and the sudden drawing in of her breath. For a moment he felt almost sorry for her. 'One word of advice, Mrs Hopkins,' he said more quietly, 'keep Matthew happy, give him what he wants, it might save you a great deal of grief in the long run.'

The next morning, he called in to the office to pick up some papers he needed and as Brian Thomas was not yet in, he poured over the books just to reassure himself that his profits were increasing. After a time, he took his hat and coat from the stand, he had no intention of remaining all day in the office. In any case, Brian Thomas would be back any time now, he could look after things, that was what he was being paid for.

Now it was time for Paul to see Hewson, give him the sharp edge of his tongue. Tell him he knew Hewson was greedy, couldn't keep his trap shut. Warn him to ease up a little on the Widow Hopkins, pushing too hard might only serve to crack her and then she would go whining to the police.

Paul went first to the drab but respectable boarding house where Hewson was staying, the man had some sense, he didn't make a show of the money he'd suddenly acquired. On the other hand, the lady who owned the place was not unattractive, a little on the full-blown side, her features rather heavy, but Mrs Griffiths was passable and Matthew was doubtless paying some of his rent, at least, in kind.

'*Duw*, not here, not Mat, not this time of the day, you'll find him in the public bar of the Castle if I'm any judge, don't know when he's going to find a decent job.'

She was talking like a wife already, Paul observed, they were all the same, give them an inch and they took a mile. Well, no, not all of them, not his little Carmella, she was different. A glow of satisfaction spread through him, he'd go to the Castle, have a word with Matthew and then go home and take Carmella to bed. What was the use of having plenty of money if he didn't do what he wanted with his time?

The bar was crowded, smoke-filled and in the corner a ragged, vociferous group of men were playing cards. The floor was covered in sawdust and the furniture comprised of old beer barrels sawn in half and upturned. Paul spotted Matthew at once, he was a big man, handsome too if you cared for the rugged type. And yet the man was no dullard. He was quite literate and particularly articulate which was one reason Paul had decided to use him. But he needed putting in his place, reminding who was boss.

'Afternoon,' Paul stood beside Matthew, Paul the shorter by almost six inches but with the whip hand for all that.

'Afternoon, Marchant.' Paul was not thrilled with the over-familiar tone of the man's voice but in the circumstances he could hardly protest. For a moment he wondered if by getting rid of Charlesworth and taking on Matthew he'd only substituted one problem for another.

'We need to talk. Get me a mug of ale.' Paul moved to a chair near the window where it was fairly quiet. He hadn't missed Hewson's rather indignant raising of the eyebrows at his tone but right at this moment, he didn't care.

'Anything wrong?' Matthew thumped the mug of ale

on the table spilling some of it but Paul ignored the man's obvious ill humour.

'Could be,' he said. 'The Widow Hopkins has been to see me, a little irate she was, too.' He paused to allow his words to sink in and Matthew, for a moment, looked suitably uneasy.

'What's the bitch been saying?' He sat and hunched his big frame forward on the upturned barrel.

'That you opened your big mouth.' Paul went on the attack. 'You must bite your tongue in future, I don't like you slinging mud at my good name, it might just stick.'

Hewson was silent and Paul relaxed in his chair. 'On the other hand, I don't see why we shouldn't make use of the little lady.'

'We?' Matthew appeared genuinely surprised. 'What's it got to do with you?'

'I paid you good money to keep quiet, that's what,' Paul said with emphasis. 'You couldn't keep your mouth shut but perhaps there's no harm done just so long as you remember we are in this together.' He took a sip of his ale, it was good and strong, tasting of the wood in which it had been stored. 'Keep her involved in our future enterprises, make her part of it so that she can't wriggle off the hook. Soon, she'll be in so deep she won't be able to get out.'

'I doubt she'll supply us with any more leather,' Hewson said sourly, 'and there's no way we can force her into selling her stock if she doesn't want to.'

'I have already bought more stock,' Paul said easily, 'this new manager Mrs Hopkins has taken on, Smithers, he and I go back a long way. He'll go on providing the leather for as long as I need it.' Paul did not see any point in adding that it had been a stroke of pure luck he knew Smithers, let Hewson believe Paul had had everything under control from the beginning.

Paul saw Hewson's guarded look of admiration and it made him feel good. 'The wagons from Glyn Hir have already delivered a fresh load of skins to the saddler, I

245

don't waste any time putting my plans into action, you see.' Paul paused, savouring his own cleverness. 'Smithers realizes how well he'll be paid if he does what I say. I've taken the trouble to grease his pockets, soon we'll have Mrs Hopkins so tied up that she won't be able to threaten us with anything.'

He was aware that Matthew was looking at him with respect and he smiled. 'If you play this game properly,' he said slowly, meaningfully, 'there's no reason why we both shouldn't make a fine profit.'

Matthew wasn't stupid, he was being told that he was a bit player in the game, Paul was the star. It was a role Matthew Hewson seemed able to accept and Paul felt a sense of triumph. 'So long as we both know where we stand, we shall get along fine.'

'Poor Charlesworth,' he added seemingly without reason. 'Didn't know when he was well off.' Matthew would know what he was saying all right, Paul had rid himself of one thorn in his flesh, he was capable of doing it again.

Out in the street once more, Paul breathed deeply of the fresh winter air. The clouds lay low over the hill tops, obscuring the peaks, wreathing them in greyness. The sea, running swiftly into the shore was pewter, cold looking, even the white caps appeared to be touched with ice. Well, winter might be holding the town in an icy thrall but Paul felt nothing could spoil his sense of well being. At last, he was his own boss, he answered to no-one, indeed, folk jumped when he told them to jump.

He sighed in self-satisfaction and lifted his hand to hail the cab that was standing idle in the gutter, the horse, head down, moving restlessly between the shafts as though eager to move away from the hard cobbles. Soon, Paul thought as he settled back in the cold leather seat, soon he would be home in the big, comfortable house that was now his, and very soon, he would be in bed with Carmella making sweet love to her, it was a good life.

Ellie returned home feeling drained and helpless, it seemed there was nothing she could do to rid herself of Matthew's unwanted attentions. She knew he would take everything he could from her, even her dignity if she would allow him. He would impose himself upon her physically if he could, simply to teach her that he had the upper hand. Well, she would kill herself rather than let him touch her.

Smithers was in the yard, overseeing the loading of the wagons with the heavy skins. The manager was no youngster, his hair was greying at the temples and he had a thick body and short neck so that his head seemed sunken onto his shoulders. But his references had been good, he had spoken simply and honestly at the interview, he was strong and had a determined thrust to his chin and Ellie had been happy to take him on.

'Everything under control?' Ellie asked pausing by the waggons, rubbing the soft head of one of the horses.

'Aye, missus, everything is under control.' His tone was clipped and she nodded and moved on, she didn't want to interfere, she was paying him to take charge and that was just what Smithers was doing.

'Well, where have you been?' Martha was sitting near the fire looking up from her sewing, her face was tinged with red, a sign that she was displeased.

'I've been to see Paul Marchant if you must know,' Ellie said lightly, 'I know I should have asked you to come but you were having a little doze and I didn't like to disturb you.'

'I wasn't asleep!' Martha said quickly. 'I was just resting my eyes. Anyway, what's it all about?'

'Just business.' Ellie had no intention of involving Martha in what was, to say the least, an unsavoury situation.

'Well I would have liked a walk in the fresh air.' Martha grumbled but her tone had softened, she could not be angry with Ellie for long.

'When you were out, guess who called?' she said, her eyes glinting.

Ellie's heart lifted. 'Don't say Daniel's been here and I've missed him?'

'Aye, Daniel has been here and you have missed him and it serves you right for not telling me where you were going because he would have come to look for you.'

Ellie felt uneasy, if Dan was searching for her it could only mean one thing that he was going away to college and soon. Well, there was nothing she could do, she could hardly go chasing after him, it wouldn't be proper to go to his parents' home, not until she and Dan were officially engaged. She certainly didn't feel she could look for him in the offices of *The Swansea Times*, that would certainly set tongues wagging. There was nothing she could do but wait for him to call again.

She sighed and Martha smiled mischievously. 'It's all right, he's going to call again this evening,' she said relenting.

Ellie shook his head, 'You heartless woman, you had me worried there for a minute, I thought he might have gone away without seeing me.'

'No,' Martha said soberly, 'he wouldn't do that, not Daniel, he loves you too much. Anyone ever tell you you're a lucky woman Ellie Hopkins?'

While she was getting ready for Daniel's visit, Ellie was able to forget, for a while, the business of Matthew Hewson and his threats. She wanted so much to be with Dan, to be close to him. He was a fine man, all she could wish for in a husband, though that happy state of affairs was still very far away. In the meantime, he would work hard as a vicar, he was the kind of man who needed to follow what he looked on as his vocation but she knew once he had left for college, she would only be able to see him occasionally. She would miss him so much.

When he arrived, Ellie had to force herself to sit still while Rosie showed him into the sitting room. It was bright now with a fire glowing in the hearth and the curtains drawn against the cold. Daniel came across to Ellie and took her hand in his. She smiled up at him, his scent was of the cold, fresh air, the sea, the pine of the trees, she breathed him in, loving him so much.

After a few moments, Martha made an excuse to leave them alone and Daniel moved closer to Ellie on the huge, cushioned sofa.

'Ellie, I'll be leaving for the college on Monday,' he said softly. 'Don't look so distraught, Lampeter isn't all that far away and I'll write every day. Promise me you will, too.'

'Oh, Daniel, of course I'll write to you. Will you be happy there, at the college, I mean?'

'I'm very lucky to get in there, I will be older than most of the other students, you see,' he smiled, 'though at least I have a grounding in some of the subjects we'll be studying so I won't be at too much of a disadvantage.'

'How long will it take, before you are a priest, I mean?' Ellie asked, fearful at the thought of being separated from him.

'A few years, I suppose. But don't let's talk about my leaving, I'm here now, with you.'

He drew her gently towards him, looking down at her, as though drinking in the very essence of her. She closed her eyes, knowing he was going to kiss her. Her heart fluttered within her as though she was a silly girl who had never known the touch of a man. How she wished that was true, she regretted so much that she hadn't been able to offer herself to Daniel as a pure and innocent wife.

His mouth touched hers softly at first and then his kiss became deeper, more searching. His arms closed around her and she held onto him, her head spinning, her senses alive in a way she had never experienced before. The kiss seemed to go on for ever, it was as though they could never be closer than they were at this moment, no intimacy could be greater than this unspoken promise between them.

When at last he released her, Ellie had tears in her eyes. She touched Daniel's cheek with her fingertips. 'My love,' she whispered, 'my own love.' He would have taken her into his arms again but with an unnecessary amount of fuss and bustle, Martha was returning to the room, in her arm a snowy cloth, a sewing needle between her teeth. Daniel still held onto Ellie's hands, as though he couldn't bear to be separated from her. Martha turned away from them, pretending she needed the light from the lamp for her task.

Ellie smiled. 'It's all right, Martha, you're not intruding, come on, talk to us, we know you find it difficult to keep a still tongue in your head.'

'Cheek!' Martha said but she was smiling. 'I sometimes feel that being a chaperon is a harder job than folk think. Talk about being in the way.' She shrugged, 'But at least no-one can talk about you two, not while I'm around.' Ellie knew to whom Martha was referring, Rosie was a good worker but loved to gossip.

Daniel rose and walked across the room and stared out into the darkness. Ellie, watching him felt herself melt with tenderness, he was so young, so untried that for a moment she feared for him. Still, she told herself, he would be safe in college, he would be with like-minded men. She bit her lip, Daniel would have no defence against a man like Matthew Hewson, she must make sure that nothing ever happened to bring about a confrontation between them. She had been tempted to tell Daniel about the contraband smuggling, ask his advice, but now she thought better of it, she must protect him while she could from men who had no scruples, men like Matthew Hewson and Paul Marchant.

Matthew stretched a lazy arm outside the bedclothes and took up the unfinished glass of whisky, allowing the burning, amber liquid to slip along his throat. At his side, Dora Griffiths lay with her eyes closed, a sated look on her round features. She might not be all that much of a looker but she certainly knew how to please a man.

After a while, she sighed and opened her eyes, staring up at the cracked ceiling of his room. 'That was lovely, Mat,' she said softly, 'I enjoyed every minute of it.'

'I know,' Matthew said smugly, still it was good to hear a woman say it, a man needed to be told he'd proved himself.

Dora turned over towards him, her arm brushing his chest. 'A man came looking for you the other day,' she said, 'forgot to tell you. Posh geezer, he was, good line to his clothes but a manner you could cut with a knife. I told him you'd be down the Castle, was that all right?'

'Aye, I saw him,' Matthew said and he took another swig at the whisky, draining the glass. He hadn't been too pleased by Marchant's high-handed attitude, who did he think he was? He might be paying Matthew a good screw but then Matthew had him by his balls, he could drop him in trouble right up to his snooty nose if he chose.

'Get me some more whisky, girl,' he said and, obediently, Dora slid out of bed and padded naked across the room. He watched her, her hips and buttocks were a little rounded for some tastes but when she turned to come back to the bed, he saw her magnificent breasts, nipples hard in the cold and he forgot his momentary bad humour.

'Come here,' he said hoarsely, 'let's get back to business, shall we?'

Afterwards, Dora bade the serving girl to bring up jugs full of hot water for him to bathe, she knew how to look after a man and Matthew felt he could do far worse than stay where he was, at least for the time being. It was still early evening and he was restless, perhaps it was time he went to visit little Ellie Hopkins again, put a bit of pressure on her, got her to hand over some money. To hell with what Paul Marchant advised, he'd told him to lay off, go easy on the girl, perhaps he wanted to bed her, Paul Marchant was as susceptible as Matthew himself when it came to a pretty woman.

He dressed carefully, his suit was good worsted, brand spanking new, the only thing he'd felt able to splash out on. He knew he had to be careful, it wouldn't do to let folk see that a man out of a job had money to splash around. Soon, of course, he would be bound to sail with Paul's ship again, but this time he would have a bigger stake in the goods carried in the hold of the *Marie Clare*. For the moment, he needed Paul, needed the ships he used to bring in the contraband goods, needed the man's organizing ability. In any case, as it was, Matthew was taking very little risk, he couldn't be accused of anything except working on board a ship bound for Ireland.

If the Customs and Excise men were ever to raid the ship, he would simply be part of the crew, Paul Marchant would be the one to take the blame for any irregularity that might be found. And yet a slight uneasiness filtered into Matthew's mind, Paul had taken the trouble of involving Ellie, up to her neck, wouldn't he have taken the same precautions concerning Matthew himself? He would have to tread very carefully, he must take great pains to ensure there was nothing concrete to tie him in to the smuggling business.

Ellie was not at all pleased to see him. She met him in the dimly lit hallway of the house bordering the tannery and Matthew could tell from the voices issuing from the drawing room that she had company.

'I want paying,' he said bluntly, 'I'm sick of playing around, I want some money and fast.'

'All right,' Ellie said at once, 'I'll pay you, if that's what it takes for you to leave me alone.'

'Anything wrong, Ellie?' The pup Daniel Bennett was standing in the doorway as if he was master of the house, his eyes were guarded as they looked at Matthew.

'Keep out of this,' Matthew said. 'It's none of your business, get it?'

'If you are upsetting Ellie then it is my business.' The

newspaper man was as tall as Matthew himself but much slighter. He looked as if he'd never done a real day's work in his life.

'It's all right, Dan, really,' Ellie said quickly.

'Aye, you tell your fancy man to keep his nose out of this or it might just get busted.'

'There's no need of that,' Ellie said, 'I've told you I'll pay you, I'll get the money out of the bank tomorrow, come up here about three in the afternoon, I'll have it ready.'

'This had better not be a trick,' Matthew said, 'any funny business and you'll be sorry.'

'Will you leave this house and now?' Daniel said in a hard voice. Matthew moved forward, his fists bunched under Daniel's chin. 'And what if I don't little boy?' he sneered. 'What will you do about it, I could kill you and you know it.'

'Please Dan,' Ellie begged, 'let it go, I'll deal with it myself, I happen to owe Matthew some money, that's all.'

'Well he hasn't got a very gentlemanly way of asking for it.' Daniel had not backed away as Matthew had expected, he grasped him by the front of his starched shirt.

'Go back to your mother's milk, sonny,' Matthew said between gritted teeth, 'you can play with the big boys when you've grown up a bit.'

To his surprise, the young reporter moved rapidly, his fist lashed out, catching Matthew a blow to the nose. His head snapped back and he felt blood run down his chin.

'You bastard!' He lunged forward but another blow caught him across the eye, Daniel Bennett was stronger than he looked.

'Just leave it now,' the reporter had the gall to say, 'I don't want to fight you.'

'It's a bit late for that, I'm going to thrash you to within an inch of your miserable life.' Matthew flung himself forward thinking his weight would bear the lighter man to the ground but suddenly Daniel was not there. Confused, Matthew looked around just in time to feel a fist connecting painfully with the side of his temple.

It began to dawn on Matthew that Daniel Bennett was not the milksop he'd taken him to be, somewhere, somehow he'd taken lessons in boxing but a kick between the legs would knock all that nonsense out of him. Even before the thought was put into practice, Daniel had caught his raised foot and twisted it so that with a cry, Matthew was on the ground, his face crushed against the floor, Bennett's foot against the back of his neck.

Anger flowed in a blood red stream before his eyes and Matthew lay for a moment, winded, gathering his strength; a blind urge to kill filled him and he made to rise. Before he could move, Daniel was dragging him upright, twisting his arm behind his back, propelling him towards the door. He was outside then in the cold night air, his face stinging, his knee agonizingly painful as he tried to stand upright.

He turned for one last venomous look at Daniel. 'You think you're very clever but all the boxing tricks in the world won't stand up against the weight of an iron bar.'

He limped away from the tannery, his head full of thoughts of revenge. They would pay for this humiliation, both of them. Oh they might be laughing now but he, Matthew Hewson, would be the one to have the last laugh of all.

CHAPTER SEVENTEEN

Bridie sat in Jono's parlour looking out at the greyness of the winter day. She felt as cold as the frost that rimmed the windows. She felt a great sadness that Paul had kept her sons away from her over Christmas, the very time they should have been with her. Now, he'd sent them away, out of her reach, God knows where. It seemed he was determined to punish her even though he was the one who had betrayed every marriage vow he had ever made.

Well, Paul was part of her past now and even though she had lost her material possessions, she had found something else, the steady, undemanding love of Simon Collins. For love her he did, it was becoming more and more apparent every day.

She rose to her feet and leaning on her stick, moved close enough to the window to look into the garden. There he was, emerging from the coal shed, his shirt sleeves rolled up, as if he didn't feel the cold. He carried the heavy coal scuttles with ease, his hair, fine and blond fell over his face and Bridie felt her heart contract.

She studied him, he was young and strong, a virile man, what did he see in her? She had been a shrewish mistress, always carping and criticizing and yet when she was at her lowest ebb, it was Collins who had been at her side supporting her.

He had changed in the weeks they'd been at Clydach; he'd become straighter, more confident as though the burden of servility had been lifted from him. She had changed too, Bridie realized, the last remnants of the old, selfish Bridie James seemed to have been knocked out of her, firstly in the way Paul had betrayed her and later in her efforts to walk again. But in that she had succeeded. Encouraged not only by Collins but by her cousin Jono she was becoming stronger every day.

When she was reunited with her children, they would see not an invalid but the upright mother they had always known. That Paul would make every attempt to turn the boys against her she didn't doubt but she had taken the precaution of writing to them, telling them only that she was taking a holiday with Uncle Jono in Clydach until her health improved. She could only hope that Paul had sent her letter on to their sons.

A splash of bright colour near the gate caught Bridie's eye and she saw a woman coming towards the house. As the slight figure drew nearer, she recognized Ellie Hopkins, her face pale, her hair drawn back away from her face. She was still in mourning for her clothing was dark except for the yellow scarf she wore around her shoulders.

Bridie returned to her chair, her ability to walk was something she would keep secret, for now at least. She didn't want anyone going to Paul, telling him how well she was. She was biding her time, waiting until she was fully recovered and then she would take on Paul and a whole fleet of sailors if need be in order to have her inheritance restored to her.

Bridie was aloof as Ellie was shown into the parlour, she hadn't forgotten the angry scene at the docklands when Ellie had struck out at her. Not that she didn't deserve it, she had behaved like a fishwife, still it was with a grave face and even graver reservations that she looked up at the other woman.

'I'm surprised that you should come looking for me, of all people,' Bridie said when Ellie was seated in a chair at the other side of the room. 'No-one could call us friends.'

'I need to talk to you,' Ellie began with a rush, it was

clear she was nervous. Had Paul made the woman promises and then let her down? It was more than a possibility.

'Well talk away then, I'm listening.' Bridie's tone did not soften, she didn't see why she should be kind to this woman who for all she knew had slept with her husband.

'Your husband . . .' Ellie began and Bridie raised her hand impatiently.

'Whatever he's done, I don't want to hear it,' she said coldly. 'I have enough problems of my own without taking on yours too.'

'I thought we might work together,' Ellie said softly, 'I'd like to explain. I am being dragged into your husband's illicit dealing and being blackmailed by a man who used to work for me.'

'You must have done something wrong then, otherwise you wouldn't be subject to threats would you?'

'I sold leather to your husband, I had my wagons take the skins to the saddler's. I didn't know that the leather was being made into horse-collars and filled with contraband goods. I didn't know that your husband was paying me far more than the leather was worth, either.'

If Bridie was surprised she had no intention of allowing this woman to see it. 'You should know better than to become involved with a married man and you a widow,' she said unforgivingly.

'I was not involved with your husband, not in any way. I was never, I repeat, never unfaithful to Jubilee, I hoped you'd have come to realize that by now.'

'Why, what should have changed my mind?' Bridie asked guardedly, there was something in the way this woman spoke that rang true.

'Your husband has installed his woman friend from Ireland in your house as his so-called housekeeper, at least that's what the gossips are saying. That sort of relationship doesn't develop overnight. I'd have thought it perfectly obvious that Paul Marchant was not

257

interested in me except as someone stupid enough to be used by him.'

Perhaps Ellie was telling the truth, what she said made sense. Still, she wouldn't put it past Paul to indulge himself with the rich widow while having a fling in Ireland at the same time.

'Why should I believe anything you say?' Bridie asked, interested in spite of herself.

'Because I am telling you the truth and we can help each other,' Ellie spoke with conviction. Bridie attempted to look past the pretty, delicate appearance Ellie Hopkins presented to the woman within.

'Together we might manage to defeat Paul Marchant and Matthew Hewson,' Ellie was leaning forward earnestly. 'I'm sure you want your ships back, don't you? What *I don't* want is Jubilee's good name being dragged through the mud.'

'Of course I want my ships back but I don't particularly want my husband exposed to all the world as a criminal,' Bridie said carefully. 'What have you in mind?'

'I have a plan but I can't put it into action alone, I'll need help.'

'I'm listening,' Bridie said not hoping for too much yet unable to contain the rising excitement within her.

'I've learned that my manager is still supplying your husband with leather. My wagons take the skins to the saddler's workshop to be made up into tack. Later, my men collect the collars, saddles, and bridles and deliver the finished goods to the docks. The collars by now are filled with opium.'

Bridie nodded, this was just what she had suspected. 'Go on.'

'Two of my trusted drivers will change the load of horse collars, replace them with collars containing only rye grass.'

Bridie was not slow to realize the implications of what Ellie was proposing. Paul's connections in Ireland would not be happy to be duped, they might even turn ugly, something he would want to avoid at all costs.

'I see what a threat this would be to Paul, I don't love him any more, indeed, I think I despise him but he is the father of my children, I wouldn't want him harmed.'

'This is where I'll need help,' Ellie said. 'Someone must go to Ireland and you have the right contacts. Whoever you send must offer to bail your husband out on condition that he signs a few papers.'

'I see, it might just work. Paul would be so frightened he'd sign anything. I'd have my fortune restored to me, my ships would be under my control again. But what about you, what good would all this do you?'

'Well, if your husband would sign another document, absolving me and Glyn Hir Tannery from any involvement in his schemes, Matthew Hewson would have no hold over me.'

Bridie considered the matter for a moment and then suddenly made up her mind, 'I'll go to Ireland myself.'

Ellie looked at her in surprise, she glanced at the wheels of Bridie's chair but seemed reluctant to say anything about Bridie's disability.

Bridie decided to trust her, she had little option really and the scheme did seem sound, it might really work. In any case, Bridie had no better ideas herself. She rose from her chair. 'Don't worry, I can walk,' she said, 'with a little help.'

Ellie smiled, 'I'm glad I came to you.' She sounded sincere and Bridie realized, reluctantly, that she might have been mistaken about Ellie Hopkins all along.

'Tell me the truth, it doesn't matter to me now,' Bridie said 'but I like to know where I stand. Was there ever anything between you and Paul?'

'Nothing. I give you my word before God, I will swear it on the Holy Bible if it will convince you,' Ellie said softly. 'I am still in mourning for my late husband but when the year is over, I'm going to marry a man I love very much.'

'Then I'm sorry for the way I've behaved,' Bridie said at last. It was difficult for her to apologize. 'For a time I was so overwrought, so insanely jealous that I was ready to believe anything of anyone.'

She studied Ellie's face, she was so open, so young and beautiful as well as being rich, she doubtless had her pick of the young men of Swansea. Why should she settle for someone like Paul?

'Perhaps when this is all over, we can be friends. It seems I've misjudged quite a few people.' Once the words were spoken Bridie felt better. It was as though she had crossed some sort of threshold. Was she becoming more fair-minded or was she simply older and wiser?

Ellie looked at her levelly. 'I hope we can. I must admit that I behaved like a fool too, going down near the docklands quite unprepared. Jubilee took me to task over it, told me I should have taken one of the men from the tannery with me but I wanted to show my independence.'

'It's all water under the bridge now,' Bridie said, 'let's both forget it ever happened.' She held out her hand and Ellie took it, shaking it firmly.

'Let's pray that nothing goes wrong,' Bridie said and Ellie bit her lip before replying. 'I'm wondering if it's wise for you to go Ireland alone.'

Bridie looked out into the garden to where Collins was leaning, in the process of locking the coal house door. He straightened, looking up at the darkening sky, the strong column of his neck exposed in spite of the cold weather.

'Don't worry,' she said softly, 'I won't be alone.'

Paul looked at the faces of the two men sitting opposite him in the smoky bar of the Burrows Inn. A raucous laugh from across the room broke the brooding silence that sometimes falls on a crowded room and instantly, as though at a signal, a buzz of voices started up again.

'What do you think is going on?' Paul asked, leaning back in his chair.

Matthew Hewson placed his tankard of ale on the table in front of him and shook back his fall of dark hair. 'I'm not sure but she's definitely up to no good. You just ask Smithers he'll tell you.'

The third man at the table leaned forward, his pugnacious face somehow threatening. 'Had some collars made up in a place outside of town, it's all very suspicious if you ask me. Worth a few quid to you to know that, isn't it, Mr Marchant?'

'Look, Smithers,' Paul said hiding his irritation, 'I appreciate that you came to tell us about this new load of tack but it doesn't really have any significance, does it? Perhaps some other customer wanted tack, plenty of people have stables full of horses, it's nothing unusual.'

'Well, I think it's worth something that I'm keeping an eye on things for you.' Smithers was surly now, sensing defeat.

'I don't think you really have any further business here, do you?' Paul said coldly.

'Oh, I'm not got rid of that easily.' Smithers' eyes were narrowed.

Paul regarded him carefully for a moment and then deliberately turned his attention once more to Matthew. 'I suggest you keep an eye on things and when you have something of real importance to tell me then I'll think about paying you.'

Paul rose to his feet, he'd had enough of the smoky bar and of the two ruffians who sat opposite him. He didn't trust them, not one inch, they would need watching, closely. He dropped some coins onto the table and nodded his goodbyes and then he was outside on the cold, frosty street. He breathed deeply, damn Smithers and damn Matthew Hewson, they had spoiled what had promised to be a good day for him, a day spent alone with Carmella.

When he reached home it was to find his wife sitting

in the drawing room waiting for him. His stomach lurched unpleasantly, the last person he wished to see was Bridie. She had doubtless come to make a scene.

'How did you get here and what do you want?' Paul said edgily, he'd had enough aggravation for one day.

'I am not here to make trouble, I just need to ask you a favour,' Bridie said evenly. 'My cousin is adding buildings to his house and I feel I might be getting in Jono's way. I thought to take a trip over to Ireland. I'd like to sail tomorrow on the *Marie Clare*.'

Paul looked at her carefully, 'Are you serious?'

Bridie nodded. 'I think I'd like to go down to Kinsale for a day or two, have some fresh air, a change of scene, blow away the cobwebs, is that too much to ask?'

There was more to it than that, much more, but what did it mean? He was silent for a moment aware that Bridie was watching him carefully. 'What about yout state of health, how would you manage aboard ship with your disability?'

'I'll take Collins with me, of course,' Bridie said as if that settled the matter. Paul considered the problem; if he refused to take her, Bridie might realize he had something to hide, she might even have her suspicions already that his cargo was not all it should be, she was many things but she was not stupid. He did not want her going to the authorities and causing trouble for him.

'Very well, if that's what you want.' Let her go, he reasoned, the cargo would be safely aboard by then, what harm could she do? She would not be able to get into the hold to examine the cargo. Even if she persuaded someone else to do the deed for her, they would find only horse-collars and patent fuel blocks, goods he had carried to Ireland many times before.

He moved to Bridie's side and took her hand in his, 'No-one can say I'm not a generous man.' He saw Bridie's face redden and he smiled in satisfaction, his barb had struck home, they both knew that Paul could afford to be generous now that he held her fortune in his own hands. Serve her right for pestering him.

The landlord was lighting the lamps in the Burrows Inn, the room was fuller now and smokier than it had been earlier. Matthew Hewson leaned back in his chair, a feeling of triumph curving his lips into a smile. 'I think just a few of the packets of opium will make us a nice little profit, why don't we help ourselves to them while we have a chance?'

'I don't think Marchant is the sort of man you can double-cross and get away with it,' Smithers said doubtfully and Matthew began to feel irritated with him.

'If you don't want to take any risks then get out now,' he said aggressively, sizing Smithers up with a practised eye. The man was not tall but he was strong enough, his biceps bulging beneath his flannel shirt. But he was short on brains, he could be outmanoeuvred with no trouble.

'No need to talk like that,' Smithers said backing down at once, 'I'll go along with whatever you say.'

'That's better.' Matthew relaxed, people were so easy to handle when a man knew what he was about. 'Let's have another tankard of ale, the night is young, I need to find myself a woman.'

Smithers looked him over, 'I know a place, lovely doxies, do anything for me. Take care of them I do, if there's bother with a customer.'

'I'm not paying for any woman,' Matthew said bluntly, 'they can nail me in my coffin when I can't get up a skirt without offering money.'

'No need to pay, I'm always welcome to take my pick of the girls, any sort of girl I like, Chinese, Indian, African, they're all bit of a change from the pale girls you get round the docks.'

'Why not?' Matthew said looking round at the pipe-smoking men in greasy caps, at the sawdust-covered floor and the beer-soaked tables. All at once he felt he would enjoy a woman who didn't demur, didn't pretend to be virtuous but allowed a man to take freely of his pleasures.

Smithers rose to his feet, 'What if Marchant finds out we've taken some of his precious opium?'

'I'm more than a match for Paul Marchant,' Matthew said, 'don't you worry about that.'

The bawdy house was brighter than Matthew had expected, clean with drapes that were rich, if faded, and furniture that was cared for and polished. It was a good sign.

'Evening, Mrs Preece Williams.' Smithers addressed the woman, who sat in the opulent chair that resembled something like a royal throne, with obvious respect. She inclined her head regally and Matthew saw that once she had been very beautiful.

'Good to see you so early, Mr Smithers, I do not theenk there will be trouble tonight, no many boats come into the docks this week so trade is, what you might say, slow.'

Was she really a foreigner, Matthew wondered, or as her name implied was she as firmly rooted in Wales as he was?

She snapped her fingers and a young girl came out of the shadows carrying a tray containing a crystal decanter and some balloon shaped glasses. 'Brandy for the gentlemen, Seranne.' The girl was quick to obey, she was dark and with the colouring of a country girl and her eyes slanted towards Matthew with approval.

Mrs Preece Williams saw the look and tapped the girl lightly on her bare arm. 'Patience, Seranne, let the man have his dreenk. In any case, our visitor might like to peruse our other girls before he makes his choice, might you not Mr . . . ?'

'Mat,' Matthew said quickly, he was somewhat suspicious, not willing to give his full name and the woman smiled.

'Mat it shall be. More brandy for Mat, Seranne, and

264

you Mr Smithers, a whisky and an hour with little Sal Huang as usual, is it?'

Smithers, with a quick glance at her, nodded but Matthew was looking at Seranne who was bending before him, her sweet, full breasts rising seductively above her bodice.

'I think Seranne will suit me just fine,' he said, liking her scent, her provocative way of looking at him, everything about her. She was seductive, knowing and completely undemanding and for the moment that was just what he needed.

'Show Mat to the best room, Seranne, and look after him. Take the rest of the brandy with you.'

Mat glanced back at Smithers but the man was disappearing through a doorway obviously anxious to get on with the matter in hand. Seranne led the way up the carpeted stairs and along the corridor to a small but elegant room. 'Make yourself comfortable, Mat,' she poured him another drink and he sipped it, realizing that it was good, strong stuff.

'Not too much of that or you'll find me a disappointment,' he said pulling her to him. She responded at once and he sighed in satisfaction, this was the life, take a woman when you wanted her and then leave her. This was merely a dalliance, a chance encounter, a little bit of spice to his boring existence.

Seranne was everything he could have wished for, she did not push him, or appear too eager, she waited on him like a handmaiden, doing anything he bade her with swift sureness that excited him. He did not care that she had practiced her art with other men, many other men, indeed the thought lent a piquancy to the event as if it were not quite real.

At last, he lay beside her sated and as if by magic, a drink was presented to him. 'Well, why not?' he said aloud, he was beholden to no-one, he might just as well make a night of it.

'Another few drinks,' Seranne said persuasively, 'will

give you back your strength. You are a wonderful lover, Mat, the best man I've ever had.'

He believed her and feeling good, he drank deeply from the glass. When Matthew opened his eyes, it was daylight, he turned his aching head and saw that he was alone in the large bed, Seranne had vanished. He rose and his ablutions were perfunctory, the water in the jug was cold as he splashed it into the basin careless of the drops falling onto the pale marble of the washstand. The door opened and Smithers entered the room, a big mug of steaming tea grasped in his hand.

'Good night?' he asked and Mat nodded, feeling none too pleased that the other man seemed clear-headed, none the worse for his night of carousing.

'Good enough,' Matthew said flatly. 'Isn't it about time you were getting back to work, don't want your boss suspecting anything.'

'No, that would never do,' Smithers agreed readily. 'But it's only just gone five, I start work at six. Perks of being in charge, the other men are hard at it by the time I get to the tannery.'

Matthew sniffed, 'You don't need to tell me, I worked at Glyn Hir for years, remember?'

Smithers ignored Matthew's ill temper. 'There's a good, cooked breakfast waiting down in the kitchen when you're ready.' Smithers backed towards the door. 'When is the *Marie Clare* sailing for Ireland?'

'Today,' Matthew said briefly and brushed his thick, dark hair wishing the other man would go away and leave him in peace.

'So when do we make our move?' Smithers persisted. Matthew turned to him, his face hard. 'When I tell you,' he said. 'Now get the hell out of here.'

The door closed and Matthew stared at it for a long moment. In only a day or two, he would be able to quit the sea, he would have a little nest egg all of his own. Then to hell with everyone, Paul Marchant, the odious Smithers and most of all Ellie Hopkins who had been the one who had got him in this situation in the first place, dismissing him as if he was a nobody.

He left the room and walked down the carpeted stairs feeling a great deal better than he had when he'd woken up. Soon, he would be able to afford a fine house of his own, he would be looked up to, he would have money in his pocket and then the whole town of Swansea could look out.

CHAPTER EIGHTEEN

'I've missed you so much, Daniel, and I'm so glad you could come home for the weekend.' They were walking side by side in the garden at the back of Glyn Hir, as far away from the smell of the tannery as they could get. The air was cold, crisp, with a light fall of snow covering the ground but Ellie felt warm as she looked up at Daniel. She felt her heart lift, in his dark suit covered by his big topcoat, he looked so handsome with a powdering of snow in his hair. 'What's the bishop of St David's like, have you come to know him any better?'

Daniel shook his head. 'He's so far above me in all sorts of ways, I'm half frightened to speak to him. I obviously don't appear as stupid as I feel because he seems to think I'm a suitable candidate for a career in the church.' Daniel took her gloved hand and hugged it close to his side. 'I think it's going to work out all right, I'm determined to make a success of it.' He paused. 'I won't be very well off, though, Ellie. I won't have much to offer you but when I've finished at Lampeter college, I'll be ordained, I'll be appointed curate, probably to some fairly small parish. Will you come with me, Ellie, where ever I go?'

'I'll be like Ruth in the Bible,' Ellie said. 'Your people will be my people, that sort of thing.' She became serious, 'Dan, there's something I have to talk over with you.'

'What is it?' He looked at her quickly, 'You're not in any trouble, are you?'

'Not exactly but I've planned something and now I'm having a conscience about it. I wanted to protect you from the truth but now, Dan, I need to know if I've done the right thing.'

He laughed. 'I'm sure you have but tell me everything and then I can really decide if you're a wicked woman or not.'

'It concerns contraband goods,' Ellie said hesitantly knowing how absurd it sounded. 'I've learned that opium is being smuggled through Ireland without any duty being paid.'

Daniel frowned. 'I don't know how you've come by this information but surely, Ellie, the proper authorities should be alerted as soon as possible.'

'It's not as simple as that.' Ellie spoke quietly. 'The opium is being concealed inside horse-collars made from our leather.'

Daniel looked down at her, she had his full attention now. 'This really is serious, are you sure about it Ellie?'

'I'm sure. What's so awful is that Matthew Hewson is involved along with Paul Marchant. Matthew threatened that if I didn't keep my mouth shut and give him a substantial amount of money, I would be implicated in the whole sorry mess.'

'Go to the police,' Daniel said at once, 'don't allow anyone to intimidate you, Ellie, you are innocent, anyone with eyes would see that.'

'I wish you were right,' Ellie frowned. 'But my wagons take the leather to the saddler and collect it when it's ready, who would believe I didn't know anything about the contraband? In any case, I think people will believe anything they hear, especially about me. I haven't exactly had an unblemished past, have I?'

She paused seeing Daniel rub his eyes, carefully considering what she had said. 'I think you could establish your innocence, Ellie, I really do. I think you must put the matter in the hands of the authorities, alert the Customs and Excise men about what's happening.'

'Listen, please Daniel, there's more. I instructed the men from the yard, Harry, Luke and Boyo to switch the loads of leather goods. What Paul Marchant is shipping to Ireland will be horse-collars, simply that.'

'I see. What then? Will you turn the contraband over to the customs men, is that your plan?'

Ellie shook her head. 'I hadn't thought of doing that, my idea was to exchange the real contraband cargo for Paul Marchant's signature on some documents. He would have to sign his wife's fortune back into her hands *and* sign a letter absolving me of any involvement in his schemes.'

'But Ellie,' Daniel's voice was soft, 'you'll be allowing these men to profit from the misery of others. The opium will be sold on the open market, don't you understand what that means?'

Ellie shook her head. 'I'm not sure, Dan, I know people smoke opium but no-one seems to come to any harm from it.'

'Ellie, you are so unworldly,' Daniel shook his head, 'opium is addictive, taken in excess it will kill.'

'But Dan, laudanum is derived from opium, it is a medicine, you know that as well as I do. The trade in opium is not illegal, what Paul Marchant is doing is smuggling simply to avoid paying the duty on the goods.'

'The selling of opium should be illegal and it will be very soon, mark my words. Whatever way you look at it, Paul Marchant is breaking the law, you realize that, of course.'

'Yes, I do realize that,' Ellie took her hands away from Daniel's grasp, piqued at his tone, 'I'm not completely stupid you know.'

'Ellie, I didn't mean to imply that you were, it's just that you can't in all conscience just hand the contraband cargo back to these men.'

Ellie turned her back on Daniel, for the first time she felt out of sympathy with him. 'Don't you realize the implications, Daniel? Marchant could be harmed if he doesn't deliver the load as promised. In any case, it's too late to change my mind now, Bridie has gone across to

Ireland, she is going to confront her husband, give him an ultimatum.'

Daniel rubbed his head. 'I can't condone what you are doing, it's just not right.'

Ellie bit her lip. 'Dan, are we having our first quarrel?'

He shook his head. 'I will not quarrel with you, Ellie, I accept you acted for the best.' He stood behind her and drew her back against him. 'I can only pray that no harm comes to either you or Bridie Marchant, I'm sure you don't realize just what sort of vicious men you are dealing with. You are playing a dangerous game, my love, I wish you'd talked to me before you got into this mess.'

She turned in his arms and faced him placing her hands against his cheeks. 'It will be all right, you'll see. Paul Marchant will sign anything just so he can save his own skin and after this is over, he will have to give up the smuggling for good, too many people know about it for it to be safe any more.'

'Perhaps you're right,' he sounded doubtful. 'I still think you should have gone to the authorities and I still think you are taking, silly, dangerous risks.'

Ellie suddenly shivered, she had felt the cold touch of Daniel's disapproval and it was a feeling she didn't much care for.

Boyo was in love. He stared across the aisle of the Catholic Church to where the O'Conner family were sitting. There were four of them, the parents, stiff in their Sunday best, Mr James O'Conner looking fierce and large with a heavy moustache and beard and his wife Irfonwy, gentle and pretty as a summer's day. Beside them were their two daughters, April and Cathie, both pretty, both with an abundance of thick hair tied back beneath old-fashioned straw hats. It was April, the elder of the two girls who interested him, who had brought him to this unaccustomed place of worship on a Sunday.

He allowed himself another glance at April, he should

271

have bought her something really special, a locket on a gold chain, perhaps. She was very well aware of his scrutiny; she glanced his way often, only to lower her golden eyelashes the moment his gaze met hers. She was, he thought, about sixteen years of age, her sister quite a bit younger.

April was well-built already, her breasts were full, straining sweetly against the crisp cotton of her dress. She had the healthy look of a farmer's daughter which was exactly what she was.

Boyo had seen the family in Swansea many times, of course, only it seemed that lately April had turned from a chrysalis into a butterfly without him being aware of it. He had sometimes collected milk and eggs from the farm for Ellie but lately she had been sending Rosie, claiming she needed Boyo at the tannery. Just his luck.

Boyo frowned, the tannery wasn't the happy place it used to be before Smithers had come to work there. He was a poor manager and his air of self importance stuck in Boyo's craw. The atmosphere at Glyn Hir was different, colder. The men resented the newcomer, he wasn't experienced in the way that Harry was, or even Luke, either of them would have made a better manager. It was just a shame that Ellie didn't think the same way.

Mind, it was the old hands she turned to when she wanted anything special done, like the swapping of the loads of collars for instance. Not that he understood what it was all about but if it was what Ellie wanted, it was all right by him. The original consignment of collars was now stored in the barn at the side of the house where Boyo used to sleep. There must be something special about those particular leather goods because Ellie had employed a locksmith to put a huge lock on the barn door.

Boyo looked up as he became aware of the bustle of people preparing to leave the church but at the last minute, the priest held up his hand. 'There will be a social evening for young people and a special mass on

Monday next.' He beamed beatifically at the congregation with the awesome regard for children given only to those who have none of their own.

Outside the church, Boyo saw that April had fallen behind and was standing a little apart from her family, apparently tying up the laces of her boots. He moved quickly towards her. 'Excuse me, Miss O'Conner,' he began hesitantly. She looked up at him and then looked quickly away again, her cheeks blushing red beneath her bright hair. 'Might I have the pleasure of seeing you at the social on Monday?'

'April! Come on slowcoach!' Cathie was calling loudly and April threw her an angry look. There was no time for undue modesty.

'Yes,' she said desperately, 'I'll see you inside the church hall.' April gave him a last, heart-stopping smile and hurried to catch up with her family.

He whistled cheerfully to himself all the way back to Glyn Hir, his mind was filled with thoughts of April, of her sweetness, the soft rose scent of her, the brightness of her hair, the incredible green of her eyes. The smile faded when he reached the tannery and heard loud angry voices from inside the currying house. This was the spot where the men forgot the worries of home and work for a while and sat round a fire, drank a few mugs of ale and played some music.

This was where he had his first experience of women, the night of Rosie's seduction. He felt a pain within him as he remembered how it had felt, the exquisite joy, the sense of becoming part of a man's world. Sadly, he realized that he knew now what Ellie had meant when she said he'd regret it. He wished in that instant that he had stayed chaste so that he would be worthy of April.

As he drew nearer to the currying house, he saw what the noise was all about, Harry and Luke were arguing with Smithers. The foreman was leaning aggressively forward, bellowing insults, it was clear he was the worse for drink.

'You are not going to break into the barn, not while I have breath in my body,' Harry was shouting. 'Listen to sense, man, I was working here before you ever came on the scene.'

'I'll handle the affairs of the tannery the way I want and there's not a damn thing you can do about it.' Smithers was big and ugly and Boyo knew Harry would have very little chance of defending himself if the verbal insults developed into a fist fight.

'Come on, you lot, knock it off.' His words were ignored as Harry spoke again more heatedly. 'You know Ellie doesn't want anyone handling the store of leather in the barn, she's given us express orders on it.'

'I'm manager here and I don't have to answer to you, shut your mouth and get out of my way.'

Harry moved reluctantly to one side and Smithers grinned in satisfaction. 'Keep your long nose out of what doesn't concern you, in future, right?'

Harry turned away, mumbling to himself and Smithers looked over to where Boyo was standing. 'And you, young pup, you'd better learn who is boss round here, keep out of what don't concern you.'

At that moment, Ellie came into the yard and sized the situation up with a quick look. 'You men had better get off home,' she said briskly. 'No sense in hanging around the yard on a Sunday, is there?'

Boyo watched as Smithers moved away with ill grace, his big head lowered, his sharp eyes glancing towards the locked barn.

'You going up to the house, boy?' Smithers was close to Boyo, his voice low. Boyo nodded. 'Well don't go clecking to the boss, right? What goes on down here in the yard is between us men and don't you forget it.'

Boyo was not likely to, not with Smithers' big shoulders leaning towards him in a way that could only be described as threatening. In any case, Boyo had other things to think about, he wanted to be alone in his narrow bed, he wanted to look out at the star-studded

274

sky and most of all, he wanted to reawaken his happy thoughts of April O'Conner. All at once Boyo was frightened and excited at the same time, the thought of intimacy with April was too exquisite to bear. He brushed the notion aside, it was improper and irreverent. Yet he was roused, he knew he was, whenever he was near her, smelt her sweetness, saw the soft swell of her breasts beneath her bodice, he wanted to hold and protect April, he wanted to possess her. Well, there would be an awful lot of water under the bridge before anything like that happened.

Monday passed in a dreary haze, the cold winter weather seemed to creep into all the nooks and crannies of the grinding house. Boyo kept his spirits high, even as he carried the bags of oak bark chippings to the yard. There was no sign of Smithers, he'd gone with the wagons to fetch the leather goods from the saddler and Boyo was relieved.

'Bugger off,' Harry said, 'you might as well finish early, you're like a cow with a musket there, lad, no use to anyone.'

Gratefully, Boyo stripped off his clothes, regardless of the cold and stood at the pump in the yard, washing the stink of the tannery from his body. Shivering, he went to his room at the top of the house and sank onto the bed, lying back for a moment, considering the evening's pleasure before him. First, he would contrive to sit next to April at the mass. Later, they would be together at the social, drinking home-made pop and eating biscuits.

One or two of the bolder youngsters would give what the father called 'a turn' singing or reciting, playing to the audience. Boyo cared for none of that, all he wanted was to be close to April. It was afterwards that the testing would come, would April let him walk her home? All the way uphill to Honey's Farm, it was a delicious thought. Perhaps her father, he of the large build and the fierce beard might come to meet her, that would certainly be a blow to Boyo's plans for taking

April's soft little hand in his. He looked down at his own hands, they were calloused from handling the oak bark, stained and brown in places as though he had smoked many cigars. He couldn't help that, it was proof of his honest labour, no girl could object to that could she?

He dressed carefully in his best clothes, normally kept neat for Sundays and then slicked down his hair with water from the jug on the marble table. The mirror hanging slightly askew on the wall showed a face that was filled with anticipation and Boyo attempted to wipe the smile from his face.

April was seated next to her sister when Boyo arrived at the church. She glanced over her shoulder a smile of welcome on her face. He sat beside her, warmed through and through by her nearness. Even the mass which was long and tedious passed all too quickly. When the priest declared that the social part of the evening was about to begin Boyo leaned towards April taking his courage in both hands.

'Is it all right if I walk you home?' he asked diffidently. She bent her head low so that he couldn't see her face. 'Cathie will be with us, mind,' she said.

'I don't care about that,' Boyo said quickly, 'though I would rather be alone with you, of course.' He wondered for a moment if he'd been too bold but April looked up at him, her smile radiant.

Under the cover of the folds of her spreading skirt, he took her hand and her fingers curled warmly in his. He felt the heat run through his body, he was ten foot tall, he could conquer whole worlds so long as he had April at his side.

Later, they walked home together in the cold darkness. Cathie, impatient, had raced up the hill ahead of them. There was a constriction in Boyo's throat but he had to speak. 'Will you be my girl, April?'

She sighed softly, 'Yes, Boyo.' The words were just loud enough for him to hear them.

They stood quite still for a long moment and from the distance came the sound of Cathie calling to them.

April smiled. 'That's that then,' she said, boldly, 'we're walking out together.'

The rest of the walk took on a dream-like quality, the sky was bright, even the cold wind singing in the bare branches of the trees seemed kinder. It was as if the world had taken on special brushstrokes of colour. This thing called love was a powerful emotion, just how powerful Boyo was only just beginning to find out.

Later, as he lay in his bed, he looked up at the pattern of light on the ceiling and pictured April's face. He went over every word, every expression in his mind. He could not sleep, he turned over in the bed and pulled the sheets up to his chin. He wondered what it was like in her house, where it was she slept, how she spent her days.

It was almost dawn before he closed his eyes and then it was to be plagued by erotic dreams that finally woke him only a few hours later. He felt tired and yet he looked forward to the day. He rose from bed and washed at the marble-topped table, finishing off the water in the jug.

He looked at his face in the mirror, he needed a shave, his beard was growing stronger, he was sure of it. It even looked in the early light as though he had a moustache. He was growing up, he had the urges of a man, urges that now needed to be contained. Later, as he walked out into the cold greyness of the yard, Boyo looked up at the sky and saw only April's shy smile and the soft gold of her eyelashes as she looked up at him and suddenly, it was a beautiful day.

CHAPTER NINETEEN

Bridie waited in the hotel room in a fever of anxiety. She glanced out of the window not seeing the softness of the Irish skies above the huddle of picturesque streets or the simply furnished room where she waited. Her hands were damp with perspiration and she prayed she would have the strength to carry out the task she had come to Ireland to do.

Bridie felt, rather than saw her husband come into the room. She glanced round with difficulty, seated as she was in her chair and saw the glower of anger burnt into his features. For a moment she wished she had accepted Collins' offer to stay with her during the difficult interview to come. 'So Paul, you've come to see me.'

'For God's sake woman,' he said without preamble, 'what have you done with my cargo?'

'That would be telling, wouldn't it?' she spoke with forced lightness. 'Now, let's get down to business.' She took out of her bag the thick, folded documents and held them out to him.

'What tomfoolery is this?' He asked, slapping the documents from her hand. They fell to the floor and lay there like a silent rebuke. 'Don't you know this is a matter of life and death, woman?'

'You will pick those papers up and read them or you will never see your cargo again.' Her voice was no longer light but heavy with anger and an unexpected feeling of sorrow. 'Oh, Paul, how low you have sunk.'

'Don't moralize to me, woman.' He paced around until he stood before her. He leaned forward and spoke coldly, 'Life with you had become intolerably boring, do you understand? At dinner parties I would look at you and do you know what I thought? How plain my wife had become, how *old* and I looked for something else.'

His words hit at her like stones, it was only the knowledge of Collins' devotion that prevented her from bursting into tears. 'So you took a mistress.' The desire to strike back was strong within her. 'One you could impress with your pathetic show of wealth, *my* wealth. You stole my inheritance, Paul, and I want it back, that's what those papers are all about. Read them, I think you will find that they have been properly drawn up by Ellie Hopkins' lawyer.'

'So that bitch is in this too!' Paul said, looking down at Bridie with such hostility that she had to resist the temptation to shrink back in her chair. 'I will not sign. I feel you have got all you deserved.'

'How do you reckon that, Paul?' Bridie forced herself to speak sharply.

He thumped his hand onto the table. 'You were cheating me, your husband, you were raking in the money from the deep sea loads and handing me the crumbs. Well, Miss High and Mighty, I outsmarted you and that is something you will just have to live with.'

'Not if I sell your cargo myself,' Bridie's words, quietly spoken silenced him. 'What would your *friends* think of that, the ones waiting for the cargo? I shouldn't think they would be very pleased.'

He bent over her chair, his eyes gleaming with anger. 'Where is it?' he said threateningly and she forced herself to meet his gaze. 'You won't intimidate me, Paul, so don't try, I have the upper hand this time.'

For a long moment, he looked as though he would take her by the throat and shake the truth from her and then, to her relief, he backed away. 'Bridie,' his tone had changed, become a self-pitying whine that grated on Bridie's nerves. 'They'll kill me if I don't deliver the load, don't you realize that Monkton is not a man to fool with.'

So the name of his contact was Monkton, that was

something to hold on to, a piece of information which might be useful.

Paul turned to her pleadingly. 'You can't let them harm me, I am the father of our sons, after all.'

She looked at him unable to keep the scorn from her voice. 'Did you think of that when you took the boys away from me? And didn't it occur to you that you could go to prison if you were caught avoiding duty on the cargo of opium? What would our sons think of you if that happened?'

He thrust his hands into his pockets, putting on the hangdog, little-boy expression that once would have melted her heart. Now it had no effect.

'Just sign those papers, Paul, and you'll have your load delivered to you here by Monday,' she said tiredly.

'Monday, that's two days away!' His lips drew into a tight line. 'You're bluffing,' he said, 'where is the cargo, what ship have you used to bring the stuff over here to Ireland, not one of mine, I'll be bound?'

She forced down her anger at his words. 'You forget Paul, I owned the bigger part of the fleet, it was I who built up the business. You forget too that my father was in shipping all his life, he had friends in the business, friends who were ships' owners and masters. Oh, I still have some power, believe me.' She was tired of all this beating around the bush. 'Now, if you know what's good for you, Paul, read those documents and sign them, it's the only way to get yourself off the hook. If you are threatened by this man Monkton, I will not raise a hand to help you, believe me. One way or another, I'll get my inheritance back from you.'

Paul reluctantly picked up the documents and, sitting at the table in Bridie's hotel room, flattened the thick pages out before him, reading steadily. 'You want every-thing,' he said at last, 'you want the whole damn caboodle, you are not even leaving me my own ships.'

'Why should I?' Bridie's voice was hard, 'Isn't that exactly what you did to me? Left me without anything.'

280

'And this,' Paul waved the last of the papers in the air, 'absolving Ellie Hopkins of any responsibility, I won't do it, why should I help her?'

Bridie sighed. 'Because she's innocent. Sign *all* the papers Paul or I have nothing more to say.'

'What if I won't sign, what if I keep you here until you come to your senses?'

'Keep me prisoner, you mean?' Bridie said, 'I've only to ring the bell and one of the maids will come to see what I want.'

'Ah, but you can't get to the bell and I'm certainly not going to ring it for you, I'm not that stupid.' He moved to the bed and sank against the pillows, hands behind his head. He stared at her with a smile curving his lips, the lips she had once kissed with passion, what a fool she had been.

Bridie rose from her chair in one movement and walked with studied calm to the door. With satisfaction, she saw that Paul was staring at her in disbelief. 'Yes, I can walk again, I'm taking control of my life you see, Paul, and you do not feature in it, not one little bit.' Her hand was on the brass handle. 'Collins is waiting outside, he's bigger than you are and much more of a man. He is on my side in a way that you have never been. Now, if you want to save your miserable skin, you'll sign those documents.'

Paul sat upright. 'They are waiting for me,' he said desperately, 'Monkton and his men, they want assurance that I'm going to deliver the load to them as expected, what am I to say?'

'Tell them there was an unexpected delay, tell them what you like but first sign those papers or face the consequences.'

Paul seemed uncertain, he took up a pen from the table and stared down at the papers as though still not decided what course of action he should take. 'Bridie, you can't leave me penniless,' he said looking at her desperately.

'Why not?' She looked at his stooped shoulders, his downcast eyes and relented. 'When this is over, providing you give up the smuggling, we'll come to a settlement, I'll see you are provided for which is generous of me in the circumstances.'

Quickly, as though afraid he would change his mind, Paul signed the documents. He flung down the pen with venom and turned, crashing his fist against the wall.

Immediately, the door opened and Collins stood on the threshold of the room, his big fists bunched, his eyes sharp as they rested on Paul.

'Get out!' Paul said, 'I'm talking to my wife, keep your place man, have you forgotten you are merely a servant?'

'Correction,' Bridie said, 'Collins is no longer a servant, he is now managing my affairs. Another thing, I ceased being your wife in anything but name a long time ago. Now you may leave us, Paul, give your colleagues the good news that they will shortly have their goods.'

Paul moved to the door and Collins stepped inside the room allowing him to exit.

'Oh Paul,' Bridie said, 'I've made a few enquiries about your little mistress, ruled by her strict mama, a lady to whom morality equates with riches. Well you are no longer rich, not by anyone's standards, so I should say goodbye to your little romance, I can't see it lasting very long, not now.'

When he had gone, Bridie sank down onto the bed, she was trembling. Her hands were shaking so badly that even when she clasped them together, they continued to tremble, she knew that her last barb had been unworthy of her, Paul was a beaten man.

Collins sat on the bed beside her, an unprecedented familiarity and put both his arms around her, holding her close. Bridie closed her eyes, breathing in his strength, his masculine scent and knowing in that moment she loved this man more than she had ever loved anyone. He had wanted her when she had nothing, when

282

she was a penniless cripple, his love was good and honest, it was real love. 'When this is all over,' she said, 'we'll be together, Collins, somehow, we'll be together.'

He said nothing but his arms tightened imperceptibly around her. She knew he wanted to kiss her, she knew too that he dare not, he still held her far above him in station even though she had been destitute. It was Collins who had been the one to find employment, he who had brought in the money which had paid for their trip to Ireland. Was paying now for the hotel room where they sat. Jono was kindness itself but it had been a point of honour on Collins' part that he didn't live on another man's charity. Bridie loved him for it.

She sighed heavily and tipped her head up, so that their lips were almost touching. She heard Collins' indrawn breath and her heart sang. 'Collins,' she said humbly, 'will you kiss me?'

'I'll have it here in two days time, you go and tell them that, Hewson.' Paul Marchant was looking down at him as if he was a piece of dog shit and Matthew didn't like it one little bit. He had not wanted to come on this last trip at all, he had watched Paul Marchant idling on deck with his Irish colleen with a bitter taste in his mouth. Above all, he had known in his bones that something was going wrong. Now, all he wanted was to get paid and to return home in safety. 'I'm not going to see that shark Monkton alone,' he said, 'not me, you can face the music yourself.'

They were sitting in the bar of Murphy's lodging house, the smell of beer mingled with the pungent odour of cigars. Matthew rubbed his foot through the sawdust on the floor and wondered if he had been a fool to ever get mixed up in what was turning out to be a dangerous business.

'We'll go together,' Marchant said at last. 'Where is Monkton, where did he go when he stormed out of here yesterday?'

'On board his ship, I suppose,' Matthew said sulkily. 'He's too much of a skinflint to pay for lodgings ashore.'

Matthew thought of the nasty scene the previous day when Paul had been forced to tell Monkton there had been some mistake, the wrong cargo had been loaded on the *Marie Clare*, only empty horse-collars had arrived. It had become clear to Matthew then why Ellie Hopkins had bought a new load of tack, the one Smithers had been so concerned about. Paul had been a fool not to take the man seriously, he was not so clever after all.

'Right, we'll go over to the docks, then, tell him everything is all right, there's been a bit of a delay but it's sorted out now.'

'Do you think that will satisfy him?' Matthew was doubtful, he never had liked the look of the man Monkton, slit eyes, dead of expression, a mean mouth and a receding chin, a man to steer clear of.

'The goods will be here in two days, that's all I can promise.' He took out the bill describing the cargo as boxes of leather tack which Bridie had given him in exchange for his signature. It gave him the right to collect the cargo from the *Glorianna*, a steam packet which Bridie had acquired some time ago and which Paul had sold off as an unnecessary expenditure to one of Bridie's colleagues. He clutched at the bill, it gave him something to show Monkton, a little bit of evidence that all was well.

'Shall we have another drink first?' Matthew said realizing that he was nervous. Perhaps there was some way he could back out of the deal before any real harm came to him. On the other hand, if he went now, he would forfeit the big wad of money that was his due. No, there was nothing for it but to go through with the whole thing. Monkton knew that Matthew was only a sidekick, a name he had resented, but for which he was grateful now.

Marchant rose to his feet. 'Better get it over with,' he said and he sounded as reluctant as Matthew felt.

Matthew glanced round, wishing there was some way out of this dilemma in which, somehow he had become involved. Then Paul Marchant was making for the door and all Matthew could do was to follow him.

Bridie sat in a chair looking up at Collins with worried eyes. 'Have I done the right thing? I don't wish any harm to come to Paul whatever he's done.'

'Now come on, Bridie,' her name still didn't flow easily from his lips. 'Did you have any alternative but to make him sign those papers? Was there any other way you could have claimed back what was rightfully yours? Just ask yourself that.'

'Come here. Hold me,' Bridie said and closed her eyes as Collins took her in his arms. 'That's right, hold me close to you, make me feel safe.'

'We'll go home,' Collins said firmly, 'we'll go home as soon as possible, there is no point in staying here a moment longer. You have what you came for.'

'All right. We'll leave tomorrow, on the early tide.' Bridie said. 'But,' she smiled, 'we might as well make the most of tonight, we will have a little drink to celebrate together, shall we?'

Collins looked at her somewhat wistfully as if he had not heard her speak. 'It won't be the same when we get home will it?'

'What do you mean?' Bridie asked but she knew what he meant. She would no longer need to live at the house in Clydach with her cousin Jono, she would be able to return to the luxury of her own home if she so wished, the home where Collins had been nothing but a servant. She was once more mistress of a large shipping fleet. 'Nothing will ever be the same, not now that I've found you. Collins,' her voice was breathless, 'don't you know how much I love you? I didn't know what love was before. I want you with me always, you know that, Collins.'

There, it was said. She trembled at her temerity, what

if he rebuffed her? 'I wouldn't have survived at all without you, you must realize that, Collins.'

'I'm not in your class, Bridie, people can be so cruel. There has been so much gossip already what with you leaving home. You don't want to add fuel to the flames.'

'I've made up my mind,' she said suddenly, 'I'm not going back to Sea Mistress. I shall buy a little cottage, live in Clydach, near Jono. No-one will talk about us there.'

'That's a sudden decision.' Collins' eyes were warm as they looked down into hers. 'But are you sure about this, you'll be giving up so much?'

'Nothing that is important to me. Why should I want to live in that big house again, it's full of memories, most of them bad. I'll shake myself free of the dust of my past once and for all.'

She threw back the bedclothes. 'Come along, Collins, I think it's high time we were in bed, it's been a long, difficult day.' She waited for him to take her in his arms, he did so tentatively at first and then as she clung to him, she felt him become aroused. She sighed softly, the bad times were over, now she was going to experience real happiness for the first time in her life.

The morning sun was stretching pale fingers into the room as Bridie came awake. There was a repeated knocking on the door and it was that sound which had intruded into her dreams.

'I'll go,' Collins said. He drew on his clothes before opening the door a few inches and Bridie heard a soft Irish voice, heavy with the sound of tears and guessed, with a flash of anger, who it was.

'Let Miss Murphy come in,' Bridie said and turned to see the young, so young, girl, heavy-eyed with weeping, standing before her, shoulders hunched in an attitude of total misery. As Collins held the door open, she stepped hesitantly into the room.

'I think Paul has abandoned me,' she said, 'I haven't seen him since we came ashore, he didn't come home all night and I love him so much I can't bear it.' She took a deep breath. 'I knew it was wrong, knew I'd somehow be punished by God for sinning. He is your husband and I committed adultery with him, it wasn't right but I couldn't help myself.' The words spilled from her. 'Now I'm going to have his baby, I know I should be ashamed but I want it, I want this baby. Do you think he'll come back to me?'

Bridie had drawn on a robe and had seated herself beside the dead grey ashes in the fireplace; she searched for some kind words to say to this girl who was little more than a child herself. She could find none. 'What about your parents?' She wondered if Paul had tired of the Irish girl, it was quite within his character and yet he had seemed so fond of her.

The girl looked up, her eyes dull. 'They'll turn me out,' she said. 'If Paul has left me, they won't put up with the disgrace.'

'Then they shouldn't have encouraged you to sleep with him in the first place,' Bridie said and hearing the sharpness in her tone immediately felt remorseful.

'I wanted him, no-one forced me to do anything, I love him, do you understand that?' There was no hostility in the girl's manner just a pitiful humility.

'Look,' Bridie said, 'come back to Wales with me, Paul will have to return sometime and then you can sort things out between you.'

A small spark of hope began to grow in the girl's eyes. 'You think he'll still love me, even though I'm expecting?' She was so wistful, so sad that Bridie could not find it in her to be harsh. In any case, Carmella had not stolen anything of value from her, not really.

'That I can't answer,' Bridie said with some asperity. 'All I can offer is to help you return to the house in Swansea.'

'You are good and kind and I have wronged you,' the girl said, 'and when Paul comes back to me, everything will be all right, you needn't bother with me any more.'

'Go home,' Bridie said. 'You'll have to pick up whatever you need for the trip back home. We shall be sailing with the evening tide.'

It was silent in the room when Carmella had gone. The wonderful mood of the night before had evaporated. Bridie looked up at Collins longingly. 'Let's forget Paul, forget everything. I want you to come back to bed, Collins, I want you to hold me, to kiss me, to make me feel like a woman again.'

He took her in his arms and held her close. Their kisses became more passionate, his hand reached to caress her breast beneath the thin cloth of her nightgown. His breathing became ragged, he kissed her deeply, his tongue probing. Then they were undressing each other with frantic hands. He was a good lover, much as he wanted release, he wanted to make Bridie sing with happiness and passion and as she moaned in delight, she knew that everything she wanted, except for the return of her sons, was right here in this room.

Afterwards, they lay together entwined as though they had always been a couple, familiar with each other's bodies. Bridie propped herself up on one elbow and looked down at him, tracing the line of his moustache with her fingertip. 'By the way, Collins, I have one more important task for you to do before we leave, is that all right?'

'I'd better do anything you say.' He was teasing her and she knew it. 'And what is this important task?'

'As if you didn't know.' She smiled up at him before drawing him, once again, towards her eager body.

CHAPTER TWENTY

'Well, Mac,' Arian Smale tapped her teeth with her pencil, 'you'd better go and interview Mrs Marchant yourself, this looks like an interesting story.'

'Her husband has chosen not to come home, what's so interesting about that?' Mac said, dropping ash from his cigar onto the polished surface of his desk.

'Bridie returns home from Ireland without her husband but with the so-called housekeeper in tow, there's a mystery in that, somewhere, believe me, I can smell it. Go to it Mac, find out what you can.'

Arian sat at the desk Mac had vacated and looked around her in satisfaction, her newspaper was successful beyond her wildest dreams. But then, she had a good team working for her and of all her reporters Mac was the most talented, he had an amazing gift for ferreting out a story from the tiniest bit of gossip. If there was any mystery behind Paul Marchant's disappearance, Mac would, before long, be in possession of all the facts.

A feeling of well-being settled over her; Arian closed her eyes for a moment, hearing with pleasure the hum of voices, the clatter of typewriting machines, all the sounds of a busy office. At last, after many failures, she had pulled her life together, made something of herself. All the times she had tried to get on her feet and fallen again were amply compensated for by her present success. She could hold her head high, she had achieved something positive in her life.

The doorbell jangled startling her out of her reverie. Arian looked up, a man in a stout mackintosh was at the front desk, head bent forward in what appeared to be earnest conversation. For some reason which she didn't understand, Arian felt a prickling of apprehension. The clerk was turning, looking towards her as if in doubt as to what she should do next. Arian rose to her feet and moved forward, the polite smile felt frozen on her lips.

'Could we talk somewhere in private, Mrs Simples?' She felt as though she had been struck, it was so long since Arian had been called by her married name, a name which brought her nothing but unpleasant memories. She led the man to one side of the office, a little way off from the noise of the typewriters. 'What is it?' she asked but with a sinking of her heart she already knew.

'It's your husband, Mr Simples, he's been taken poorly.'

Arian stared at the man. 'But he's in that place because he's – he's poorly, as you call it.' She heard the thin sound of panic in her voice and made an effort to control the trembling that had seized her.

'You don't understand, this is different, Mr Simples is sick in body, very sick. I think you should come to see him.' Before it is too late, the words hovered in the air without being said.

'I'll get my coat.' Arian was surprised how normal her voice sounded but her hands still shook as she hurried upstairs to her apartment.

Gerald was sick, how sick? Guilt hung like a heavy weight inside her, she hadn't been to see him in a long while, she had meant to go; every weekend she had promised herself she would take the trip to the edge of town and visit her husband but the weekends came and went as, feebly, she made up excuses, any excuse not to go to the special hospital where Gerald now spent his days.

It was wet in the street outside the offices of *The Times*, the paving stones shimmered in the mist, treacherous, uneven, a trap for the unwary. A thin fog hung over the rooftops, obscuring the chimney stacks, mingling with the smoke from many fires. It was a cold, cheerless

February day. Arian was grateful to settle into the cab the man had waiting. She glanced at him, trying to read something in his expression. 'I'm sorry, I didn't get your name,' she said quietly. 'I think your news upset me so much that I forgot my manners.'

'Upset you? I'm sorry.' Was there a hint of sarcasm in his tone or was it just her conscience, she wondered. He spoke again. 'I'm Dr Thornton, I was coming into town and I thought I'd call and see you personally, convey the bad news myself.'

She couldn't make out if he was rebuking her or merely being polite. 'How bad is he?' The words had to be forced from between her lips. She had never loved Gerald and yet she owed him a duty and even in that she had failed miserably.

'He has an infection of the lungs, both lungs,' the doctor said evenly. 'I'll be blunt Mrs Simples, this condition has been with him for several days and it has worsened overnight. I don't expect Mr Simples to recover, I'm sorry but there's no other way to say these things.'

'I see, well thank you for your frankness.' She paused. 'Don't you think I should have been informed of Gerald's condition before this?'

'Our policy is not to alarm the relatives of our patients unnecessarily.' Dr Thornton said smoothly. 'Patients who are on drugs, who are largely inactive, do unfortunately develop all sorts of complications. Sometimes the symptoms pass without anything serious occurring, sometimes, as now, the situation becomes grave.'

Arian wished in that moment that Calvin was beside her, helping her through the ordeal that was most certainly coming. What did she feel? She tried to picture Gerald's face, he had been handsome but never, never had she felt the slightest liking for him let alone love. He had trapped her into marriage and she had never forgiven him for that and she couldn't now, not even if he was on his deathbed.

The stark walls of the hospital loomed up out of the mist and Arian felt her spirits sink even lower as she imagined herself walking in through the doors, the chains and locks that had to be undone, leading to what?

When she was led by a nurse into the hospital ward where Gerald was lying, Arian gagged at the smell, stale urine and formaldehyde mingled together in a pungent cocktail of despair. Gerald was almost unrecognizable, he had grown so thin in the weeks since she had last seen him. His cheekbones jutted grotesquely, his nose and chin were gaunt against the parchment of his skin.

Arian stifled a gasp, how could anyone be so sick and still go on living? His breathing was noisy, his lips blue, he looked as though he was already dead. She sat beside the bed not sure what she should do. She reached out a tentative hand and then drew it back, repelled by the sight of the man in the bed.

'How long has he been like this?' Arian glanced up at the nurse who shook her head.

'Don't know, madam, I only came on duty this morning.' She moved away in a rustle of starched linen leaving Arian alone with Gerald.

It was as though he had been waiting for that moment, he opened his eyes and stared directly at her and she started back in her chair, frightened by the lucidity in his face.

'I'm not ready to go yet,' his voice was faint, reedy but there was a demonic glow in his eyes that frightened her.

'I won't let you be free of me, ever,' he said, 'I'll come back and haunt you even from my grave, you are my possession, Arian, no other man can take my place.'

'Hush,' she said quietly, 'don't try to talk.' She was surprised that he was so rational, his ravings seemed to have gone, his senses were restored. Perhaps it was just a temporary state brought about by the cessation of the sedative drugs that were usually in his system. Perhaps

292

even the worst sort of mental sickness was overcome by the will of the dying.

He closed his eyes as though very tired and turned his thin face away from her. Arian wanted more than anything in the world to run out of the hospital, to go home, to wash away the stink of the hospital, wash away any thoughts of Gerald Simples. But she sat, frozen in misery looking down at the man in the bed, her husband.

The nurse returned and hovered near the bed, Arian looked up hopefully. 'Can I speak with Dr Carpenter?' she asked almost pleadingly.

The nurse nodded. 'He's waiting to see you in his office, madam.'

With a last desperate glance towards the still figure in the bed, Arian left the ward and followed the nurse along a maze of corridors. Her head had begun to ache, she felt sick with fear and remorse, she had virtually deserted Gerald these past months and his words echoed in her mind, his threat that he would return after death to haunt her. What if he could reach her from beyond the grave? But that was absurd, she was being morbidly fanciful, influenced by the dreadful atmosphere of the hospital.

'Eddie,' she went gratefully into the light, airy office where Eddie Carpenter was sitting behind a cluttered desk and, leaning over, took his hands in hers. 'Eddie, is he going to die?'

'Sit down, Arian. Would you leave us alone, nurse?' The girl rustled away and Arian sank into a chair facing across the desk.

'I don't think he has very much longer,' Eddie said evenly. He leaned forward and his eyes were suddenly brimming. 'I know I hated the man, still do, for what he did to my daughter but by God he's had his punishment in full.' He bent his head to hide his grief and Arian thought of his daughter, beautiful, young, besotted by Gerald, her life snuffed out by him.

'Eddie, Gerald will haunt us all all our lives, he's right

about that, we'll never be able to forget the evil he's done.'

'Even while I've hated him, I've treated him to the best of my ability.' Eddie straightened and looked at her, clear-eyed now. 'His madness seemed to be intermittent but the last weeks, he's been worse than ever, his fury, his madness, has burnt him out. This is why I waited until now to send for you, I wanted to spare you as much pain as possible.'

'I know.' Arian spoke quietly. 'I feel so guilty, Eddie, I've been getting on with my life, being happy and fulfilled and I've neglected Gerald badly.'

'There was nothing you could have done even if you'd been here every day.' Eddie's words comforted her a little. 'And don't lose sight of the fact that the man was never any good to you, you must not allow yourself to feel guilty.'

Arian was silent for a moment and then she asked a question, dreading the answer. 'Should I stay?' Relief flooded through her as Eddie shook his head. 'No point, I'll be giving him some medication in a minute, he'd sleep then, peacefully, perhaps.' He paused. 'There will be matters to discuss, however painful they might be, the funeral arrangements to be made, I'm sorry but it has to be done.'

Arian shuddered. 'Will you let me know when . . . it sounds so callous to say it but you know what I mean.'

'I'll let you know,' Eddie said rising to his feet. 'Now go home, put it out of your mind for now. The end will come soon enough and then you can get on with the rest of your life.'

'And you, Eddie?'

He smiled grimly. 'I should be thanking God for what I have left, my loyal wife, my career, my friends. But I can't forget my first born daughter and the day she died in some hotel room like a common whore.' He rubbed his eyes. 'It's marked me, Arian, it's a nightmare I must live with for the rest of my life.'

294

Impulsively, Arian went to him and held him close, her head against his chest. Once they had been lovers, long ago, one summertime, now they were just two people joined by mutual misery.

When she was back in town, Arian went directly to her rooms, she couldn't face the bustle of the office. Gone was her euphoria of the morning, gone was the sense of achievement, the wonder at the way she had made a success of her life against all the odds. Instead, she felt her senses were blunted. The smell of the hospital seemed to be in the very folds of her clothes and she took them off and pushed them into a basket ready to be washed.

Once she had bathed and was dressed in a clean skirt and blouse, she felt better. She had the maid bring her some hot coffee and she leaned back in an easy chair, her feet stretched out towards the fire and tried to regain her equilibrium.

A knocking on the door roused her and she called 'Come in,' automatically. She had hoped it was Calvin, Calvin who would take her in his arms and erase all the bad memories. It was Mac, his eyes alight in a way that could only mean one thing. 'You've got a story.' It was a statement. He dropped his long frame into a chair and allowed himself a smile.

'Have I got a story!' He stared at her waiting for some reaction and she searched her mind frantically for a clue as to what he had been working on.

'Tell me,' she said at last.

'Not only has Paul Marchant disappeared in very suspicious circumstances indeed but it appears that the man might have been involved in some sort of smuggling racket.'

Arian leaned forward interested in spite of herself, her apathy vanishing. 'How did you find out all this?' she asked in surprise. 'You haven't skipped over to Ireland and back by some sort of magic carpet have you?'

'Didn't have to, just spoke to a sailor off the *Marie Clare*, one Matthew Hewson.'

Arian frowned. 'We'd better keep this quiet for the moment, just until we know more about the situation. We don't want to be accused of scandalmongering, not until we have more than this man's word to go on, after all Matthew Hewson isn't exactly famed for his honesty is he? Still, well done, I always knew you were a gifted reporter Mac, but I certainly didn't realize you could do my job better than me.' She frowned suddenly. 'What about Bridie, how is she taking all this?'

'Mrs Marchant does not seem unduly upset that her husband is not in Swansea with her. What she did tell me was that shortly she will be selling up her extravagant house and moving somewhere quiet. It seems she has got her fortune back in her own hands, somehow.'

Arian shook her head. 'The mystery deepens. I don't know how you do it, Mac, but I'm so glad you belong to *The Times* and not to any other newspaper.'

'You are very lucky to have me, Arian Smale.' He pinched her cheek. 'Now, how about you telling me what's happened to make you unhappy.'

'You are perceptive on top of all the other talents,' Arian said softly. She moved to the window and stared unseeingly into the street far below. 'It's Gerald,' she said, 'he's dying.'

'You'll pardon me if I say that's good news.' Mac's hands were suddenly on her shoulder. He turned her to face him and looked down at her with a stern expression. 'You've done your best in that quarter,' he said, 'and don't forget it.'

She shrugged hopelessly. 'What have I done but begrudge him every visit I've ever made to that place?' She paused. 'I haven't even done very much of that lately.'

'You've paid for him to have the best attention, remember? You could have abandoned him to his own fate. After all the evil that man did, anyone would have forgiven you for turning your back on him. He deserved to spend the rest of his natural life in a mad house.'

Arian sighed heavily. 'At least if he dies he'll be at peace at last.'

'That's a good thought,' Mac said, 'hold on to it.'

When Mac left the room, Arian remained where she was, staring down into the grey, wet street. She didn't know what she should feel, remorse, regrets, what? She searched within herself and all she knew was that there was a deep gratitude that her obligation to a man she hated was almost over.

Matthew Hewson had never been so glad to be walking the streets of Swansea even in the dank, winter weather and mists that pervaded the town. He had escaped from Monkton by the skin of his teeth, Marchant had not been so lucky, he'd been detained on board until the shipment of opium was delivered. Bridie Marchant had been very clever, perhaps how clever she didn't even realize herself. And where did it all leave him? He was back in Swansea, safe from Monkton's wrath but his pockets were empty except for the paltry few shillings that reporter chap had given him. Still, he hadn't revealed too much of his story, he reasoned the information might come in handy later.

He thrust his hands into his pockets, he wasn't sure just how much Bridie Marchant had found out about the illegal trade in opium and his own part in the transactions. He was a little afraid of Bridie Marchant, she was a strong, perhaps a ruthless, woman. She had turned the tables on her husband with very little trouble, she might just be too clever for Matthew. The only option left to him was to tackle Ellie Hopkins. He knew he could make her feel guilty, make her feel she owed him something and so she did, he thought bitterly.

With renewed sense of purpose, he turned towards the outskirts of the town in the direction of Glyn Hir

Tannery. He felt unaccountably nervous, unsure of his reception.

It was Rosie who answered the door to his insistent knocking. She looked at him without emotion and he deliberately smiled at her, trying to charm her. 'You're looking more lovely than ever, Rosie, a real treat for these jaded eyes of mine.'

'Wait here.' Obviously, his charm no longer had any effect on her. He thrust his hands into his pockets feeling let down, betrayed almost, how fickle women were, all over a man one minute and the next as cold as ice.

Eventually Rosie returned and Matthew was shown into the kitchen. He stood there feeling awkward, waiting for Ellie to put in an appearance. She entered the room so quietly, he scarcely heard her and she looked at him with expressionless eyes. 'What do you want, Matthew?' she asked without preamble.

'What do you think?' He might as well be as blunt as she was, he decided. 'I want some money. If I can't have the shares I'm due then I'll take hard cash instead.'

'You are joking with me, aren't you, Matthew?'

'But you said you'd pay me, that time . . .' his voice trailed away.

'That time Daniel gave you a hiding you mean?' Ellie said dryly. 'Well that was to prevent you fighting and it didn't work. You should have taken the money when you had the chance. Now it's too late.'

He moved a step nearer her. 'I could go to the police, tell them about your dealings with a certain drug smuggling racket. Don't think it would be my word only, Smithers would back me up.'

'Smithers?' Ah, he had shaken her confidence now. He looked at her with scorn in his eyes.

'Aye, Smithers, he was working for us, for me and Paul Marchant, he kept us informed of what was happening. More than that, he continued to supply the leather we required.'

'Then he wasn't very good at his job, was he?' Ellie's voice had taken on a hard note.

'Never mind all that,' Matthew spoke belligerently, on the defensive now. 'None of that makes no odds now except that you could still lose your good name.'

'You are wrong,' Ellie said, 'it's quite obvious that Paul Marchant hasn't taken you into his confidence.'

'I don't know what you mean.'

'I mean he signed some papers, he not only restored his wife's fortune to her but he cleared me of any involvement in the whole sorry business.' She smiled suddenly, 'I'm afraid you don't come out of it so well.'

'Why, what did he say about me?' Matthew felt his throat become dry.

'Just cut your losses, Matthew, go away and don't let me see you around here again or my conscience might trouble me, I might find it necessary to inform the authorities about your little schemes.'

'You're bluffing, you'd implicate Marchant too, if you did anything so rash.'

'Try me.' Ellie lifted her chin and stared directly into his eyes. He moved to the door, he knew he was defeated. He felt anger burn within him. He paused and turned towards her. 'Don't think you've got away with this, I'll get what's rightfully mine if it takes me a lifetime. You'll never know when I'll turn up, Ellie Hopkins, but I'll be there, just biding my time.'

Ellie followed him to the door. 'On your way out of the yard, tell Smithers he no longer has a job at Glyn Hir, there's a good man.'

Matthew threw her a venomous look. 'Damn you! Do your own dirty work.' He strode away, impotent anger boiling within him, he felt like reaching out, taking Ellie Hopkins by her frail throat and strangling the life out of her.

Boyo was in the yard, he looked up at Matthew with indifference and then turned away again. Matthew went over to him, turned him round and smacked him square

299

on the mouth. The boy fell to the ground; looking up, dabbing at the blood on his already swollen lips. He got to his feet. 'I owe you for that, Matthew, and one day you are going to know all about it.'

'Fat chance! Tell your boss that's for her,' he said and then he walked out of the yard, away from the stink of the tannery, heading for town.

'Good riddance to bad rubbish,' Martha said angrily. 'How dare he come here and make trouble like that.'

'I don't think we'll see him again.' Ellie sank into a chair. 'I should have realized about Smithers though, I caught him hanging around the barn when I had the contraband hidden there, at the time I thought it was just idle curiosity. Well, I can't have him working here any longer.'

'Instant dismissal, that's what's called for.' Martha folded up her sewing and put it away. 'It's too bad when you can't trust the people who work for you.' She took off her spectacles, handling them with care, they were new and she treated them like a prized possession. She had even worked an embroidered case especially to hold them. 'Pity Daniel was away at college, he'd have given Matthew Hewson short shrift.'

'I have to deal with these things myself,' Ellie said, 'at least until I can get away from the tannery for good.'

'You mean to sell up then, one day?'

'I'll have to. If I'm to go with Daniel to wherever his job takes me, I can't have the worry of the tannery too.'

'I think you should train Boyo to run the place, good man that, got brains and he's got spirit, I like that.'

'You're right,' Ellie said. 'It's a fine idea, I should have thought of it myself.

'Aye, it would give the boy a good chance to better himself, he hasn't had many chances in that young life of his, has he? Something else you want to think of, too, my lady, the year is almost up, the year of mourning for your husband. Soon you must take off your widow's

300

weeds, buy some decent colourful clothes for heaven's sake! Just look at you, black skirt, black bodice, even jet beads, you will be an old woman before your time if you don't watch out.'

Ellie smiled. 'All right, don't nag me, Martha, I am quite aware of the time passing, indeed, I'm counting the days until Dan comes home from college.'

There was a knocking on the front door and the sound of Rosie's hurrying feet across the hall.

'Good heavens, you are popular today,' Martha said in a resigned way that belied the curiosity in her eyes.

Ellie rose to her feet with a smile when the door of the sitting room opened to admit Bridie with Collins behind her. 'What a terrible smell!' Bridie said coming forward and kissing Ellie's cheek. 'How do you manage to live with it?'

'We won't have to for much longer,' Ellie laughed.

'Don't tell me you are house-hunting, too,' Bridie said warmly. 'Collins and I are going to move to Clydach, I'll buy a small cottage, somewhere easy to keep warm and clean.'

Ellie smiled, Bridie's idea of a small cottage was probably something with five bedrooms and servants' quarters. 'Sit down, please, make yourself comfortable. Tell me, what can I do for you?'

Bridie looked towards where Ellie was sitting. 'I've come to give you the note Paul signed and to say goodbye, I doubt we'll see much of each other once I move away.'

'Clydach isn't that far, I could always come up to see you. As for the note from your husband, I've already made use of that.' Ellie smiled at the surprise in Bridie's eyes. 'I pretended I already had it in my possession, Matthew Hewson was quite put out, believe me.'

'Matthew Hewson is home?' Bridie asked. 'Perhaps I should track him down, ask him what he knows about Paul's reluctance to return to Swansea.'

'I doubt he'll tell you anything,' Ellie said, 'not unless

you offer him a hefty bribe, money seems to dominate Matthew's every thought.'

'Do you know where he lives?' Bridie asked and Ellie shook her head. 'I've never cared to find out, I'm sorry, Bridie.'

'Ah, well, we'll see. Paul will get in touch when he's good and ready. In the meantime, let's just enjoy each others company while we have the chance.'

The evening shadows were closing in when Ellie stood in the doorway, waving to her departing guests. Ellie sighed, it was a good time of year with winter losing its grip on the land, the trees budding, the earth coming to life once more. And soon, very soon, she would be sharing her life with Daniel.

CHAPTER TWENTY-ONE

April was nervous. She stood in the window of the farmhouse and stared out into the garden bright with daffodils and to the fields beyond. It was lambing time, Jamie was very busy but he was prepared to give up some of his precious time in order to have tea with his stepdaughter's new friend.

'Do you think we'll have enough cake?' Fon bustled into the spotless kitchen, her slim figure encased as always in a crisp white apron. 'I don't want your young man to tell folks we don't eat well up at Honey's Farm.' She smiled and pinched April's cheek. Before April could reply, Jamie came into the kitchen, his hair sparkling with droplets of water, he looked fresh and clean and wholesome. He kissed April's head and hugged Fon in a bearlike embrace.

April shook her head at them but she understood their need for shows of affection well enough. Fon and Jamie had lost both their sons and tried to compensate for the loss by being extra loving to each other as well as to Cathie and April. Her own mother, as far as April remembered, had been a stoic, independent sort of woman who showed no-one affection. She had died when April was just a small girl and Jamie and Fon had taken April into their home, treated her like a daughter. Yet April had always felt there was something lacking. Now she had Boyo, she knew what it was, it was someone of her very own to love.

'He's coming.' Cathie bounced into the room, 'I saw him through the window. He's got his best suit on, *duw*, he looks like a dog's dinner.'

April glanced around the room, it looked bright and cheerful, a fire gleamed in the black-leaded hearth, the brasses shone and April knew she must give Fon full credit for that. The back door stood open, the fresh March breezes ruffled the white cloth on the table, April waited until Boyo knocked and then she allowed Cathie to move to let him in, not wanting to appear too eager.

His face was reddened though if it was because of the breeze or embarrassment, April couldn't tell. He took off his cap and twisted it in his hands and for a moment there was silence.

'Come in and welcome lad,' Jamie's big shoulders were bent forward as he shook Boyo's hand. 'Make yourself at home.'

Boyo sat stiffly on the edge of the chair, his glance swept towards April and she smiled tremulously.

'How are your family, lad?' Jamie was attempting to make conversation but it was the worst question he could have asked. Boyo went even redder. 'I'm an orphan, sir, came from the workhouse. Jubilee Hopkins took me in when I was young, gave me a roof over my head. Jubilee and Ellie are the only family I've ever known.'

'Tough start for any young man,' Jamie said.

April glanced at him, she was grateful to Jamie for trying to put Boyo at his ease but Boyo was shifting awkwardly in his chair.

'Why don't you show Boyo over the farm?' Jamie said. 'Tea won't be ready for a while, will it Fon?'

'Not for half hour or so, there's plenty of time. Take a shawl, April,' Fon cautioned, 'it's quite chilly out in the fields, mind.'

It was good to be in the fresh air, walking side by side with Boyo. April wanted to reach out and take his hand but she didn't quite dare. She glanced up at him and he turned his head and met her eye. 'I suppose I've cooked my goose, now, with your father, I mean.'

'No of course you haven't.' April knew at once what was worrying him. 'The fact that you grew up in the

304

workhouse won't bother Jamie one little bit, he wouldn't stop us getting married, don't you worry.'

She flushed suddenly, 'We will marry one day, won't we?' Boyo turned and faced her. 'Of course.' His eyes were blue, very blue against the brownness of his skin. She wondered briefly what his origins were, perhaps his parents came from abroad, Italy or Spain. She found the idea exotic. She held out her hand, her heart beating swiftly and he took it, curling his strong fingers around hers. She felt a thrill run through her as, linked, they walked away from the farmhouse and towards the open fields.

'Do you think you've done the right thing?' Fon asked, turning from the window to look at Jamie. 'Isn't sending them off alone like that asking for trouble?'

'I trust April to be a sensible girl,' Jamie said.

'I know but I'm still worried, what sort of future would April have with a boy like him, he has nothing.'

Jamie took her in his arms and tipped her face up to his. 'He has his pride,' he said gently. 'He's earning his keep, he's neat and clean, she could do a lot worse.'

Fon sighed, 'I suppose so.' Fon sniffed the air. 'Good heavens! I'd better take the scones out of the oven, they'll be done to death!' She bent over and lifted the tray of scones and placed it on the window-sill to cool. Perhaps it would be rather nice when April was wed, one less to wash and feed in the busy household. It was time, after all that the girl spread her wings.

She well remembered the time April had threatened to leave the farm. She had applied for a position at Glyn Hir Tannery as a maid but fortunately the post had gone to an older girl. April had sulked for a few days and then forgotten all about her intention to leave home.

Cathie came in from the garden where she had, apparently, been keeping watch. 'They're coming back,' she announced. 'He's holding her hand, dad, soppy thing.' Fon hid a smile, Cathie was at the age when she wanted nothing to do with boys. According to her they were noisy, smelly creatures.

When the couple came into the kitchen, April was flushed, her eyes shining. Fon felt tears come to her eyes, April's delight was an innocent emotion, something so beautiful, so young that Fon all at once felt old and jaded.

'Sit down, Boyo,' Fon smiled at him. 'The scones are hot from the oven and I've got a nice pot of jam put away for a special occasion and I think this is it.'

'Did you enjoy your stroll around the farm?' Jamie took a seat at the table next to Boyo, leaning on one strong arm, talking as though man to man.

'It's an eye-opener,' Boyo said. 'I didn't realize how tiny the lambs were. And the cattle, they are so docile, makes me feel a bit guilty really.'

Fon put the plate of scones on the table, 'Why should you feel guilty?'

'Well, I see only the skins,' Boyo spoke awkwardly, 'it's not very nice.'

Fon nodded. 'But then, you don't kill the beasts, that's all done at the abattoir.'

'True enough,' Boyo agreed. 'Still, it's much better seeing the cows alive and grazing in the fields than having to work with the skins all day long.'

'Perhaps one day you'll be a farmer,' Jamie said but without too much conviction. Farming had to be born and bred into a man, the long hours, the back-breaking work, the toiling in rain and shine, it was not the idyllic life many townies supposed it to be.

Boyo smiled. He really was a good-looking boy, Fon realized as she took her seat next to April. 'Ellie, Mrs Hopkins has plans for me,' Boyo spoke proudly, 'she wishes me to train up to take over the management of the tannery when she gets wed.'

'Ellie Hopkins is getting wed?' Fon asked, her interest aroused. Boyo flushed bright red. 'Sorry, I shouldn't have said anything, it's all a secret, just for the time being.'

'Well my mam and dad won't say anything,' April said comfortingly. Boyo smiled at her, obviously besotted.

The chatter became more general and Fon found that she was growing to like Boyo, his frank, open manner and his polite deference to herself and Jamie was reassuring. In any case, it was foolish to take the relationship between her stepdaughter and this young man seriously, no doubt April would have many young lads dancing attendance on her before she settled down.

Later, when the youngsters were in the parlour, Fon said as much to Jamie. He looked thoughtful. 'I don't know, they seem serious enough to me. If they're truly in love, I for one won't stand in their way.'

'Nor me,' Fon said quickly, 'but I hope that they don't rush into anything before they're sure of their feelings.'

She paused, watching Jamie shrug on his coat, he was a big handsome man and she loved him dearly, if April should be so fortunate in her choice of man then Fon would be happy for her. She reached up and hugged Jamie and he looked down at her, his eyebrows raised. 'What was that for?'

'Just to say I love you.'

Jamie pinched her cheek. 'I know you do and rightly so, aren't I the best catch for miles around?'

She flicked a cloth at him. 'Go on, off with you, you big idiot!'

She watched him as he walked away from the house and a smile curved her lips. He was right, he was the best catch for miles around and he was all hers.

Gerald's condition had become critical. By the time Arian arrived at the hospital, he was gasping for breath, his mouth blue, his face sunken and gaunt. She stood near his bed, looking down at the husband she never loved with pity.

'It won't be long now.' The doctor entered the room and stood beside her. Arian looked up at him and saw that Eddie Carpenter was rubbing at his eyes tiredly. 'We've done all that we can for him but I'm afraid it wasn't enough.'

'I'm grateful to you,' Arian said softly, 'I don't know how I would have coped without this hospital.' She sighed, 'I can't help feeling guilty that I didn't do enough for him myself.'

'You did all that was humanly possible.' Eddie spoke reassuringly. 'He needed constant medication or he would have become violent again. You have nothing with which to reproach yourself.'

'You are a nice man, Eddie Carpenter,' Arian said gratefully. She heard a sigh from the man in the bed and turning, saw that Gerald's eyes were open. He was staring upwards and though his eyes appeared clear, he seemed lost in a world of his own. 'May God forgive me,' he said and his voice was thin, reed-like in the silence of the room. And then he died, in contrast to the way he had lived, quietly and peacefully.

Arian stared down at him for a long moment seeing only the sad husk of the man who once seemed possessed with demonic strength. She could not cry, there were no tears for Gerald Simples in her. She bent her head and prayed for forgiveness for her coldness of heart. Eddie's hands were gentle upon her shoulders then, drew her away from the bed, and out of the room. She was led into an office, seated in a chair and a cup of hot tea was placed before her. She sipped it gratefully.

'Is there anything I can do?' Eddie was seated on the other side of the desk now, leaning over it, staring at her anxiously. Arian shook her head. 'No thank you, Eddie, I'll manage.' She sighed. 'I'll call into the undertakers on my way home, I don't suppose there will be much else for me to do, will there?'

'There will be no difficulties this end, Simples' death

was of natural causes, he'd been very sick for some time and his health had deteriorated over the years, there will be no problem, I assure you.'

When Arian left the hospital, she lifted her head to the cool breeze coming in from the sea. The air was softer today, it held the promise of spring. Already daffodils were waving triumphantly in the hedgerows, defying the March winds.

Later, with her unpleasant business completed, the funeral arranged, Arian made her way to Calvin's house. The maid showed her in, an expression of curiosity on her face, it was rarely Arian called without prior notice. Calvin came at once from his study, he was wearing a deep wine-coloured jacket and a crisp white shirt and he looked so wholesome and alive that Arian wanted to go straight into his arms. He led her into the drawing room and once he'd closed the doors, he held her close. 'It's over, isn't it, he's gone?'

Arian nodded wordlessly. Calvin held her closer, kissing her glossy hair. 'You did your best for him, always remember that.'

He led her to a chair and she sank down gratefully, her legs were suddenly trembling. She put her hands to her face feeling the hotness of her cheeks.

'I should be sad for him and all I feel is relief.' She looked appealingly at Calvin. 'Am I very wicked?'

'Of course not, my darling. That man put you through hell, what do you think you should feel?'

'I feel I should have tried to help him, tried harder to find a cure for his illness. At the very least I should have gone to see him more often than I did, he was my responsibility.'

'Look,' Calvin took her hands, 'whenever there's a death, those in contact with the sick person feel guilt, it's natural enough but believe me, you must shake yourself out of it. Gerald was cruel, he was a murderer and he became addicted to laudanum, what could anyone do for him that you didn't do?'

'I know what you say makes sense.' Arian rubbed her eyes, 'but . . .'

'No,' Calvin interrupted her, 'there are no "buts", what you did for Simples was over and above your duty.' He smiled. 'Come on, I'm going to take you out for a drive, we'll breathe the fresh air and look at the dawning of spring and we'll talk about our future together.'

Arian felt a glimmer of happiness, Calvin was right, there was nothing more she could do for Gerald Simples other than give him a decent Christian burial. She sighed softly and then there were tears in her eyes, though who she was crying for, she wasn't quite sure.

She rose to her feet, 'I'd like to take a drive with you, Calvin but I'll need to get back to the office, I'm not one of the idle rich like you, remember.'

He took her in his arms again. 'Will I see you tonight?' he asked softly. She nodded. 'Yes please.' She hugged him to her and then moved resolutely to the door. 'I must catch up on my work.' It was she realized what she most needed right now, to lose herself in her paper. She paused and looked up at Calvin. 'It's over, the past, my marriage, it's over at last.'

The funeral took place several days later. The rain seemed in tune with Arian's feelings as it poured grey and cold over the freshly dug earth. She looked around her, there was no-one to mourn the passing of Gerald Simples, no-one but the wife who never cared for him. The curate intoned the prayers and over his quietly spoken words, Arian heard the singing of a bird. It was like an omen, a symbol of her freedom. Was she callous to think that way?

After the brief ceremony had ended, Arian thanked the curate and seeing that he was impatient to be away to a warm fire and a change of clothing, made her way out of the cemetery and onto the road where she had a cab waiting for her.

'Excuse me, Miss Smale, might I talk to you?' A young man was standing before her, a pencil and notebook clasped in his hand. 'I'm from the *Cambrian*, we are going to write a piece about the death of Gerald Simples, I understand the man was a murderer, I wondered if you wished to make any comment?'

Arian shook her head. 'No, except you should learn to use a little tact if you want to become a good reporter.'

Alone, she drove home to her rooms above the press and considered the future that was unfolding before her. Soon, she would put the past behind her, she would feel free to marry Calvin. She experienced a dart of unease at the thought and then pushed the feeling aside. She wanted to be with Calvin, of course she did, have everything out in the open with no need to hide in corners but there would be ample time for that, later, much later. He had wished to accompany her to the funeral today but she had dissuaded him, it was pointless fuelling the flames of the gossips, enough had been said in the past about Arian Smale and her affairs.

The clip-clop of the horse's hooves slowed and Arian realized that she was home. She paid the driver and hurried indoors, locking the door behind her. Upstairs in her rooms, the fire burned in the grate and Arian sank down on the carpet feeling the warmth of the flames penetrate the coldness that had settled over her.

Later, she bathed and changed into fresh dry clothing and then tucked her feet up under her skirts for warmth. She had asked Calvin not to come around this evening, she needed to be alone. There was no question that she wished to be Calvin's wife or was there? She loved him but did she really want to live with him in his grand house? She glanced around her, the room was comfortable, familiar, it was hers and it was home. Outside she could hear the distant sound of traffic, the sound of horses' hooves on the cobbles, of street vendors calling their wares to entice the passer-by. She was in the heart of Swansea and she liked that. She supposed she had settled into a rut during the past years, she had become quite selfish in her independence but it was a good feeling to be answerable to no-one, to be mistress of her destiny. Marriage to Calvin would change all that, was that what she really wanted?

Even when she retired to her bed, thoughts still plagued her, doubts about her future loomed large. She would sleep on it, she decided and then, when she was calm and clear-headed, she would make her decision.

It was late the next evening by the time she saw Calvin, she had been busy with the paper, there had been more than the usual petty irritations to mar her day. The tide tables had been wrong again and a family who had been named in a trial at Swansea courts was claiming it was a case of mistaken identity. Mac had lost his temper and dismissed one of the junior reporters and the young man's fiancée from the typing room had burst into tears and declared she was leaving too.

'Had a hard day?' Calvin asked when she arrived at his house and flung herself into the nearest chair sighing with gratitude at being off her feet.

'You could say that.' Arian unlaced her boots and kicking them off, wriggled her toes with pleasure.

'Well, that will all be over in a month or two.' Calvin poured her a good measure of port. 'You'll be a lady of leisure when you're my wife.'

'I'm not quite sure I understand you.' A prickle of apprehension made Arian's voice more sharp than she had intended. 'I would still expect to run the paper, Calvin, there's never been any question of me giving that up.'

'But you can't work when you are married to me,' Calvin was genuinely surprised, 'you'll be Lady Calvin Temple, you need never work again.'

'I need never work again as it is,' Arian replied tartly, 'I have enough funds to keep me in modest comfort for the rest of my life but that's not the point.'

Calvin looked grave. 'Then what is the point?'

Arian shook her head. 'Calvin, I've been having doubts, not of my love for you,' she added hastily, 'that is without question but am I really cut out for marriage, I wasn't much of a wife to Gerald Simples was I?'

He turned away from her and she knew he was hurt. She rose swiftly and went to him but he held the two glasses of port between them as though they were a shield.

'How can you love me if you don't wish to marry me?' His voice had taken on an edge and Arian moved away from him and stared down into the fire.

'You know I need a son,' Calvin said, 'I thought you were of a mind to give me an heir.'

'I know and I would love to have your child, our child, but Calvin, I can't give up the newspaper, I really can't, not even for you.' Her pathway was clear now, she knew what she must do.

'Calvin, I can't marry you, I've been having doubts about it and now that you have put forward your ideas of what our married life would be like, I know it would be wrong for me.' She paused and then spoke more gently. 'Can't we just carry on as we have been doing all this time, please?'

Calvin put down the glasses and came to her, taking her in his arms. 'I need you, Arian, I want you to be the mother of my child, isn't that natural?'

'Yes, of course it is,' she said, 'but . . .'

'There are no buts,' Calvin's voice was hard, 'either you love me enough to give up the paper or the relationship is ended.'

'Don't give me ultimatums.' Arian drew herself away from him. 'I can't be forced into a mould, it's far too late in my life for that. I've been used enough, now I am a woman in my own right, a successful woman. I love working on the paper, I raised it up from nothing but rusting machinery and a dilapidated building, I've made *The Times* one of the most popular papers in Swansea, I can't give it up.'

'We both know that the paper could function very well without you,' Calvin said. 'Mac is talented, he's more than capable of managing the affairs of the business alone so don't make me excuses, Arian.'

Arian sat on one of the elegant chairs and drew on her boots, lacing them up with short angry stabs of her fingers. 'I'm a person, not an object to obey your commands, how dare you talk to me like that?'

'You bent to Simples' will but you won't bend to mine, is that it?'

Arian looked up at him. 'That's not fair and you know it, Gerald was always unstable, he used coercion and force, I had expected more of you.'

He was kneeling beside her then, trying to take her hands in his, 'I'm sorry, I didn't mean all that, I was angry, forgive me, my love.'

She let him hold her but she was unresponsive, tense in his arms. When he released her she looked into his face, his dear face so close to her own.

'But you won't let me be your wife and the proprietor of *The Times*, is that correct?'

Her tone angered him and he rose to his feet, thrusting his hands into his pockets, moving away from her. 'You've summed up the situation with your usual swiftness of mind.' He was being sarcastic and they both knew it.

'Then there's nothing more to be said.' She moved out into the hall and by the way the maid appeared swiftly from the shadows and helped Arian with her coat, it was clear she had been listening. Tomorrow, the word would be all over Swansea, that now, even though she was a widow, Calvin Temple was not going to make an honest woman of Arian Smale.

Well to hell with them and to hell with Calvin, she had managed alone before, she would do so again. She began to walk towards the town where the lights were flickering from the streets and where the sea, silver in the moonlight, washed into the shore.

She had half expected Calvin to come after her, she listened for the sound of a horse and the wheels of the

314

carriage but the silence fell thickly around her. The street lamps were nearer now but they shimmered as the tears filled her eyes. What had she done? She had alienated Calvin perhaps for ever. And yet she knew that if she had to make the choice between marriage and the newspaper all over again, she would have come to the same decision.

Well, she was on her own now, a widow but a rich and successful one. She held her head high as she entered the Strand and as the sign above the door of the newspaper office came into sight, ghostly in the lamplight, she felt her spirits lift a little, she was coming home.

CHAPTER TWENTY-TWO

Ellie had retired early, worn out after a day of helping in the grinding house. Martha had been horrified. 'You'll spoil your hands, they'll be calloused and stained, not the sort of hands a vicar's wife should have.'

'It has to be done,' Ellie had protested, 'we're two men short; with Smithers gone and Harry taken to his sick bed, there's nothing for it but to get on as best we can.'

'Let Rosie do it, then,' Martha replied. 'She's a robust girl, more fitted to the work than you are.'

'I'd rather Rosie carry on with the housework, the washing, the cooking, that sort of thing, she does it well, much better than I ever did.'

Martha had not been appeased and now, lying in her bed, Ellie felt that Martha had a point. Ellie's bones ached, her head ached, she felt as though she had been kicked from one side of the yard to the other. She was getting soft.

She needed to take on more hands; Harry, Luke and Boyo were good workers but they couldn't be made responsible for the entire running of the tannery. The currying, unhairing and fleshing, the soaking of skins in a solution of oak bark, these were time-consuming operations. As well as hard physical effort, skill was involved if good leather was to be produced and the high standards of the Glyn Hir tannery were to be maintained.

Boyo had been working like a Trojan in the grinding house, doing the work of two men. He had been carrying in the plates of oak bark, feeding the greedy wheels of the hopper as well as carrying the bark chippings out to the yard. He couldn't keep that sort of pace going, however willing he was and today Ellie had taken pity on him. She unearthed her old skirt and top and had gone into the grinding house to help him. Now she was overtired, she couldn't sleep.

She thought of Daniel, wondering if he was awake in his college room in Lampeter, looking out at the stars. The same stars she could see through her own bedroom window. She felt a stab of disquiet, had he got over his disapproval of her involvement in the opium business? She had done her best in a bad situation but her best did not measure up to Daniel's moral scruples.

She turned her face away from the moonlit window and firmly closed her eyes but sleep would not come. Her thoughts were racing around her head like the slivers of bark inside the hopper. Was what she had done to protect herself so wrong, she wondered? Perhaps it had been selfish of her to wish for a way out of Matthew's blackmailing scheme, perhaps she should have gone to the authorities straight away and told them about the contraband just as Daniel had wished. But what was the use of thinking of what might have been?

Ellie sat up and lit the lamp. She plumped up her pillows against the hard brass bedhead and looked around her at the shadow-filled room. She wished Daniel was here with her now so she could tell him how much she loved him. He was a man of strong principles and she admired him for it but he was young, untried, he didn't yet know the pitfalls the world could hold in store.

Ellie lifted her head, suddenly alert, she had heard a sound out in the yard, she sat up straighter, listening intently but there was only silence. She sighed and doused the lamp and then slipped from her bed and pushed aside the curtains, opening the window wide. A bright moon was shining, she could see in the distance the shape of the wall around the tannery. The shadow of the buildings were in stark contrast to the splashes of moonlight, it was a fine, crisp spring night.

She was just about to close the window and return to bed when she scented the hint of smoke in the air. She raised the window higher and leaned out and the sharp tang of burning wood was unmistakable. She saw it then, a flame rising from the roof of the currying house and even as she watched, it sprung higher, shooting sparks into the night sky.

The oak bark was dry, it hadn't rained for several days, it would burn fiercely. It was out in the middle of the yard and though it should not have posed a threat to any of the buildings, the fire was spreading. The beam house was alight too now and Ellie was suddenly galvanized into action.

She pulled on a robe and hurried into Boyo's room. 'Wake up, Boyo, the tannery is on fire!'

He was awake at once, as though he had not long been asleep. He sat up, wide-eyed and saw the flames outlined against the closed curtains of his room.

'I'll get help.' He slid from his bed and drew on his trews and neither Ellie nor he had time to be embarrassed by his state of undress.

'I'll call Martha, I doubt if the fire would spread this far but it's best to be on the safe side.'

Martha, in contrast to Boyo was slow to wake, she sat up and rubbed her eyes and Ellie had to repeat herself several times before the older woman rose reluctantly from her bed. 'Don't know what the world is coming to,' she grumbled, 'never had fires in the middle of the night in my young days.'

Ellie met Rosie on the landing, the girl was rubbing her eyes, her hair hanging loose to her shoulders. Ellie ushered her downstairs, 'Come on, Rosie, wake up and make sure Martha doesn't go back to sleep. I'm going to investigate, I won't be long.'

Ellie hurried outside and was struck at once by the acrid smell of burning leather. As she neared the tannery, she could see that most of the buildings were well alight.

As if by an unseen signal, Harry arrived at the tannery,

he looked unshaven and bleary-eyed, he should not really be out of bed, Ellie thought with a stab of concern. Close on his heels was Luke, he stood, hands on hips staring at the flames with disbelief. '*Duw*, there's not a lot anyone can do here,' he said mournfully. 'The whole place is going up like a tinder box.'

'Aye,' Harry wiped his brow as a piece of smoking bark touched his hair. 'Someone's done a good job here, Ellie.'

'Do you think it was deliberate then?' Ellie asked and Harry nodded sagely. 'Oh, aye, no accident this, nothing here to ignite the timber, see? This is deliberate, no question.'

Ellie heard a bell ringing, it echoed faintly against the roar of the burning buildings.

'Fire brigade is on its way,' Luke said. 'Bit late, if you ask me.'

'Boyo went for them as soon as we saw the fire,' Ellie said, 'I suppose we should have realized it was useless, the wooden buildings were bound to go up in minutes.' She felt suddenly weary. 'I might as well go back to the house. Tell the leading fireman to come up to see me when he's finished here.'

Ellie rested her hand on Harry's shoulder. There was nothing she could do and standing in the yard shivering was not helping anyone. As she turned away from the flames, she realized she was still in her nightclothes.

'Aye, go on you, Ellie, we'll see what we can salvage from this little lot.'

Up at the house, Martha was fully awake and dressed, she looked up questioningly as Ellie entered the kitchen. Rosie was peering into the fire, carefully shovelling coal onto the fading embers.

'Is it bad?' Martha was white-faced but her greying hair had been brushed carefully into place. She would meet her maker looking impeccably tidy, Ellie thought as Martha continued to speak. 'I can smell the burning leather from here.'

'I think the lot is ruined.' Ellie sank into a chair and drew her robe closer, she was suddenly very cold. 'Jubilee would be so distressed if he could see the tannery now, hardly a building left undamaged.'

'Will it be a great loss, financially, I mean?' Martha sounded anxious and Ellie shook back her long hair. 'I'll have no money problems, Jubilee left me very well provided for, it's just sad to see all he worked for going up in smoke.'

'How do you think it started?' Martha leaned across the table, 'It's not likely it was an accident, is it?'

'I bet it was that Matthew Hewson,' Rosie looked up, her face was smudged with dust, 'no-one else wicked enough to deliberately set light to the tannery is there?'

Ellie privately agreed with Rosie, Matthew was more than capable of carrying out an act of arson. 'We don't know who is to blame,' she said firmly. 'The firemen will soon have the blaze under control and perhaps they can tell us exactly what has happened.'

Rosie brightened, 'The firemen will be coming up to the house? Oh, I think they're so brave, they rescue people an' all, don't mind putting themselves in danger.'

'I think you'd best get some clothes on.' Martha's tone was acid.

'*Duw*, there's nothing to see, me and Ellie are both wrapped up like babies in a shawl,' Rosie protested. 'In any case, it looks as if it's too late, if I'm not mistaken there's the sound of voices in the garden, the men are here all ready and gasping for a cuppa, I bet.'

Ellie sighed in resignation as there was a knock on the door and Harry entered the kitchen. 'I've got the boys from the brigade here,' he said, 'can they come in for a minute?'

'Of course, Rosie, you'd better put the kettle on.' Ellie drew her robe more tightly around her. 'Come in, find a seat, boys, tell me the worst.'

The leading fireman took off his helmet and pushed back a tuft of hair that was dark with sweat. 'Not much left, missus,' he said. 'Definitely a case of arson because we found traces of oil-soaked rags next to the currying house.' He smelled of burning wood and his face ran with rivulets of sweat. 'The seat of the fire was at the pile of oak bark you had stacked in the yard, easy enough to set light to those, dry as tinder they were.'

Ellie sighed, it could only be Matthew who had set the fire, no-one else would have been so wicked and irresponsible. Harry and Luke stood in the doorway, faces blackened with smoke and Ellie felt a dart of pity for them. From today, there would be no work at Glyn Hir.

'Will you rebuild the place?' Harry asked as though reading her mind. Ellie rubbed at her eyes. 'I don't know, Harry, I really don't know what I'll do.' She looked around. 'I must talk to Boyo, anyone seen him?'

'He was in the yard, looking for clues, so he said.' Harry looked grim, 'Like the rest of us, he has a fair idea who started the fire.'

Ellie frowned worriedly, 'Do you think you'd better go and look for him, Harry? I don't want any harm to come to him.'

Harry nodded and left the room and Ellie sank into a chair, staring round her in bewilderment, not able to believe what was happening.

Rosie was in her element, she made pot after pot of tea, supplying the firemen with as much as they could drink. Watching her, envying Rosie's energy and enthusiasm, Ellie felt tired and depressed, nothing seemed to be going right in her life any more. It was frightening to think that she had made such a bad enemy of Matthew Hewson that he would set light to the tannery and burn it to the ground.

Harry returned. 'No sign of him,' he said, 'boy's gone off somewhere on business of his own, I reckon.'

'You sure he's not lying hurt somewhere?' Ellie asked anxiously. 'I haven't seen him for ages.'

'He's all right, that lad can take care of himself,' Harry

said. 'He was standing with us as bold as brass when the fire was put out so he's quite safe; he's got his own reasons for going off the way he has, don't you worry.'

At last, the firemen piled out of the small kitchen leaving it suddenly empty. Ellie rubbed her eyes with her hands, afraid she was going to cry. Martha banged the empty teapot on the table and sank into a chair. 'I thought they'd never go and leave us in peace. They must all be awash with tea,' Martha sniffed looking pointedly at Rosie.

'Don't be ungrateful,' Rosie replied. 'Them boys are brave, mind, you wouldn't like to put yourself in danger every day like they do, would you?'

'Come on, you two,' Ellie said quietly. 'It's still only early morning, let's try to get some rest.'

'I won't go back to sleep, not now,' Martha said. 'Go on up, you, I'll occupy myself with a bit of sewing.'

Ellie climbed the stairs wearily and sat on the bed, still wearing her robe. She knew she wouldn't sleep but she needed to be alone, needed to quieten her thoughts. There were big decisions to be made and in her present frame of mind she was very worried that she might make the wrong ones.

Once the firemen had finished their job, something had caught Boyo's eyes, a small movement, a glimmer of light, he wasn't sure what but obeying his instincts, he'd quietly made his way out of the yard.

The moon had obligingly reappeared from behind a cloud and Boyo had seen the tall figure of Matthew Hewson striding along the lane leading to the road as if he was out on a daylight stroll.

Boyo had traced him to the boarding house where he was staying, saw him entering the door using his own key and knew that Matthew had made a cosy home for himself. Boyo took note of the address, it might come in useful. He rubbed his chin, he still smarted from the way Matthew had hit him, casually, as if he was nothing but a punch bag. Well he would show Matthew Hewson that he had brains, a much more useful asset than brawn alone could ever be. One day, Matthew Hewson would have his just deserts and when that day came, Boyo would be there, watching.

Daniel was coming to see her. Ellie was luxuriating in hot water in the large zinc bath, the warmth of the kitchen fire casting a rosy glow on her breasts and arms. She wondered what Daniel would say when he came home, with luck he would have put the business of the opium smuggling out of his mind.

Later, in her room, she combed her hair; long, curling hair, lit with golden lights, she wanted to be as perfect as possible for the man she loved.

Downstairs, Rosie was washing up the dishes in an enamel bowl, she looked up in approval when she saw Ellie. 'Excited are you?' Rosie's eyes were alight, 'it must be lovely to be promised to such a good man.' She sighed.

'Rosie, I don't want any gossip about me and Daniel getting married, not outside these four walls, anyway.'

There was a knock on the door and Ellie rose to her feet, her heart beat swiftly in anticipation. 'Go answer it, Rosie, tell him I won't be long.'

She took a last look at herself in the mirror over the fireplace and then, slowly, not to appear too eager, she went towards the doorway. In the hall, Rosie was giggling like a little girl and Ellie felt disappointment fill her as she realized that the caller was not Daniel but Caradoc Jones. She forced herself to smile, she had completely forgotten this was his night to do the books.

'Sorry to hear of the fire, Ellie.' Caradoc seemed to have difficulty tearing his eyes away from Rosie's smiling lips. 'Dreadful thing to happen, dreadful.'

Ellie led the way into the parlour. 'Come on in, Caradoc, there's a nice fire burning in the grate.'

Caradoc was looking back over his shoulder. 'Lovely little lady, Rosemary, so sweet and innocent.' Caradoc's eyes were alight in his plump face. As was his habit, he stood back to the fire and lifted his coat to feel the full benefit of the warmth. 'Yes, such innocence is rare these days.' Caradoc repeated.

Ellie hid a smile, innocent wasn't the way she would describe Rosie. Caradoc looked at her properly for the first time. 'You are very smart, Ellie, expecting company are you?'

'Daniel Bennett should be here any time now, so I hope you will forgive me if I leave you alone,' Ellie said, 'but please, make yourself comfortable, Rosie will bring you some refreshment in a minute.'

Daniel was late. He came into the hallway on a breath of cool evening air and handed Rosie his hat and coat. Rosie disappeared and Daniel took Ellie in his arms. 'I'm sorry,' he said, 'last time we talked I acted like a pompous prig, I should have known better.

'And now I find the tannery razed to the ground, what's happened here Ellie? Why didn't you get a message to me? I'd have come at once.' He didn't wait for a reply, 'Have the police found out who was behind it?'

She shook her head. 'No, not yet, I don't suppose they ever will either.' She smiled. 'Never mind, I feel better now that you are here with me.'

She felt a tingling sensation as he ran his hand lightly over her back and up to her neck, caressing the warmth beneath the thick braid of hair.

'I don't think I can wait until I've finished my training,' he spoke softly. 'There's nothing to keep you here, now, why don't we get married right away?'

The door to the kitchen opened and Martha poked her head round it, peering short-sightedly at the couple in the hallway. 'Aren't you going to say hello to old Martha then?' she said with mock anger. Daniel moved forward and kissed Martha on the cheek. 'Same old grouch,' he said playfully, 'haven't you got a smile for me?'

Martha made a pretence of cuffing Daniel and turned back to the kitchen fire.

'Where's Rosie?' Ellie asked, 'I'd like her to make sure Caradoc is taken care of.'

'She's making sure of that all right, she's still in there,' Martha jerked her head towards the parlour. 'Been in there some time, she has, Caradoc is right taken with the girl and she revels in it.'

Martha drew Daniel towards the chair near the hearth. 'Should have been here on the night of the fire, flames shooting right up into the sky there were, mind, took the firemen hours to put out the blaze.'

'I would very much like to know how it started,' Daniel said grimly.

'So would we all.' Martha rose and gathered together her sewing and her glasses, 'I'm going off to my bed, I think I can trust you two to behave yourselves.' She left the room quietly and Daniel turned to Ellie.

'What are you going to do?'

'About the tannery you mean?' She stretched her hand across the scrubbed surface of the table and rested her fingers on his. 'I don't know, Daniel, I suppose I will have to close it down, there doesn't seem much point in trying to rebuild. It might be better if I sold up the house and the land as it is.'

Daniel rubbed his chin thoughtfully. 'It's a pity to let years of work go to waste, I think it might be well worth thinking about rebuilding.' He smiled, 'Though if we get married soon, you won't be able to work the place yourself.' He paused, 'I know I'm being unfair but I'm asking you to become the wife of a poor clergyman.'

'We won't be poor, Dan,' Ellie said gently, 'you know very well that Jubilee left me more than adequately provided for.'

'I don't want you to use your money,' Daniel said quickly, 'you keep that in case of a rainy day.'

She was silent for a moment and then she took a deep breath. 'You're right, about rebuilding the tannery, it meant a great deal to Jubilee. In any case, I did promise Boyo that he could eventually run the place. Harry and Luke would be grateful to still have a job, as well.'

'There you are then.' He looked across at her intently. 'Now, are you going to answer the question I asked ten minutes ago?'

Ellie smiled at him, her face illuminated with happiness. 'Do you really want to marry me as soon as possible, Dan are you sure?' She was silenced by Daniel's mouth on hers.

It was late by the time Daniel left the house. He was the last to go, Caradoc having departed a little after ten-thirty. Ellie stood in the doorway and watched until he was out of sight and then, she made to close the door on the darkness of the night.

Suddenly, she was forced backward as the door was flung open. A large figure blocked the doorway and Ellie put her hand to her mouth to prevent herself from crying out in fear. 'Who is it, what do you want?' Her voice sounded small, shaky and Ellie swallowed hard, trying to summon her courage.

He came into the hall, closing the door behind him and Ellie saw his face for the first time. 'Matthew, what do you think you are doing here this time of night, are you mad?'

He didn't answer, he reached out and caught her blouse, pulling at it with rough fingers. The fabric was strong and impatiently, Matthew swore. Ellie backed away from him, frightened by the look on his face.

'I want to teach you a lesson you won't forget.' Matthew caught her and pressed her up against the wall. His hand was lifting her skirts, pushing them aside. His intentions became all too clear.

Ellie opened her mouth to scream but he clamped his hand over her lips. With a quick movement, he pushed her to the floor, pinning her with his weight. 'So you want to play it rough do you?' His eyes were fevered, it was clear he had been drinking.

Ellie struggled frantically to free herself, 'Don't do this, Matthew, you'll be sorry, I warn you.'

His hand was rough on her bodice, pulling open the buttons, hurting her with his grip. 'Ah, what pretty breasts and look at that darling little beauty spot just on your shoulder there let me kiss it.' His mouth was hot against her bare flesh and Ellie shuddered. 'Leave me alone, please leave me alone.'

He wasn't listening, he lifted himself upwards loosening the thick belt at his waist. Ellie, looking beyond Matthew's shoulder, saw a slim figure loom out of the darkness. She saw the glint of a spade, heard the noise as it came hammering downwards.

Matthew remained poised for a moment as if frozen before falling away from Ellie, blood pouring down his forehead. She put her hand over her mouth as she saw Boyo, his face white, standing over Matthew's still form. She couldn't believe so much had happened in the space of a few minutes. She staggered to her feet and as Boyo dropped the spade from his nerveless fingers, she put her arms around him and held him close.

Rosie came rushing down the stairs and into the kitchen, her hair tangled about her face. When she saw the figure on the floor, she gave a small scream, her eyes wide. 'Is he dead?' Her voice was muffled. Ellie was too frightened to answer her. It was Martha, coming more slowly into the hallway, who had the presence of mind to bend over Matthew and feel the pulse in his neck.

'He'll live,' she said. 'I reckon you'd best run and fetch the constable, Rosie.'

Ellie made an effort to gather her wits. 'Wait, you don't know what happened here.'

'I'm not daft,' Martha said, 'this villain,' she looked scornfully at Matthew's unconscious body, 'he tried to rape you. Boyo here, he defended you the best way he knew how.'

327

'I don't want the police brought into this,' Ellie said, 'I can do without the scandal it will cause.'

Martha appeared doubtful. 'But look at the state of you, you're trembling,' she said.

'Yes and that's all I am, shaken. I'm not harmed, my clothing isn't torn, who'd believe I didn't lead Matthew on?'

'What are we to do then?' Martha was less certain of her ground now, seeing sense in Ellie's reasoning.

'Boyo, get one of the horses hitched up to a waggon, we'll take Matthew into town, leave him somewhere he'll be found at first light.'

Boyo spoke for the first time, 'You stay here, Ellie. I know where Matthew lives, I'll take him there, say I found him unconscious in the street. I doubt he'll want to tell the truth about what happened here tonight.'

When the cart had rumbled away across the yard towards town, Rosie set to clearing up the mess. A table had been knocked over in the struggle and a lamp tipped onto the floor. Oil was making a stain across the polished boards.

'Leave that, Rosie, come along, we'll sit in the kitchen,' Ellie said, 'it should still be warm in there.' The women sat in silence until, about an hour later, the sound of wagon wheels could be heard outside in the yard.

'Thank God!' Ellie whispered, 'Boyo's come home.'

He was smiling. 'All done,' he said, 'Dora Griffiths, the lady who owns the boarding house, took in my story hook, line and sinker, seen him drunk before, I expect.'

'What did you tell her about the bump on his head, how did you explain that?'

'Didn't have to,' Boyo said, 'she decided herself that he must have fallen and cracked his head on the cobbles. Said I was a good lad for fetching him home. He started to come round then, so I scarpered. I bet he has a thick head and served him right.'

Ellie pushed back her hair, 'Perhaps I deserve all the

328

grief Matthew's giving me, I should just have given him the money he asked for in the beginning.'

'One like him would never be satisfied,' Martha said quietly. 'Give him an inch and he'd take a mile, keep coming back for more until he'd bled you dry. He's the type who never forgets a grudge.'

Ellie shivered, it was as though someone had just walked over her grave.

CHAPTER TWENTY-THREE

It hadn't taken Bridie very long to find just the house she wanted. It was built on a hillside between Clydach and Pontardawe facing the open countryside.

The house was of old stone, mellowed by the years into a pale biscuit colour. The windows were long and numerous, allowing for greater penetration of light into all but the northernmost corners of the building. The ceilings were high, with a delicate tracery of plasterwork reminiscent of icing on a cake. It felt like home and Bridie loved it at once.

'Do you think we'll be happy here?' she took Collins' hand as they stood in the drawing room, innocent of furniture, the boards bare, the windows uncurtained. Sunlight spilled in from the spacious gardens to the front of the property and on the perimeter of the grounds, trees added a green fringe to the lush, overgrown lawns.

'I'd be happy with you anywhere, Bridie.' He still spoke her name shyly and Bridie loved him for it. She smiled at him, wanting him to be as happy as she was.

How she could have overlooked Collins' qualities when he was simply her butler, she just didn't know. He was such a warm, caring man, so strong in every way and she had treated him as a mere servant, not even noticing his fine looks and dignified bearing.

'Will you bring any of your furniture with you from the Swansea house?' Collins moved closer, his arm encircling her waist as though he wanted to reassure himself that she was a real flesh and blood woman and not a figment of his imagination.

Bridie shook her head emphatically. 'No, I want to

make a clean break. Once Paul comes back to Swansea he can take charge of Carmella and I can sell Sea Mistress. I can rid myself of all the bad memories the place holds for me.' She looked up at Collins, her eyes pleading. 'I can make a home for my sons here, you *will* take to them won't you, Collins?'

He turned her to face him. 'They were always good boys and they are part of you, I'll fall in love with them just as I did with you.'

'What do you really think of them?' Bridie brushed a speck of dust from his lapel and Collins smiled at the proprietary attitude Bridie was adopting towards him.

'Two healthy, noisy little boys, normal as any others.'

Bridie sighed. 'Paul arranged things so that the boys were never home. Once I left him, he vowed I would lose them, he sent them away to relatives out of sheer spite. Will they blame me for this sorry mess, Collins?'

'When they come home, they are going to have to adjust to a great many changes, give them time, Bridie, just don't be too impatient.'

She knew he was right. She moved to the window and stared into the garden. 'Would you like a child of your own, Collins?'

'Is this question academic or is there something you're trying to tell me?'

She laughed. 'No, I'm not pregnant, I don't suppose I ever will be again, at least that's what the doctors told me.'

'Well, doctors,' Collins shrugged, 'they are often wrong aren't they?'

'That's true, if I'd believed them I wouldn't be standing here on my own two feet, now would I? Anyway, you didn't answer my question.'

'I am content, more than content with what I have now,' he said. 'God has been good to me, allowing me to have the woman I love, someone I believed was out of my reach. I wouldn't dream of asking for more.'

'But,' Bridie persisted, 'you *would* like a son, most men want to have an heir don't they?'

'Even if they have nothing to leave?' Collins's voice was teasing. 'Yes, I suppose I would like a son but only if you were his mother. As it is, I have all I want or need right here.'

Bridie closed her eyes as he came close, holding her to him. She listened to his heart beating against hers and breathed in the scent of him. Tears of happiness came to her eyes and she let them run unchecked down her cheeks. She held Collins tightly and they remained standing entwined in each others arms for a long moment before Bridie released her hold.

'We must make arrangements to have our house cleaned and refurbished ready for us to move into as soon as possible,' she spoke softly, dreamily, looking around the sun-warmed room and then back to where Collins was standing watching her, his head on one side. It was as if, even now, he could not believe what was happening to him.

'Come on,' Bridie said more briskly, 'we'd better make tracks for Swansea, I have a great many arrangements to make.'

He bowed mockingly, 'Your carriage awaits, my lady.'

Bridie flipped him playfully across his arm and swept out of the room, her head high, playing the haughty lady. In the carriage, she glanced sideways at Collins, his profile was strong, not really handsome but with a fascinating charm that made her heart melt. Once he would never have sat beside her but would have been up top, in the front of the carriage with the driver, but even then Collins had had an air of being his own man. Now he was her man and she meant to hold on to him.

It was painful walking up to the door of Sea Mistress again, she had been wise to return to Jono's house in Clydach, Bridie decided. The front door stood open and as Bridie entered the large hall, one of the maids greeted her with relief. 'Oh, Missus Marchant, I'm so glad to

332

see you! The girl, the Irish lady, she's been taken bad, it looks as if she's losing the baby.'

Bridie turned to Collins and he nodded, knowing what was needed without being told. 'I'll fetch the doctor at once.'

Carmella was in bed, gowned in voluminous white night attire, her young face a mask of pain.

'It's going to be all right,' Bridie said softly, 'it's going to be just fine, I promise you, the doctor is on his way.'

'I want Paul, why isn't he here? I want my mother, I want a priest, Oh God help me!' Carmella's voice was thin with fear, she clutched at Bridie's hands, 'I'm hurting so much, I think I'm going to die without being absolved of my sin.'

'You are not going to die,' Bridie said firmly.

Carmella clutched at her stomach, her face contorted in anguish, she held on tightly to Bridie's hand as though afraid she would be left alone. Bridie felt a sudden pity for the girl and an anger against Paul for landing them all in this mess.

It was a relief when the doctor, a young man, new to the district, entered the room breathing confidence as he came. 'Dr Squires, at your service.' He bowed to Bridie, 'Let's have a look at the little lady then.'

Carmella shrank against the pillows, shaking her head from side to side. 'No, not a man,' she gasped, 'I can't let a man touch me, it's not right.'

'Carmella, this man is a doctor, it's his job to help women in labour, don't be silly.'

But Carmella was adamant, she pushed the doctor, her eyes wide with terror and after a moment he moved away from her shrugging his shoulders. 'No point in upsetting her further, she's almost hysterical as it is. Bring in a midwife, there's a good nurse lives only half an hour away by carriage, send your man to fetch her, there's nothing I can do here.' He sounded regretful, thinking possibly of the fat fee he'd been anticipating.

'You will be paid for your time and trouble,' Bridie

said ushering him from the room, 'just send me your bill.'

Dr Squires left the house with the same jaunty step as he'd entered, it looked as if he was coming out of the bargain very well, no effort had been required on his part and yet he was being paid for his time, quite a good evening's work.

Carmella's ordeal was a long one. She was lying inert on the bed, looking near to death when at last, she miscarried of her child. The nurse looked down at Carmella and shook her head. 'Poor little mite, not cut out for this malarkey is she?' Her gaze moved to Bridie.

'You are small, madam, if you will pardon me saying so, but you have good hips, built for carrying. Two sons you've got, I understand? Well it will be a girl next, mark my words.'

Bridie bowed her head as a feeling of regret washed over her for what could never be. She coughed to hide the rush of emotion but the nurse was busy tidying up, washing her hands, rolling down her sleeves. She had not noticed the effect her words had upon Bridie.

'I'll call tomorrow, see how the little lady is doing. Once she recovers,' she nodded to the figure in the bed, 'she'll be as right as she's ever been.'

Bridie saw the midwife to the door, she wondered if she should leave Carmella to rest, but the girl's voice called to her thinly from the bed.

'I want to go home to Ireland,' Carmella said pleadingly, 'say you'll arrange it for me.'

'If that's what you want then I'll see to it as soon as you are up and about.'

Carmella fell back exhausted, beneath her eyes were blue shadows, she looked pinched and ill and Bridie felt pity drag at her. Why was it that everyone Paul touched, he hurt?

Carmella began to cry, 'Paul hasn't deserted me, has he? Surely he'll come for me in Ireland. I'm sorry, he's *your* husband but he loves *me*.'

'Don't worry, I fell out of love with Paul a long time ago,' Bridie said flatly. 'I knew he had other women, I suppose I became used to the idea.' She saw Carmella flinch and regretted her words at once. 'But perhaps you're right about him being in love with you.'

Carmella looked up at her anxiously. 'I wasn't the first one he'd been with since he was married, then?'

Bridie rose from the bed. 'I'm afraid not. Rest now, you'll need all your strength if you want to travel home soon. In the meantime I'll arrange to send a letter to your parents, I'll tell them to expect you within the month.'

'Bridie,' Carmella's voice was soft, 'do you think he's gone off with another woman, then, is that why he hasn't come home?'

Bridie shrugged. 'I just don't know, Carmella, he's never been the predictable kind, he might well have gone off on a ship somewhere for all I know.'

Bridie left Carmella to rest and stood for a moment on the spacious landing. Sunlight was streaming in through the stained-glass window, falling patterns of light splashed the walls and the carpet with myriad colours.

Strange how the world turned around, she mused, once, not very long ago she would have been bitter, unforgiving, hating the girl who had stolen Paul's affections. Now, all she felt was pity for Carmella, the girl would just have to learn that Paul was an incurable womanizer. She had believed his protestations of love but now it must be clear even to Carmella that Paul was a man no woman could ever be sure of.

The sounds of activity from the yard penetrated the kitchen where Rosie was roasting a chicken for lunch. She moved to the window and stared out at the half-dozen tradesmen, small figures in the sunlight of the open ground leading to the tannery. The wooden buildings were taking shape, the walls were in place already

335

although it seemed only a few weeks had passed since the fire.

Rosie wiped the beads of perspiration from her forehead, the kitchen was hot even though the back door stood open. Rosie's mouth curved into a smile, she would bathe later, wash her long, thick hair, make herself beautiful. She stared unseeingly into the sunlight, anticipating the evening. Caradoc Jones was coming to do the books, she would see him tonight and a sudden sense of excitement filled her.

In moments of calm reflection, Rosie didn't really know what she saw in Caradoc. He was young enough, just a few years older than she was, but he was plump and somewhat plain. Until he smiled, that is, and then great dimples appeared each side of his mouth. It was when he smiled that his eyes became crinkled with humour; lovely blue, honest eyes which looked on her with obvious pleasure.

At first she had not taken a great deal of interest in Mr Caradoc Jones, he was a bookkeeper, a very clever man, an educated gentleman. He had a fine house near the docks, a fashionable house with heavy curtains at the window and a door knocker shaped like a lion's head which had been polished to within an inch of its life. Rosie knew all this because she had followed him home one night and stood outside mooning over him like a love sick girl.

It was then, standing in the darkness, seeing the light from the lamps gleaming in the windows that she knew she wanted to be there with him, inside the warmth of his house, she wanted more than anything to be Mrs Caradoc Jones.

'You fool!' she said the words out loud and sank down into a chair. What should he want with the likes of her, a humble servant? And what would he say if he knew of her past, she being a woman who had known more than one man?

Her face softened as she remembered the way he

looked at her, with such brightness in his eyes. He smiled at her often. He made excuses to be with her. He came into the kitchen on some pretext or other and then sat with her half an hour or more just talking about anything under the sun. So Rosie hoped and waited and prayed that one day, Caradoc would pluck up the courage to speak to her of his feelings.

She believed him to be an honest man and yet sometimes doubts filtered through the haze of her happiness. Did he just want a quick roll in the grass with her, was he looking for a fancy piece to while away a few hours? She had no means of knowing because Caradoc was a man shy of showing his feelings. Rosie heard the spitting of the roasting meat in the oven and with a sigh, returned to her work.

'Well,' Ellie smiled, 'you have progressed really well, I'm very pleased at the work you're doing for me.'

'Thank you, missus.' The foreman stood, cap in hand, his grey beard bobbing as he spoke. 'We does our best, see?'

'So you think you'll be finished in a few more weeks, is that right?'

'Aye, providin' the rain holds off, see missus?'

'Well, thank you for the report on your progress and of course you must feel free to order any goods you might need.'

The man inclined his head in acknowledgement and left the room and Ellie listened to his heavy footsteps crossing the hallway. She looked ruefully at the spot where he had been standing, sawdust had fallen from his boots onto the carpet, Rosie wouldn't be too pleased about that. She liked the place to be nice when there were visitors coming.

Caradoc Jones wasn't exactly a visitor but Rosie treated him as such. Indeed Rosie treated him as a very special guest. Ellie smiled, she saw more than Rosie realized. Caradoc, ostensibly, was coming over to double check the books, a task he was taking upon himself with increasing enthusiasm. He had agreed readily to her suggestion that he tutor Boyo, teach him his own efficient methods of accounting and Ellie felt as though she had offered Caradoc an ever open door at the tannery house.

But at least the new regime suited Boyo, he was looking forward eagerly to his next lesson. He had spent the last few days writing out columns of figures, adding and subtracting, worried that he might appear slow to a man like Caradoc. Ellie had told him not to concern himself. 'Caradoc knows you are just a novice at all this,' she had touched Boyo's cheek. 'It will all take time, be patient.'

'Have I ever said how grateful I am, Ellie?' His voice had been resonant with feeling. 'I don't know where I would have ended up if it hadn't been for Jubilee and for you.'

Ellie sat now in the darkening room and sighed, knowing that soon she must light the lamps. She hated this time of day when the sun was going down and the darkness drawing in. It was then, when she had time on her hands, that she missed Daniel the most.

But soon things would change, soon they would be married and they would be closer than ever before. Daniel would still have to attend his college, of course, she accepted that but at least the times they were together would compensate for his long absences.

When she had questioned Daniel about the Bishop's response to his decision to marry, he'd been vague. It had occurred to Ellie that the Bishop might have urged Daniel to wait at least until he was ordained before taking such a step but she pushed the disquieting thought aside.

Sighing, she rose, the house was quiet, Martha had gone to visit an old friend and Rosie was upstairs in her room. Ellie stood at the window, looking out at the dusk settling over the land. The hills rose steeply around the valley and the stark shapes of the half finished tannery

338

buildings stood out against a night sky that was streaked still with red.

In a few weeks, the tannery would be functioning once more and Ellie was glad, feeling that Jubilee would have approved of her efforts. The decision to rebuild had been a difficult one, it would have been so easy to leave the tannery as it was, razed to the ground, but with a warm feeling in her heart, Ellie knew she had done the right thing.

Rosie was brushed and shining by the time she opened the door to Caradoc Jones. She bobbed him a quick curtsey and stood back for him to enter the hallway. The light from the lamp fell on his curling hair as he took off his hat and he bent forward towards her, smiling down into her face, his dimples in evidence.

'Evening, Rosemary, how are you this fine night?' He stumbled over the words as though he wasn't in complete control of his tongue.

'I'm very good, sir.' She debated whether to add 'all the better for seeing you' but decided against it, thinking it too forward.

'Miss Ellie is in the parlour, Boyo's there too, would you like to go through, sir?'

'Not right away, I'll have my pot of tea first, in the kitchen, if I may. Ellie knows my funny ways by now, she knows I can't start work until I've fortified myself with a little refreshment.'

Rosie was pleased, he wanted to be with her, she was sure of it. She went before him into the kitchen and pushed the kettle, already boiled once, onto the fire. Immediately it began to issue steam and Rosie saw from the corner of her eye that Caradoc was smiling.

She lifted the kettle but it was overfilled and the rush of steam gushed outwards catching her hand. She gasped and banged the kettle down and at once Caradoc was at her side.

'Have you hurt yourself, let me look, oh, dear, your

339

poor hand.' He lifted it suddenly to his lips and kissed the soft flesh. He looked up and met Rosie's eye and blushed a fiery red. He dropped her hand suddenly and moved away from her.

'Forgive me, Rosemary, I'm not usually that forward.'

She took a chance. 'There's nothing to forgive, I liked it, very much indeed. You are a kind man, Mr Jones.'

Emboldened, he took a deep breath. 'I wonder if you like me enough to come walking with me, one evening,' he rushed the words out as though fearing they would never be said. Rosie hesitated, telling herself not to appear too eager. 'That would be very nice, Mr Jones.' She glanced up risking a bolder, more encouraging look. 'I'm off on Thursday, as it happens.'

'Thursday, it is then. Now let me pour the water on the teapot, that kettle really is too heavy for you.'

Rosie felt a warmth steal through her, she had always been regarded as a fine built woman, strong and a willing, able worker. It was wonderful to be treated as a delicate little lady, too weak to lift up a kettle of water. If only he knew; when anyone in the house bathed, it was Rosie who carried kettleful after kettleful up the stairs to the bedrooms.

When at last Caradoc took his leave of her, Rose leapt up in the air, waving her arms in triumph, she and Caradoc Jones were walking out together!

Thursday seemed as though it would never come but at last, Rosie found herself dressing carefully, anticipating with high excitement her evening with Caradoc Jones. She had told Ellie about it and Martha, Old Elephant Ears, had heard and done her best to put a damper on Rosie's joy.

'Don't you go anywhere alone with him,' she warned. She meant well, Rosie knew it, but she wished the old woman would mind her own business.

'Some men are out for what they can get, especially when it comes to taking out a serving girl,' Martha spoke in dire tones and Ellie laughed. 'Have a heart, Martha,

Caradoc Jones isn't exactly the type to prey on defence-less women, is he?'

'That's as may be but when it comes down to it, they all want to have their wicked way with a woman, don't they?'

Rosie hoped so though she forbore to say as much aloud, she didn't want to shock Martha or Ellie come to that. In any case, Caradoc was special, she knew enough about him to tell her that he had principles. She hoped he was the sort who wouldn't think of taking a woman to bed without putting a ring on her finger first. The thought thrilled her. Mrs Caradoc Jones, it sounded wonderful.

He called for her promptly at seven. The sun was still shining, casting long shadows over the trees, giving a silver edging to the few clouds that were about. It was a lovely day, a most wonderful day.

In silence, they walked away from the tannery and down into the town. There, as they neared the pier, the air was tangy with the smell of salt and tar.

Awkwardly, they sat side by side on one of the struts of wood under the pier and watched as the sea rushed inwards and then was dragged back again into the basin of the bay. Rosie searched her mind for something to say, why was she so tongue-tied with this man when she could usually tease and taunt with ease?

It was Caradoc who broke the silence. 'I don't know what to say to you, Rosemary, I'm afraid you'll think me dull or worse a fool.' She was amazed to hear Caradoc give voice to the same doubts she'd been harbouring. She turned to him warmly and looked into his face. 'I know what you mean, I feel just the same.'

He took her hand tentatively. 'I hope you do feel the same because Rosemary, I think, no, I *know* I'm falling in love with you.'

She felt an unexpected blush rise to her cheeks. 'Oh, Caradoc!' She squeezed his fingers, she who had lain with men, had taught them how to enjoy a woman, she was absurdly shy with the one man who mattered so much to her.

'And you, Rosemary, do you feel, do you think you could bear to be walking out with me, properly, I mean, as my betrothed?'

She could hardly breathe for the joy of it all. She closed her eyes and leaned towards him and as she had hoped, he pressed his lips to hers and kissed her. At first, he was tentative, she let him be, knowing he must find his own way. Growing bolder, he put his arms around her, drawing her close, kissing her more deeply and with greater passion. The kiss seemed to go on for ever and Rosie was filled with happiness and excitement.

She knew she wanted this man, wanted him in every way. She wanted him to make love to her but more, she wanted their love to be of a more lasting sort than the merely physical. She realized in that instance that she had held herself too lightly, she had grasped at gratification not realizing that there was more, far more to a union between two people than the coupling of bodies.

They drew apart at last and Rosie put her head on Caradoc's shoulder, feeling the warmth of the dying sun on her face, hearing the lap of the sea with heightened sensibilities. She was in love.

'Well, that's my duty done,' Bridie said as she turned away from the docks. 'Carmella is safely aboard, on her way home to Ireland. Whether she will find Paul again, who can say?' She sighed in satisfaction. 'Why do I feel so relieved, is that mean of me, Collins?'

He put his arm around her shoulder. 'You are too hard on yourself. The girl is lucky, not many women would have been so kind in the circumstances.'

Bridie smiled up at him. 'I can be kind because I'm happy. You have made me happy, Collins.'

'Then I can't ask for more,' he said quietly. Bridie

looked at him wondering if he was teasing but his face was deadly serious.

She slipped her arm through his and he glanced down at her. 'We're in Swansea, mind, not Clydach, aren't you afraid of the gossips?'

She shook her head. 'What can they do to me now?' Paul's disappearance had been the source of tremendous speculation; most people concluded, probably correctly, that he had run off with another woman.

So she walked arm and arm through the streets with Collins, her head high, her shoulders proud. That she could walk at all was due to the dedication of the man who had been her servant, the man she loved.

Her spirits sank a little as she drew nearer to Sea Mistress. The house sat on a hill, elegant and classical in line, the Grecian Doric pillars giving the entrance a grand appearance. Once, she had been happy there but that was a long time ago. Now all she wanted was for the place to be sold. With Carmella returned to her own country, the matter would be dealt with right away.

At the doorway, Collins paused and turned her to face him. 'Let me take you to Clydach, not to your cousin's but to our own house,' he said persuasively, his hand rubbing her shoulder.

'But there's no furniture,' she protested, 'the drapes are in place and so are the carpets but there is no bed.' She lowered her eyes as she felt the colour rise to her face. Collins laughed in amusement.

'In any case,' she said hurriedly, 'though the kitchen is equipped there's no staff to cook for us.'

'Don't be silly, I will cook for us,' Collins said. 'Come on, Bridie, let's go home.'

She turned away from the ornate front entrance of the house and began to retrace her steps along the driveway. 'We'll take a cab,' she said eagerly, 'we'll be there within the hour.'

In the busy streets of Swansea, it was easy to pick up a cab. The driver, seeing Collins's raised hand drew the

343

horses to a halt and though his eyebrows raised slightly when he heard the name of their destination, he nodded affably enough. The good fare would more than compensate for his time.

Bridie leaned back in the leather seat, comfortable and safe in the curve of Collins' arm. 'You know I'm a very demanding woman, don't you?' she said softly. 'It won't only be the cooking I'll want from you.'

Collins caught her chin in his hand and turned her lips towards him. 'I am yours to command, my lady,' he said and then he kissed her.

CHAPTER TWENTY-FOUR

Arian sat in her apartments high above the noise of the busy street carefully studying the latest edition of *The Swansea Times*. Normally, she would have felt the glow of pride that always came with a sense of having done a good job but now she felt only an emptiness, without Calvin, her achievements seemed meaningless.

What had happened to their vow to make the most of their lives? When Calvin had saved Arian's life almost at the expense of his own they had believed they were destined to be together. Now they had parted in anger, she unwilling to give up her work, he convinced that if they married she should be happy to live her life as Lady Calvin Temple. She was independent, had made her own decisions albeit sometimes unwisely. She had made a success, at last, of her life; she had built a newspaper she could be proud of, how could he expect her to give it up so lightly?

It was some days now since she had seen him, days in which she had felt lost and alone. She missed Calvin badly and yet she knew she could not go back on her decision. She needed the newspaper, needed her success perhaps more than she had ever needed Calvin. But the pain of losing him went deep.

She heard the distant ringing of the doorbell and moved to the window, staring out at the figure standing in the street. The maid was out, the offices downstairs were closed, the shutters drawn and yet the man who stood outside appeared determined on gaining a response to his repeated rings. The bell sounded again, the very note of it expressing impatience.

Arian made her way along the passage and began to descend the stairs, apprehension gripping her. Perhaps, she thought with rising panic, someone had come from Calvin, he could be sick. The matter certainly must be urgent for the caller to be so persistent. She opened the door to a man who appeared vaguely familiar.

'I'm sorry to trouble you.' He was well set, presentably dressed and quite good-looking.

'My name is Matthew Hewson, I used to work for Ellie Hopkins. I have some information that I think might interest you.'

She remembered then that this was the man who had spoken to Mac about the smuggling. 'Come into the office,' she opened the door wider. 'We can talk in here.'

She indicated a chair behind the long counter, 'Please, sit down, make yourself comfortable.' She took up a pencil and a pad and faced him. 'In your own words and in your own good time, tell me your story.' She spoke encouragingly and Matthew Hewson nodded, leaning forward slightly in his chair.

'It's about the opium smuggling,' he began and Arian looked at him warily. 'It's a good story.'

'Do you know where Paul Marchant has gone? That would be what I would call a good story.'

'He was being kept on board ship against his will, I was there with him but they let me go. I know the name of the man who was buying the contraband.'

'Go on,' Arian said.

'First I'd like to know how much you will pay me, Miss Smale,' he spoke smoothly, obviously sure of himself.

'Give me something to go on,' Arian said, 'and then I'll decide how much it's worth.'

Matthew Hewson nodded, 'All right, Paul Marchant might be dead, Monkton is the boss man, he's not one to cross but before I say any more, let's talk money, shall we?'

*   *   *

It was Ellie's wedding day. She was dressed in an oyster satin gown, the neck was square and the bodice decorated with frills, the overskirt was folded at the front, dipping longer at the back. The sleeves were elbow length with puffs of cream coloured chiffon. Her shoes were the latest court design made of oyster satin to match her gown.

'You look lovely, Ellie.' Rosie stood looking at her admiringly and Ellie took a deep breath, feeling her hands tremble in nervous anticipation.

'Don't look so worried,' Martha was smiling, 'it's a wedding, remember?'

'I know.' Ellie could scarcely speak. 'I just hope I'm doing the right thing, Daniel hasn't finished college yet, he's going to be away a great deal of the time.'

'So, when he is home you'll be able to spend all your time together.'

She was right, Ellie bit her lip, she loved Dan, she was happy to be his wife, why then was this niggling doubt plaguing her?

'The carriage is here,' Martha said, peering through the window. 'And there's Caradoc Jones, dressed up in all his Sunday best, ready to stand up for you. Oh, I do love a wedding.'

Rosie was suddenly animated, flinging open the door and rushing outside with such haste that she almost tripped over her new shiny boots.

'Here's your parasol,' Martha said briskly, 'and your bag, they match beautifully, you really do have such good taste Ellie.'

How Ellie forced her shaking legs to carry her towards the coach she didn't know but she found herself seated near the window with Caradoc Jones beside her and with Martha and a flushed Rosie on the opposite seat. The carriage jolted into movement and Ellie glanced back at the rambling house where she had spent the last five years of her life. A lump came to her throat as she thought of Jubilee, dead now over a year, surely if he was looking down at her at this moment he would be wishing her happiness?

The old buildings of Swansea seemed to fly past the window, insubstantial, ghostly. Ellie looked at the streets, so familiar to her and scarcely saw them. What if Dan changed his mind, what if he hadn't made the journey last night from Lampeter, what if he'd been held up somehow, delayed, had an accident on the road? But she must stop panicking, it was foolish of her, it did no-one any good.

At last the towering pinnacle of the church spire came into view and Ellie took a deep breath, trying to control the beating of her heart.

When the carriage jerked to a halt, Caradoc stepped down and turned to help her into the roadway. A few people had gathered outside the church, anticipated a wedding as the bells pealed out into the still air and Ellie held her head high as she walked towards the entrance porch.

Inside, it was cool and dim after the brightness of the sun. The unmistakable smell of old bibles and wax polish drifted towards her mingling with the scent of fresh flowers placed before the alter.

He was there. Daniel stood tall and proud, his shoulders erect, his head high. Beside him was his brother. They were alike and yet different, with Dan standing at least six inches the taller of the two men. She stopped beside him and his hand reached out and took hers in a firm grip and all at once her nervousness vanished.

The vicar began to speak. 'Dear friends, this is a marriage between a charming young lady and an ordinand, a man who intends to take my job from me, one day.' A small ripple of appreciative laughter went through the congregation. 'I wish them every happiness and may God's blessing be always with them.'

Ellie smiled proudly up at Daniel, happy that his place in the church was being recognized.

The vicar began the ceremony and Ellie, conscious only of Daniel's nearness, scarcely heard the words of it being spoken. She made her vows with a quiet but firm voice. Daniel said his vows clearly, in strong, precise tones, already he sounded like a cleric. It seemed to go on for a long time, the sun shone in through the windows, a bee droned, searching the flowers for honey and Ellie thought she had never been so happy in all her life.

Then it was over, the organ music swelled, filling the church with magical sound and Ellie was walking towards the sunshine holding the arm of the man she loved.

They stayed the night in the Macworth Hotel in High Street. The room was cool and looked out onto the busy roadway. Shadows slanted across the carpet and dulled the colours of the covers on the bed.

As Ellie undressed, she felt a sense of unreality, it was all so strange, the opulent room, the heavy, unfamiliar drapes, the long corridors outside housing other people, strangers, it was all so unsettling.

Daniel came to her and took her in his arms. 'Don't be afraid, Ellie,' he said softly, 'it's very strange for me, too, let's learn to be husband and wife together, shall we?'

He helped her to undress and hung her gown carefully in the heavy wardrobe. She smiled, he was very neat, putting away his clothes so that they wouldn't crease. Doubtless being at college had taught him that to take care of his clothes saved him effort in the long run.

'Don't laugh at your husband's funny little ways,' he said catching her eye, 'I can't help it if I'm a compulsive tidier, can I?'

She slipped into the big double bed, the sheets felt cold, unaired and for a moment, homesickness gripped her. She wished in that instant that she was at Glyn Hir safe in her own familiar room. Alone.

Daniel was beside her then, taking her gently into his

arms. He held her close and kissed her hair. She closed her eyes and clung to him praying she would not disappoint him, that she would always be a worthy wife to him. Love-making wasn't new to her, she had had a vigorous lover in Calvin Temple. She knew too, what it was like to lie night after night with Jubilee who had been a heavy sleeper but a restless bedfellow. But now, everything was changed, she was making a new beginning and she wondered if she was able to cope with all the emotion that was filling her.

She allowed Daniel to kiss her, to divest her of her new nightgown, she felt him tremble and knew his uncertainties were just as real as her own. A warmth filled her, she clung to him, pressing herself against him. He was the man she loved, her darling Daniel, the man she would spend the rest of her life with.

She felt a moment of pure joy when Dan took her, the feeling transcended anything she had ever known. He was gentle and sure, his touch delicate, his every move designed to make her happy. She found tears springing to her eyes. She clung to him, wanting to be closer, to be part of him. Passion and happiness fused together and she pressed her lips against the firmness of his shoulder to prevent herself from crying out in joy.

Later, they lay side by side, Dan smoothed her neck and shoulder, his finger coming to rest on the mole just above her breast. 'A lovely beauty spot, for my eyes only,' he said gently.

A shadow fell over Ellie's happiness, those words had been said before, by another man, by Matthew Hewson. She realized in that moment what harm he could do her if he so chose and she shuddered.

'What's wrong, Ellie, a goose walk over your grave?' Dan said drawing her close to him. 'It's all right, everything is all right, nothing can harm us now, we're man and wife together and no man shall put us asunder.'

*　　*　　*

350

Arian looked down at her notes and a frown creased her brow, she didn't know if she could use this story, the information about Paul being held on board this man's ship was all speculative at the moment without any proof to back it up. Regarding the smuggling, Matthew Hewson knew what he was talking about, no doubt about it. He had dates and times and a thorough knowledge of the methods used to transport the opium to Ireland. Leather from Glyn Hir tannery had been used to conceal the smuggled cargo and it was the Marchant ships which had carried the contraband on regular trips across the Irish Sea.

At last, Arian put down her notes, she would go downstairs, see Mac, ask him what he thought about it all, perhaps he could unearth some other facts, facts that might determine what exactly had happened to Paul Marchant.

Mac looked up from his desk as Arian stood before him, her face grave. 'What's up, looks as if you've swallowed something sour,' he said in his usual irreverent manner.

'I want to talk to you.' Arian closed the door of his office, shutting out the noise from the larger room where the other reporters sat at their machines, typing up their latest efforts.

'Read these.' Arian put the notes on the desk and Mac bent over them adjusting his newly acquired glasses. After a moment he looked up. 'Nothing really new, is there, this is more or less what Hewson told me before.'

'Except for the fact that Paul Marchant might be held prisoner, might even be dead.'

He looked up at her. 'Do you want to go with it?'

'Not yet,' Arian said slowly, 'I want you to find out a great deal more. I'd like you to . . .'

'I know,' Mac rose to his feet, 'you'd like me to dig a little, see what I come up with.'

'Exactly. Find out why this Matthew Hewson has it in for both Ellie and Bridie Marchant, if he's trying to implicate them in this smuggling racket there must be some very powerful motive behind it. But most importantly try to learn what has happened to Paul Marchant.'

'What did you pay him, this man Hewson?' Mac, as usual came straight to the point. Arian grimaced. 'I take your point, Hewson's motive might simply be greed. You're right, of course.'

'Well, might as well give my own brain a challenge,' Mac said pulling on his white scarf and his battered hat, setting it at a jaunty angle on his head. 'Things have been a bit too quiet around here for my liking, about time we had a shake up.'

'If we learn what's happened to Paul Marchant there'll be a shake up, all right,' Arian said dryly. 'But we must be sure of the facts before we publish anything.'

'Aren't we always?' Mac bent down and kissed her cheek. 'You do know you're looking decidedly under the weather, don't you?' He leaned back on his heels and studied her face. 'Not enough love life these days, that's what's wrong with you.'

She slapped him playfully, 'Get on with your job and leave the homespun philosophy to others more qualified.'

'And who is better qualified than a gifted journalist?' Mac smiled. 'People like me can read the minds of lesser mortals, didn't you know that?'

'Out!' Arian smiled as Mac retreated towards the door in a pretence of being frightened by her tone.

'I'm going boss lady, I'm on my way.' He left the door open and Arian paused listening to the chatter from the other room. The voices that rose above the clatter of the typewriting machines were eager, young and she suddenly felt very jaded.

'It's our anniversary today,' Daniel held a bouquet of roses before him and smiled down at Ellie.

'Quite right,' she said smiling, 'it's a week today since

352

I gave up my freedom to become a slave to the kitchen sink here at Glyn Hir.'

'Huh!' Daniel pressed the flowers into her hands. 'Poor hard done by wife, my heart bleeds for you.' He leaned forward and kissed her lightly.

'Dan,' she said quietly, 'do you realize that this is our last night together, tomorrow you'll be off back to college?'

'I know,' he sighed, 'but you'll have plenty to occupy you, you'll have to find us a house, a modest one mind, I'm not a rich man and you must remember that.' He looked round, 'We can't live at the tannery for ever, can we? I sometimes wish you didn't own the place.'

'Dan, why not let me . . .' her words trailed away as he held up his hand.

'No, you let me,' he said. 'I know you have far more money than I could ever earn in a lifetime but at least allow me to pay for the roof over our heads.'

'All right,' Ellie said, 'a modest house it will be, then. Can we afford to have Martha with us and Rosie too, of course?'

'I dare say I can run to a small staff,' Daniel said soberly, 'it's only fitting that the wife of a cleric should live respectably.'

'I'm going to miss you dreadfully,' Ellie said, attempting and failing to keep her voice light.

'I'm going to miss you, too, my little sweetheart.' Disregarding the flowers, Daniel took her in his arms and held her close. 'Just remember that God intends us to be together, you will make me a perfect wife,' he whispered against her mouth. Ellie felt a touch of unease, Daniel was building his hopes too high, he was placing her on a pedestal.

'Dan,' she placed her hands on either side of his cheeks, 'please don't forget I'm only human and that I'm fallible. I'm no saint, never was never will be.'

'Your past is over and done with,' Daniel said firmly, 'you are a different person now, you are older and wiser.'

'But Dan, I don't have your unshakable faith,' the words were spoken in little more than a whisper. 'I felt the power of Evan Robert's words, of course I did and I want to be good enough for you, good enough to play the role of a vicar's wife but don't expect too much of me, will you?'

He released her. 'I'm going into the garden, I'm going to have a last puff of my pipe and I don't want to have Martha reading me the riot act so tell her I'm taking my evening constitutional.' He smiled, 'Out of sight, out of mind.' He tweaked a curl of Ellie's hair. 'You see, I'm not perfect, either, I'm not above a little bit of deception if it will give me the quiet life I crave.'

Ellie sighed softly as the door closed behind Daniel, she wanted to be with him every moment, she even begrudged this small parting from him. All too soon, she would have to manage without him, she in Swansea and he sixty miles away in Lampeter.

She took a deep breath and walked towards the parlour, she might as well join Martha for a little while. Her mouth curved into a smile, before too long, if she knew Daniel, he would suggest an early night and then they would lie in each other's arms until dawn washed the floor of the bedroom with rosy light.

Daniel looked up at the cloudless night sky, the stars were bright, appearing close enough to touch. It was warm still, it had been a balmy summer's day, a day he would hold to him, a memory of the time spent with Ellie, his dear wife.

Daniel turned, hearing a sound beyond the garden gate. As his eyes grew accustomed to the gloom, he made out the figure of a man standing on the pathway leading away from the house, he was still and quiet as though he had been watching Daniel. Behind him was the shadowy outline of a horse, head down as though weary of waiting. Perhaps they had been there a long time, Daniel thought. 'Can I help you old chap?' Daniel moved closer and then he recognized the

354

man. 'Hewson, what are you doing here?'

'I came to do you a favour – old chap.' The tone was sarcastic.

'I need no favours from you.' Daniel's hands clenched into fists, this man had the power to take all the Christian charity from his soul. He turned away but Hewson stopped him in his tracks.

'It's about your little wife, Ellie.' The words fell softly, insidiously into the darkness. In spite of himself, Daniel turned, waiting for the man to go on.

'Bedded her by now, I expect,' Hewson said leaning nonchalantly on the gate. Daniel felt anger sing in his blood, this man was attempting to sully the beautiful union between him and Ellie.

'Shut your mouth!' Daniel heard the harshness in his voice and took a deep breath. He was playing into Hewson's hands, allowing the man to rile him.

'Don't be so uppity,' Hewson's voice continued remorselessly, 'we have such a lot in common, you and me, *old chap*.'

'I don't know what you're talking about and I doubt you do either.'

'Oh but I do. That sweet little mole on Ellie's shoulder just above her breast, I never see it without feeling the urge to kiss it.'

Daniel froze, in that instant he knew that he was capable of murder. He moved forward but Hewson was too quick for him. He turned and mounted his horse.

'Give my regards to your wife,' Hewson said, 'tell her I'll be there to keep her warm while you are away.'

The sound of pounding hooves beat in Daniel's brain, his head ached suddenly, his mouth was dry. He clutched the gate for support and took a deep breath trying to steady himself. The man was a monster, he would do anything to cause trouble. And yet, he had seen Ellie unclothed, he must have done to know about the mole on Ellie's shoulder.

355

She wasn't capable of betraying him, was she? He could see her face in his mind's eye, the clear eyes, the way her mouth curved when she looked up at him. She wouldn't have slept with Hewson since she had met Daniel, he was sure of it. But could he bear it if she had been Hewson's mistress before that?

He returned to the house and without looking into the parlour went upstairs to the room he shared with Ellie. He looked down at the bed, his marriage bed and a feeling of nausea rose to grasp at his throat. Ellie must, at some time, have been intimate with Hewson and did it matter when it had happened? It shook him to the core to realize that Ellie was not the person he believed her to be.

She came hurrying up the stairs behind him. 'Dan, what is it?'

He faced himself in the mirror and saw that he was white, his eyes burning with the pain of his anguish. 'I just saw Hewson,' he said and he saw Ellie's eyes darken. Was it with dislike for the man or guilt, a treacherous voice in his head asked.

'What did he want?' She sounded anxious, well, she would be. He looked at her, searching her face for some indication of what she was feeling and after a moment moved to close the bedroom door.

'He told me how much he enjoyed your charms.' The words came out like an accusation and Ellie flinched.

'And you believed him?' Her tone held incredulity and for a moment, doubt shook him.

He moved to where she stood and carefully opened her bodice, she looked up at him in bewilderment. He pressed his finger against the mole and, sickened, remembered how he had pressed his lips to the very spot. Had Hewson's mouth been there before him? The thought was unbearable.

'He kissed you there,' he said flatly.

'No!' Ellie said fiercely.

'How did he know about it then, the beauty spot

356

wouldn't be revealed by any gown however low it was cut.'

Ellie's face flushed a fiery red. 'Let me explain, Dan, sit down, be calm, just don't . . .'

'So the man has seen you disrobed? Answer me yes or no, Ellie, please.'

'It wasn't like that,' Ellie sounded desperate, 'he came uninvited into the house, he was unwelcome, you know how much I dislike him.'

'So you're saying he forced his attentions on you.' Daniel could not stop the interrogation now if he wanted to, anger was reverberating like a drumbeat through his head.

'Yes, that's what happened.'

'And you didn't think to call for the help of your friend Martha or Rosie for that matter?'

'Of course I did. Calm down, Dan, for God's sake!'

'Taking the name of the Lord in vain isn't going to convince me of your innocence.' Daniel knew he sounded like a pompous prig but the words came of their own volition.

Ellie drew herself up, her face suddenly blank. 'Very well, you are determined to think ill of me. We will say no more of this tonight, we'll talk in the morning when you are in a better humour.'

He grasped her arm and before he knew what he was doing he had raised his hand threateningly. Aghast, he stood back from her. 'Lord Jesus Christ help me.' He shuddered, rubbing at his eyes. 'I don't know what I'm doing. See, Ellie what you have brought me to?'

He turned and left the room and made his way down the stairs and out through the front door leaving it open behind him. He didn't know where he was going, all he knew was he couldn't remain in Ellie's company or he wouldn't be responsible for his actions.

He walked away from Glyn Hir, taking the back roads into town. He intended to put as much distance between himself and his new wife as he could.

Ellie sank onto the bed dry-eyed with shock. She remembered only too well how Hewson had attacked her. The situation had been none of her making. How could Daniel even think she had encouraged Matthew Hewson, the man repelled her?

She heard the front door closing and her heart lifted with hope, had Daniel returned? She went to the top of the landing and saw Martha below in the hall with her hot water bottle, present on all occasions, even on a summer's night such as this one, and her heart sank.

'The front door was left wide open,' Martha spoke reprovingly. Her tone changed as she glimpsed Ellie's strained expression, 'Has anything happened?'

Ellie shook her head miserably. 'No, go on to bed, Martha, don't put the bolt on, Dan is out walking.'

If Martha considered the situation a little strange, she didn't give voice to her thoughts. She climbed the stairs and paused for a moment, looking at Ellie. 'Sure you're all right?'

Ellie nodded, 'Yes, I'm sure. Goodnight Martha and God bless.'

Unable to sleep, Ellie waited in her room for a moment for Martha to settle and then crept down the stairs to the kitchen. Rosie was there setting the table for breakfast.

'What's wrong?' she asked as Ellie sank down into a chair, her head in her hands.

'What's the matter, you can tell me?' Rosie said gently. 'Have you and that handsome husband had a lover's tiff, is that it?'

All at once, Ellie began to cry. She put her arms on the scrubbed surface of the table to cushion her head. She felt Rosie's hand warm on her back and heard the girl's soft voice. 'There, there, it happens all the time, it's only natural, mind.'

Ellie drew a shuddering breath and looked up at Rosie, the girl was looking at her with sympathy and Ellie felt that Rosie was so much wiser than she was in experience of the world.

'It's Mat, isn't it, he's been making trouble again. I saw him lurking outside. I watched from the window as he leaned on the gate like he owned it and spoke to Daniel.' Rosie was unashamed of her attempt to eavesdrop. 'I could hear raised voices but I couldn't make out what they were saying. I could see Daniel was very angry though.'

She drew her chair to Ellie's side. 'Take my advice, don't quarrel over Mat, he's just not worth it. He's a real bad lot is that one and I should know.'

'I didn't really have much choice,' Ellie said, her voice hoarse with tears, 'he's been turning Dan against me, telling him that him and me, well that we . . .' She broke off unable to put the terrible accusation into words.

'Daniel should have more sense than to listen to him,' Rosie said stoutly, 'he should know you wouldn't touch Matthew Hewson with a bargepole.' She sighed. 'But then men haven't got much sense, not when it comes to love they haven't.'

Ellie sighed heavily, thinking over Rosie's words. The clock struck the hour and she glanced up at it, worried about Daniel. What if he'd gone in search of Matthew, what if it came to blows between the two men, Dan might be hurt.

'You go to bed, Rosie, I'll wait up, Daniel won't be long now, I'm sure of it.' She wasn't sure at all, indeed, she wasn't sure of anything at this moment. Rosie hesitated and Ellie forced a smile.

'As you say, it's just a lover's tiff, go on up, you have to rise early in the morning, you need your sleep.'

Ellie sat dry-eyed and wide awake in the kitchen until the cold, grey light of early morning poked prying fingers in through the window. She admitted to herself then that Daniel wasn't coming back, not today, perhaps not ever.

CHAPTER TWENTY-FIVE

Boyo watched with a critical eye as the rebuilding work at the tannery progressed. Gradually, the ruins were being replaced by new structures which rose phoenix-like from the ashes of the fire.

Glyn Hir was where his future lay; here, God willing, he would bring April as his bride when the time was right. Of course, they were both too young yet to make a serious commitment but in his heart he knew there would never be anyone else for him.

Sometimes he felt guilty about his past, he would watch Rosie with her voluptuous figure and feel the hot sweet sensation of lust sweep through him. At those times he prayed to God to take away his unworthy thoughts. Once, Harry had caught him, head bowed, hands pressed together and asked him what he was praying for. When Boyo told him, he'd flung back his head and laughed.

'*Duw anwyl*, the good Lord never intended man to be a faithful creature,' he said. 'The Lord knows everything and he knows how frail a vessel he's built. Since Adam sinned we have all been tarred with the same brush, we look upon a woman and we want her, it's natural, see?'

Boyo, knowing that Harry rarely entered the door of a church, took leave to doubt his views on morality. Still, God was merciful, he would forgive and Boyo felt his conscience ease a little.

He still lived in the house on the edge of the tannery and though Ellie was married now, nothing really seemed to have changed. Daniel Bennett had returned to college and life had continued in the same even pace as before. Except that Ellie seemed to have lost all her joy in loving and living. Had her marriage been a mistake he wondered?

At first, she'd seemed happy and contented, very much in love with her husband. It was only in the last few weeks that she mooned about the place with sad eyes and a long face.

Ellie came out of the house at that moment and crossed the ground between the house and the tannery wall. She walked stiffly as though holding herself in check and Boyo saw with a shock of alarm how thin she had become.

'Ellie,' he stood six inches taller than her now, his body had filled out, he was a man and he was proud of it. 'Ellie, it's awful to see you like this, what's happened, what's wrong with you, are you sick?'

'Sick at heart, Boyo.' She put her hand on his arm, 'I can't talk about it but please try not to worry, it will all sort itself out in time.' She didn't sound as if she believed her own words and Boyo frowned. 'Can I help, Ellie, is there anything I can do?' He thrust his hands deep into his pockets, he might be a man on the face of things but he was still full of uncertainties when it came to handling emotions.

Ellie shook her head, 'No, love, no-one can.' She changed the subject adroitly. 'Have you remembered Caradoc is coming tonight? You will be here to have your coaching in the book work, won't you?'

Boyo frowned, Caradoc was kind enough and intelligent but he didn't seem eager to impart his knowledge too quickly. Boyo had more than a sneaking feeling that Caradoc was more interested in sitting in the kitchen talking to Rosie than instructing him in the facts and figures of tannery affairs.

Ellie gave Boyo one of her rare smiles. 'It's taking a long time, isn't it, are you finding the lessons very difficult?'

'Well, no, it's not that,' Boyo didn't want to sound critical, he searched his mind for something to say and failed and he just shrugged.

'Shall I have a word with Caradoc on your behalf?' Ellie leaned her arms on the warm stone wall and her bodice flapped around her thin frame like washing on the line.

'No, there's no need,' Boyo said quickly. 'It's just that Caradoc likes to take his time.' He smiled. 'He's getting very keen on Rosie, that's what it is and if I learn too quickly, his visits won't be necessary.'

Ellie didn't seem surprised. 'Rosie and Caradoc?' she said thoughtfully, 'I thought so.' She put her head on one side consideringly. 'I think you are right, Caradoc *is* getting serious about Rosie.'

Boyo knew damn well he was right, he knew the signs; didn't he suffer from the same symptoms himself?

'I'm surprised Martha hasn't noticed anything,' Ellie said thoughtfully, 'she's usually the first one to make comment on affairs of the heart.' Ellie sighed. 'But then I haven't been very good company of late, I've been too wrapped up in myself to notice what's going on under my nose.'

Greatly daring, Boyo rested his hand on Ellie's thin shoulder. 'I can see you're unhappy and it worries me, what is wrong, Ellie?'

Ellie chewed her bottom lip. At last she spoke. 'It's just that Matthew Hewson has been causing trouble again,' she closed her eyes for a moment as though in pain. 'Matthew spoke to Dan, gave him the impression that he and I had been, well, close. Remember the night Matthew attacked me? Well he saw a mole on my shoulder and taunted Daniel with it.'

'What a pig!' Boyo said fiercely. 'No-one knows better than me how much you despise Matthew Hewson, you wouldn't want him within a mile of you. Shall I talk to Daniel, tell him what really happened that night?'

Ellie shook her head. 'He hasn't shown a great deal

of faith in me, has he? He should believe *me*. No don't speak to him, Boyo, if Daniel can't take *my* word for it then perhaps we've made a terrible mistake by getting married so soon.'

Her words echoed Boyo's own doubts but he spoke up stoutly. 'Don't you believe it.' Boyo wanted to hug her but he didn't dare presume so far. 'You and Daniel Bennett were meant for each other, anyone can see that a mile off.' It might not be what he really believed, indeed, he didn't know what he believed but his words seemed to comfort Ellie.

She smiled up at him gratefully and Boyo felt a wave of anger run through him. He had never liked Matthew Hewson, Boyo would not forgive him for the uncalled for slap he'd aimed in Boyo's direction for no other reason than that he was in a foul mood. As for the sound beating Matthew had given him, well that *was* called for, Boyo had done him wrong and it was only fair that he take the consequences. But now Matthew had picked on Ellie, had tried to ruin her marriage, such mischief was unforgivable.

Ellie straightened and her voice became brisk as she changed the subject. 'The buildings are nearly finished; soon, Boyo, you'll have a job to work at, will you be pleased?'

'I can't wait,' Boyo frowned, his future was becoming clear, a smooth path stretched before him and yet there was one thing worrying him. He wondered if this was the right time to talk to Ellie about it, she had enough on her plate as it was and yet wouldn't his problems take her mind off her own?

'Come on, out with it,' Ellie said softly in her usual perceptive way, 'I can see you are dying to ask me something.'

'It's my name,' Boyo said self-consciously, 'it's not bothered me before but how can I think of asking any girl to marry me when I haven't even got a proper name?'

Ellie studied him for a long moment and then she took

his arm. 'I see your dilemma. Come on, let's walk back to the house.'

She was silent for so long that Boyo wondered if she'd heard what he said. Then, with some of her old sparkle, she looked up into his face. 'I could go to the workhouse for you, find out if they have any records there of your birth.'

Boyo felt hope grow within him, it was such a simple idea that he wondered why he hadn't thought of it himself. On the other hand, should he begin making enquiries himself, the powers that be might not feel inclined to divulge any details they might have of his birth. Ellie, however was a respected member of the community, she had been Mrs Jubilee Hopkins for some years and now she was married to a man taking the cloth. If any information should be available, Ellie would have a good chance of learning what it was.

He took a deep breath. 'Will you do that for me, Ellie, I'd be so grateful?'

'I'll go down to the workhouse as soon as I can, I promise you.' She squeezed Boyo's arm. 'It's about time I thought of someone else's problems other than my own.'

It was the reaction he had hoped for and Boyo felt a moment of triumph, in a way it was as though he had solved two problems in one fell swoop. Together they went into the house and the hallway was cool after the early September sunshine outside. Boyo had always loved this house, it had been his only real home. He'd been taken from the workhouse when he was about eight or nine years old and he remembered it as though it was yesterday.

He shuddered as he thought of the workhouse, the grey old buildings, the long bare dining room, the rough benches at the tables, the poor quality of the food. He supposed he'd been lucky that he had been the right age to begin work and a healthy child to boot. Lucky too that Jubilee had taken an instant liking to him and had decided upon taking him to live at Glyn Hir.

Jubilee had made him a home over the stable, a comfortable place, somewhere of his very own. In return, Boyo had worked hard. The work had been tiring, long hours and heavy labour, but it had given Boyo a sense of his own worth. It was only after his fight with Matthew that Ellie had insisted on Boyo living in the house.

He glanced fondly at Ellie as they stood together in the hallway, she was the one who had given him his real chance in life, Ellie had faith enough to train him to be in charge of the tannery when she eventually moved away. His heart swelled in pride at the prospect of being boss, more than a foreman, he would be a manager. The position offered security, he would have a real future, something solid to offer April when they were married for they would be married, he was determined upon it.

Caradoc Jones was there before them, he must have come round to the back of the house, Boyo surmised, otherwise he would have seen the accountant's approach. It was patently obvious why he would choose to enter the back door, the kitchen was where he would find Rosie. Caradoc smiled somewhat sheepishly at Ellie as he emerged from the passageway leading to the hall, 'Day to you, Ellie, I called a little early so Rosemary gave me a cup of tea, I hope you don't mind.'

'Of course I don't mind,' Ellie said, 'you are doing me a favour by coming here, I appreciate it.' She smiled up at Caradoc. 'Is your pupil shaping up well?'

'Pupil? Oh, aye, Boyo's a bright lad, no trouble teaching him, indeed, he learns a little too quickly for my liking, I can see I'll be out of a job if he keeps this up.'

Ellie smiled. 'No fear of that, we'll always need your expert eye on our business. Jubilee was good with the books but he always appreciated your ability to spot any errors.'

She turned towards the parlour. 'I'll leave you to get on with it then. See you both later.'

Boyo followed Caradoc into the study, he was full of anticipation, he liked the book work, was quick at figures and the challenges with which Caradoc confronted him from time to time stimulated his mind. And later, when the sun cooled and the hazy autumn evening fell, then would come the moment he'd been waiting for, the moment when he and April met on the patch of ground that sloped away beneath the warm stone buildings of Honey's Farm.

'I want you to think very carefully about your future,' Fon was saying but April scarcely heard her, she was turning and twisting before the mirror, trying to see if the frock she'd chosen for her meeting with Boyo was flattering to her complexion.

'You could go to college,' Fon continued, 'you could even learn to be a typewriter operator, work in an office or something, you have your whole life ahead of you.'

April stopped posing and looked round at Fon, a smile curving her mouth. 'All I want is to be married to Boyo,' she said.

'Well, you're young yet, you have plenty of time to settle down, why not explore all the possibilities before you first?'

'Would you change *your* life?' April asked quietly and Fon shrugged. 'My life was sort of mapped out for me, I came here to work at Honey's Farm as a young girl, I fell in love with Jamie and then there seemed nothing else to do but marry him.'

'You see?' April was triumphant, 'You married the man you loved and that's what I want to do.'

'But things are different these days,' Fon protested, 'there are so many things a young lady can do.'

'I don't want to do any of them,' April replied patiently, 'I only want to marry Boyo.'

Jamie came into the kitchen. 'You two arguing again?' His tone was good-natured, he knew Fon too well, knew

366

she wasn't the sort to provoke a row if she could help it.

'Fon wants me to think about my future,' April said, 'she wants me to go to college or something. *You* like Boyo, don't you Jamie?'

'Of course I do, I like him very much, he's a fine lad but I think you should listen to Fon nonetheless, you are very young still.' Jamie sighed. 'I don't want to sound harsh but there are disadvantages about not knowing your parentage, there could be all sorts of inherited sicknesses, have you thought of all that?'

April hadn't and she didn't intend to worry herself with what might be. 'No,' she said shortly, 'I don't go looking for trouble.'

She saw a glance of amusement pass between Jamie and Fon and then she was hugged in Jamie's big arms. 'You're right, we mustn't look for trouble. Bring the boy in for supper, he's always welcome at my table.'

As she left the farmhouse behind her, April was smiling. Fon might nag a little but it was only because she cared. The thought was warming.

As she breasted the hill, she drew a deep breath of sheer excitement, he was there, waiting for her, his tall rangy figure outlined against the pale evening sky. She resisted the urge to run towards him but her eyes were drinking him in.

When she came to stand before him, he held out his hands and took both of hers in a firm grip. He bent forward and kissed her cheek and she longed to turn her face so that their lips would meet.

'You look very nice,' Boyo spoke as though he had difficulty getting the words out. His eyes stared down into hers and April felt her colour rising. She felt tongue-tied and shy in Boyo's company, she was so anxious to do and say the right things, it was unthinkable that she disappoint him in any way.

'You are looking very smart too, Boyo,' she said but her voice was stilted and he looked down at her anxiously.

'Is everything all right?' His tone was as off-hand as hers had been and April knew this wasn't the way either of them wanted it to be. She took her courage in both hands and smiled at him without raising her eyes to his.

'Everything is wonderful now that I'm here with you.' The words came out in a rush and as soon as they were spoken, April blushed a fiery red.

Boyo reached out tentatively and took her hand and very gently turned it over, kissing the softness of her palm. 'April.' There was a world of tenderness in his voice and April felt tears come into her eyes. She loved him so much that it hurt, she wanted to nestle close to him, to have his arms around her holding her close. But that was a joy to be reserved for when they were married. Hugging and kissing could lead to other things and April wasn't ready, wasn't equipped, to deal with passion, not yet.

Boyo seemed to sense her feelings, he took her hand and tucked it under his arm and they sat staring down at the world spread out below them behaving more like old friends than lovers.

Ellie stood in the parlour, staring at Daniel's set face, trying to control the trembling of her limbs. He had arrived at Glyn Hir unexpectedly and hope had risen within Ellie's heart, hope that he'd reconsidered all that Matthew had said and decided the man was lying. But it was not to be so. From the moment he'd entered the house, Daniel had avoided her eyes, his manner had been stiff, almost formal, as though they scarcely knew each other. Not even Martha's effusive greetings had softened his attitude.

'What have you come here for, Dan?' Ellie asked quietly. 'It's obvious you are not looking for a reconciliation.'

'We are married,' Daniel said flatly, 'for good or ill you are my wife and I have an obligation to you.'

His words were like knife wounds and Ellie sank down

into the old rocking-chair, her legs refusing to support her. She kept her composure, outwardly at least and looked at the man she loved with clear eyes. 'You have no obligation where I am concerned. You forget, I am a wealthy woman in my own right, I have need of no man's charity.' Her words were intended to wound as she had been wounded.

Daniel took a deep breath. 'It's not charity I'm offering you, Ellie,' he said evenly, 'I'm suggesting that we try to pick up the pieces, forget what is done and try to make some sort of future for ourselves together.'

She looked at him wearily. 'Sit down, for heaven's sake, Dan, don't stand on ceremony, not in this house where you've always been a welcome guest.'

'So have other men, obviously.' His tone was sharp but he took a seat facing her and she saw the pain in his eyes and her heart missed a beat.

'Dan, nothing happened between me and Matthew Hewson, he wanted it to, yes, he tried to force himself on me but I loathe him, I could never welcome his advances, you must be mad not to see that.'

He sighed heavily as though the weight of the world was on his shoulders. 'I wish I could believe that, Ellie, I really do but that time, when he came into the kitchen, when your husband had died, when he resented my attempts to comfort you. I had a feeling even then that he was more to you than just a workman.'

She was becoming angry and she tried to curb her emotions; there would be nothing gained by an exchange of cruel words. 'What do you know about Matthew Hewson, Dan, is there anything in his character to suggest he is truthful, honest, an individual who can be trusted?'

'He's a cheat and a liar, he's everything you imply he is but that doesn't prove anything.' Daniel rubbed his hand through his hair. 'Women are often attracted to scoundrels, I saw enough of that in my newspaper days to be convinced of it.'

369

'Dan, believe me, I was never attracted to any man, not until you came along. Are you so blinded with anger and jealousy that your sense of reason has deserted you?'

'I don't know what to think.' Daniel bowed his head for a long moment and then, taking a deep breath looked up at her. 'Let's try again, at least try, shall we?' he said evenly, 'I don't want to quarrel with you Ellie, I love you in spite of everything.'

'But you can't find it in your heart to trust me and believe in me?'

'It's difficult, Ellie, you are a frail woman when it comes to men, you must admit that much.'

Her face grew hot, he was referring to her affair with Calvin, how dare he? 'So my past is to be dragged up, I am to be goaded by my one mistake every time a man looks at me, is that it? Do you think I'm so "frail" that I'd fall into any man's arms then? Do you think I've bedded Harry and Luke too, they've been around me all the time I was married to Jubilee remember?'

'Don't be coarse, Ellie.' He looked away from her ashamed and she knew her barb had hit its mark.

'So the doubt is there, is it? You think I'm a whore.' She rose to her feet bitterly hurt, hating him in that moment. 'Go away Daniel and don't come back, do you understand me?'

She moved to open the parlour door and hung back to allow him to pass. As he stood looking down at her, he shook his head. 'I hate to leave matters this way,' he said. 'I thought to solve something of our problems by coming here and making my peace.'

'Well you have a strange way of making peace when you practically accuse your wife of taking to her bed any man she meets.'

He left her then without a word and she closed the door after him, feeling the tears hot on her cheeks. She didn't return to the parlour for fear Martha would come and question her, instead, she hurried up to her room and bolted the door and flung herself face down

370

on the bed she had shared with Daniel for such a short time.

It was a few days later when Ellie made a journey through town and up the hills of Mount Pleasant to the workhouse. The untidy spread of gaunt buildings seemed forbidding in the grey, misty day that had greeted her when she awoke. Still, she had made a promise to Boyo and it was one she intended to keep.

At the gate, the porter, seeing that she was a respectable, well dressed lady asked her to wait while he arranged for someone in authority to see her and he left her standing on the steep slope leading from the roadway to the main body of the building. Presently, the porter returned and led her in through the door and across a wide, cold entrance hall towards an office located near the back of the main building. Ellie was ushered into the room and saw she was facing a formidable woman dressed in the garb of a matron, the stiff, cotton cap crackling as she turned her head.

'Good morning, what can I do for you, Mrs Bennett?' The woman's tone was not welcoming. It implied she was extremely busy and had little time to spare for trivialities. 'Are you collecting for some charity perhaps?'

'No,' Ellie said, 'it's nothing like that.' She took the seat the woman indicated with a quick, impatient gesture of her hand and pulled her gloves more firmly over her fingers in an unconscious move, as though to impress on this officious woman that she herself was more than a little busy too. 'It's about a boy, taken into my husband's employ some eight or nine years ago. All I know about him is that he's called Boyo.'

'We'll need a great deal more than that to go on, Mrs Bennett, your husband, Mr Bennett can't he enlighten you?'

Ellie shook her head, this was going to be difficult, the matron's attitude didn't exactly encourage confidences.

'I was married before, to Jubilee Hopkins, owner of Glyn Hir tannery. It was he who took Boyo from here.'

'Ah, yes, Jubilee Hopkins, a fine old man.' Ellie looked at her was it her imagination or did the woman emphasize the word 'old'?

'Not been gone from this earth very long, has he?' The tone was definitely censorious. Ellie chose to ignore the question.

'I am anxious to know what Boyo's origins are, my present husband, the Reverend Bennett believes it necessary now that the lad is getting older.' She guessed that her little exaggeration of Daniel's position in the church would impress and it did. The matron visibly warmed. 'Ah, *that* Bennett family, good stock and the son a fine upright man, you are a very fortunate lady if I may say so.'

There wasn't much the formidable matron would not dare say, Ellie suspected.

'I remember the case of the boy very well indeed,' the matron allowed herself a tiny smile. 'I would advise you to speak to your late husband's lawyer on the matter, Mr Bernard Telforth is in possession of all the relevant facts concerning this boy's forebears.'

It was clear she knew something that she was not prepared to divulge. Ellie rose to her feet. 'Thank you for your time, Mrs . . . ?'

For an instant the matron looked uncomfortable. 'It's Miss Bowden,' she said 'but everyone calls me Matron.'

Ellie was glad to leave the grey, depressing buildings behind her. Surrounded as they were by high walls they resembled not so much a place for unfortunates as an abode for habitual criminals.

She walked back down the hill towards the town, pausing for a moment to enjoy a glimpse of the sea and the splash of sunlight that shone briefly between the buildings. She wondered if she should go to Bernard Telforth's offices straight away but suddenly, she felt tired and her spirits were low. She paused to sit on a flat stone on the bank leading upwards from the busy streets of Swansea examining her feelings. The visit to the workhouse had saddened her, if it hadn't been for the intervention of Jubilee, wonderful, kind Jubilee, she might well have ended up there herself.

She took a deep breath and entered the busy streets, hearing the sounds of wagons, of horses' hooves on cobbles; of a street vendor's raucous tones exhorting the good citizens of the town to buy *The Swansea Times* and she was possessed by a feeling of unreality. All around her people were living their lives, working in offices or shops, sharing the joy of companions and she, Ellie Bennett was alone. Was she destined to be that way always?

Had she not lain with Daniel, become his wife in fact as well as in name, the marriage could have been annulled. Is that what he would have wanted? She felt tears constrict her throat, she loved Daniel so much, why had he turned against her, how he could choose to believe a scoundrel like Matthew Hewson was beyond fathoming.

She passed the door of a public bar and heard the sound of raised, happy voices, someone was laughing uproariously and suddenly she felt she was on her own against an unfriendly world.

373

CHAPTER TWENTY-SIX

Ellie looked at her reflection in the mirror that hung in the hallway of the house at Glyn Hir, nothing about her outwards appearance, except perhaps for the shadows beneath her eyes gave any indication of her inward turmoil. She had been preparing to go out when the letter had come from Daniel. She had opened it with hands that trembled and scanned the contents eagerly, her throat constricted with a mixture of hope and fear.

A feeling of relief washed over her, he was coming here again this afternoon, he wanted to see her, he had missed her, he needed to talk to her. She reread his words and had hugged the note paper, the only frail link between them, and tears misted her eyes.

She took off her hat and placed it carelessly on the stand and returned to the mirror, tidying her hair, wondering how she would look to Daniel. Would he see the woman he loved, the woman he'd married or would he see one who had betrayed him? What did his letter mean?

She moved to the parlour where Martha was sitting bent over her sewing. 'Not going out after all?' she said breaking a piece of thread in her teeth. 'I thought this meeting with Mr Telforth was important.'

'Not as important as my marriage,' Ellie spoke breathlessly and waved the letter. 'Dan is coming home again, he wants to talk to me, oh, please God let it be all right this time.'

Martha put down her sewing and turned to face Ellie. 'It's to be hoped that he's come to his senses.' Her tone was unusually sharp. 'I never could understand why he was so angry with you, he should have known you would never do anything to hurt him.' Martha rose to her feet. 'I'm going up to my room, I'll give you a bit of privacy so that you can get this foolishness sorted out once and for all.' She smiled. 'Rosie isn't likely to bother you, she's entertaining Caradoc Jones in the kitchen.'

'Oh, is she? I didn't see him arriving.' Ellie sank into a chair, 'It's not his day to go over the books, is it?'

'I think he has other matters on his mind these days besides columns of figures. He's come courting and I trust his intentions are honourable because I think Rosie's really in love this time. I wouldn't like to see her hurt for all her faults.' She shrugged, 'But there we are, you can't live a body's life for them.' Martha left the room and closed the door quietly behind her.

The afternoon seemed to drag by and it was almost an hour later when the bell rang out harshly, echoing through the hushed silence of the house. It was Dan and he was behaving like a visitor to Glyn Hir not her husband.

Ellie waited a moment, listening intently, hearing Dan's vibrant tones with a lifting of her heart.

'Ellie, it's Mr Bennett,' Rosie was at the door of the parlour, on her face was an expression of triumph, it was almost as though she had conjured Daniel out of thin air by her own cleverness.

'Thank you, Rosie.' Ellie was on her feet, her eyes on Daniel's face searching his eyes, his mouth for any signal that she was forgiven. Ellie stared at Daniel for a long moment, almost afraid to speak. He returned her gaze longingly and she saw, with a catch at her throat, there were tears in his eyes.

As the door closed behind Rosie, they moved together and then Daniel was holding her, his face pressed into the warmth of her neck. 'Ellie . . .' he began but she pressed her mouth to his, silencing him. Words could hurt, could cause misunderstandings and she wanted nothing to spoil the safety of being in his arms.

They remained for a long moment, just holding each other and then he kissed her so tenderly that she knew that somehow, by some miracle everything was all right between them.

'What a fool I've been,' Daniel whispered the words in her ear, 'a fool to doubt you. I've missed you so much, Ellie, I can't live without you, I know that now.' He held her away from him. 'I've spent time on my knees praying for guidance, I remembered the times when together we listened to Evan Roberts preach, I thought of your honesty about your past and I came to the conclusion at last that I should believe your word before any other.'

He kissed her again, very gently. 'I have a confession to make, I've had a letter from Boyo, he told me the whole story, how you'd reacted after that bastard tried to attack you. How Boyo had fended him off with the sharp end of the shovel. What an awful time you must have had and I didn't make it any better.' He paused. 'I'm sorry for doubting you, Ellie, I'm so very sorry.'

'It's all right,' Ellie hid her disappointment that it had taken an outsider to convince her husband of the truth. 'It's over and done with now. You are here with me, that's all that matters.'

'I meant to make it right, convince you of my love,' Daniel said earnestly, 'even if it had taken me all night.' Ellie leaned against his shoulder.

'It might well do that,' she said, softly, 'take you all night, I mean.' And as she looked up into his eyes, a smile curved her lips.

The next day, even after Daniel had left for Lampeter, Ellie felt his presence, his love surrounding her. She sang as she walked around her garden, she felt alive again, part of the world, not just an unhappy spectator.

So engrossed was she in her thoughts that she jumped when she heard footsteps on the path behind her. She turned quickly and saw the tall, rangy figure walking towards her. 'Boyo, come and talk to me.'

They sat together on the warm wood of the bench

situated between two tall alders. The leaves of the trees were gold and red, some of them already making a carpet in the grass. Boyo looked down at her, the questions in his eyes not lost on her.

'Thank you for writing to Dan.'

'I know you told me not to,' Boyo said, 'but I thought it for the best, I couldn't just wait around doing nothing. Is everything all right, now?'

'Everything is fine. Now we have to sort your affairs out.'

Boyo's features lit up. 'You learned something of my past?' He was tense and she felt a tinge of guilt that she had put his worries out of her mind.

'Not yet,' she hated to dampen his hopes. 'But I have a lead, I might know someone who will be able to tell me everything we need to know.'

'Oh, I see.' He sounded disappointed and Ellie reached out and touched his hand.

'Have patience, Boyo, it will all come right, believe me, I can feel it in my bones.' He was silent for a moment and then he nodded his head.

'Right then. Now to business, I suppose you'd better come to talk to the foreman of the builders, it seems the workmen have hit a snag or two, run out of supplies, ordered too little timber, the usual sort of thing.'

'Can't you deal with it, Boyo?' Ellie was too happy to spend her time organizing the work on the buildings. 'It's about time you started taking the reins into your own hands. How old are you now, seventeen isn't it?'

He nodded, 'Aye, that's right. Are you that confident of my ability that you'll allow me to take up my responsibilities so soon?'

'Boyo, if you can't authorize the spending of a little Glyn Hir money, then I'm a Dutchman! Of course I have confidence in you.'

He beamed at her. 'Ellie, I love you,' he said and she leaned forward and hugged him.

'I know,' she said, 'I'm like a mother to you, aren't I?'

'Well, not quite,' he grinned. 'There was a time when I had quite a fancy for you, before you became Mrs Bennett, of course.'

'Ah, well, you've grown up now, found a lady love of your own. Are you happy, Boyo?'

'Happy as I can be. It's just now I have this burning wish to learn who I really am. I suppose I won't be content until I know something more about my background.'

'I've made an appointment with Jubilee's solicitor, Mr Telforth, according to the matron of the workhouse, he has the details of your birth.'

Boyo leaned forward. 'Why, what has Jubilee's solicitor got to do with it?'

Ellie shook her head. 'I won't know until I see him. I failed to turn up at my first appointment with him when I knew Dan was coming home but I'm going to town tomorrow and as soon as I know anything, I'll tell you, I promise.'

Boyo rose to his feet. 'I'd better get on, I'll take money from the petty cash then, get these timber supplies on their way.'

Ellie watched him walk away down the garden path. At the gate he turned and waved and she waved back feeling a wash of affection for him. He was young, very young, but he knew the running of the tannery perhaps better than anyone. He would make a fine manager given a few years in which to mature.

Ellie returned to the house. She would go to her room ostensibly to rest but what she wanted most was to lie on the bed she had shared with Daniel and dream about her husband.

'It's so good to see her happy again.' Rosie slid two maids of honour onto his plate. Caradoc liked good cooking and never failed to compliment Rosie on her skill. He didn't fail now. 'These cakes are so delicious, so light they melt in the mouth, you really are a wonder, Rosemary.'

He was the only one who never used the diminutive of her name. He was a precise man, he liked the figures in his books to add up and he carried on this trait into other aspects of his life with a meticulous care that charmed Rosie.

She sat opposite and looked at him, trying to see him with the eyes of a woman who didn't love him. It was impossible of course, others might see a rather plump young man with thinning hair but Rosie saw the kindness in his eyes, the humorous curve to his mouth, revealing his sense of fun, the one thing that saved him from being pompous.

'Why are you staring at me, Rosemary, I'm no oil painting, am I?'

'You look wonderful to me,' Rosie spoke softly, 'a knight in shining armour.'

He leaned across the table and caught her hand in his. 'I've a surprise for you, Rosemary,' he said. 'I was keeping it for when we went out together this evening but I can't wait any longer.'

He delved in his pocket and brought out a package. Rosie watched, her excitement mounting. He unwrapped the tissue paper and then held out a leather-covered box. Rosie looked at him for a long moment and then took it with eager fingers, snapping the lid open feeling almost breathless with excitement. Nestling in the velvet interior was a ring. The square cut emerald gleamed in the light from the fire and the two diamonds flanking it sparkled up at her with such brilliance that she blinked a little.

'Oh, Caradoc, this can't be for me, it must have cost you a king's ransom.'

'It was my mother's,' he said simply, 'until now I was not fortunate enough to find a lady worthy to wear it.'

She went to him and put her arms around his

shoulders, hugging him to her. His head was against her full breasts and he groaned, unable to bear the sweet-smelling nearness of her without feeling the urge to ravish her there and then.

'Will you marry me and soon?' he asked in a husky voice. She pushed herself onto his knee. 'Of course I will, I thought you were never going to pluck up enough courage to ask me. Here.' She handed him the ring carefully. 'Put it on my finger for me.'

'It fits,' he said as proudly as though he had made the ring to fit her himself, 'I knew it would.'

Rosie held her hand away from her admiring the sparkling gems, feeling her heart full of happiness. It wasn't just that the ring was precious in its own right, it was what it meant to her and what Caradoc had felt in giving it to her.

'Can I go and tell Ellie?' she asked him smiling down into his eyes, mesmerizing him. He nodded, unable to speak and she slipped away from him.

Ellie looked up as Rosie entered the parlour and speechlessly held out her hand. Martha was the first one to respond.

'Rosie, my dear girl, you are going to marry the delightful Mr Jones, how wonderful.' She sounded genuinely pleased and Rosie smiled at her. They had not always seen eye to eye and yet there had sprung up a sort of tacit understanding between them; in spite of everything Rosie was fond of Martha.

Ellie took Rosie's hand and stared down at the ring in admiration. 'He really must love you very much,' she said, 'that's a beautiful ring.'

'It was his mother's,' Rosie said proudly, 'he said I was the only girl fit enough to wear it after her.'

'I wish you every happiness,' Ellie said, 'but does this mean I'll have to look for a new maid?'

'Well, not just yet,' Rosie said, 'though Caradoc does want us to be married as soon as possible mind, but I won't leave you in the lurch.'

'I should hope not,' Martha had assumed her usual tone of asperity but Rosie smiled understandingly.

'I'll miss you all,' she said, 'this is the first home I've had, the first place where I've been treated like a real person and I'll never forget it.'

'You are a wonderful homemaker,' Ellie said, 'and always so cheerful, we'll miss *you*, believe me.' She hesitated for a moment. 'Bring Caradoc into the parlour Rosie and then fetch us a bottle of Jubilee's best port. No, on second thoughts, I'll fetch the port, this is *your* celebration.'

Rosie dimpled and turned at once towards the kitchen. She dragged a shy and reluctant Caradoc into the parlour and pushed him bodily into a chair.

'Ellie's bringing us a drink,' she said and Caradoc looked up as Ellie came into the room with the port.

'This really is most kind of you, Ellie,' he said, 'I do hope you don't mind me coming to call uninvited like this but I really can't stay away from Rosemary for very long, I'm a lost cause where she's concerned I'm afraid.'

'You are always welcome in my home,' Ellie said, 'Jubilee thought highly of you and so do I.'

'Most kind,' Caradoc repeated, his eyes fixed on Rosie longingly. Ellie knew how he felt, she loved Dan to distraction, she only wished she could be near to him as easily as Caradoc could be with his Rosie.

Ellie held up the bottle of port she had taken from the cellar and stared down at the dusty label. She recognized it of course, it had been one of Jubilee's favourites. She paused thinking of him for a moment, dreaming in the silence, remembering his kindness, his love, with real gratitude. She had been fortunate with the men in life, even Calvin had been good to her, he'd given her everything except his name. Her fate must have been pre-ordained, she decided, because had she married Calvin, she would not now be so happy. In all probability she would never have even met Daniel, what a dreadful loss that would have been.

She shook off her thoughts, they were too profound for this time of evening when the shadows lengthened and she felt the sharpness of being without Daniel so acutely.

'I'll get the glasses,' Rosie leaped up, 'don't you bother, Ellie, I know just where they are.'

Ellie took a seat, happy to allow Rosie to have domain in her own kitchen. Martha looked over her spectacles at Caradoc, her eyes shrewd. 'You're getting a fine girl there, you know,' she said, 'a good manager of all her duties, prudent and particular as to how her house is kept.'

'I know that,' Caradoc said softly, 'I can see I'm going to have an enormous task making her take things easy when we're married.' He smiled, his mouth curving at the corners. 'Pity help any maid I employ, she'll have to be excellent to measure up to Rosemary's high standards.'

'You are not wrong,' Martha agreed dryly. She watched as Rosie bustled into the room with four glasses on a tray.

'I've just been talking to your fiancé and he tells me you'll be waited on by a maid of your own when you're married.'

Ellie watched Rosie with amusement, if astonishment was the reaction Martha had expected, she was not to be disappointed.

'What, me have a maid?' Rosie looked at Caradoc, her mouth agape.

'Certainly you'll have a maid,' he said firmly, 'I already have a good lady who does my cooking and my laundry and she will remain as part of the household, naturally. But with the extra work and the entertaining we will undoubtedly do, we'll need a tweeny as well.'

Rosie sank into a chair and flapped at her face with her hand. 'Well, *duw, duw*, I never!'

'Good enough' Martha said, 'about time you took life a bit easier my girl, you do the work of two around here, what we'll do without you I just don't know.'

This was praise indeed coming from Martha and Rosie looked at her shaking her head. 'I never!' She repeated parrot-like. Ellie smiled. 'Stop teasing, Martha,' she said sternly, 'give Rosie a chance to think of the future in her own good time, you'll only vex her if you keep on about it.'

'Only giving praise where it's due,' Martha said primly. 'In any case, Rosie will need all the help she can get when the little ones come along.'

'Little ones,' echoed Rosie, 'she talks of little ones Caradoc, do you hear her and us not yet married.'

'She has a point,' Caradoc said. 'I want a son and heir like any other man.'

Rosie put her hands to her cheeks and stared up at everyone as though she couldn't believe what she was hearing.

'Have some port,' Ellie said filling the glasses, 'it might help to calm you down a little.'

Rosie smiled up at her. 'You're very kind, Ellie, can I ask one favour of you?'

'If it's within my power to grant you a favour then I will.'

'Can I be married from here? It's the only home I have.' Rosie's voice was wistful. Ellie sat beside her on the comfortable sofa and took her hand.

'Of course you shall be married from here, there's no question about it. We'll see you well on your way with a reception and flowers and all the trimmings.' She waved a hand at Caradoc as he moved to protest. 'I won't hear a word against it, I have more than enough money, you above everyone should know that, Caradoc Jones, so let me give you my wedding present in any way I choose.'

Without any warning, Rosie began to cry, she bent her head in her hands and sobbed like a little child. Caradoc moved, quickly for a large man, and kneeling before her hugged her in his big arms.

'There, there,' he said softly, 'there, there, everything is going to be all right.'

383

Rosie looked up at him, her eyes brimming. 'Oh Caradoc, I've never been so happy in all my life.'

Later, as Ellie lay in her bed, she envied Rosie, tomorrow she would see her Caradoc again. As for Ellie, it might be weeks before she could lose herself in her husband's embrace. She turned on her side and buried her face in the softness of the pillow and if a few tears fell from her eyes there was no-one to see them.

Matthew was tired of waiting. Each day he'd looked in the pages of *The Swansea Times* and each day he'd been disappointed. What was wrong with Arian Smale, why didn't she print the story he'd given her, was she mad? But then, she was probably hand in glove with both Bridie Marchant and with Ellie Hopkins. Well, he would wait no longer, if *The Times* didn't wish to print the story of the smuggling then someone else would.

It was a brisk day in late autumn, the trees were transformed into emblems of summer's end. The sun was a mellow glow against the sky but Matthew saw none of it. He walked, head high, hands thrust into his pockets, seeing only the money he would get for his story.

In the offices of the *Gomerian*, he had difficulty at first in seeing someone in authority. The young man at the front desk was obstructive, almost rude until Matthew caught him by his immaculate shirt front and almost dragged him over the counter. 'Get me someone in charge before I punch your head in.' He released the lad who fell back, straightening his clothes, his face white.

The editor looked at him without smiling, it was clear he'd been informed that the man standing before him was dangerous, he kept well away from the counter staring at Matthew as though expecting him to attack at any moment.

'I'd like to talk to you in private,' Matthew said in a reasonable tone of voice which took the man by surprise.

'On what subject, sir?' The editor moved uneasily from one foot to the other.

'On the subject of some of the top merchants in the town being involved in illegal trade. I could go to one of your competitors with the story, of course.'

'No need of that sir, come along to my office, I'm sure we can do business.'

With a feeling of triumph Matthew followed him along the corridor and into a plushly furnished office. He took the big chair set before the desk without waiting to be invited and after a moment's hesitation, the editor took the chair facing him. Matthew leaned forward. 'I have dates and times and even the amounts of money made from these nefarious dealings, I have names, of course, and all this information is yours – for a consideration.'

'Have you informed the police?' The editor asked smoothly and Matthew made a wry face.

'Of course not.'

The editor rose indicating the interview was at an end. 'I'm sorry, sir, without proof, real, rock-hard proof, I dare not print anything.'

Matthew wondered for a long moment if there was anything to be gained by smashing the man in the face. At last, he contented himself with overturning the desk so that the man leaped back against the wall in fear. 'Sod you then! I'll go elsewhere,' he said furiously.

When he left the office of the *Gomerian*, Matthew turned into the doorway of the Swan and slumped down at one of the tables. He needed a drink, more than one drink if it came to that. He placed some money on the table and watched as the landlord came swiftly to his side. Money certainly got people's attention. Pity he didn't have more of it, Matthew thought sourly.

He didn't notice the tall, rangy man who came and sat a few tables away from him. In any case, if he had seen and recognized him, he wouldn't have cared. He took up his mug of ale and drank deeply and settled down for the evening.

Across the room, Mac was watching, he had been

following Hewson for some time. He'd seen him go into the offices of the *Gomerian* and hoped that the editor had not been fool enough to pay any money over to the man.

Matthew was very drunk by the time he left the Swan and Mac was easily able to catch up with him. Mac was just behind Matthew when he slipped and fell into the gutter and quickly he moved to help him to his feet, dusting down his jacket in a helpful manner before leading him back towards the doorway of the Swan.

'Let me treat you to another drink, old man,' Mac said smoothly, 'it seems to me there's a lot you would like to get off your chest.'

Later, as Mac walked along the quiet roadways towards home, he was smiling his slow, triumphant smile; a smile which Arian would have recognized as a sign of Mac's satisfaction of a job well done.

CHAPTER TWENTY-SEVEN

'So what have you found out?' Arian was sitting at her desk staring up at Mac in anticipation. She could read him well, he was obviously pleased with himself. He stood, shuffling a sheaf of papers in his hands, his hat tilted back on his head, the usual cigar between his lips. He took off his hat and seated himself opposite Arian, she waited, hearing the muted sounds of activity from the large office beyond her door. 'Mac, you are a devious old thing, we both know that. Now will you please talk to me?'

'Marchant has been trading in opium which we knew. Mrs Marchant, it seems, managed to swap the loads so that the *Marie Clare* carried only legitimate cargo on Marchant's last trip. She held back the contraband until her husband agreed to her demands.'

'I see. Very clever of her, so that's how Bridie got her inheritance back?'

'Quite. In order to have the opium returned to him Marchant was forced to sign all his assets over to her.' Mac paused to light a cigar. 'Marchant is probably being held prisoner by his contact, he might even be dead. Hewson was involved but only in a small way. He was given his marching orders, Marchant was not so lucky.'

'Should we inform the authorities?' Arian asked hesitantly. Mac rose to his feet and placed his hat on his head. 'It's the only thing we *can* do. We could print, of course but there is no real proof that Hewson is speaking the truth. If he is and the story breaks, it could be Marchant's death knell.' He sighed. 'I'm off home, this is one problem only you can tackle. See you tomorrow.'

When Mac left the office Arian rubbed at her eyes wearily. She felt jaded and uncertain. Where was her enthusiasm for a story, why was she not prepared to take the matter to the limits, print the story and damn the consequences? Was it that the paper was no longer enough for her? She had believed it to be her whole life, she had even told Calvin so, or as good as. And yet without him she felt empty and hopeless. She was missing Calvin more than she had believed possible, she might as well admit it to herself if not to anyone else.

She rose impatiently and moved to the door, she had work to do. Bridie must be consulted, she must be told about her husband's predicament, given an opportunity to decide the best course of action.

Arian paused at the door of her office and squared her shoulders, she must face the crowded outer office with an air of calm composure. She was determined that to the world she would appear confident, in charge. She opened the door and stepped out into the noise and bustle and the smell of ink that was the life blood of *The Swansea Times*.

'So the story of your past has had to wait then?' April picked a blade of grass and chewed at it thoughtfully. She looked at Boyo's downcast face and admitted to herself that secretly she was relieved that the day of judgement, as she had come to think of it, had been postponed. 'Well, I can understand why, Ellie was troubled, worried about her marriage. She will find out something as soon as she can, I know she will.'

'Look, Boyo,' April spoke softly, 'it doesn't matter to me who your parents are, I love you for yourself.' She blushed as she spoke and Boyo's face softened.

'I know that and I'm proud of you.' He shrugged, 'But I have to know, I just have to know who I really am.'

'I realize it's no fun to be an orphan, Boyo, I've felt many times that I'm imposing on the O'Conners. Good as Fon and Jamie are to me, I'm not really one of them, it hurts sometimes.'

Boyo put his arm around her. 'But you have a name of your own even if you don't choose to use it. You are a Thomas, you know who your mam was and you still have a brother living somewhere. I'm out in limbo, I can't seem to settle until I have an identity of my own.'

April changed the subject. 'Have you heard the gossip that's going round about Mrs Marchant? Her husband missing and her living with a servant up in Clydach, or so they say. What do you make of that, isn't it a come down for a rich lady?'

Boyo shrugged, 'Well what's important is she doesn't think like that. Live and let live, I say.' He bent and kissed April's nose.

April drew away from him unwilling to let the subject drop. 'Mrs Marchant was born rich, those sort seem to be able to do just what they like and get away with it, they flout the law in any way they choose.'

'Do you know much about it then?' Boyo asked and April shook back a curl that had come loose from the ribbons. 'The law, I mean.' His tone was teasing.

'I read as much as I can about it, I suppose I could become more interested if I was given the chance.'

'Why not take it up seriously then?' Boyo asked, 'I mean why not do as Fon suggests and go to college?'

'Don't you start that,' April said. 'If I left Swansea, you'd have forgotten all about me by the time I came back. In any case, all I want now is to be your wife.'

'What, Mrs Boyo?' he laughed. 'See, I really will have to find out who my parents were, won't I?'

April rose to her feet and brushed the leaves from her skirt. She looked down across the town to where the sea curved against sands, pale gold in the late autumn sunshine. Suddenly she felt sad, it was the last glimmering of an Indian summer, it had been such a beautiful summer. She had fallen in love, found a soulmate, someone who loved her back. Now, it seemed it was over, all gone like the leaves that had fallen leaving the trees bare.

She shivered and turning to Boyo buried her head in his shoulder. 'We will be together for always, won't we?' Her voice was muffled so that he had to put his head close to hers to hear what she was saying. She breathed in the clean scent of him and suddenly, she was afraid.

'Come on, you're shivering, I'm going to take you home,' Boyo whispered against her hair. 'I don't want my best girl catching a chill, do I?'

As they walked, hand in hand across the fields of Honey's Farm, April knew that she must enjoy every moment she had with Boyo. She hoped that soon he would learn who his parents were so there would be no barriers between them. Suddenly it seemed urgent as though time was slipping away from them.

But that was absurd, they were both so young, so healthy, so full of love and life. And yet the feeling persisted even as Boyo held her in his arms and kissed her and told her he would always love her.

At Glyn Hir the building work was finished. A fresh stack of oak-bark plates stood in the yard and the distinctive smell of soaking leather permeated the air.

Ellie, standing outside in the garden, smiled, it seemed Boyo had taken her at her word, got on with the job and started production immediately. Some of the old leather had been salvaged from the fire but that would soon be used up. It would take three years before the new leather would be ready to sell and until then, she would need to buy in stocks from another tannery simply to keep her regular customers supplied. There would be little profit in it but there was the goodwill of the people with whom she did business to consider.

She went indoors, looked around at the big rambling house that had been her home for five years and knew the time had come to move out. As soon as she could, she would rent a place near the sea until Dan had finished college and then she would go with him to wherever his job led him.

She heard sounds from the kitchen, heard the rise and fall of voices and knew exactly where she would find Martha and Rosie. A cheerful fire roared in the grate and Ellie made straight for it, holding her hands out to the blaze. She looked up to see Rosie and Martha watching her.

'Soon, ladies, I'm going to start looking for somewhere to live,' she said quietly. 'I can't stay here for ever more, can I?'

'I couldn't bear to be parted from you now,' Martha said quickly. '*Duw*, what would I do on my own?'

Rosie sighed. 'I don't know how long it will be before I get married but until then, I'll gladly work for you, wherever you go.'

Martha looked round her, 'What will you do with this place, Ellie, will you sell it?'

Ellie shook her head. 'I'll let Boyo live here for as long as he wants to, he's going to be in charge of the tannery anyway so he might as well be on the spot.'

'That's kind of you, Ellie, very thoughtful, I know Boyo has been working like a Trojan here, getting the place shipshape again.' Martha patted her skirts as though Boyo's head was resting in her lap. 'Harry and Luke are back in work too, they haven't deserted us for another job. Good men you have there, mind.'

'I know,' Ellie looked at Rosie. 'Bring my coat, there's a love.'

'Going out again?' Martha asked, her eyebrows raised.

'Afraid so, I have to see Bernard Telforth on business.'

'There's mysterious,' Martha said, 'are you going to tell us about it?

'You'll know, all in good time.' Ellie took her coat from Rosie. 'I won't be long, keep the fire going in the parlour, it gets so chilly in the evenings.'

Later, as she entered the lobby of Mr Telforth's offices, Ellie wondered what she would learn from him.

The old man welcomed her warmly, 'Sit down, my dear, I hope you are keeping well?'

She took the seat he indicated and leaned forward, her hands clasped together. 'I need to discuss something with you, Mr Telforth, I'm not sure if you can help or not.'

He looked at her strangely. 'I think I know what this is about,' he took a file of papers from his drawer, 'it's Boyo, isn't it, you want to know his real name?'

'How did you know?' Ellie asked.

'It was bound to come up sooner or later. Once the boy started asking questions, you would be the first to offer help.' He flipped open the file and glanced down at the information inside. 'Hopkins, that's his name.'

'Hopkins?' Ellie said, her throat suddenly dry, 'how can that be?'

'Patience, my dear.' Bernard Telforth looked at her over his glasses. 'You'll have to prepare yourself for a shock.' He paused and then, as though encouraged by her silence, he continued. 'Jubilee had an affair, a very brief affair many years ago before his unfortunate sickness. The woman left town and in due course gave birth to Jubilee's daughter.' He took a deep breath. 'The woman contacted me and though I recognized her, I chose to discount her story, she died shortly afterwards.' He looked at Ellie as though trying to assess her feelings. 'Her daughter, Marian, lived for a long time in Cardiff with an aunt who knew nothing about the child's father.'

'But how . . . ?' Ellie broke off mid-sentence as Mr Telforth held up his hand.

'History has a way of repeating itself, the daughter Marian, in the fullness of time also bore an illegitimate child – the one we know as Boyo.'

'I still don't understand,' Ellie said, 'I can't believe Jubilee would have left any kin of his to be brought up in a workhouse.'

'Jubilee knew nothing about it.' Bernard shut the file.

'Boyo was transferred to Swansea from Cardiff when he was a few years old.'

'Then how did he come to be working with Jubilee at Glyn Hir?'

'Jubilee wanted to give an orphan a home, I was sent to the workhouse to sort out the legalities of the matter. I saw the documentation concerning the boy's forebears, I put two and two together.'

'And Jubilee never knew the connection between Boyo and himself, never knew he had a grandson?'

'In my wisdom, I thought it best not to tell him,' Bernard Telforth shrugged. 'Who knows what might have happened, the boy's relatives might have turned up and claimed all Jubilee had worked for. The background was not reassuring, there could have been instability, mental illness, something in the child's blood, I couldn't take a chance.'

'So why are you telling me all this now?' Ellie asked in a strained voice. 'I feel such a fraud, as if I've taken everything that belongs rightly to Boyo.'

'I am old, I can no longer make decisions with the confidence, or arrogance I had in my youth so, my dear lady, I entrust this burden of truth to you.'

He handed her the file. 'In my capacity as your solicitor, I suggest you make an allowance to the boy, I think he deserves that much.' He shrugged. 'But as I said, it's up to you now.'

Ellie left the offices in a daze. So much had happened in the last few days, so many upheavals, she felt she could scarcely cope with this fresh revelation about Boyo's birthright.

She wandered towards the beach, the salt tangy air filled her nostrils and she breathed deeply trying to be calm. She settled herself on a spar staring out to sea. What should she do? Boyo was the rightful owner of Glyn Hir, should she sign it all over to him?

Daniel, she thought in anguish, if only you were here now. She looked up at the clouds scudding across the skies, winter was creeping upon the town, the nights would lengthen and she would be alone. 'Daniel, I need you!' Her voice was carried away by the cold wind and the wash of the ocean. Only the distant screech of the sea birds could be heard above the noise of the gathering storm.

CHAPTER TWENTY-EIGHT

With winter came the worst sickness Swansea had seen in a long time. Influenza of a most virulent kind was sweeping through the huddled streets of the town touching almost every household with terrible results. There seemed little the doctors could do to contain the illness; the hospitals were full, funerals were an everyday occurrence and the shops were eerily empty. Even the maids from the big houses, shopping in the market place, had ceased to haggle over prices and did their business as swiftly as possible before hurrying away from the silent streets.

'Good thing we don't live any closer to the town.' Martha, as usual, was busy sewing, her glasses perched on the end of her nose. 'Lucky we hadn't yet found a house to rent, the tannery might be smelly but at least we're out of danger up here.'

Ellie raised her eyebrows but kept her doubts to herself, the sickness, she knew, could be carried in by any one of a dozen means. There were deliveries to be made both to and from the tannery, Rosie needed occasionally to go into town for supplies; contact with people who might be infected was inevitable. The tradesmen, those who were not stricken, still called to the door of Glyn Hir and as for Harry and Luke, goodness only knows where they spent their evenings, most likely in the crowded smoky rooms of one of the public houses of the area. Still, if it comforted Martha to think them safely away from danger, then so be it.

Ellie stared into the fire, deep in thought and after a long silence, Martha spoke again. 'What's eating you,

Ellie, not worrying about that husband of yours, are you? He's young and fit and what's more he's all the way down in Lampeter, I doubt if they have even heard of the influenza there.'

Ellie shook her head. 'It's not Dan I'm worried about, it's Boyo. My conscience is troubling me, I feel I'm failing in my duty towards him. I'll have to talk to him and soon, tell him what I've found out about him but somehow I can't bring myself to find the right words.'

'Want to confide in me or is this too private a matter?' Martha put down her sewing and gave Ellie her full attention.

Ellie debated for a moment and then decided she could do with Martha's commonsense approach to the problem of Boyo's ancestry. 'When I went to see Bernard Telforth a few weeks ago, it was about Boyo.' She paused, biting her lip, she had not even been given the opportunity of talking all this over with Dan yet, still, she could hardly stop now, Martha's eyes were alight with anticipation. 'Boyo wanted to learn about his background,' she continued, 'that's natural enough, especially now he's walking out with April O'Conner.'

'And?' Martha urged, 'did you learn anything interesting?'

'Oh, yes,' Ellie smiled dryly. 'Very interesting. Boyo is Jubilee's grandson.'

'What?' Martha leaned forward in her chair. 'How can that be, I thought Jubilee was barren?'

'I know,' Ellie nodded, 'so did I and so did he. Apparently he had one brief love affair. It all happened a long time ago, well before he had the sickness. To cut a long story short, Boyo is Jubilee's next of kin, for all I know, his only kin.'

Martha looked at her in silence for a long moment. 'I can read you like a book,' she said, 'now you feel guilty because you have inherited all of Jubilee's money. Well the solution is simple, share it with Boyo.'

Ellie looked across at her. 'I feel he deserves it all,'

she said softly. 'The whole estate, the tannery, the money, it does, by right, belong to Boyo.'

'Rubbish!' Martha rose to her feet and brushed down her skirts, 'That's nonsense! You were Jubilee's legal wife, you would naturally be looked after however many children Jubilee had.'

'But would he have bothered to marry me if he'd known he had a grandson?' Ellie said in a small voice. 'That's what I keep asking myself.'

'Look, all anyone would expect of you is that you give Boyo a decent share of Jubilee's money. Some people wouldn't even do that much, believe me.'

Ellie sighed heavily. 'I know you are right, I only wish Dan was here so that I could talk to him about it, he's so wise.'

'And you haven't told Boyo any of this?'

'No, first I want to be sure in my mind what I'm going to do with the estate.'

'He won't demand anything, not if I know Boyo,' Martha said evenly. 'That lad has more sense than many twice his years.'

'I must do what's right,' Ellie said. 'What I think Jubilee would have wanted. But should I talk to Dan first and then talk to Boyo, what do you think?'

'I think you should put Boyo out of his misery as soon as possible,' Martha said dryly. 'It's not fair to keep him waiting. Just tell him the facts and worry about making any decisions concerning the money afterwards.'

'I suppose you're right. I know Boyo is really anxious to learn all he can about his past. I'll talk to him first thing in the morning, I promise.'

'Good girl.' Martha folded up her sewing. 'I think I'll turn in early, I'm feeling just a little tired.' She rubbed her eyes and Ellie looked at her in concern. 'Are you sure that's all, you're just tired, you don't feel ill?'

'Don't fuss, girl,' Martha softened her words with a smile, 'I'm strong as a horse, you know that as well as I do.'

'I'll get Rosie to bring you up a cup of hot milk,' Ellie said, 'it will help you to sleep.'

'That sounds nice.' Martha sighed heavily. 'Can she bring me a hot water bottle as well, do you think?'

'Go on, up to bed, I'll see to everything.'

Later, Ellie sat in the kitchen with Rosie, glad of the girl's cheerful company, tonight she felt unaccountably lonely.

'Where's Boyo?' Rosie glanced at the clock. 'He's late isn't he?'

'I expect he's taking his time walking home from Honey's Farm.' Ellie smiled warmly, 'He's in love, really in love for the first time.'

'But not the last, I'll wager,' Rosie smiled. 'He's a fine boy, whoever gets him will be a lucky woman. I'm very fond of Boyo.'

Ellie looked at her and smiled. 'So I heard.'

Rosie had the grace to blush. 'I don't want Caradoc to hear of it, mind, nor anything about Matthew Hewson. I don't think he'd like it very much.'

'No need for him to know, not if you don't want him to. What's past is past and we all have our skeletons in the cupboard remember.'

'You'll make a lovely vicar's wife,' Rosie said warmly. 'You don't make a body feel awful and wicked, you're such an understanding person.'

Ellie grimaced. 'I don't know, I don't feel good enough for Daniel, not really.'

'He's very lucky to have you,' Rosie said stoutly, 'you'll do him proud, that you will.'

Ellie rose. 'Well, there's no sign of Boyo, he can let himself in, I'm going to bed.'

She was relieved not to have to face Boyo and the questions in his eyes until morning. She knew Martha was right, she must talk to him as soon as possible, put his mind at rest. He deserved that much. But not tonight.

'I'll just bank up the fire and then I'll come up too,' Rosie said. 'Good night Ellie, God bless.'

Lying in bed, Ellie looked up at the moonlight, sharp, crisp and wintry as it shone in through the window. She wished Dan were at her side, wished she could talk to him ask him what was right. She sighed, ah well, she would sleep on her problem and perhaps in the morning, she would have all the answers.

It wasn't to be. Early, before daylight, Ellie awoke to hear sounds of coughing coming from Martha's room. She rose quickly and pulled on her robe, tying the belt firmly around her waist. The polished boards were cold beneath her feet as she crossed from her own room over the landing to where Martha slept.

Ellie quickly lit the lamp and took it to the table beside the bed. Martha's eyes were closed, her cheeks flushed, the glitter of perspiration beaded her forehead. Ellie, her mouth dry, realized that Martha had contracted influenza.

Rosie, awakened from sleep, stood in the doorway, worried but reluctant to intrude. 'Can I do anything, Ellie, is Martha sick?'

Ellie turned to the girl and nodded slowly. 'We'll bathe her and dress her in a fresh gown,' she said attempting to be calm and practical. 'Can you bring some water, Rosie?'

'Aye, I'll do that and while I'm at it, I'll see to the fire, might as well make sure it stays alight now.'

Boyo emerged from the back bedroom rubbing his eyes. 'What is it, Ellie?'

'It's Martha, she's not well.' She moved to the door and spoke in whispers. 'I'm not sure but I think it's the influenza.'

Martha began to cough again and Ellie returned to her side. 'It's all right, I'm going to give you something to ease your chest.' She looked over her shoulder at Boyo. 'Fetch me the bottle of elixir from the shelf in the pantry, Boyo, and a spoon as well, please.'

Martha opened her eyes as though with a great effort. 'Ellie,' her voice was little more than a croak, 'I've caught it, haven't I?'

'It looks like it,' Ellie didn't bother to prevaricate, she knew Martha would not appreciate half-truths. 'But you are going to be all right, Rosie and I will take care of you until daybreak and then Boyo can go for the doctor.'

Boyo's footsteps sounded on the stairs and he entered the room with the brown bottle in his hand. 'Here we are,' he glanced down at Martha and smiled encouragingly, 'this will make you feel better.'

'Go on back to bed, Boyo,' Ellie said softly, 'there's not a lot you can do now.'

'Might as well stay up now I'm awake,' Boyo said firmly. 'I'll make an early start in the yard.'

Rosie returned with a jug of water and poured it into the bowl on the washstand. 'I managed to take the chill off it with what was left in the kettle,' she said in a low voice.

When Martha had been given the elixir and was changed into a fresh gown, Ellie sank into a chair beside her. 'Feel any better, Martha?'

Martha didn't answer, she seemed to have sunk into a deep sleep, it was probably the medicine working, Ellie thought as she leaned over the older woman anxiously.

'Come on downstairs,' Rosie whispered, 'you look all in.'

Ellie glanced uncertainly at Martha and Rosie shook her head. 'She won't wake now, not for a while, best let her rest easy.'

It was warm in the kitchen and, gratefully, Ellie sat near the fire. Boyo was putting more coal on the flames and Rosie slumped over the table and rested her head in her arms. Ellie touched her lightly on the shoulder. 'Go back to bed, get a couple of hours, it's still on four o'clock.'

Rosie sighed, 'I think I will. Call me if you need anything, mind.'

After she had gone, Ellie leaned back wearily in her chair. She knew the moment had come when she must speak to Boyo about his past and it was not going to be easy. She wasn't sure how he would react, would he resent being robbed of his heritage, would he blame Jubilee for what had happened so long ago?

'What is it, Ellie?' Boyo asked quietly, 'I can see you are worried, is it Martha, is she very sick?'

Ellie shook her head. 'It's not about Martha, Boyo, it's about you.'

He took a deep, steadying breath. 'You've found out who my parents were?'

'Not exactly,' she looked down at her hands. 'What I do know for certain is that you are a Hopkins, you are Jubilee's grandson.'

He was stunned into silence for a moment, a mixture of emotions fleeting across his face. At last, he cleared his throat and spoke. 'How can that be, Ellie?'

She took a deep breath. 'Jubilee had an affair when he was young. The girl left Swansea in disgrace and he never saw her again. What he didn't know was that the girl was pregnant by him.'

'I can't take this in,' Boyo rubbed his eyes, 'Jubilee my grandfather and he never knew it, is that what you are saying?'

Ellie nodded. 'Jubilee's daughter grew up not knowing who her father was. Eventually, she had a child, that child is you.'

'So my mother was never married?' Boyo asked. 'I am a bastard.' His voice was filled with bitterness. He rubbed at his eyes as though trying to clear his head. 'I suppose she gave me the name Hopkins out of some sort of pride, perhaps she hoped I would trace my roots one day.' He looked directly at Ellie. 'Did my mother give me a first name?'

Ellie swallowed hard. 'I don't know very much, Boyo, except that when Jubilee wanted a boy from the work-house, he took a liking to you. His solicitor Mr Telforth checked all the details and discovered the ties between you.'

'And he didn't tell Jubilee?' Boyo shook back a lock

of hair that had fallen over his eyes. 'Why, Ellie, why didn't he tell Jubilee that I was his kin, it would have meant so much to him and to me?'

'He was afraid Jubilee would be put under pressure from your mother's family, I suppose,' Ellie said quietly. 'Mr Telforth did what he thought was best for his client and at the same time ensured you had a decent future.'

'He played God with my life,' Boyo's voice had an edge of sadness to it and Ellie reached out and touched his hand.

'We know who you are now,' she encouraged, 'and we'll sort out the matter of the inheritance, don't you worry about that, I wouldn't cheat you out of anything that is rightfully yours.'

His fingers curled into hers and he smiled, his gloom lightening. 'Don't you think I know that, Ellie?' He didn't move for a long moment. He shook back his hair and gazed up at the ceiling. 'Well,' he said at last, 'at least I know that on my grandfather's side I come from decent stock, Jubilee was a good man, I loved him in my own way. My mother, now that's a different story.'

'Don't be so ready to judge,' Ellie cautioned, 'none of us are perfect, are we? You just have to take our household into account to see that we have all made mistakes.'

Boyo nodded. 'You're right, Ellie.' He released her hand and sank back into his chair. Suddenly he seemed to relax. 'I can offer April something of a background to my life, I'm grateful for that, very grateful. Thank you Ellie.'

'You are more than welcome.' Ellie looked beyond Boyo's shoulder to the window where the light was beginning to turn from blue-black to grey. 'It will soon be daybreak.' She rose to her feet. 'I'd better go and check on Martha. Will you go fetch the doctor, Boyo?'

As Ellie made her way up the stairs, she heard the click of the latch as the door closed behind Boyo, knowing that for him, life was just beginning, nothing would ever be the same again.

It took almost a week for Martha's fever to break, a week during which she coughed and moaned in pain and discomfort and, when she was lucid, wept tears of fear and frustration. But at last, she was sitting up against her pillows, pale but obviously well on the mend.

'It's all thanks to you.' Martha's voice was still thin with fatigue but with much of the old spirit returned to it. 'You've been better than any kith or kin could be.'

Ellie smoothed out the bedcovers and plumped the cushions. 'Well, I suppose I'd better make the most of the compliments while they are offered, we'll all be getting the rough side of your tongue soon enough.'

As she left the room, there was a feeling of jubilation in her heart, Martha was well again and soon, quite soon, Dan would be home on holiday.

Paul paced the boards of the small cabin with short angry strides. He had been kept prisoner for long enough on Monkton's ship and anger was replacing his initial sense of fear and uncertainty. Monkton's ship had been in deep water for weeks with Paul locked in the small cabin like an animal. Now, the ship was back on familiar ground, in Cork harbour.

Paul began to thump on the door, shouting out loud, kicking at the lock. He must be heard, Monkton must release him now they were back in the Irish port. He fell back as he heard the lock turn on the cabin door and pressed himself against the bunk. Monkton came into the room flanked by two burly crewsmen.

'You are making a lot of noise, I can't have that, Marchant, I can't have that at all. I've been lenient so far, taking you with me on my journeys. Now you have become troublesome, I am undecided what I should do with you. This is my last call on Ireland so it's time I made up my mind, one way or the other.'

'Look, if you are worried that I'll say anything . . .'

Paul stopped speaking abruptly as Monkton held up his hand. 'It's you who should be worried. You see, you know too much about me. I'm considering a burial at sea for you. That would be one way of silencing you for good.'

Paul felt a chill run through him. 'I can hardly tell anyone about your activities without implicating myself, can I? And what about Hewson, you released him?'

'Hewson knows nothing of importance, in any case, he's a nobody,' Monkton said reasonably. 'You, on the other hand, have some influential friends.' He paused consideringly. 'I could take you on another little trip and dump you off somewhere quiet.' He turned away. 'I have until tonight to think about it, in the meantime, I would advise you to be sensible.'

When he was alone, Paul stared at the closed door knowing he must make a move before it was too late. If he could pick the lock on the door, he could get out of the cabin and up onto the deck, at least that way he would stand a chance. There was no point sitting around any longer waiting to see if Monkton meant to kill him or not. He knelt down on the boards and saw that one of the nails had worked loose. He tried to prize it out with his fingers but it held fast. On the table was a tin mug along with the remains of his breakfast. Paul felt sweat run down his face in spite of the coldness in the cabin. He jammed the rim of the mug under the nail and levered it upwards. It came free, rolling along the boards with a sound like a drum beat to Paul's straining ears.

It took him longer than he had anticipated to pick the lock but at last it opened beneath his touch and he breathed a sigh of relief, there was no bolt on the outside. Monkton, it seemed, had relied on Paul's fear of reprisal to keep him a prisoner.

Paul shivered a little in the cold air, there was a thick frost along the side of the ship as he moved silently onto the deck. His mouth was dry as he crept towards the gangway, almost afraid to breathe. There was a great deal of activity taking place, large wooden crates were being lowered into the hold. Voices were raised as dockers called instructions to each other and Paul breathed easier, realizing he couldn't have chosen a better time to escape.

He straightened, moving across the deck with studied casualness, forcing himself not to look over his shoulder. He walked past one of the sweating sailors who was attempting to hold a crate steady against the roll of the tide and the force of the north-easterly wind that had sprung up.

Paul focused his attention on the gangway, it was less than ten feet away, ten feet to freedom. Scarcely had the thought come into his mind when he heard a voice shout out behind him.

'Stop him! Stop that man!' He would recognize that voice anywhere, it was Monkton's. He felt a moment of blind panic and then he began to run. The boards were wet with icy water, Paul's breath was rasping in his throat, the gangway seemed to come no nearer. There were more shouts and the thud of feet pounding behind him. He felt a hand grasp his shirt and he struggled to free himself.

The deck heaved, Paul caught a glimpse of cold water far below him. The hands released him and he teetered for a moment before falling with heart-stopping slowness over the side. He knew from experience what would happen, he had seen it many times before. He had time for one short scream before the roll of the ship brought the bulk of the side towards him crushing him against the hard stone of the jetty.

'So you see,' Boyo was seated in the kitchen at Honey's Farm, his face red, his hands twisting his cap into a knot, 'it turns out that I'm Jubilee Hopkins' grandson.'

April's face shone with happiness as she beamed

around at Jamie and Fon. 'There,' her tone was triumphant, 'I told you everything would be all right.' She looked at Boyo with clear eyes. 'Not that I cared one jot who his parents were.'

Boyo felt warm, how he loved April, she was his ally when he needed one, she cared for him through good or ill, she was everything a wife should be. And now he had something solid to offer her.

Jamie took out his pipe and Fon stared up at him disapprovingly. 'You are not going to smoke that foul thing in here, are you?'

He smiled good humouredly but carried on puffing his pipe regardless of her protest, he knew it was lightly made. 'So, then, Boyo, what are your future prospects, any idea where you stand?'

Boyo met his gaze. 'Not yet. What I do know is that I can depend on Ellie to be fair and just.'

Jamie nodded. 'I would agree with that, son.' He smiled at Boyo and there was a mutual liking between them that was growing stronger the more they came to know each other.

April rose from her chair and moved to the door and Boyo, with a glance towards Jamie, saw the older man's almost imperceptible nod and followed her.

Boyo was glad to be out in the cold winter air, he saw the fields hard with frost, the hedgerows dusted with silver. The air cut keenly through his wool coat but at least he was alone with April. He put his arm around her shoulder and hugged her and she looked up at him her eyes alight. He stared down into her face, in spite of her happiness, she looked pale and her eyes were shadowed and his heart dipped within him. 'You feel all right, don't you, April?' he asked. 'You seem to be under the weather.'

'It's nothing, just a headache, I'll be all right, really I will. Don't look so worried.'

'When we're married, I'll make sure you don't have to lift a finger when you feel like this,' he said firmly.

'I'll cosset you and care for you and you won't know you've even been off colour.'

She smiled, 'You always make me feel good, Boyo.' She squeezed his hand. 'I'm glad you've found out about your past though more for your sake than for mine.'

April's voice quivered a little and Boyo imagined for a moment it was with emotion but when he looked down at her, April was clutching her chest, her face deadly white. She slumped against him and he held her in his arms, his heart beating rapidly. She was sick, really sick, anyone with any sense could tell this was no ordinary chill. He lifted her in his arms and she fell against his shoulder, small moans escaping from her lips. Her eyes were closed emphasizing the blueness of the shadows beneath them. He carried her back to the farmhouse and into the warmth of the kitchen and Fon took one look at his face and moved forward at once.

She put the back of her hand to April's brow and bit her lip. 'Can you carry her up to bed for me, Boyo?' she asked quietly. 'I'll send Jamie to fetch the doctor.'

Boyo climbed the stairs taking care not to jar April more than he could help. Fon hurried up the stairs behind him and pushed open one of the bedroom doors. Boyo carried April inside setting her gently on the bed.

'Go on downstairs and see to the fire for me, there's a good boy,' Fon said quickly, 'I'll get April into her nightgown and make her comfortable.'

'Is it the influenza?' Boyo asked thickly. Fon met his eyes, her gaze steady. 'I'm very much afraid it is.'

The doctor when he came, confirmed their fears. He could do little but advise Fon to keep the girl dry and warm. He left after only a few minutes and Boyo bit his lip, frightened by the way the doctor shook his head as he went out the door.

Fon did her best, Boyo watched as she made a mustard plaster and carried it upstairs. He knew it was an attempt to relieve the rattling in April's thin chest.

'You'd best go back to the tannery,' Fon said at last. 'They'll be worried about you, won't they?'

He nodded. 'I suppose so. Can I come back in the morning?' Fon took his arm. 'Of course, if they can spare you from work, that is.'

He walked home not feeling the cold bite of the winter night nor seeing the brightness of the stars in the crisp, clear sky. All he could see was April's white face, her blue-shadowed eyes and a great fear was within him.

CHAPTER TWENTY-NINE

Arian put down her pen, her wrist was aching and she wished most heartily that she had taken the trouble to learn how to operate one of the typewriting machines in the office below. She felt overworked and anxious about her newspaper, cursing the epidemic that had swept the town. Most of her staff had fallen prey to the influenza, there was only one junior reporter still active as well as herself and of course the indestructible Mac was, as usual, a tower of strength.

Arian leaned back wearily and rubbed her eyes, she had reported the deaths of some of the most prominent citizens in Swansea. It was a harrowing time and one Arian prayed she would never have to repeat. And through it all, at the back of her mind, she asked herself what she was doing estranged from Calvin Temple at a time like this.

The outer doorbell pinged and Arian heard the sound of footsteps crossing the room. Her own door swung open and Mac came in, his face reddened by the wind and cold. 'It's like a ghost town out there.' He slumped into a seat and threw his hat in the general direction of the stand in the corner. It landed on the floor and he ignored it. 'It's as if the great plague had come to Swansea, doors and windows are closed and the only people about seem to be funeral directors in black coats.'

Arian closed her eyes for a moment. 'Any news of Calvin?' The words were forced through stiff lips and she looked up to meet Mac's eyes half fearing his reply.

'He's fine, looks as healthy as ever. I saw him in the

street, just been visiting a sick friend, a lady friend. Well-heeled she was, by the look of her house.'

'Was?' Arian asked tentatively. Mac nodded. 'Aye, that's the word. She died this morning.'

Arian was suddenly angry with Calvin, what was he doing putting himself at risk, visiting those afflicted with the influenza, was he that careless of his own health?

'Loyal man, that Calvin Temple,' it was as though Mac had read her thoughts, 'takes guts to put yourself in the firing line the way he did. Could have stayed at home out of harm's way, couldn't he?'

'Let's close up the office.' Arian rose from her chair so abruptly that it tipped backwards and teetered for a moment before falling with a crash against the wall. Mac righted it without comment and then followed Arian from the room.

Upstairs, it was gloomy with rain beating against the windows. Only the fire burning low now gave any sign of warmth. Arian bent and placed more coals in the grate and Mac watched her laconically.

She looked up and caught his eye. 'The maid's sick, gone into the infirmary, I don't think she's going to last the night, poor girl. Hang on, I'll get us some brandy from the kitchen.'

Mac came into the kitchen after her and sank into one of the chairs. 'Why don't we stay in here? It's much warmer than the sitting room, brighter, too.'

Arian nodded. 'You're right, this side faces the sea and catches what little light there is. Oh, how I hate the cold winter days.'

'You have to have the bitter to enjoy the sweet, my dear Arian.'

'So wise and so damn smug and a cliché to boot!' Arian poured the brandy and sat opposite Mac, enjoying the warmth of the liquor in her mouth.

'You could go away for a week or two,' Mac suggested. 'You could even afford to take a trip abroad, somewhere you'd see the sun. Why not?'

'I don't think there would be a paper if I took time off, you can hardly run the place single-handed, can you?'

He shook his head. 'You're right there. I could get someone in though.'

Arian shook her head. 'Mac, we're selling more papers than ever, the people who are not sick are buying it just to see who has died.'

Mac laughed mirthlessly. 'I've noticed, I think it gives some people a sense of satisfaction that they've outlasted their peers.'

'Don't be cynical, Mac.'

'I'm being realistic.' Mac held out his empty glass and Arian refilled it. 'It's only human, it's a case of thank God it's not me.'

Arian returned to the subject uppermost in her mind. 'Calvin, how did he look, did he mention me?' She hated herself for asking and yet she felt she had to know.

Mac bent his great head with its shock of greying hair and looked into his brandy. 'No. I volunteered the information that you were well and carrying on with the business.'

'Hm! I bet he made some sarcastic comment about business coming first.'

'He didn't as a matter of fact.' Mac looked up and met her eyes. 'He appeared as anxious to know more about you as you are about him.'

'That's not the impression I've got, not from what you've said.' Arian felt her depression deepening.

'Ah, well, you weren't there, you didn't see the expression on his face when I mentioned your name.' Mac drained his glass. 'Anyway, I've got work to do, I'd better get down to the printing room see how many of our workers are still on their feet.' At the door of the kitchen he paused. 'Why not go to see him, Arian? Put yourself out of your misery.'

'I don't know.' She rubbed her eyes, 'I just don't

know, Mac. Shouldn't he be the one to come and see me?'

'Heaven save me from a stubborn woman.' She heard the sound of the door to her apartments closing and suddenly, she was alone in the silence.

She sighed, putting her head for a moment into her arms as they rested on the kitchen table. 'Calvin, Calvin, why don't I know what it is I really want?'

Eventually, she rose and moved purposefully to the door, she had work to do and she might just as well get on with it as sit here brooding.

April was dead. Jamie it was who had come to the tannery to break the bad news. Boyo had not cried, not even when Jamie had hugged him as if he was his son but now the numbness was wearing off and all he felt was pain. Her funeral was the darkest day of his life and Boyo felt he would never recover from the horror of it all.

Boyo went about his work in the tannery with fierce determination, trying to concentrate on something other than his gut-ripping grief.

'*Duw, duw*, slow down, man, you'll kill yourself.' Harry was in the currying house scraping a hide clean of the coarse hair that clung to it. He was sweating in spite of the cold weather and Boyo stared at him uncomprehendingly.

After a moment, his vision cleared and he saw that Harry was tired, there were lines about his mouth and his eyes were shadowed. 'I'll have to get more hands in,' he put down the scouring brush and rubbed his palms on his leather apron. 'We are all working too hard, we need at least three more men.'

'Aye, both the casual labourers died in the epidemic, poor sods but thank God, the worst is over now.' Harry smiled cheerfully. 'And we *are* keeping up with the orders in spite of everything but that's down to your efforts. I reckon you've increased our trade to double what it was in Jubilee's day.'

'More call for the leather,' Boyo said flatly but of course, that was only part of the answer. Mostly, the upturn in business was because of his selling abilities. He'd gone out on the road, clad in a new suit and a crisp shirt with a fresh white starched collar and had canvassed the businesses in the area with great results. It seemed he was a natural salesman, his grave manner served to impress potential buyers as did his knowledge of his subject.

Under the tutorship of Caradoc Jones, his acumen with figures and his ability to work out complicated sums in his head gave him a great advantage, for while clients were scribbling on paper, he had the answer to costings on the tip of his tongue.

As for the influenza epidemic, for a few weeks it had slowed up sales but as Harry said, the worst was over. For some people, but not for Boyo, never for him. He swallowed hard as he left the currying house, he needed to see Ellie, to talk things over with her, it was only right he consult her about the hiring of any new hands.

Ellie was sitting in the parlour with Martha who was almost completely recovered from her illness. Rosie was just bringing a batch of rock cakes out of the oven, her cheeks flushed and her hair falling about her face in wisps. She smiled when she saw him.

'There you are, Boyo, just in time for a nice hot cake.' She was trying her best to cheer him up and even as he returned her smile there was no lightening of the pain inside him. He shook his head. 'No, I'm not staying, I've been working in the currying house and my clothes stink to high heaven.'

Ellie wrinkled up her nose. 'We had noticed. Come on, sit down, for heaven's sake. I want to talk to you.'

He pulled back a chair, the legs scraping the flagstones and sat down heavily.

'You are tired,' Ellie leaned towards him, 'are you doing too much, Boyo?'

'We all are.' He replaced his cup in the saucer. 'I need

to employ more hands, at least three. That's why I'm here.'

'Well that's entirely up to you, Boyo,' Ellie said, 'you don't have to ask my permission, you're the boss now.' She put her hand over his. 'It's kind of you to consult me, Boyo, but it really isn't necessary.' She sighed. 'I have abandoned any idea of renting a house in Swansea, the terrible influenza epidemic made me realize that time is precious, I feel I simply must go and live with Dan in Lampeter.' She looked at Boyo worriedly. 'I've already discussed this with Martha and Rosie and they are both in agreement. I'm sorry to break this to you so abruptly but you do understand, don't you?'

Boyo nodded. 'Aye, I understand and I'll miss you but I'll manage, don't you worry.'

'It won't be for ever,' Martha smiled encouragingly at him, 'once Daniel has finished college we'll come back home to Swansea, won't we Ellie?'

'And I won't be far away, mind.' Rosie paused wiping her floury hands on her apron, 'When Caradoc and me are married he'll still be coming to look over the books and I'll be with him.'

'You're not a bad bunch.' Boyo tried to smile but it was a half hearted attempt and everyone knew it. 'I might as well wash and change and go into Swansea this afternoon. I'll call in at *The Times*, put in an advertisement for some hands.'

'That's fine by me, Boyo. I don't want to see you wearing yourself out doing the work of three men.'

He left the kitchen and made his way upstairs to his room. There was water in the jug on the table and he splashed some into the bowl and stripped off his working clothes shivering a little in the cold air. He glanced through the window, the skies were as grey and as dark as his own feelings. He bent his head. 'April,' he whispered his eyes tightly closed, 'oh, April my love, how am I going to face the rest of my life without you?'

* * *

Arian was standing in the outer office talking to Mac when the doorbell jangled and a rush of cold air heralded the arrival of a visitor. She looked up to see the young man from Glyn Hir Tannery standing inside the doorway, smartly dressed, hat in his hand and with his hair slicked down flat across his head.

'Good afternoon,' she smiled warmly, she had found Boyo pleasant on the few occasions they'd met but she saw now that there was a new air of gravity about him as though in the last few weeks he had grown from a boy into a man. Hadn't there been some talk of him walking out with April O'Connor, the young girl who had died in the epidemic? If so, it was no wonder he seemed so subdued.

'Good afternoon, Miss Smale.' He came closer and she could smell the cold of the winter air on him. 'I need to place an advertisement for some hands,' he said. 'I want experienced men but not too old and I want workers who live in the vicinity of the tannery.'

Well he certainly had no difficulty in making up his mind or in communicating his thoughts, Arian mused. She watched as Mac hastily scribbled the requirements on a piece of paper and then handed it to Boyo for his approval. After a moment, the young man nodded.

'Will you send the bill to me at the tannery, please?' He turned to leave and Arian, on an impulse, stopped him.

'I understand you are the new manager up at the tannery, these days?'

'That's right.' Boyo, it seemed, was not going to volunteer a great deal of information unless pressed.

'You do realize you are very young to be in such a position,' Arian persisted, 'it would make a good story for my paper, human interest, we call it. Would you allow me to interview you?'

'What now?' He looked surprised.

'Why not? Unless you have a pressing engagement somewhere else.'

Boyo shook his head. 'No, I haven't. What sort of thing do you want to know?'

'Well, where you came from, your background, are you betrothed, that sort of thing.'

He gave her a long look that made her feel slightly uncomfortable. 'Then I will have to disappoint you on all counts,' he said. 'I grew up in the workhouse, I knew nothing about my parents until now and as for being betrothed, I was once but she died.'

His bald statement of facts made Arian feel as if she had been prying, which of course, she had. 'I am so sorry,' Arian said quickly, 'I didn't mean to re-open any wounds.'

It was only when he had gone, striding out along the grey street that Arian realized the full import of their conversation. Boyo had known nothing about his background, he'd said, not until now. So there was a story there after all and it might be interesting to find out what it was.

Calvin sat before the window staring out at the rain soaked grounds. Trees dripped incessantly, swept by the wind and above them the skies were lowering and heavy with more rain to come. His visitors would be back from their trip to the shops soon and would be looking for the warmth of the fire.

His aunt meant well, she was the last of the Temples of his mother's generation. She had never married but was bringing up the daughter of a dead friend, a pretty girl and very rich. It was clear what Aunt Margaret had in mind. She had not yet broached the subject but soon, any day now, she would get around to the point of her visit and start trying to play the matchmaker. Well Calvin had no intention of getting married to the girl, suitable and pleasant though she might be. Aunt Margaret would just have to go back to the country and admit that her visit had been a failure.

A copy of *The Swansea Times* lay on the table before

him and he thought of Arian, her pale skin, her clear eyes, how he wanted her, her sweetness, the soft scent of her, the feel of her silken hair against his skin. Curse her!

Perversely, his next thought was to thank God she had escaped the influenza epidemic that had taken the lives of several of his neighbours in the close-knit community on the hills outside of Swansea. The lower orders had fared worse than their betters which was an indictment of the way they lived, he supposed. The poor endured bad sanitation, inadequate meals and drank far too much raw liquor. The poor of Swansea, for the most part, eked out a miserable existence in cold, damp dwellings. Perhaps, he mused, he should put some of his not inconsiderable fortune into the improvement of housing in and around the Swansea area. It was something he should seriously consider.

Unless he and Arian were reconciled, there would be no heirs, no-one to make use of Calvin's money. He might as well do some good to someone rather than the fortune go into the state coffers. Not that Calvin wanted to be a replica of Lord Shaftesbury, who everyone knew had done great work for the poor of his own area in his own time, but at least he might work quietly to make the town a better place for all to live in.

Was he growing soft? He glanced down at *The Times* once more, he always took it, read every page as though somewhere there would be a message from Arian for him but it was a vain hope. Perhaps he should make some effort to see her but could their differences ever be reconciled? He rose to his feet and thrust his hands into his pockets. He still thought it entirely reasonable that she give up the proprietorship of the newspaper; as Lady Temple she would find her social life increasingly demanding. It simply wasn't possible for her to spend hours, sometimes late into the night, down at the offices in the Strand. And yet she had been adamant that she would continue to run *The Swansea Times*. Could they perhaps come to some sort of compromise where she spent most of her time at home and only a small part of it at the office? It was worth discussing with her, surely, for his life had become empty without her.

He moved over to his desk and seated himself before drawing a sheet of paper towards him. After a moment's hesitation, he began to write. 'My dear Arian.' He paused, his pen falling onto the sheet as he searched his mind for just the right words that would bring her to him.

Arian wrinkled her nose as the cab came to a halt outside the rambling house at Glyn Hir, how anyone could bear to live in such surroundings, she just did not know. The horses moved uneasily between the shafts as though anxious to be away. 'Can you collect me in about an hour?' Arian paid the driver and the man lifted his cap in acknowledgement.

Rosie opened the door, drying her hands on her spotless apron. The smell of baking permeated the house, a fragrant improvement to the odour outside.

'I've come to see Ellie, is she at home?'

Rosie nodded. 'Come in, miss, there's a nice fire in the parlour, I'll go get her, she's upstairs, packing some things.'

'Packing, she *is* leaving then?'

'She will be soon, just as soon as Dan, that's her husband, comes to take her down to Lampeter.'

It was warm in the parlour and the furniture shone with constant polishing. Arian sat in an upright, upholstered chair, shabby and old but comfortable, her thoughts racing as she waited for Ellie to put in an appearance.

'Arian, there's nice to see you.' Ellie was a pretty girl, Arian noticed Ellie's pale beauty as if seeing her for the first time. She was small, appearing delicate with her fair skin and hair, but she was tougher than she looked. What Arian didn't see was that she and Ellie were very

418

much alike in appearance as well as in sturdiness of character.

'I'm sorry to call unannounced,' Arian smiled. 'I know it's rude of me but I heard from one of my reporters that you might be leaving town, I thought it would be a nice gesture if I came to wish you luck. Perhaps I could put a piece in *The Times* about your move from Swansea?'

'Don't apologize, you're very welcome.'

The women sat for a while making small talk. Ellie seemed a little remote, her thoughts somewhere else and Arian wondered at the wisdom of her visit. They had never been close friends but they once had something in common, a love for Calvin Temple.

'I was talking to the young tannery manager, Boyo, I was very impressed by his manner. Will he be taking charge when you leave? Or will the tannery be put up for sale?'

Ellie was quiet for a long moment and Arian rushed to fill the uncomfortable silence, 'Forgive me, I'm prying.'

'The future ownership of Glyn Hir is in the balance at the moment,' Ellie said softly.

Arian accepted defeat and tried to amuse Ellie with the trivial affairs of the townsfolk but after a while, she rose to her feet. 'I won't keep you any longer but if there's anything I can do, please get in touch.'

'Look, I haven't been very good company today. Why not come up to see us Saturday evening, Dan has to return to Lampeter for the Sunday services so that's the only opportunity I'll have to talk to you before I leave. I can tell you a little bit more about the tannery then, only I'm not sure how important you'll think it once you hear what it is.'

'If it concerns the lives of the people of Swansea then it's of interest, not only to me but to my readers. We'll all be glad of some relief from the awful news of the influenza epidemic.' She studied Ellie's face, she was quite obviously happy in her marriage, a light had come into her eyes when she had mentioned her husband and yet something was troubling her.

Later, as Arian returned home in the jolting cab, shivering against the cold leather seat, she racked her brains to solve the puzzle of Ellie and Boyo. There was some definite connection there but what was it?

Arian was glad when she arrived home and, as she alighted in the wet street, she glanced up to her rooms where the lamps gleamed in the widnows; Megan was a good girl. Arian's last maid had recovered from the influenza but as she had no wish to return to service Arian had advertised for another girl. It wasn't just that Arian needed help in the house, someone to tend to the fires and the stove but she needed company in the lonely evenings, another body and soul to share the solitude of the large building. Megan was a hearty girl, cheerful and a good worker, she had a strangely motherly approach even though she was a good few years younger than Arian.

Arian paid the driver and gave him a large tip and he nodded down at her, raising his cap imperceptibly from his head. Inside the passageway leading to the upstairs rooms, it was dark and silent and Arian wished she had a candle to light her way.

Megan beamed at her as Arian came into the brightness of her rooms. 'Heard the door, miss, let me take your things. *Duw*, you're wet and cold, I've put a bottle in your bed to warm it for you.'

Arian let Megan take her coat. 'That's a good girl, it's freezing out tonight.' She followed Megan into the kitchen where it was warm and bright, the stove filling the room with radiance. 'I think I'll just sit in here with you for a bit and get myself thoroughly thawed out.' Arian felt in need of company, she was fast turning into a lonely old maid, she told herself not without a touch of irony.

Megan seemed not the least flustered by her mistress' strange actions but then this was her first position as maid and she had no preconceived ideas about how the rich were supposed to behave. 'I saw the maid from the big house up on the hill, you know that one his lordship lives in,' Megan said conversationally. 'Seems he's been having a lady caller visiting him, full of it is Dotty.'

Arian felt her stomach turn as she tried to compose herself. 'Oh, is this lady staying with his lordship?' She hated herself for prying but she couldn't help it.

'Looks like it, been treating her to fine dinners and the best wine from his cellar, too, so Dot says.'

Arian, for a moment was back at the big house, fetching wine from the cellar for the preparation of Calvin's meal. Inadvertently, she had brought the best of his stock and had received the sharp edge of cook's tongue for her troubles. But all that was a long time ago. Another life time. 'What's this lady's name, did Dotty tell you?'

'Oh, aye, a rich heiress come from the country for the winter, a Miss Southerby. Course, her mam or her old aunt or someone goes visiting with her, it wouldn't do otherwise would it?'

'No, I suppose it wouldn't.' Arian felt suddenly ill. So Calvin was no longer waiting for her to change her mind. It seemed he'd cut his losses and was searching for a wife. Well, he never pretended with her, he'd told Arian more than once that he needed an heir, that it seemed was his prime consideration. Well, she couldn't really blame him could she? 'I think I'll turn in, Megan, I'm feeling a bit washed out.'

It was a long time before she slept. She kept seeing Calvin in her mind's eye with a lovely young girl on his arm, walking up the aisle to the surge of organ music. Turning her face into her pillow, she cursed herself for being a fool.

It was not until the morning, until she went downstairs into her office, that she saw the letter in the familiar scrawl that made her heart dip with emotion.

421

She opened it with shaking fingers and read the short note quickly.

'I need to talk to you. Can you come up to the house on Saturday evening?

Yours ever,'

It was signed with Calvin's usual flourish. She sank back in her seat, she was supposed to go up to Glyn Hir Saturday night. In any case, Calvin was probably going to tell her something she did not wish to hear, offer her yet another ultimatum, that she accept his terms and marry him or he would turn his attentions elsewhere. Well she would not, she could not be pushed into a mould, not even to suit Calvin. Slowly, she screwed the note into a tight ball and then dropped it with a mass of other papers into the waste-bin beside her.

CHAPTER THIRTY

Matthew Hewson was sitting in the public bar of the Ship Inn staring out moodily at the dull, winter weather. Marchant was probably sunning himself in some foreign land and what had Matthew to look forward to? He was alone, all his money gone, practically friendless and from no fault of his own.

It was Ellie Hopkins who had cheated him out of what was rightfully his, who had started his run of bad luck. She had sacked him like a dog, sent him packing from a job he had held for a long time, a job he had been good at. It was time he had his revenge. He brooded over the injustices that had been done to him, making a catalogue of them in his mind and as his anger grew, his fist clenched around the handle of his mug of ale, the knuckles gleaming white.

She had outsmarted him all along the line, he mused bitterly, she had denied him the shares which were rightfully his. She had scarcely been bothered by the fire at the tannery, with her money rebuilding some sheds was no great inconvenience. She was a whore posing as a lady, married now to a mealy-mouthed priest. Well, *he* would be getting a nasty shock too, Daniel Bennett would soon find out he was not so clever. Ellie had even come out of the smuggling game unscathed in spite of the fact that her wagons had been delivering the opium. There must be a lucky star shining over her head. Well, he, Matthew Hewson would, soon extinguish it.

Matthew felt like hitting out at someone, he sunk lower into his chair, he burned with anger and frustration. They were all winners except for him. Ellie Hopkins, sitting pretty, owning a vast fortune, Daniel Bennett the new husband of the rich widow and Marchant who was running away from all his problems in some sunsplashed spot while he, Matthew, was still down in the gutter.

Well, Ellie, at least, was not going to get away with it. He moved his foot to reassure himself that the bag was still there beneath the table and smiled unpleasantly as his toe gently came in contact with the explosives.

It hadn't been easy acquiring what was virtually a bomb but with the help of Dai, the gunsmith, he had managed it. Crude, it might be but it was enough to blow Glyn Hir and everyone in it to kingdom come. Ellie Hopkins had it coming to her, if he couldn't share Jubilee's money then she would have none of it either.

He had spent his last shillings paying the gunsmith to make up the charge from a mixture of nitre, charcoal and sulphur, urging the man to mix in the sulphur well, he needed the explosive to keep until he found the right opportunity to use it. Dai had protested that he was no expert in the field of explosives, he could only use the outdated methods of his father's generation but Matthew had ignored him. Did it matter what methods were used so long as the bomb did the job?

He scowled into his ale, half drunk, his ill humour obvious in every line of his body. Today he had been asked to leave his lodgings, he hadn't paid his landlady rent for many a month and because of his growing obsession with getting his revenge on Ellie Hopkins he had even been failing between the sheets. Finally Dora Griffiths had run out of patience and she had ordered him in no uncertain terms to quit his room. And it was all Ellie's fault, oh, yes, she had a great deal to answer for, she had ruined Matthew's future. Well, he was determined she would pay for what she had done and pay for it even if it had to be with her life.

Bridie was sitting in the window of the modest house in Clydach, looking out at the fields stretching out before

424

her in a rolling pattern of fresh greens and muted yellows. From upstairs came the sound of her sons laughing, chasing across the floor, no doubt encouraged by the young nanny Bridie had engaged.

It was good to have the boys home but it seemed what God gave in one hand, he took away with the other. She looked down at the letter, she had read it a dozen times. It had been sent by an employee from a shipping office in Ireland. It told her in stark terms that her husband was dead. She covered her face with her hands, poor Paul, he had not deserved to die. He had been all sorts of a cad, stripping her of her fortune and her dignity but to end his life crushed between the side of a ship and the dock was a cruel accident of fate.

It was ironic that the letter had come now when she had been so happy. Guilt had seared her, the feeling that she might have been the cause of Paul's death. And yet now, rereading the brief words, she realized there was nothing anyone could have done to save Paul. He had served the sea and the sea had been the means of taking his life.

She folded the letter carefully and locked it away in a drawer. Then she returned to the window once more, spring was not far away. Life was beginning anew, she must forget the past and look forward to the future.

She rested her hand on her stomach and her eyes shone with dreams. What if her suspicions were true, could such a miracle be possible after what the doctors had once told her?

Collins came in from the garden, she heard him kicking off his boots near the back door and a smile curved her lips. She felt her heart beating in anticipation as it always did when he came near to her. She realized that until she had grown to know Collins as a man, she had never experienced real love. Her feelings for Paul had been those of an immature girl, in love with the image of a man and not the reality. The reality

425

had been a self-centred, even ruthless, man who had manipulated everyone, including her.

Once perhaps, she too had set great store by money, by amassing even more of it, she had equated money with security, what a false notion that had turned out to be. Money, she concluded, could be snatched away at the stroke of a pen, love was more enduring.

Collins came into the parlour in his stockinged feet, a smear of earth on his cheek, he'd obviously been working on his vegetable garden. Bridie smiled and held out her arms to him. He knelt before her and she cradled his head against her breast feeling tears of happiness spring to her eyes. 'Have I ever told you how much I love you?' she asked softly. He raised his head and looked at her. 'Once or twice but tell me again.' He stretched up and kissed her mouth and she clung to him for a long moment. He took her face in his hands and looked into her eyes. 'Why are you crying, you can't alter anything, Paul's death was nothing to do with you, please can't you believe that Bridie?' He frowned worriedly.

'I know what you say is true but it will take me a long time to forget how Paul met his death. I know the sea, know her cruel ways and I know that accidents happen but I wish I'd had the chance to straighten things out between us.' She sighed softly. 'Still, there's no point crying, I must just count my blessings. I'm being silly and foolish; women in a delicate condition are often foolish, didn't you know?'

He sat back on his heels, his mouth broadening into a smile and she saw with pleasure the whiteness of his teeth in his weathered face. He was so wholesome, so lovable, how could God have handed her such gifts when she had been a cold, selfish woman?

'Are you saying what I think you're saying?' He gathered her hands in his and held them tenderly, as though they would snap beneath his strong fingers.

'I'm not sure yet, but yes, I think, I'm *almost* certain

426

there is going to be another little Collins about the place before too long.'

He held her and kissed her eyes, her nose, her cheeks, her hair as though he could never give her enough of his love. 'Bridie, I will take care of you, I will wait on you hand and foot, I will be your slave. You must have plenty of rest, on no account will you overdo things. Bridie,' he was suddenly very serious, 'I love you so much I don't think I'd want to live if I lost you.'

Collins knew her history, knew of her disastrous last pregnancy as all the staff at Sea Mistress had known. She shook her head. 'Nothing is going to happen to me, I just feel it in my bones that this is right, it's meant to be. Oh, Collins what if we have a little girl, a daughter, wouldn't that be wonderful?'

He held her close, gently stroking her hair. 'When will we know for sure?'

Ellie turned her mouth close to his. 'The doctor is calling this afternoon, when he's examined me, he should have a very good idea one way or another.'

'I will be on tenterhooks all day.' Collins rose to his feet. 'Now, I must bring you food, you must build up your strength.'

Bridie laughed. 'We really will have to employ more staff, especially now because I won't want you in the kitchen not when we've a baby to look after.'

Bridie settled back in her chair and stretched her arms above her head. 'You know what, Collins? I feel young again, young and beautiful and happy. Am I tempting fate by being so happy?'

He shook his head. 'I'm here now, the bad times are over and I mean to see that only good times lie ahead.'

As he left the room, a momentary cloud of fear settled on Bridie then she brushed it aside, it was just the foolish superstition of a woman with child she told herself, and the words warmed her so that the smile returned to her eyes.

Dr Jones arrived at two o'clock sharp, the appointed

time, and he breezed into the house, young, fresh-faced and eager to please. His examination was carried out without delay and he was deft and very thorough. When the doctor was leaving, Collins saw him to the door and then came hotfoot up the stairs. He stopped breathlessly and looked at her his brow furrowed. 'Well?'

'Yes, it's yes! He's quite sure I'm with child and so am I. Oh Collins, isn't it wonderful?'

He came to her and drew her close. After a moment, Bridie held him away from her. 'We'll be married quietly, up here in our own home if possible. We won't invite anyone to the wedding, I just want it to be me and you and afterwards—' she broke off mid sentence as a thought struck her. 'You *do* want to be married to me, don't you?'

'Of course I do,' Collins said soberly, 'but I didn't dare to ask lest you thought I was interested in your money.'

She threw back her head and laughed, 'You! I've never met anyone less interested in money in all my life.' She looked at him more soberly. 'I'll never forget how wonderful you were to me when I had nothing.' Bridie looked at Collins thoughtfully. 'I wonder,' she said softly and Collins looked at her indulgently.

'What do you wonder?'

'I wonder if Ellie's husband Daniel Bennett could marry us, he's a priest isn't he?'

'What if we take a trip to Swansea and find out, shall we?' Collins asked quietly.

'When shall we go?' Bridie leaned forward eagerly.

'The sooner, the better.' Collins stretched over the table to kiss her mouth. 'The sooner the better, my love.'

Ellie was surprised when a letter was delivered by hand from Bridie Marchant requesting a visit the following night. She had heard about Paul Marchant's death, of course, as had everyone else in Swansea. But what Bridie could want from her, Ellie was not quite sure. Ellie

428

hastily scrawled a reply and sealed it into an envelope and handed it to the young boy. She gave him six-pence and he looked at it wide-eyed before doffing his cap and climbing back on his cycle.

'Do you want any butter, missus?' the boy asked, his foot resting on the ground. 'I had some deliveries to make but one of my customers wasn't home and I'll have to go back to the shop if I have anything left over.'

Ellie took the butter and opened her bag but the boy shook his head. 'No, don't pay me, missus, the boss, he likes to collect the money himself.' He grinned, 'There's a big bag of flour, too, very useful and it will keep.'

'Very well, I'll have the flour but nothing else, right?'

The boy grinned. 'My boss will be happy that I've found him a new customer.'

'Who is your boss?' Ellie smiled at the lad's cheek. He grimaced and lifting his cap rubbed at his head. 'Harry Parkins, got shops in Swansea, Clydach and Neath. Family business it is see but old man Parkins keeps his hands on the purse-strings, mind.'

'Well, ask him will he bring me up a little sugar, tea and salt when he brings the bill. And tell him to come soon because I'll be going away shortly.'

'Thank you, missus, he might crack a smile for once in his life when I give him your message.' He rode away, his thin legs beneath his checked trousers pumping the pedals as he tried to get up speed. Ellie heard his cheerful whistle as she turned back into the house, the notes hung hauntingly for a moment on the still air.

'What is it, Ellie?' Martha came out of the parlour, her glasses perched on the end of her nose.

'A note from Bridie asking can she visit tomorrow night. I've said yes, even though Dan will be home, I could hardly refuse, could I?'

'I suppose not.' Martha followed as Ellie went along the passage towards the kitchen. 'I'm sorry about Mr Marchant, no-one deserves to die young like that do they?'

'Not even a man like Paul,' Ellie agreed. 'Here, Rosie, extra butter, put it on the cold shelf in the pantry, will you?'

Rosie took the butter and sniffed it. 'Mm, good Welsh salt butter this, see the little drops of water oozing out of it, shows it's got plenty of salt in it.' She weighed it in her hand. 'A fair pound, spot on, I'd say.'

Ellie smiled, Rosie was the expert in such matters so she had no intention of arguing. 'I expect you're right.'

'How much did it cost?' Rosie was ever practical. Ellie shook her head. 'Do you know, I'm not sure? I believe a Mr Parkins will call at some time to collect his money, I'll tell you then.'

'Dear enough, I'd say,' Rosie looked as if she had to pay for the butter herself. 'A bit more added on for delivery too. Better to buy it in the market like always.'

'Rosie,' Ellie changed the subject, 'do you think you could bake up a batch of scones and things for tomorrow night?'

Rosie's face brightened. 'Aye, that I will, I'll do it straight away, the Reverend will be home soon, won't he?'

'Daniel is not a Reverend yet Rosie, and yes, he will be home this evening, I hope. Tomorrow we'll be having visitors, Bridie Marchant is coming over and I'm expecting Arian Smale, as well.'

'Quite a going-away party,' Rosie beamed, always anxious for a chance to show off her culinary skills, 'I'll do some cutlets of lamb in mint jelly and some . . .'

Ellie held up her hand. 'No need to go to any trouble, Rosie, really, I'm sure our visitors will have eaten.'

'The Reverend will be starving, Mr Dan is always starving. I'd better make some nice hot pasties for tonight then and some game pie as well.'

'All right, make what you like, you will anyway,' Ellie grumbled good naturedly. 'Come on Martha let's get back to the parlour and the warmth of the fire, shall we?'

It was soothing sitting in the cheerful room with the

lamp casting warm shadows and flames leaping from the coals in the grate. The ticking of the clock was the only sound, the regular marking of time having a soporific effect on Martha so, after making herself comfortable in the chair, she began to doze. Ellie looked at her with affection, she was glad Martha was going with her to Lampeter, it would have been lonely without her and with Dan at college all day. Rosie, because she would be married soon, would remain in Swansea.

The plan had been that she would be married from Glyn Hir but now, Ellie proposed to return for the wedding and take over one of the hotels for the day in order to give Rosie a good start in her new life.

Martha opened her eyes, suddenly as alert as though she had not been asleep. 'I'm looking forward to Rosie's wedding.'

'Have you been reading my mind?' Ellie asked dryly.

Martha smiled. 'Maybe. She's a good girl, deserves the best, I like Rosie.'

'You surprise me,' Ellie said with her eyebrows raised. 'I always thought you two were at loggerheads.'

'Well, perhaps we were but it was only done to add a bit of spice to the proceedings. We've rubbed along well enough most of the time.'

Ellie sat back in her chair and began to dream, content to let Martha do most of the chatting. Tonight, Dan would be with her. He would hold her in his arms, make love to her, make her feel she was truly alive. And tomorrow, he could help her entertain her visitors, it would be good practice for him. She smiled to herself, everything was going so well, did she deserve to be this happy? She closed her eyes for a moment, savouring her feelings of euphoria and then Martha was prodding her. 'Wake up sleepy head, your husband is home.'

CHAPTER THIRTY-ONE

As Arian made preparations for her trip to Glyn Hir, she felt the first flutterings of unease. She stood before the mirror, hatpin poised above the crown of her velvet hat and stared at her reflection. She thought of Calvin waiting for her to come to him and bit her lip, was she doing the right thing? Tonight could be her last chance to patch things up between them. 'You know what this means, don't you?' she said to her reflection, 'it means that once and for all you are putting your paper before your love for Calvin Temple.'

She thrust the hatpin more securely into her hat and picked up her gloves and bag. What she was feeling was only a last minute bout of nerves, she knew what she wanted and that was to keep her independence. If Calvin really loved her, he would be willing for her to continue working on her newspaper. And if she really loved him, loved him enough, a small voice said in her head, she would give up all for Calvin Temple.

Soon it would be spring but today it was cold in the street, her breath hung in puffs of vapour on the chill air. Above the buildings in the Strand, the sky was heavy and grey. A thin drizzle began to fall and Arian walked to the edge of the kerb and hailed a cab. She gave the driver the address and climbed into the rocking carriage, shivering as she sat back in the cold leather seat. How she'd hated the winter months when her only escape from the depressing weather was to concentrate on the paper, on her work. She couldn't relinquish it, she would die of boredom sitting at home all day playing the great lady. In any case, it was all academic now, Calvin would not be slow to realize the implications when she failed to meet him tonight. The journey did not take long. Arian looked out of the window, hearing the sound of the horses' hooves against the roadway and glimpsing the silver ribbon of the river Tawe, she wondered again if she was doing the right thing but it was too late now, the familiar smell of the tannery permeated the air.

She felt a tinge of excitement, she had learned that Bridie Marchant would be here and Arian was curious to learn more about Paul's death. It appeared to be accidental but was that the truth? She paid the driver. 'Perhaps you will call back for me about ten o'clock tonight?' she said and the man grunted and gave what she took to be a nod of assent, though by the look on his face, it wouldn't do to rely on him too heavily.

Rosie let her into the house and took her coat with a smile. 'In the parlour, miss, there's a lovely cheerful fire burning in the hearth. The other visitors have arrived already and Mr Daniel is home from college.' She giggled, 'It's quite like a party, mind.'

Arian was surprised and a little disconcerted, she had hoped for a quiet chat with Bridie. For a moment she was inclined to flee, she wasn't sure she could cope with a crowd of people right now. But then, she was being welcomed into the room by Ellie who took her hands and led her to a chair near the warmth of the fire.

'You look frozen, come on, warm yourself, have some mulled wine, it's delicious.'

The first few minutes of her arrival were taken up with greetings, polite enquiries were made regarding her health and Arian accepted a glass of warm wine with a feeling of being swept away on a tide.

Bridie leaned forward, her eyes shining, her hair falling in curls around her forehead. She looked surprisingly young and beautiful but then she was obviously in love with the man who hovered so attentively at her side, Arian thought with a stab of envy. It did not seem

433

appropriate to raise the matter of her husband's death, not in the face of such happiness.

'Collins has decided to make an honest woman of me,' Bridie said quietly.

What a change in a woman, Arian thought, once Bridie had been a bitch of the first order but then an awful lot had happened to her over the last few years. Pain and loss had tempered her nature, apparently bringing out the best in her.

Daniel entered the room followed by Caradoc and Boyo, the men were laughing noisily. Arian felt alone, a woman without a man in tow. 'Congratulations,' she said quietly to Bridie, 'I hope you will be very happy.'

'I'm sure I will,' Bridie said slowly, her eyes on Collins who had gone to stand in a group with the other men. Arian leaned back in her chair as Dan moved into the centre of the room.

'We have been discussing Evan Roberts, the man who headed the revival in Wales last year. It seems he had gone into hiding in Leicestershire with the Penn Lewises. Been burning the candle at both ends, by all accounts, and needs to rest.' He paused for a moment and then, as a silence greeted his words, he continued to speak. 'Still, the effects of his ministry are being felt everywhere, the criminal lists are non-existent, the courtrooms empty, he has accomplished a great deal in his short career.' Another silence caused him to colour. 'I'm sorry, I'm being a bore, acting the preacher.' He smiled, 'All that is about to change, we men are going outside to take a look at the tannery buildings. Boyo wants to discuss some alterations he feels would improve the production of the leather.'

It was Martha, the elderly woman sitting back a little from the others, who spoke. 'Going out to the nearest public bar to have a drink and a smoke, more like it,' she said dryly.

Dan held up his hands. 'Caught, I confess it all. But we won't be very long, I promise you that.' He smiled,

'It will give you women a chance to talk about weddings and babies and things dear to all your hearts.'

Arian felt disgruntled, weddings and babies were the last things she wanted to talk about. She felt a moment of panic, the time was slipping away and Calvin would be waiting for her. Was she making the biggest mistake of her life by not going to him?

The cheerful voices of the men died away and as if on a given cue, Bridie began to speak. 'I hope you'll all bear with me,' she looked across at Ellie. 'I want to ask Dan about marrying us, Collins and me. I would like the ceremony to be conducted at home, in my little house in Clydach, would Dan be able to do it, do you think?'

Ellie shook her head, 'But Bridie, I thought you were a Catholic, wouldn't you rather be married in a church of your own faith?'

Bridie looked a little shamefaced. 'Not in my condition,' she said. 'In any case, I want it done quickly so that my child has a secure future. I don't want a public affair which it would be in a Catholic church, you understand? In any case, Collins isn't a Catholic, so it would be very difficult to arrange.'

Arian watched as Ellie shook her head. 'Dan isn't ordained yet, he couldn't conduct the ceremony himself if he wanted to but I'm certain he'll find someone willing to carry out the service in your own home if that's what you really want.'

Arian suddenly felt the urge to be away from here, from the cosy talk of weddings. Bridie must have caught her look. 'I'm sorry, I'm being selfish, monopolizing the conversation, it must be a real bore for the rest of you.'

Arian felt ashamed for that's exactly what she had been thinking. 'No really, but I have another appointment, I should have been there at least an hour ago.' She could still make it if she hurried, she could still be with Calvin, surely they could find some sort of compromise that would suit them both?

'But it's so cold,' Ellie said following Arian to the door,

435

'you don't want to walk all the way back to town, do you?'

'I'll go down to the nearest street and get a cab, don't worry.' Arian couldn't wait to be away, she had been a fool to try to put Calvin out of her life, she loved him and she needed him. Why had she left it so long to tell him so?

They were in the hall now and Ellie was about to speak again when the door was pushed roughly open. Arian saw a man standing against the light, he looked huge in a greatcoat that reached almost to his ankles, his hair stood up wildly as if he'd been running bareheaded in the wind.

'Back, away from the door,' he said in a harsh voice. 'Back in the room there and at the double.'

He edged closer. 'I've got explosives tied around my body and any sudden movement might set them off then we'd all be blown sky high so I am warning you, don't try anything silly.'

Arian moved forward, this man was mad but then she had dealt with a madman before, she had been married to one. No-one was going to intimidate her, not ever again. 'I'm walking out of here,' she said, 'do your worst.'

She saw his hand lift and then it was as though a sky full of stars was bursting inside her head. Then, abruptly, everything became black.

'Matthew!' Ellie looked down at Arian's senseless figure on the floor and made to bend over her. The sound of laughter drifted from the parlour and Matthew stiffened. 'Who have you got here?' he asked gruffly and Ellie felt a sudden surge of hope.

'I've got visitors, the menfolk will be returning soon, you'd better go now, while you can.' As soon as she spoke, she realized she had made a mistake, she had let Matthew know that the women were alone.

'Get in there.' He gestured towards the parlour

436

and, bending, caught Arian's arms. No-one moved as Matthew dragged the unconscious form of Arian into the lighted room. Ellie was pushed savagely against the wall. 'Anyone else in the house?'

Ellie shook her head. 'No-one.'

'You are lying, where's Rosie?'

Ellie bit her lip. 'I don't know, I think she went out.'

Matthew stood in the doorway and bellowed Rosie's name. She came hurrying out of the kitchen, rubbing her hands on her apron. When she saw Matthew, she stopped in her tracks and stared at him in bewilderment. 'What on earth?'

'Get in here with the other women,' Matthew said coldly and Rosie obeyed him knowing by the tone of his voice that it wouldn't do to protest.

Inside the room, Matthew turned the key in the lock. 'You women,' he said, 'push that table against the door.'

'What on earth do you hope to achieve by all this, Matthew?' Ellie asked coldly. 'The men will return soon, I mean it, they'll be all over you.'

'Shut your mouth.' His eyes were glittering and hard. 'I'm the boss here now and you will all do as you are told or I'll set this thing off and we'll all be dead.'

He shrugged off his coat and Ellie saw that a strange metallic box was strapped to his waist.

'So you'd blow yourself up, too?' Ellie asked with sarcasm and Matthew glared at her. 'If I don't get what I want that is exactly what I'll do. Now sit down all of you and keep quiet.'

'What do you want?' Ellie asked. She glanced at Bridie who was white-faced, her hands pressed together as if she was praying. 'Perhaps we can settle this before the men return. That way, we will all be spared a great deal of grief.'

'I want money, what else?' Matthew said. 'I didn't expect a reception committee, I expected only you and that mealy-mouthed husband of yours to be here. As it is,' he looked round with satisfaction, 'my bargaining power will be that much greater.'

'How can anyone get you money at this time of night?' Ellie said reasonably.

'You know the bank manager personally, don't you?' Matthew's tone was equally reasonable. 'If you were to go and plead with him, tell him that it was a matter of life or death, which it is, I'm sure he'd open the vaults for you.'

Arian groaned and Ellie saw her struggle to sit up. She took her arm and helped her into a chair. A small trickle of blood was running down her temple. Arian looked around her as though dazed and then her eyes cleared and became wary as she sized up the situation.

Into the silence came the sound of knocking on the door. Matthew looked up, his neck stiff. 'Who is that?' He moved silently to the window and twitched he curtains. 'It's a delivery van,' he said, 'are you expecting anyone?'

Ellie felt the absurd desire to laugh. 'It must be Harry Parkins, come to collect his money I expect.'

The knocking sounded again, louder this time. Ellie made a movement but Matthew shook his head. 'No, stay quiet, he'll give up eventually and go away.'

The knocking continued, the sound repeated persistently, beating into Ellie's brain until she felt she could scream. But at last, there was silence.

'What now?' Ellie asked. 'Will you go with me to the bank? Then I can try my best to get you the money you want.'

He shook his head. 'I've a better idea.' He looked round the room. 'Let us see, there will be several men, I take it?'

No-one spoke and Matthew took Ellie's hair in his hands, twisting it cruelly. 'Well, let's figure it out for ourselves then. There will be the toerag Mrs Marchant is living tally with for a start, Daniel Bennett our preacher, of course.' His gaze wandered around the

438

room. 'Who else? Ah yes, Rosie's new boyfriend, the fat Mr Caradoc Jones and lastly that shrimp Boyo, quite a party.'

'So, they'll be back soon, you can't hold out against all of them,' Ellie said defiantly.

'Ah, but I hold all the aces,' Matthew smiled without humour. 'I have you ladies and I have the explosives.'

'What are you planning to do?' Bridie asked fearfully. Her hands were clasping her stomach as if to protect her unborn child.

'Why, I'm going to send your worthy menfolk to the bank of course, I'm sure one of them will sway the balance in my favour, it would be in their own interest, wouldn't you say?'

Ellie tried to appeal to Matthew. 'Look, just take me with you now, we'll go to the bank together, I'll get you all the money you want.'

He seemed to consider the matter and Ellie's hopes rose, at least if Matthew agreed, the others would be out of danger. Especially Dan, she didn't know what he would do when he came home and found the women virtually under siege.

Just then, there was the sound of hooves on the roadway that ran between the house and the tannery. Swiftly, Matthew moved to the window and peered out through the curtain. 'Damn and blast!' he cursed. 'That fool tradesman is back again, he's anxious for his money isn't he, Ellie, how much do you owe him?'

'It's a considerable amount,' Ellie said quickly, 'I told him to collect it tonight because we would be moving out soon, that's probably why he's so persistent.'

'Right, get enough money to pay him and watch what you say, I'll be right behind you.'

While Matthew cleared the furniture from the doorway, Ellie took some coins from her bag trying to think clearly, something must have happened to bring Harry Parkins back to the house so soon, he'd scarcely had time to cover even a mile. She moved to the door and opened it, looking out into the darkness, acutely aware of Matthew standing behind her, just out of sight, his hand on the contraption strapped to his waist.

'I'm sorry to keep you waiting,' Ellie said trying to read the man's expression. She looked past him to where his van was standing a little way off from the house. In the shadows, she fancied she could see dark figures moving across the garden and round towards the back of the house.

Her hopes rose, Dan must have seen Harry Parkins coming away from the tannery and asked him his business. The man had probably complained, emphasized that he was owed money. Dan would have put two and two together, guessed that if no-one had answered his repeated knocking, then something must be very wrong.

She counted out the money, and then stepped back into the hallway. 'Thank you Mr Parkins, I'm sorry . . .' she got no further, Matthew kicked the door shut and pulled Ellie into the parlour. 'You must think me a fool, I wasn't going to let you stand there giving that man signals that you needed help.'

'I wasn't doing anything, just being polite,' Ellie protested. 'You didn't want me to rouse his suspicions, did you?'

He flung her away from him and she fell heavily against the edge of the table. She gasped in pain and then Rosie was helping her to her feet. Arian was sitting white-faced in a chair, she looked at Ellie in concern and Ellie shook her head warningly. She crouched on the fender box, wondering what Dan was planning, whatever he did, it would be dangerous because Matthew could set the explosives off at any time he chose.

And then everything seemed to happen at once. The door from the hallway burst open and Collins stood framed in the light, his eyes ablaze with anger. He glanced at Bridie who put her hand to her mouth to stifle her cry of fear.

The window was smashed in with a resounding crashing of glass and Daniel stood crouched on the sill. He measured the distance between himself and Matthew with his eyes and then he sprung. Matthew was forced onto the ground, someone screamed but Ellie was moving forward, dragging at the belt at Matthew's waist.

'Look out, he's got some sort of explosive device!' she gasped as Matthew struggled fiercely, trying to twist free.

There was a rush of footsteps and then Caradoc and Boyo were in the room, joining in the struggle. In that moment, two things happened, the belt containing the device came away in Ellie's hands and Matthew twisted away from his captors.

He leapt through the window in one huge bound and his footsteps could be heard pounding across the yard. Boyo moved quickly, he took the device from Ellie's nerveless fingers and then he too had disappeared through the window.

Ellie ran after Dan as he darted through the hallway and towards the front door. She could see Matthew climbing into the van shouting at Parkins to drive away.

Boyo was pounding across the ground at a tremendous rate, he almost caught up with the van as it moved out of the roadway. Ellie saw his arm come back and then the metal device was arching through the air, in through the wildly swinging doors of the vehicle.

The explosion, like the sound of cracking thunder, suddenly shook the van. Flames shot out of the open doors and black smoke belched upwards. The van was torn from the shafts and the horses reared in fright, pawing the air, before racing away down the road.

Daniel was running then, towards the fiercely burning vehicle and Ellie watched, her heart in her mouth, as the other men, figures outlined against the flames, searched the area near the tannery wall. It seemed an age before Dan and Collins returned, holding the shocked and trembling figure of Harry Parkins between them.

'Hewson is dead,' Dan said. 'I don't think he stood a

chance, not in that confined space. Mr Parkins managed to jump clear as soon as he reached the shadow of the tannery buildings.'

'Aye, that I did, I wasn't going to let that madman take me anywhere.' Harry Parkins shook the dust from his coat. His face was red and there was a gash on his forehead.

Boyo came into the hallway, his face blackened by smoke. 'I'm sorry about your van, Mr Parkins, I didn't know where I was throwing that thing, I only knew that Matthew Hewson had to be stopped before he killed someone.'

Dan put a hand on Boyo's shoulder. 'You did the only thing possible in the circumstances. Come on, we'll go for the police, we must let them know what's happened here.'

Arian stood in the doorway. 'May I come with you, Daniel?' She looked back at Ellie and smiled wryly. 'I've got a wonderful story for my paper but somehow, it doesn't seem all that important any more. I think I just have time for my very important meeting. Goodbye, Ellie.'

In the parlour, Bridie and Martha still stood in shocked silence. 'Come on, Rosie,' Ellie said, 'I think we could all do with a stiff drink.' Her voice cracked with weariness and strain and it was Bridie who came to her and took her arm. 'We'll get off home, I think it's best.' She glanced through the broken window at the smouldering van. 'You were so brave, Ellie, I think you saved our lives.'

Ellie shook her head mutely. She drew a ragged breath, watching as Collins put his arm around Bridie. 'Come on, my love, let's get back to Clydach,' he said dryly, 'at least it's quiet there.'

Ellie took the drink Rosie held towards her and then, with Martha and Caradoc, sat waiting for Dan to return. When he did, it was with two policemen and a senior officer who came into the house and looked round the wrecked room with raised eyebrows. 'You were all here when this . . . when the accident occurred?'

Ellie nodded and the officer smiled at her reassuringly. 'You are Mrs Bennett I take it?'

She nodded again watching as he drew up a chair and sat facing her. 'I think you'd better tell me all about it,' he said and his tone was so fatherly, so normal that suddenly Ellie began to cry.

'There, there Mrs Bennett, take your time, I'll try to get this all over as quickly as possible, I know you have all been through a dreadful experience but it's going to be all right now.' He patted her hand. 'We'll have that . . . that wreck taken away as soon as possible. When you go out in the morning you won't even know anything happened here.'

Ellie doubted that but, haltingly, she began to tell him what had happened from the moment Matthew had come into the house until the men had burst in. He kept nodding his head and when she had finished, he checked her story with the others. After a time, he rose to his feet, touching his hat. 'That's it then, I'll bid you good night,' he said genially. 'Don't come to the door, I'll see myself out.'

Dawn was almost upon them when at last Ellie and Daniel sat alone in the kitchen, enjoying the warmth of the fire. It had scarcely seemed worthwhile going to bed, in a few hours, they would be on their way to Lampeter.

'Look, Ellie,' Daniel said, 'if you can bear to live on a vicar's stipend, why not sign the tannery over to Boyo, shake the dust from your heels completely?'

Ellie looked up at him. 'That's just what I wanted to hear.'

Dan moved to the window and opened the curtains and a rosy dawn poked fingers of light into the room. 'Today,' he said softly, 'we begin our new life.'

Later, with her bags packed and loaded into the waiting cab, Ellie stood aside for Martha to go on ahead, watching as Dan helped the older woman into her seat, then she turned and kissed Rosie warmly. 'Have a good life with Caradoc,' she said. 'I hope you will be very happy.'

Boyo was at her side then, taking her awkwardly in his big arms, his face red, his eyes suspiciously moist. He didn't say anything, he just held her close.

Ellie struggled to speak though it was difficult with tears gathering in her throat. 'It's all yours now, Mr Boyo Hopkins, as it should have been from the beginning. Promise me you'll employ a nice respectable lady to take care of you, and mind you eat enough, hear me?'

She released him and hurried towards the cab. As Dan took her arm to help her up the step, she turned for a moment and looked back.

'Goodbye,' she whispered, her eyes blurred with tears. Then she turned away from the house, from the place where she had known happiness and pain. The house in which she had lain beside Jubilee and loved him like a daughter. Glyn Hir, where she had, at last, grown into a woman.

Daniel was right, her life was just beginning, a whole new world was unfolding before her. She reached out and twined her fingers in his and Daniel's clasp was firm and warm. Across the carriage, Martha pretended to doze and outside the window Ellie imagined she could see, through the unyielding earth, the first shoots of a new year forcing their way towards the sun.